EX LIBRIS

VINTAGE **CLASSICS**

THE WAY BACK

Erich Maria Remarque was born in Osnabrück in 1898. Exiled from Nazi Germany and deprived of his citizenship, he lived in America and Switzerland. The author of a dozen novels, Remarque died in 1970.

Brian Murdoch was born in 1944. He is Professor Emeritus of German at Stirling University.

ERICH MARIA REMARQUE

The Way Back

TRANSLATED FROM THE GERMAN BY
Brian Murdoch

VINTAGE

2 4 6 8 10 9 7 5 3 1

Vintage
20 Vauxhall Bridge Road,
London SW1V 2SA

Vintage Classics is part of the Penguin Random House group
of companies whose addresses can be found at
global.penguinrandomhouse.com.

Penguin
Random House
UK

First published in Germany as *Der Weg zurück* by Propyläen,
Berlin in 1931
First published in Great Britain in translation by A.W. Wheen as
The Road Back by Putnam in 1931
This new translation by Brian Murdoch first published by
Vintage Classics in 2019

www.vintage-books.co.uk

A CIP catalogue record for this book is available
from the British Library

ISBN 9781784875268

Typeset in 10.5 pt/13 pt Bembo
by Integra Software Services Pvt. Ltd, Pondicherry

Printed and bound in Great Britain by Clays Ltd, Elcograf S.p.A.

Penguin Random House is committed to a sustainable future
for our business, our readers and our planet. This book is
made from Forest Stewardship Council® certified paper.

Translator's Preface

It may seem odd to talk about a sequel to *All Quiet on the Western Front*, a novel in which the narrator and principal character is famously killed at the end, and is thus unable to experience the post-war world, which he was, however, prepared to face as best he could. However, for the new novel, which is again a (mostly) first-person narrative, Remarque effectively brought that main character, Paul Bäumer, back to life. The narrator in *The Way Back* is Ernst Birkholz, whose very name is an echo: *Baum* means 'tree' and *Birkholz* is 'birchwood'. Ernst is presented as a classmate of Paul, hence one of the group of those who went straight from the grammar school into the war. If one follows the directions in the novel on a map of Osnabrück, too, Ernst seems to live in pretty well the same place. Other characters whom we had met through Paul Bäumer in *All Quiet on the Western Front* appear again in *The Way Back*, some of them adapting to the new world successfully, others less so. The point is, of course, that both young men are representative of the huge numbers who fought. Some were killed, some were not.

This was a work which Remarque himself declared that he had to write. In *All Quiet on the Western Front* things happen which the narrator of that work has to accept for the time being, even if he does not understand them, and sometimes he even tells us that he will have to think about them after the war. He himself cannot do so, but Ernst Birkholz does, and various points raised in the first novel are developed in the second. One of them is the question of comradeship, which in the first novel is referred to as the best thing that the war had brought about. But it did *not* survive the war, it was simply a fellowship in adversity. One of the principal themes of the second work is to show precisely how that comradeship was dictated exclusively by the circumstances of war, and how it very quickly breaks down in post-war civilian society, sometimes even violently. Remarque did not want anyone to think that because the war had engendered a close comradeship between soldiers, that this was somehow a point in favour of the war as such.

During the fighting, Paul had no time to think beyond the famously circular justification that 'war is war'. In *All Quiet on the Western Front*, when Paul, having just made it back to his own lines, is shown a sniper picking soldiers off, he comments that he could not do that, and in the second novel, Ernst visits a former sniper, now a comfortable family man, who is still proud of his score card and who has not the slightest doubts about his activities at the time. He – as did many – still believes in and uses the old cliché: war is war, after all.

Some of the material in the first novel is picked up and replaced in the post-war situation. Paul comments in the first novel that only a field hospital can really show you the damage war can do, and in the second Ernst (and the reader) observes a procession of the war-wounded, paraded in front of him as they campaign for better treatment. The question of rehabilitation is nowadays – at last? – being treated with greater awareness and sympathy, but in the circumstances of Germany after 1918 the effects on those who survived but who were physically impaired are devastating. The psychological adjustment of any of the former soldiers is less visible, but no less problematic, and this is another major theme of the second novel. Scenes set in an asylum make that point in the new work particularly graphically, but the long-term effects on all of the returning soldiers, whose youth had been taken from them when they were sent to the trenches, is made clear in all kinds of variations.

That one group of the young men had been plucked out of school and sent to the front led in the first novel to mocking discussions of the uselessness of their formal education in the situation in which they now found themselves. When members of that same group try to resume their education in the new work, this point – the disruption of their lives – is worked out fully. Their teachers want them simply to continue where they left off, and this is impossible, as they point out vigorously to those teachers. That Ernst tries – and fails – to become a teacher himself is also telling.

Above all else, this new work, which is set at the end of 1918 and into 1919, shows that the gunfire and the killing did not stop with the armistice. There are three significant shots fired in the new work after the war is over, and a further principal character commits suicide; every one of these incidents picks up ideas from the first work. With the breakdown of comradeship and the rise of political polarisation, one of the ex-soldiers shoots a former comrade because he is now on the other side of a political divide. The second shot is when a former soldier shoots a man he finds with his girlfriend, arguing in court that he has spent years killing people he did not hate, so why should he not shoot someone he *does* hate? The third shot, close to the end of the work, is once more at the old front line, to which one of the group has returned; he shoots himself, unable to cope with the post-war world, and his suicide is a classic case of survivor guilt. The other suicide in the work – this time significantly not by a gunshot – is that of another of Ernst's close friends, who had contracted syphilis in a field brothel. Although he can be cured, he cuts his wrists to let out the poison of the real disease in his blood, the one he cannot shake off and which cannot be cured: the war itself.

All these points link the two novels as the survivors try to make their way in a new and changed society, to move forward along the way back. Most chilling, however, is one of the final scenes of the work, one which points onwards historically, rather than backwards; the former soldiers, who only a short time ago were still in the trenches, see a group of lads who are presumably part of one of the right-wing youth movements which sprang up after the war, playing at soldiers on a mock-exercise, and who jeer at Ernst and the others as cowards and Bolsheviks. Such youth movements did indeed come into being (on both sides of the political divide) very soon after the war; but one side would become very prominent indeed only a very short time after this new historical novel, *The Way Back*, was written at the start of the 1930s.

★ ★ ★

It is appropriate to add a brief note on the names of those mentioned in the new novel.

Although it is for the most part once again a first-person narrative, a great many former soldiers are named in *The Way Back*, making the point that in spite of the slaughter, a lot of young (and also older) men *did* come back and had to adjust to the new world. Some of the men killed in *All Quiet on the Western Front*, including the narrator, Paul Bäumer, are named at the beginning as comrades and/or schoolmates of the survivors. The rest of the names are mostly new ones. Another young soldier, Heinrich Wessling, is killed in the new work at the very end of the war, and therefore even later than Paul Bäumer.

The new narrator is Ernst Birkholz and his closest friends are Ludwig Breyer and Georg Rahe. Remarque sometimes gives both names, sometimes just a surname, and he switches between the two in single passages. Others in Ernst's immediate circle include Willy Homeyer, Valentin Laher, Ferdinand Kosole, Tjaden (who was also in the previous novel, and who is definitely a survivor) and Jupp. Some play major parts in separate episodes: the older man Adolf Bethke, who has an unfaithful wife; Gerhard Giesecke, who is in an asylum; Max Weil, who is shot by a fellow soldier; and towards the end, Albert Trosske. Some former soldiers do well in the post-war world, most notably Arthur Ledderhose, and Karl Bröger. Two former officers, Heel and Seelig, are presented negatively. Many more ex-soldiers are mentioned in the context of the school, such as Julius Weddekamp, Alwin Westerholt, Helmuth Reinersmann, Paul Rademacher and others. Still more crop up in individual episodes, such as Franz Wagner, Anton Demuth and Franz Elstermann. Remarque could sometimes be careless with names, and here on one occasion refers to someone who is not apparently present in the incident when it is described in detail, and I have corrected this.

★ ★ ★

This novel was first published in English in a translation by A. W. Wheen as *The Road Back* (London: Putnam, 1931), a title used also for a film version. Since this title is far less well-established than that of the work to which it is a sequel, *All Quiet on the Western Front*, I have used a different and slightly more literal translation of Remarque's *Der Weg zurück*, in order to underline the fact that the soldiers are trying to find their way back into life.

In case anyone is inclined to compare this version of Remarque's second war-novel with Wheen's, however, it must be noted that (stylistic differences aside) the latter is not, strictly speaking, a translation of the same book. Wheen usually worked from a pre-publication typescript, and there are fairly frequent passages in his version – in many, though not all, cases only a sentence or two at a time – which were *not* included by Remarque in the final and definitive text published by Ullstein under their Propyläen imprint (there had also been a pre-publication serialisation in a magazine). More substantial passages left out of the book edition by Remarque include a longish comic section on the soldiers' teacher-training examinations, and some extended graphic details of the war-wounded whom Remarque allows to pass in procession past the reader; but even smaller cuts may appear significant, as in the trial scene of Albert Trosske. It must be emphasised, therefore, that the fact that there are passages in Wheen's version which are absent here does *not* mean that this has been abridged or censored; it is, I think, the first English translation, and as accurate a translation as I have been able to make it, of the author's final German book edition (Berlin: Propyläen, 1931). I have also had to hand the most recent KiWi paperback (with a valuable afterword by Tilman Westphalen; Cologne: Kiepenheuer und Witsch, 1998), and this, though essentially the same as that first book edition, has a few minor differences (a line seems to have been omitted at one point, for example, probably a typographical error), plus some corrections for the sake of consistency. I have in principle followed the 1931 first edition, however, also in respect of its section-divisions, which are again slightly different in the recent paperback.

All that aside, the usual translation difficulties remain, and the translator must do whatever is possible to indicate, for example, the deliberate contrast of the familiar with the polite form of address in German. It is interesting, too, that the separate opening and closing portions are *not* styled 'prologue' and 'epilogue' by Remarque, but literally as 'entrance' and 'exit'. Further, literary or political allusions (now) unfamiliar to the English reader can sometimes, if not always, be clarified by (it is hoped) discreet and brief expansions, although a footnote would have been needed to remind the reader that Friedrich Ebert had been a saddle-maker, and footnotes are not possible. Sometimes, however, liberties simply *do* have to be taken. I have changed the name of a vicious dog, for example, because 'Pluto' might anachronistically and inappropriately evoke a Disney cartoon; and if my attempt to offer something plausible for the untranslatable title of a revue leads some sharp-eyed critic to chastise my apparent unawareness that the Rumpler Taube was not in fact a bi-plane, then so be it.

Brian Murdoch, 2019

STARTING POINT

All the men that there are left of Number 2 Platoon are dozing in a battered and blasted section of trench behind the front line.

'That's a funny sort of shell ...' says Jupp suddenly.

'What do you mean?' asks Ferdinand Kosole, half sitting up.

'Listen for a minute,' replies Jupp.

Kosole cups a hand behind his ear and listens. We all do the same, straining into the night to hear. But there aren't any other sounds apart from the dull noise of artillery fire and the high-pitched whistle of shells. From over on the right there is the rattle of machine-gun fire as well, and the occasional scream. But we've been used to all that for years, and it's nothing anyone would waste his breath on.

Kosole gives Jupp a look.

'It's just stopped, just now,' he counters, embarrassed.

Kosole gives him another sharp look. But when Jupp still looks calmly back at him he turns away and simply grunts:

'It's just your guts rumbling, that's your funny shell noises. You'd be better off with a bit of shut-eye.'

With that, he scrapes some earth together to make himself a headrest, and stretches out carefully, so that his boots can't slip into the water. 'Bloody hell, I've got a wife and a double bed at home,' he murmurs, with his eyes already shut.

'Somebody'll be in it with her,' says Jupp from his corner.

Kosole opens one eye and gives him a hard glare. He looks as if he is about to get up again, but then he just grumbles: 'Don't push your luck, Rhineland boy.' And at once he is asleep and snoring.

Jupp beckons me to crawl across to him. I climb over Adolf Bethke's boots and sit down beside him. With a sidelong glance at the snoring Kosole he comments bitterly: 'I tell you, his sort don't know the meaning of education.'

Before the war Jupp had been a clerk in a law firm in Cologne. Even though he has been a soldier for three years, he's still pretty sensitive, and out here he sets great store by being someone with an education. Of course he doesn't know himself what that really means; but of all the things anyone ever said to him back then, it is precisely that word 'education' which has stuck with him, and he clings on to it as if it were a plank of wood in the open sea, to stop himself from going under. Everybody out here has something like that – it might be the wife, or a business back home, or a pair of boots. With Valentin Laher it's booze and with Tjaden it's the simple desire to stuff himself with beans and bacon again. Kosole, on the other hand, gets angry at the mere sound of the word 'education'. For some reason he associates it with formal stiff collars, and that's enough for him. It even has that effect now. Without even interrupting his snores he snarls: 'You bloody pen-pusher!'

Jupp shakes his head in a superior and resigned manner. We sit together silently a little while for warmth. The night is wet and cold, there is a lot of cloud, and a fair bit of rain. Then we pick up the tarpaulins we are squatting on and drape them over our heads.

On the horizon we can see the light of the artillery flashes. You get the feeling that it must be less cold over there, it looks so inviting. The rockets go up like coloured or silver flowers over the flashes. A great red moon is swimming through the damp air over the ruins of a French farm.

'Do you believe we're going home?' whispers Jupp.

I shrug. 'That's what they're saying …'

Jupp breathes heavily. 'A warm room and a sofa and going out in the evening – can you still imagine what all that's like?'

'When I was last on leave I tried my civvy suit on,' I reply thoughtfully, 'but it was far too small for me; I'd need new things.' How fantastic it all sounds when you are out here: civvies, sofas, an evening out … Strange thoughts come up – just like black coffee when it tasted too much of the rusty metal of the dixie it was boiled in, and you bring it up again, hot and choking.

Jupp picks his nose absent-mindedly. 'Christ almighty, shop windows – and cafés and women.'

4

'Come on, man, you'll be happy enough just to get out of all this shit,' I tell him, and blow on my freezing cold hands.

'You're right.' Jupp pulls the tarpaulin over his thin, sloping shoulders. 'What are you going to do, then, if you get out of here?'

I laugh. 'Me? I'll probably have to go back to school. Me, Willy, Albert, and even Ludwig over there.' I point backwards to where somebody is lying in front of a shell-shattered dug-out, with two greatcoats over him.

'Hell, you won't really do that, will you?' says Jupp.

'Don't know. We'll probably have to,' I reply, and suddenly I feel really angry, though I don't know why.

Something stirs underneath the greatcoats. A pale, narrow face emerges and groans softly. Lying there is my classmate, Second Lieutenant Ludwig Breyer, our platoon commander. For weeks now he's had diarrhoea with blood in it – it's dysentery, of course, but he doesn't want to go back into the field hospital. He'd rather stay here with us, because we're all waiting for peace to be declared, and then we can take him with us. The field hospitals are overflowing, nobody cares properly for anyone, and as soon as you're lying on one of those beds you're one step nearer to being dead. People all around are kicking the bucket, and if you are on your own in the middle of it all it's catching, so before you know it you're one of them as well. Max Weil, our medical orderly, has made him up some sort of liquid plaster and he guzzles that down to cement up his guts and give him a bit of relief. All the same he still has his trousers down twenty or thirty times a day.

And he has to go again now. I help him round the corner and he squats down.

Jupp waves at me. 'Listen, there it is again!'

'What?'

'The shells I heard before.'

Kosole stirs himself and yawns. Then he gets up, looks meaningfully at his great fists, squints over at Jupp and tells

5

him: 'Christ, if you're playing silly buggers with us again, your bones'll be going home in an old potato sack.'

We listen. The whistling and piping as the unseen shells rise and fall are interrupted by a strange, hoarse-sounding, long-drawn-out noise that is so new and weird that it makes our skin crawl.

'Gas shells!' shouts Willy Homeyer and jumps up.

We are all awake and straining to hear.

Wessling points up at the sky. 'There they are! Wild geese!'

Against the dull grey of the clouds there is a darker line, a V-formation. The point is headed towards the moon, and then cuts into its red disc and we can see the dark shadows clearly, a wedge made up of many wings, a procession with strange, wild, squawking cries that die away in the distance.

'There they go,' grumbles Willy. 'Damn it, if only we could just take off like that! Two wings and away!'

Heinrich Wessling looks at the geese as they fly away. 'Winter's coming on,' he says slowly. He's a farmer and knows about these things.

Ludwig Breyer leans against the revetment, weak and sad. 'First time I've seen any of them.'

But all of a sudden Kosole has become the most cheerful of us. He quickly gets Wessling to put him in the picture again, and what he wants to know most of all is whether wild geese are just as fat as farmyard ones.

'More or less,' says Wessling.

'Well, blow me down,' says Kosole, his face twitching with excitement. 'So what we've got flying through the air up there are fifteen or twenty first-class roast dinners!'

There is another rushing of wings just above us, and again we are assailed by the rough, throaty call as if some bird of prey were attacking us, and the beat of the wings merges with the drawn-out cries and the force of the ever stronger wind until it all becomes a fierce and powerful image of freedom and life.

A shot rings out. Kosole lowers his gun and looks eagerly up at the sky. He's taken aim at the middle of the formation. Tjaden is

6

standing next to him, ready to race off like a gun dog if a goose comes down. But the flock flies resolutely on.

'Pity,' says Adolf Bethke, 'that would have been the first sensible shot in this lousy war.'

Kosole tosses his rifle down in disappointment. 'If only we had a few shotgun cartridges!' He sinks into a state of melancholy as he pictures to himself what we would have done if it had worked. He moves his mouth involuntarily as if chewing.

'Right,' says Jupp, watching him. 'With apple sauce and roast potatoes, eh?'

Kosole gives him a poisonous look. 'Shut your trap, pen-pusher!'

'You should have been in the flying corps,' says Jupp with a grin, 'then you could have gone after them with a net.'

'Arsehole!' declares Kosole with an air of finality, and settles down to sleep again. It's the best thing to do. The rain gets heavier. We sit back-to-back with the tarpaulins over us, squatting in our section of trench like mounds of dark earth. Earth, a uniform, and underneath that just a little bit of life.

★ ★ ★

I'm awakened by a fierce whisper. 'Forward, forward!'

'What's going on?' I ask, still half asleep.

'We've got to go up to the front,' grunts Kosole and gets his stuff together.

I'm bewildered. 'We've just come back from there.'

'Bloody nonsense,' I hear Wessling curse. 'The war's over, isn't it?'

'Come on, forward!' It is Heel himself, our company commander, and he is driving us on. He runs impatiently through the trench. Ludwig Breyer is already on his feet. 'Can't be helped, we've got to go up the line,' he says in a resigned tone of voice, and grabs a couple of hand grenades.

Adolf Bethke looks at him. 'You ought to stay here, Ludwig. You can't go up the line with your dysentery.'

Breyer shakes his head.

Belt buckles click, rifles clatter, and the wan smell of death rises up again out of the earth. We had hoped that we'd got away from it forever, because the mere thought of peace had exploded like a rocket before our eyes. And even if we hadn't believed it, or really taken it on board, in the few minutes it took for the rumour to get about, the hope alone had been enough to change us more than the previous twenty months had done. Up until now, one year of war had simply been added to the next, one year of hopelessness followed another, and when you looked back you were amazed both that it had been such a long time, and also that it had *only* been that long. But now, when word is going round that peace could come any day, every hour seems a thousand times as long, and every minute under fire seems harder and longer than all the time so far.

The wind makes a miaowing noise over what is left of the parapets, and the clouds scud rapidly across the moon. Light and shadows are changing continuously. We move up in close file, a group of shadows, a pitiful Number 2 Platoon, shot down to a few men only – the company as a whole is hardly up to the strength of a normal platoon – but those that are left have been tried and tested. We even have three old sweats from 1914 with us: Bethke, Wessling and Kosole, who know everything and often talk about the first months of the war, when things were actually moving, and it now sounds like something from the days of the old Teutonic warriors.

Everyone finds his own corner, his own hole when we reach the position. There isn't much going on. Verey lights, machine-gun fire, rats. Willy sends a rat flying into the air with a carefully aimed kick and cuts it in half with a trenching-tool as it falls.

There are isolated shots. Over on the right we can hear hand grenades exploding in the distance.

'Let's hope it stays quiet here,' says Wessling.

'To get your brains blown out now ...' Willy shakes his head.

'If your luck runs out, you could break a finger just by picking your nose,' growls Valentin.

Ludwig is lying on a tarpaulin. He really could have stayed behind the lines. Max Weil gives him a couple of tablets to take. Valentin tells him he ought to drink some schnapps. Ledderhose tries to tell a dirty joke. Nobody is listening. We lie around. Time passes.

Suddenly I shudder and raise my head. I see that Bethke is also sitting up already. Even Tjaden stirs. The instinct of years is telling us something, no one knows yet what it is, but for sure something special is up. We raise our heads cautiously and listen, our eyes narrowed to slits so that we can penetrate the half-light. Every one of us is wide awake, with all of our senses at their sharpest, and every muscle ready for what is to come; we don't know yet what it is, but it can only spell danger. The hand grenades scrape along the ground as Willy, the best thrower, crawls forward. We are lying like cats, pressed against the ground. Right beside me I can make out Ludwig Breyer. There is no sign of sickness now in his tense features. He has the same cold, deadly expression that everyone here has, the face of the front-line trenches. A terrible tension has frozen and set our faces, so unusual is the message sent to us by our subconscious long before our actual senses recognise anything.

The fog wavers and drifts. And then suddenly I realise what it is that has put us all on the highest alert. It has simply become quiet. Completely quiet.

No machine guns, no firing, no impacts, no whistling of shells, nothing, nothing at all, not a shot, not a scream. It is just quiet, absolutely quiet.

We stare at each other, unable to understand. It is the first time that it has been so quiet since we became part of the war. We sniff the air uneasily, trying to find out what is happening. Is it a gas attack? But the wind is all wrong, it would disperse it. Is there going to be an offensive? But then the silence would have given it away well in advance. What can be going on? The grenade I am holding is wet, the tension is making me sweat so much. It's as if your nerves are trying to tear themselves apart. Five minutes. Ten minutes. 'It's a quarter of an hour now,' calls out Valentin Laher. His voice has a hollow sound in the fog, as if it were coming from a grave. And still nothing happens, no attack, no sudden darkness of leaping shadows ... Our hands relax and then tighten again. We cannot bear it! We are so used to the noise of the front that now, when it is no longer on top of us, we feel as if we are going to explode, burst like balloons.

'Hey, you know what? It's peace,' says Willy suddenly, and that hits us like a bomb.

Our faces relax, our movements become less purposeful and more uncertain. Peace? We look at each other incredulously. Peace? I drop my hand grenades. Peace? Ludwig lies back slowly on his tarpaulin. Peace? Bethke has a look in his eyes as if his face is going to break up. Peace? Wessling stands immobile as a tree trunk, and when he moves his head and turns towards us, he looks as if he just wants to start walking now and go on till he reaches home.

And then all at once – we barely notice it in our excitement – the silence is over, the dull drone of artillery fire starts again and from a distance a machine gun starts to rattle like a woodpecker. We calm down, and we are almost happy to hear the familiar sounds of death again.

* * *

It's quiet during the day. At night we are supposed to move back a little, as we have often done before. But those on the other side don't just come along after us, they attack. Before we know where we are there is heavy shelling. Behind us great red fountains spurt up, raging in the twilight. For a while things stay quiet where we are. Willy and Tjaden come across a tin of beef and scoff it right away. The others just lie there waiting. The long months have burnt them out and they are pretty well indifferent to everything when they can't defend themselves.

The company commander crawls into our shell-hole. 'Got everything you need?' he asks through the noise. 'Not enough ammunition,' shouts Bethke. Heel shrugs and passes Bethke a cigarette over his shoulder. Bethke nods without looking round. 'That's the way things are,' shouts Heel, and jumps across to the next shell-hole. He knows that they'll manage. Any one of these old hands would make just as good a company commander as him.

It gets dark. The firing catches up with us. We haven't got much cover. We dig into the shell-hole with our spades and our bare hands to make holes for our heads. Then we lie there pressed hard against the earth. Albert Trosske and Adolf Bethke are beside me. A shell impacts twenty yards or so away. We open our mouths wide when the bastard comes whistling down so as to save our eardrums, but even so we are half deafened, dirt and mud are spurted into our eyes, and the hellish mixture of cordite and sulphur rips at our throats. Bits of shrapnel rain down on us. It must have got someone, because alongside some hot metal from a shell a torn-off hand goes flying past, right by Bethke's head.

Heel jumps into our shell-hole, and in the light of the explosions we can see that he is white with rage under his helmet. 'Brandt,' he coughs. 'Direct hit. Blown to bits.'

It gets noisy again, it rages, roars, rains mud and steel, the air thunders, the earth rumbles. Then the curtain of fire goes up, is pulled back, and at that moment men rise up out of the earth, burnt, blackened, holding hand grenades, waiting and ready. 'Back slowly!' commands Heel.

The attack is over on our left. There is fighting around one of our machine-gun posts in a shell-hole. The gun barks away. The flashes from the hand grenades are jerky. Suddenly the machine gun is silent – it has jammed. Immediately the post is surrounded. A few minutes later it is cut off. Heel sees it happen. 'Damn it.' He sets off over the ridge. 'Forward!' Bullets fly overhead, Willy, Bethke and Heel lie down within range and throw their grenades, then Heel quickly jumps up again – he is like a madman in moments like this, an absolute devil. But it works. The men in the shell-hole get their resolve back, the machine gun springs into action again, and contact has been made. We dash back together to get to the concrete pillbox behind us. It all happened so quickly that the Americans haven't even noticed that the post has been cleared. Grenade-bursts are still visible in the abandoned shell-hole.

Things quieten down. I'm worried about Ludwig. But he is there. Then Bethke crawls in. 'Wessling?'

Heel turns up. 'What's going on?'

'Wessling is missing.'

Tjaden was lying next to him when we started to go back, but he hasn't seen him since. 'Where?' asks Kosole. Tjaden points outwards. 'Damn!' Kosole looks at Bethke. Bethke looks at Kosole. Both of them know that this might well be the last battle we are in. They don't hesitate for a moment. 'What the hell!' grunts Bethke. 'Let's go!' says Kosole. They disappear into the darkness. Heel dashes out after them.

Ludwig gets everything ready to go into action if the three of them come under attack. It's quiet for a little while. Then suddenly hand grenades go off and there is the noise of small-arms fire as well. We rush out, Ludwig first – then the sweating faces of Bethke and Kosole come into view, and they are dragging someone behind them on a tarpaulin.

Heel? No, Wessling, and he's groaning. Heel? He's holding them off, still firing; and then he's back. 'Got the whole lot of them in the shell-hole,' he shouts, 'and two more with my revolver.' Then he stares at Wessling. 'Well?' Wessling doesn't answer. His belly has been ripped open and looks like a butcher's shop window. You can't even see how deep the wound is. We bandage it up as best we can. Wessling is groaning for water but we can't give him any. You mustn't drink with a wound in the guts. Then he asks for a blanket. He's freezing, he has lost so much blood.

A runner brings orders for us to fall back further. We take Wessling with us on a tarpaulin with rifles stuck down each side so that we can carry him until we can find a stretcher. We move back carefully in single file. Gradually it gets light. Silvery mist in the bushes. We move out of the fighting zone. We are already sure that it's over, but then there is a soft whirring, and the flat noise of a strike. Ludwig silently rolls up his sleeve. He's been hit in the arm. Weil bandages it.

We go back. Back.

The air is as mild as wine. This is not November, this is more like March. The skies are pale blue and clear, the sun reflected in the pools of water by the sides of the path. We go down an avenue of poplars. The trees stand on both sides of the road, tall and almost completely undamaged, with just one or two missing. This area used to be well behind the lines and is not nearly as ravaged as the few miles in front, which we have had to give up day by day, yard by yard. The sun shines on the brown tarpaulin, and as we move along the yellow avenue the falling leaves keep sailing down, and some land on it. The dressing station is completely full. There are already a lot of wounded men lying by the entrance. For the moment we leave Wessling outside. A number of men with wounds in the arms and white bandages are forming up to march off. The station is already being closed down. A doctor runs about and examines the newcomers. He has a man taken inside straight away whose leg is hanging loosely, bent the wrong way at the knee. Wessling is just bandaged up again and left outside.

He wakes up from his dozing state and looks at the doctor as he leaves.

'Why is he going?'

'He'll be back,' I tell him.

'But I've got to go in, I've got to be operated on.' Suddenly he becomes terribly agitated and fingers the bandages. 'This has got to be sewn up right away.'

We try and calm him down. He has gone green and is sweating with fear. 'Adolf, run after him, get him back here.'

Bethke hesitates for a moment. But with Wessling's eyes on him he has no choice, even though he knows it is pointless. I see him talking to the doctor. Wessling follows him with his eyes as far as he can. It's horrible to see the way he tries to turn his head.

Bethke comes back but makes sure Wessling can't see him, then shakes his head, raises a single finger and mouths silently the words 'one – hour'.

We look reassuringly at Wessling. But nobody can deceive a dying farmer! When Bethke tells him he'll be operated on later and the wound just has to settle a bit, Wessling knows. He is silent for a moment, then he gasps out softly: 'Yes, there you all are, safe and sound – and you're going home – but me? – four years and then this ... four years ... and then this ...'

'They'll take you into the dressing station any minute, Heinrich,' says Bethke to comfort him.

He'll have none of it. 'Leave off.'

He does not say much more after that. He doesn't ask to be carried inside, but wants to stay out in the open. The dressing station is on a small slope. From here you can see clearly way back down the avenue we came along. It is bright and golden. The earth is still and soft and safe, you can even see fields under cultivation, small, brown, well-tilled parcels of land, right by the clearing station. Whenever the wind blows away the smell of blood and pus you catch instead the sharp scent of the ploughed furrows. There is blue on the horizon and everything looks very peaceful; that's because the view here is not towards the line. The front is over to the right.

Wessling is quiet. He is watching everything very closely. His eyes are attentive and clear. He's a farmer, and understands the landscape better than we do, and in a different way. He knows that he is going. Therefore he does not want to miss a thing, and does not look away again. Every minute he gets paler. Eventually he makes a small movement and whispers: 'Ernst ...'

I bend down to hear what he says. 'Get my things out.'

'There's time enough for that, Heinrich ...'

'No, no. Just do it.'

I lay them out in front of him. A wallet made of shabby calico, a knife, a watch, money – all familiar stuff. Loose in the wallet is a picture of his wife.

'Show me,' he says.

I take it out and hold it so that he can see it. A clear-skinned, browned face. He looks at it. After a while he whispers: 'So it's all done, then,' and his lips tremble. At last he turns his head away.

'Take it with you,' he says. I'm not sure what he means, but I don't want to keep asking, and so I put it in my pocket. 'Take all that to her ...' He looks over at the rest of the stuff. I nod. 'And tell her ...' He stares at me with a strange, wide-eyed look, murmurs something, shakes his head and groans. I try my hardest to make out what he is saying, but he just makes a gurgling noise, twitches, breathes heavily and more slowly, with pauses from time to time, then very deeply again, with a sigh ... and suddenly his eyes look like those of a blind man, and he is dead.

★ ★ ★

The next morning we are up at the front for the last time. There is hardly any firing now. The war is over. In an hour we are supposed to pull out. We'll never have to go back again. When we leave, we are leaving forever.

We destroy what there is to destroy. Little enough. A few dugouts. Then we get the order to withdraw.

It's a strange moment. We stand there together and look ahead of us. There are strands of light mist over the surface of the ground. The lines of shell-holes and trenches are clearly visible. It's true that these are only the last bits of the front line, because this area was a reserve position, but it still came into the firing zone. How often did we come up through these communication trenches? And how often did rather fewer of us make it back? The monotonous landscape before us is grey – in the distance there is what is left of a copse, a few stumps, the ruins of a village, and in the middle a solitary high wall, which has somehow managed to survive.

'Yes,' says Bethke thoughtfully. 'Four years we've spent in this.'

'Yes, damn it,' nods Kosole. 'And it's over just like that.'

'Bloody hell.' Willy Homeyer leans against the parapet. 'Funny, isn't it ...?' We stand and stare. The farm, the scrap of copse, the ridges, the lines of the horizon further way, it was a terrible world and a hard life. And now it's going to be behind us, and when we move on it will disappear further and further behind us with every step, and in an hour it will be gone as if it had never existed. How can anyone grasp all that?

So there we stand, and we ought to be laughing and roaring with delight – and yet there's a flat feeling in our stomachs as if we'd swallowed something and need to spew it up again.

Nobody has much to say. Ludwig Breyer leans wearily against the trench wall and raises a hand, as if he were waving to someone standing opposite.

Heel appears. 'Can't tear yourselves away, eh? Well, now for the real crap.'

Ledderhose looks at him in amazement. 'But peace is coming.'

'Yes, and all that crap,' says Heel, and moves away with a look on his face as if his mother had just died.

'He never got his medal, he missed out on the *Pour le Mérite*,' explains Ledderhose.

'Oh, shut it,' snaps Albert Trosske.

'OK, let's go, then,' says Bethke, but he still doesn't move.

'There are a lot of us in the ground out there,' comments Ludwig.

'Yes, Brandt, Müller, Kat, Haie, Bäumer, Bertinck –'

'Sandkuhl, Meinders, both the Terbrüggen boys, Hugo, Bernhard –'

'Christ, give it a rest ...'

A lot of us are in the ground out there, but up to now we have never felt this way about it. After all, we were together – they were in their graves, we were in the trenches, with just a handful of earth between us. They were just a bit ahead of us, because every day their number went up and ours went down – often we weren't sure whether or not we had already joined them. But the shells regularly brought them back to us, with crumbling bones flying overhead, scraps of uniform, rotting, wet and muddy heads, coming back into battle from their earth-covered dugouts in the heavy firing. It didn't seem horrible to us; we were still too close to them. But now we are going back into life, and they have to stay here.

Ludwig, whose cousin was killed in this sector, blows his nose between his fingers and then turns round. Slowly we follow him. But we stop a few more times and look around us. And we stand still again, and suddenly we feel that everything out there in front of us, that absolute hell, that ragged patch of shell-holes, is still there inside us. And we feel, damn it, that — if the idea weren't so crazy and so sickening — that it almost looks as if it were all comfortably familiar to us, painful and fearsome, but our home, and that here is where we belong.

We shake our heads over this — but whether it is the lost years that are lying out there, or our comrades, or all the wretchedness that this piece of earth covers up, there is still so much misery deep in our bones that we could howl and weep.

And then we march off.

PART ONE

1

The roads through the countryside are long, the villages are bathed in a grey light, the trees are rustling, and the leaves are falling, falling.

But along those roads the grey columns are moving onwards, step by step, in their faded and dirty uniforms. The unshaven faces beneath the steel helmets are thin and hollow from hunger and deprivation, drawn and reduced to a pattern of lines of horror, courage and death. They move on in silence, as they have marched along so many roads before, ridden on so many goods trains, crouched down in so many dugouts, taken cover in so many shell-holes, without saying much. And in the same way they move along this road towards home and peace. Without saying much.

Older men with beards and slim younger ones who are not yet twenty, all fellow soldiers, all the same. Beside them their lieutenants, themselves still not much more than children, but who have been their leaders on many a night in many attacks. And behind them all is the army of the dead. And so they move forward, step by step, ill, half starved, with no ammunition, in companies that have been thinned out, with eyes that still can't quite grasp it: they have escaped from hell and this is the way back into life.

★ ★ ★

The company marches slowly because we are all weary and we still have our wounded with us. For this reason our group falls further and further behind. The region is hilly, and when the road climbs we can see from the top of the rise in one direction the rest of our own troop ahead, moving away from us, and in the other the closed-up, endless ranks of soldiers following us. They are Americans. Their columns are moving along like some great broad river through the rows of trees, and the restless glitter of their weapons hovers above them. But all around lie the quiet fields, and the tops of the trees in their autumn colours stretch upwards, solemn and impartial, above the oncoming flood.

We have spent the night in a little village. A stream with willow trees at its side is flowing along behind the houses where we bedded down. There is a narrow path alongside it and we follow it, walking in single file in a long line. Kosole is at the front. Trotting beside him is Wolf, the company's dog, sniffing at his haversack for food.

Suddenly, at the point where the path meets the main road, Ferdinand jumps back.

'Watch out!'

In a moment we've raised our rifles and have spread out quickly. Kosole lies down in the ditch by the road ready to fire, Jupp and Trosske take cover and keep a lookout from behind some elder bushes, Willy Homeyer reaches for the hand grenades on his belt, and even our wounded men are ready to fight.

Some American troops are coming along the country road. They are laughing and chatting with each other. This is their advance party, and they have caught up with us.

Adolf Bethke is the only one of us who had stood still. Now he walks calmly a few paces back along the road, away from cover. Kosole stands up again. The rest of us also come to our senses and put our belts and rifle straps back where they should be – the fighting stopped several days ago, after all.

The Americans are taken aback when they see us. Their conversation dies away. They approach us slowly. We withdraw to a barn, to keep our backs covered, and wait to see what happens. We put the wounded men in the middle of our group.

After a full minute's silence, a lanky American detaches himself from the rest and waves to us.

'Hello, *Kamerad!*'

Adolf Bethke raises his hand too. '*Kamerad!*'

The tension eases. The Americans come forward. Almost at once we are surrounded by them. We've never seen them at such close quarters before except when they were taken prisoner or killed.

It's a strange moment. We stare at them in silence. They stand in a semicircle around us, all big, strong men, and you can see at once that they've always had enough to eat. They are all young – not a single one is anywhere near as old as Adolf Bethke or Ferdinand Kosole, and they are by no means the oldest of our lot. But none of them is as young as Albert Trosske or Karl Bröger either, and those two are still not the youngest we have, either.

They are wearing new uniforms and new greatcoats; their boots are watertight and they fit; their weapons are in good condition and they have pockets full of ammunition. Every one of them is fresh, has never been in action.

Compared to these people, we really are a mob of bandits. Our uniforms are faded from the dirt of years, from the rain in the Argonne, from the chalk dust in the Champagne region, from the watery marshes of Flanders; our greatcoats have been ripped by shrapnel and shell fragments and sewn together with great clumsy stitches, stiff with mud and sometimes with blood; our boots are worn through, our weapons nearly useless, we are practically out of ammunition. Every one of us is just as dirty as the rest, just as unkempt, just as weary. The war passed over us like a steamroller.

More and more troops come along. By now the whole area is full of curious onlookers.

We are still backed in the corner, surrounding our wounded men, not because we are afraid, but just because we all belong together. The Americans nudge one another and point at our old, worn-out gear. One of them offers Breyer a piece of white bread, but he doesn't take it, even though there is hunger in his eyes.

Suddenly one of them points with a suppressed exclamation at the bandages on our wounded men. They are made of crêpe paper and tied on with string. All the rest peer at them, then step back and

23

have a whispered conversation with each other. Their friendly faces show sympathy because they can see that we no longer even have any proper lint bandages. The man who first hailed us puts his hand on Bethke's shoulder. '*Deutsche – gute Soldat,*' he says, '*brave Soldat.*'

The others nod vigorously.

We don't say anything, because there is nothing we can say. The last few weeks have taken a terrible toll on us. We had to go into battle again and again and lost people pointlessly; but we didn't ask questions, we just did it, as we had been doing all the time, and by the end our whole company had only thirty-two men left out of two hundred. That is how we came out of it, not thinking much about it and not feeling much more than that we had done what we had been told to do, to the best of our ability.

But now, under the pitying gaze of the Americans, we can understand how senseless it all was in the end. The sight of their endless well-equipped columns of troops makes clear to us what a hopelessly overwhelming mass of manpower and materials we had made our stand against.

We bite our lips and look at one another. Bethke moves away so that the American's hand is no longer on his shoulder, Kosole stares into the distance, Ludwig Breyer straightens up, we take a firmer hold of our rifles, brace ourselves, our eyes get harder and we don't look down. We look again across the country we have come from, we are tight-lipped and emotional, and once more it all comes burning through us, all that we have done, all we have suffered, all that we have had to leave behind.

We don't know what kind of state we are in. But someone would only have to say one hard word and it would pull us together whether we wanted it to or not, we would rush forward and attack, wild and breathless, crazy and lost, and we would fight, fight again in spite of everything –

A stocky, sweaty-faced sergeant pushes through towards us. He pours out a great stream of German over Kosole, who is standing nearest to him. Ferdinand starts backwards, completely taken by surprise.

'He talks exactly like us,' he says to Bethke in amazement. 'What do you make of that, then?'

In fact the man speaks better and more fluently than Kosole does. He tells us that he was in Dresden before the war and has a lot of friends there.

'In Dresden?' queries Kosole, getting more and more baffled. 'I was there for a couple of years myself –'

The sergeant smiles, as if this were some special commendation. He tells us the name of the street where he lived.

'Less than five minutes from me,' declares Kosole, now thoroughly worked up. 'It's a wonder we never met! Do you happen to know Mrs Pohl from the corner of Johannes Street? A fat widow-lady with dark hair? She was my landlady.'

The sergeant doesn't know her, but does recall a bookkeeper called Mr Zander, although Kosole can't place him. But both of them remember the River Elbe and the castle, and this makes them beam at each other as if they were old friends. Ferdinand claps the sergeant on the arm. 'Bloody hell, speaks German like one of us and used to live in Dresden! Why the blazes were we fighting each other?'

The sergeant laughs and has no idea either. He fetches out a pack of cigarettes and offers one to Kosole. He helps himself without a second's hesitation, because any one of us would give up part of his soul for a cigarette. Our own are made of beech leaves and hay, and that's only the better variety. Valentin Laher reckons that the usual sort are made of mattress straw and dried horse dung – and Valentin is a connoisseur.

Kosole blows out the smoke with great relish. We sniff at it eagerly. Laher has gone pale. His nostrils are twitching. 'Let us have a puff,' he asks Kosole imploringly. But before he can even take the cigarette, another American holds out a packet of Virginia tobacco. Valentin stares at it in disbelief. Then he takes it and sniffs at it. His face is transformed. With reluctance he gives the packet back. But the other man refuses it, and jabs a finger at the badge on Laher's forage cap, which is sticking out of his pack.

Valentin doesn't understand. 'He wants to swap the tobacco for the cap badge,' explains the sergeant from Dresden. Laher finds that even harder to understand. First-class tobacco for a tin badge? The man must be off his head. Valentin wouldn't part with the packet now even if they made him a sergeant or a lieutenant as a reward. Without further ado he offers the American the whole cap, and eagerly fills his first pipe, his hands trembling.

We've realised now what's going on: the Americans want to trade. You can see that they haven't been in the war for very long; they are still collecting souvenirs, epaulettes, cap badges, belt buckles, medals, uniform buttons. In exchange we get a good supply of soap, cigarettes, chocolate and canned food. On top of that they even offer us a great handful of cash in exchange for our dog, but there they can offer as much as they like, Wolf stays with us. On the other hand, we have a bit of luck with our wounded men. An American with so many gold fillings that his gob is shining like a brass foundry wants scraps of bandages with blood on them, so that he can prove back home that they really were made of paper. He offers us some first-class biscuits and an armful of proper bandages for them. Carefully, and with great satisfaction, he stows the paper bandages in his wallet, especially the one he gets from Ludwig Breyer, because that has the blood of a lieutenant on it. Ludwig has to write his name, the place and his unit in pencil on it, so that everyone in America will know that the whole story is true. At first he doesn't want to, but Weil persuades him, because we are desperate for decent bandages. Besides, the biscuits are exactly what he needs for his dysentery.

However, Arthur Ledderhose makes the best deal of all. He trots out a box full of Iron Crosses that he'd found in some abandoned orderly room. An American as wrinkled as he is, with a face like a lemon, just like his, wants to get hold of the whole boxful. But Ledderhose just narrows his eyes and gives him a long, appraising look. The American holds the stare, just as unmoving and apparently quite innocent. All at once the pair seem as alike as two brothers. Something well beyond war and death has suddenly turned up, something which has survived everything: the spirit of business.

Ledderhose's adversary soon sees that he can't do a thing, and that he isn't going to put one over on Arthur – trading single items will be very much more profitable. Arthur swaps stuff until the box is empty. Gradually things pile up beside him, even butter, silk, eggs and underwear, so that when he is finished he's standing there like a bandy-legged one-man grocer's shop.

We set off again. The Americans call out after us and wave as we go. The sergeant in particular keeps it up for a long time. Even Kosole is moved, as far as this is possible for an old soldier. He grunts a few farewell noises and he waves as well; mind you, when he does, it still looks like a threatening gesture. Then he says to Bethke: 'Pretty decent bunch, eh?'

Adolf nods. We walk on without saying anything. Ferdinand has his head down. He's thinking. He doesn't do that very often, but when something gets into him he really holds onto it and keeps turning it over in his mind. He can't get the sergeant from Dresden out of his head.

In the villages the people stare at us as we go past. There are flowers at the window of a railway official's house by the tracks. A woman with full breasts is nursing a baby. She's wearing a blue dress. Dogs bark at us. Wolf barks back. In the road a cockerel is treading a hen. We smoke, and our minds are blank.

★ ★ ★

Marching, marching. Field hospitals in one area. Supply depots in another. A large park with plane trees. Stretchers and wounded men under the trees. The leaves are falling, covering them with red and gold.

A gas hospital. Serious cases, men who can't be moved any more. Blue, waxy or green faces, dead eyes, eaten up by the acid, dying men gurgling and choking. They all want to get away, afraid of being taken prisoner. As if it made any difference where they die.

We try to comfort them, telling them that the Americans will look after them better. But they don't listen. They keep on shouting after us to take them with us.

That shouting is horrible. The pallid faces look completely unreal out here in the clean air. But worst of all are their beards. They seem to have a strange existence of their own, hard, single-minded, growing and flourishing on the men's cheeks like some dark fungus which feeds on itself the more they fall into decay.

Many of the seriously wounded men hold out their thin, grey arms like children – 'Won't you take me with you, lads?' they plead. 'Won't you take me with you, lads?'

In their hollow eyes there are already deep, strange shadows lurking, and the tortured pupils peer out as if they are drowning. Others say nothing; they just follow us with their eyes, watching us for as long as they can.

Gradually the shouts get fainter. The road goes slowly onward. We're carrying a lot of stuff, because you have to have something to take home. There are clouds in the sky. In the afternoon the sun breaks through and the birches, which only have a few leaves left on them, are reflected in the puddles on the roadway. There is a soft blue haze in the branches.

As I march along, with my pack on my back and my head down, I can see in the clear pools of rain at the edge of the road the image of those bright, silvery-silken trees. The picture reflected in this accidental mirror is more powerful than the reality. Down there, embedded in the brown earth, is a little piece of sky with trees, there is depth and clarity, and suddenly it makes me tremble. For the first time in a long while I have the feeling again that something is beautiful, that this image reflected in the pool of water at my feet is simply beautiful, beautiful and pure – and with this trembling sensation my heart rises, everything else falls away for a moment, and now I can feel it for the first time: peace – I can see it: peace – I can grasp it completely: peace. The pressure that so far has never let

28

up now eases and something unknown, something new flies up, a bird, a great white bird, peace, a quivering horizon, quivering expectations, a first glimpse, an idea, hope, things bursting forth, things to come: peace.

I come out of it with a start and look around me. Behind me there are my fellow soldiers on their stretchers, still calling out to us. There is peace and they have to die anyway. But I am trembling with joy and I'm not ashamed. Strange …

Maybe that is the reason why there are always wars, because you can never completely share the suffering of other people.

2

By afternoon we are sitting in the courtyard of a brewery. Our company commander, First Lieutenant Heel, comes out of the establishment's office and calls us together. An order has come in to say that representatives have to be chosen from the ranks. We are very surprised by this. Nothing like that has happened before.

At that point Max Weil appears in the courtyard. He's waving a newspaper and shouts out: 'There's a revolution in Berlin.'

Heel turns round. 'Rubbish,' he snaps, 'there's just a bit of unrest in Berlin.'

But Weil hasn't finished yet. 'The Kaiser has fled to Holland.'

That wakes us up. Weil must have gone mad. Heel goes very red in the face and shouts: 'Bloody liar!'

Weil passes him the newspaper. Heel screws it up and stares at Weil in fury. He cannot stand him, because Weil is a Jew, quiet and calm, who likes to sit around reading books. Heel, on the other hand, is the forceful type.

'It's all nonsense,' he growls, and glares at Weil as if he'd like to tear him limb from limb.

Max unbuttons his tunic and fishes out a second paper, a news-extra. Heel glances at it, rips it into pieces and goes off to his quarters. Weil puts the pieces back together again and reads the report out to us. We sit there completely dumbfounded. Nobody knows what is going on any longer. 'The word is that the Kaiser wanted to avoid a civil war,' says Weil.

'It's crazy,' shouts Kosole, 'what if we'd come out with something like that back then? Damnation, and that's what we stuck it out for, out here.'

'Jupp, just pinch me to make sure I'm still here,' says Bethke, shaking his head. Jupp confirms it for him. 'Then it must be right,' Bethke goes on, 'but I still can't understand any of it. If one of us had done that he'd have been put up against a wall.'

'I mustn't start thinking of Wessling or Schröder,' says Kosole, and clenches his fists, 'or else I'll explode. Little Schröder, just a kid, he was lying there squashed flat, and the man he died for just scarpers! Shit and shit again!' He kicks his heels noisily against a beer barrel.

Willy Homeyer makes a dismissive gesture. 'Let's change the subject,' he suggests. 'The Kaiser's finished as far as I'm concerned.'

Weil explains that in some of the regiments soldiers' councils have been set up. The officers are no longer in charge. Many of them have had their shoulder-flashes taken off.

He wants to establish a soldiers' council for us, too. But this doesn't meet with much approval. We don't want to establish anything. We want to go home. And we'll get there one way or another.

Eventually three representatives are chosen: Adolf Bethke, Max Weil and Ludwig Breyer.

Weil tells Ludwig that he has to take off his shoulder-flashes. 'You're barmy ...' says Ludwig wearily, tapping his finger on his forehead. Bethke pushes Weil back. 'Come on, Ludwig is one of ours,' is all he says. Breyer joined the company as a volunteer and rose to be a lieutenant. He doesn't just talk to Trosske, Homeyer, Bröger and me in a friendly and familiar way – that's to be expected, because we were all at school together – but also with his other old comrades, just as long as there isn't another officer within earshot. He's highly thought of because of this.

'Heel can take his off, though,' insists Weil.

That's much easier to understand. Weil has often been mucked about by Heel, and it's no wonder that he wants to savour his moment of triumph.

We don't care one way or the other. Heel was a bit harsh, it is true, but he led from the front and was always the first one over the top. Soldiers take note of that kind of thing.

'You could try asking him,' says Bethke.

'Best to take a couple of bandages with you, though,' Tjaden calls after him. But things turn out unexpectedly. Heel comes out of the office building just as Weil is about to go in. He has a couple of messages in his hand and he points at them. 'It's true,' he says to Max.

Weil starts his speech. When he gets to the part about the shoulder-flashes, Heel makes a sharp movement. We reckon all hell is going to break loose, but the company commander merely says – suddenly and to our complete amazement – 'You are right.' Then he turns to Ludwig and puts his hand on his shoulder. 'You probably don't get it, Breyer, do you? An ordinary soldier's tunic, that's the thing. The rest is all over now.'

None of us says a word. This is no longer the Heel we know, someone who went out on patrol armed only with a walking stick, and who was reckoned to be bulletproof. This is someone who is finding it hard just to stand there and speak to us.

Later that night, when I had already fallen asleep, I'm woken up by a low conversation. 'You're dreaming,' I hear Kosole say. 'No, it's true,' counters Willy. 'Come and see for yourself.' They get themselves up and go out to the courtyard. I follow them. There's a light on in the office and you can see in. Heel is sitting at the desk with his officer's jacket in front of him. The epaulettes are missing. He's wearing a private's tunic. His head is in his hands and – but this is impossible – I move a step closer – Heel, Heel is crying.

'What about that, then!' whispers Tjaden.

'Out of here!' says Bethke, and gives Tjaden a kick. We all creep back, shaken.

Next morning we hear that a major from one of the nearby regiments shot himself when he heard that the Kaiser had run away.

Heel comes out. He is grey from lack of sleep. He issues the necessary instructions in a quiet voice. Then he leaves again. We all feel terrible. The last thing we had has been taken from us.

The very ground has been taken out from under our feet. 'It feels as if we've been well and truly betrayed,' says Kosole sourly. The column that now forms up and marches gloomily on is quite different from yesterday's. A company that has been lost, an army that has been abandoned. With every step we take our trenching tools rattle in a monotonous rhythm – all in vain, all in vain. Only Ledderhose is happy as a lark, selling us tinned meat and sugar from his American supplies.

★ ★ ★

The next evening we reach Germany. Now that French is no longer being spoken all round us we are slowly starting to believe in the peace. Up till now we've secretly been prepared to get the order to about face and go back to the trenches; soldiers have a distrust of things going well, and it is better to be prepared from the beginning for the opposite. But now a gentle feeling of excitement is gradually taking us over.

We come to a large village. There are a couple of faded garlands hanging over the street. So many troops must have passed through here already that it isn't worth putting on anything special for the last of them. And so we have to make do with a few faded and rain-soaked WELCOME signs, loosely framed with ceremonial oak leaves made out of green paper. The people hardly look at us as we march past because they are so used to it all. But it is new for us to have got here, and we are hungry for a few friendly words and glances, however much we might insist that we don't give a damn. At least the girls could have turned out and waved to us. Tjaden and Jupp try again and again to attract the attention of a few of them, but they get nowhere. Probably we just look too scruffy. Eventually they give up trying.

It's only the children who come along with us. We hold their hands and they trot along beside us. We give them what chocolate we can spare, because of course we still have to take some home with us.

Adolf Bethke has lifted a little girl up and is carrying her. She is pulling on his moustache like a horse's reins, and laughing fit to burst at the faces he is pulling. Her little hands are beating on his face. He takes hold of one and shows me how tiny it is.

The child starts to cry when he stops pulling faces. He tries to calm her but she just cries more loudly and he has to put her down.

'Looks as if we've turned into real bogeymen,' rumbles Kosole.

'The children are bound to be frightened by someone's mug straight from the trenches,' explains Willy, 'it'll give them the creeps.'

'We smell of blood, that's the point,' says Ludwig.

'Then we're going to have to have a bath sometime,' reckons Jupp, 'and that might make the girls a bit keener on us, too.'

'Yes, well, if only it were just a question of having a bath,' says Ludwig pensively.

Crestfallen, we move on. After all the years out there we had pictured our return home quite differently. We had thought that people would be waiting for us, but we now realise that everyone here is already preoccupied with his or her own life. Everything has moved on and still is moving on, and it is almost as if we have become superfluous. This single village isn't Germany as a whole, of course, but for all that, the situation sticks in our throats, and a shadow passes over us, a strange feeling of foreboding.

Wagons rattle past us, their drivers shout, people look up for a moment and then go on pursuing their own thoughts and worries. The church clock strikes, and the moist breeze whiffles over us. Only an old woman with long ribbons on her bonnet walks tirelessly along beside our column, asking in a shaky voice after someone called Erhard Schmidt.

We are quartered in a large barn. But although we have done a lot of marching, none of us can settle. We go and find a bar.

Things are very lively. There's a cloudy new wine, this year's already, and it tastes wonderful. It also has a powerful effect on the legs. We are all the more happy to be sitting down. Clouds of tobacco smoke drift through the low room, and the wine smells of earth and summertime. We fetch out our tins of beef, carve off chunks and put them onto thick slices of bread and butter, then stick our knives into the broad wooden tables beside us, and eat. The oil lamp shines down like a mother over us all.

Night makes the world more beautiful. Not in the trenches, but certainly in peacetime. We were discontented when we marched in this afternoon, but now we have livened up. The little band playing in the corner is soon augmented by our people. Not only do we have pianists and harmonica virtuosos, but we've even got a Bavarian with a zither. In addition Willy Homeyer sets up an improvised one-string bass, and uses metal covers from washtubs to add to the mix the glorious noise of a bass drum, side drums and cymbals.

There is one unfamiliar element, however, which goes to our heads even more than the wine: the girls. They are quite different from the way they were this afternoon, they laugh and they are approachable. Or are these different ones? We haven't seen any girls for ages.

At first we are both eager and shy at the same time, not very sure of ourselves, because while we were out at the front we have forgotten how to behave around them – but then Ferdinand Kosole waltzes away with one of them, a solidly built piece with an impressive superstructure, the sort of breastwork you could comfortably rest your gun on. The others follow his example.

The sweet and heavy wine is buzzing pleasantly in the brain, the girls are rustling past, the music is playing and we are sitting in the corner in a group around Adolf Bethke. 'Lads,' he says, 'tomorrow or the day after we'll be home. I tell you, lads, my wife – it's been ten months now ...'

I lean across the table to speak to Valentin Laher, who is giving the girls a cool and appraising look. A blonde is sitting next to him, but he pays her hardly any attention. As I bend forward, something in my pocket bumps against the edge of the table. I put my hand down to touch it. It is Wessling's watch. How long ago that was!

Jupp has fetched up with the fattest of the ladies present. Dancing with her, he looks like a question mark. One of his great paws is flat across the girl's massive rear, playing five-finger exercises. She's laughing, her wet lips near his face, and he's getting livelier by the minute. In the end he steers her towards the door to the courtyard and then outside.

A few minutes later I have to go out too, round the corner for a pee – but a fat and sweating NCO is already there with a girl. I wander into the garden and am just about to start when there is an almighty crash right behind me. I turn round and see Jupp and the fat girl land on the ground with a wallop. A garden table gave way under them. Fatty snorts with laughter when she sees me, and sticks her tongue out. Jupp just hisses. I disappear rapidly behind some bushes and promptly tread on someone's hand – this is a hell of a night. 'Can't you look where you're going, you great clodhopper!' roars a bass voice. 'How was I to know that some idiot would be having a lie-down in the bushes?' I snap back crossly, and eventually find a secluded corner.

A cool breeze, pleasant after the fug indoors, dark gable ends, arbours, stillness, and a gentle splashing noise as I pee. Albert comes along and stands next to me. We piss pure silver.

'Bloody hell, Ernst, what about all this?' he says.

I nod. We gaze at the moon for a bit. 'You mean that all the crap is over, eh, Albert?'

'Damn it all, yes, Ernst –'

There are creaking and cracking noises behind us. Girls shout out loudly in the bushes and are suddenly cut off. The night is like a thunderstorm, charged, feverish and bursting with life, which quickly spreads like wildfire.

In the garden somebody groans. This is answered by a giggle. Shadows come down from the hayloft. Two people are standing on a ladder. The man presses his head urgently into the girl's skirt and stammers something. She gives a coarse laugh which scratches across our nerves like a wire brush. A shiver goes down my back. How close to each other they are – yesterday and today, death and life.

Tjaden emerges from the dark garden. He is covered in sweat and his face is glowing. 'Well, lads, that's how you find out that you're alive again,' he says, and buttons up his tunic.

We walk round the building and come across Willy Homeyer. Out in a field he has made a huge fire from weeds and things, and thrown in a couple of handfuls of potatoes he has acquired somewhere. Now he is sitting peacefully and dreamily on his own by the fire waiting for the potatoes to cook. By his side he has a few cutlets, some of the American canned meat. The dog is squatting watchfully next to him.

The flickering fire sets off coppery reflections in his red hair. A mist is rising from the meadows lower down. The stars are twinkling. We sit down with him and pull the potatoes out of the fire. The skin is burnt black, but the insides are pale gold and they smell wonderful. We grab hold of the cutlets with both hands and gnaw at them as if we were playing a mouth organ. Then to go with them we drink some schnapps from our tin mugs.

How good those potatoes taste! Is the world still turning? Where are we?

Are we not boys again, sitting in that field back home, near Torloxten, where we had spent the whole day rooting potatoes out of the strong-smelling earth, while red-cheeked girls in washed-out blue dresses came along behind us with the baskets? Those potato roasts when we were young! Strands of white mist drifted across the field, the fires crackled but otherwise everything was still, the potatoes were the last harvest, everything else had been gathered in – all that was left was the earth, the clear air, the bitter, white, beloved smoke, the end of autumn. Bitter smoke, the bitter smell of autumn, the potato roasts when we were young – the strands of mist drift, drift and dissolve, the faces of old comrades, we're on our way, the war is over, everything is strange and melting – the potato roasts have come back, and the autumn, and life.

'Christ, Willy ...'

'Good stuff, eh?' he says, looking up with his hands still full of meat and potatoes ...

Oh, you twerp, I meant something completely different.

★

The fire has died down. Willy wipes his hands on his trousers and snaps his knife shut. A couple of dogs in the town are barking. Otherwise everything is quiet. No more shells. No more munitions columns rattling along. Not even the creaking of the field ambulances driving by slowly and carefully. A night in which far fewer people will die than at any point in the last four years.

We go back into the bar. But there isn't much going on there now. Valentin has taken off his tunic and done a few handstands. The girls applaud him, but he isn't very pleased. He says crossly to Kosole, 'I was a good acrobat once, Ferdinand, but this stuff wouldn't even be good enough for a local fair. My bones aren't what they were. And "Valentini on the High Bar" – that used to be a classy act once! Now I'm rheumatic ...'

'Come on, just thank your lucky stars that you've still got your bones at all,' shouts Kosole, and thumps his hand on the table. 'Music! Willy!'

Homeyer starts up with his drums and cymbals. Things liven up. I ask Jupp how it went with the fat girl. He makes a dismissive gesture. 'Well, well,' I say in surprise, 'that was soon over, then.'

He pulls a face. 'I thought she fancied me, do you know what I mean? Right, and then afterwards the slut wanted money off me! And what's more, I banged my knee so hard against that bloody garden table that I can hardly walk.'

Ludwig Breyer is sitting at the table, pale and silent. He should have gone to get some sleep long before, but he doesn't want to. His arm is healing well, and the dysentery isn't as bad as it was. But he is still withdrawn.

'Ludwig,' says Tjaden in a slurred voice, 'you ought to go out into the garden for a bit ... that's good for everything ...'

Ludwig shakes his head and suddenly goes very pale. I go and sit down by him. 'Aren't you looking forward at all to getting home?' I ask him.

He just stands up and leaves. I don't understand him any more.

Later on I come across him again outside, on his own. I don't ask him any more questions. We go back in silence.

In the doorway we bump into Ledderhose, who's just about to disappear with Fatty. Jupp grins. 'He's in for a surprise.'

'No,' says Willy, 'she is. Or do you really think Arthur is likely to part with even a single copper?'

Wine spills across the table, the lamp is smoking, the girls' skirts are flying. There is a warm tiredness behind my eyes, all edges are blurred and softened, like Verey lights in the mist, and my head sinks slowly down towards the tabletop. The night is rushing onwards, softly and wonderfully, like an express train heading homewards. We'll soon be home.

3

We are standing formed up on the barrack square for the last time. Some of the company live locally, and they are dismissed. The rest of us have to make our own way from now on. The trains are so irregular that we can no longer be transported as a group. We have to split up.

The huge grey parade ground is far too big for us. A dull November wind sweeps across it, smelling of partings and death. We are all lined up between the canteen and the orderly room and we don't take up any more room than that. The great empty space around us calls up depressing memories. There they stand, column after column of them, the invisible dead.

Heel moves down the line of the company. But walking with him are the ghosts of all his predecessors. First in line behind him is Bertinck, still bleeding from the neck, with his chin torn off and his eyes sad, company commander for a year and a half, a teacher, married, four children; and next to him, his face a grey-green colour, is Möller, nineteen years old, gassed three days after he took over the company; and then Redecker, a forestry surveyor, blasted into the ground by a direct hit from a shell after two weeks; then Büttner, already more indistinct and further away, a captain killed by machine-gun fire right to the heart; and like shadows behind all of these come the others, already nearly nameless by now and a long way back – seven company commanders in two years. And more than five hundred men. Thirty-two are standing in the barrack square.

Heel tries to say a few words of farewell. But he can't do it, and has to give up. No words in the world could make any impression in the face of this lonely, empty square, with only a couple of rows of survivors, standing there silent and freezing in their boots and greatcoats and thinking about their old comrades.

Heel goes from one man to another and shakes hands with everyone. When he gets to Max Weil he is thin-lipped as he says: 'Your time is beginning now, Weil …'

'It will be less bloody,' replies Max calmly.

'And less heroic,' counters Heel.

'That isn't the only thing in life,' says Weil.

'But it's the best thing,' replies Heel, 'what else could be?'

Weil hesitates for a moment. 'Something that sounds odd nowadays, Lieutenant: kindness and love. There's a sort of heroism in that, too.'

'No,' replies Heel quickly, as if he had been thinking about this for a long time, and his brows are drawn, 'all you get with them is martyrdom, and that's something quite different. Heroism starts where reason breaks down, the point where life no longer counts. You have to understand that it's to do with madness, with intoxication, with risk. But it has very little to do with aims. Aims – that's your world. Why? What for? To what end? – anybody who asks that kind of question just doesn't understand …'

He says this so forcefully that it sounds as if he is trying to convince himself. His sunken face is agitated. In the last few days he has become embittered and looks years older. But Weil has changed just as rapidly. He had always been reserved, nobody knew what to make of him. Now he has suddenly emerged and is becoming more and more forceful. No one would have thought that he could speak the way he does. The more edgy Heel becomes, the calmer Max Weil gets. Quietly and firmly he says: 'The misery of millions is too high a price to pay for the heroism of a few.'

Heel shrugs. 'Too high a price – purpose – payment – those are your kinds of words. Let's see how far you get with them.'

Weil looks at the private soldier's uniform that Heel is still wearing. 'And how far did you get with yours?'

Heel reddens. 'At least they've given me things to remember,' he says harshly, 'the memory of things that can't be bought for any money.'

Weil is silent for a short time. 'A memory ...' he repeats, and looks around over the empty parade ground and at the few of us drawn up there, 'yes, and also a dreadful responsibility ...'

The rest of us do not understand much of all this. We're freezing cold and reckon that talking is pointless. Talking never changes anything in the world and never will.

The columns break up. The farewells begin. The man next to me, Müller, settles his pack on his back and tucks his packet of provisions under his arm. Then he puts out his hand: 'Well, good luck, Ernst ...'

'Good luck, Felix ...' He moves on to Willy, to Albert, to Kosole ...

Gerhard Pohl comes along, the best singer in the company, who, when we were marching, always sang the high tenor part when the melody was especially florid. The rest of the time he held back, so that he had plenty of voice for the two-part passages. His face, brown and with a wart on it, looks agitated; he has just taken his leave of Karl Bröger, with whom he played endless games of cards. That farewell was a hard one for him.

'Bye, Ernst ...'

'Bye, Gerhard ...' And he is gone.

Weddekamp shakes hands with me. He used to make the wooden crosses for those who were killed. 'It's a shame I never got to make one for you, Ernst,' he says. 'You'd have had one in mahogany. I'd already put a lovely piano lid aside specially.'

'Just because it hasn't happened so far doesn't mean that it won't,' I reply. 'When I need it, I'll send you a postcard.'

He laughs. 'Keep your chin up, lad, the war isn't over yet.'

And he trots off, with his one shoulder lower than the other.

The first group has already disappeared through the barrack gates. Scheffler, Fassbender, little Lucke and August Beckmann were in that group, and others follow. We're a bit worked up. You have to get used to the idea that they are going away forever. Up to now the only way you could leave the company was by being killed, wounded or seconded. Now there is another way: peace.

It's strange. We are so used to shell-holes and trenches that we are suddenly mistrustful of the silent landscape in which we now find ourselves – as if the silence is just a trick to lure us into an unmarked minefield ... And our old comrades are all running off into it, carelessly, alone, without rifles or grenades. You feel as if you should run after them, grab hold of them and shout: what are doing going out there on your own, you should stay here with us, we have to stick together, how can we survive otherwise ...?

Round and round it goes in your head, a strange feeling; we've been soldiers for too long. The November wind whistles over the empty parade ground. More and more comrades go. It won't be much longer, and we shall all be on our own again.

* * *

The rest of the company are all going the same way home. We establish ourselves in the railway station to try and get onto a train. The station hall is like an army supply depot, full of crates, boxes, packs and tarpaulins.

Two trains go through in seven hours. People grab their doors and hang on like bunches of grapes. By the afternoon we have managed to find ourselves a place near the track. By evening we are right at the front, in the best position. We sleep on our feet.

There isn't another train until late the next morning. It's a goods train with blinded horses. Their turned-up eyeballs are bluish-white with red streaks. They stand quite still, their heads stretched out, and only in their quivering nostrils is there any sign of life.

In the afternoon an official announcement is made that there will be no more trains today. Nobody moves. Soldiers don't believe official announcements. And sure enough, another one does come along. We can see straight away that this one will do. Half full at most.

The whole station concourse is loud with the noise of men getting their belongings together and then with the violent onrush of the columns as they charge out of the waiting rooms. This ends up in a great melee when they come up against the men waiting in the hall itself.

The train glides past. There is an open window. Albert Trosske, the lightest of us, is hoisted up and climbs in like a monkey. The next minute the doors are mobbed. Most of the windows are shut. A few are shattered by blows from the rifle butts of those who want to get on at all costs, even with cuts on their hands and legs. Blankets are thrown over the jagged glass and in various places people are already climbing on board.

The train stops. Albert has run along the corridor and pulls down the window just in front of us. Tjaden and the dog are the first ones to jump in. Bethke and Kosole are close behind, helped up by Willy. The three of them then quickly take possession of the doors to the compartment, to block it off from both sides. Our belongings go in next, together with Ludwig and Ledderhose, then Valentin, me and Karl Bröger. Last of all, after once more vigorously clearing the way for himself out on the platform, in comes Willy.

'Everyone in?' shouts Kosole from the corridor, where there is a great press of men. 'In!' roars Willy. Bethke, Kosole and Tjaden are back in their seats like a shot, and a flood of men pours into the compartment, they climb on top of the luggage racks and fill up every spare inch.

The engine itself has been stormed. Men are sitting on the buffers. The roofs of the carriages are completely covered with people. The guard shouts out: 'Get down off there, you'll crack your skulls!' 'Shut it, we'll be careful!' comes the response. Five men have occupied the lavatory. One has his backside hanging well out of the window.

The train pulls out. A few who weren't holding on firmly enough fall off. Two are run over and dragged away. At once others jump on.

The outside steps to the compartments are full. The struggle to get aboard is still going on as the train pulls out.

One man is holding onto the door. It flies open and he is left hanging onto the window. Willy climbs after him, grabs him by the collar and hauls him in.

During the night our carriage has its first casualties. The train goes through a low tunnel and some of those on the roof are crushed to death and swept off. The others must have seen it happen, but from up there they had no way of getting the train to stop. What's more, the man hanging half out of the lavatory window went to sleep and fell off the train.

The rest of the carriages have casualties as well. As a result the roofs are fitted up with blocks of wood to hold on to, ropes and rammed-in bayonets. They also set up a sentry system to give warning of any danger.

We sleep and sleep, standing up, lying down, sitting, squatting, bent over packs or boxes, we sleep. The train rattles on. Houses, trees, gardens, people waving – demonstrations, red flags, guards posted at stations, shouting, special editions, revolution – we're going to sleep first, and the other stuff can come later. It's only now that we realise just how tired we've got in all that time away.

It starts to get dark. There is one dim lamp burning. The train is going along slowly. It has to stop a lot because of engine failure.

Our packs are rocking back and forth. Smoke billows up from our pipes. The dog is sleeping peacefully across my knees. Adolf Bethke moves over to me and strokes him. After a little while he says: 'Well, Ernst, we'll soon be going our separate ways.'

I nod. It's strange, but I really cannot picture life going on without Adolf – without his ever-open eyes and calm voice. He taught me and Albert everything when we first came to the front as completely raw recruits, and without him I don't think I would still be here.

'We must meet up again,' I say. 'Often, Adolf.'

The heel of a boot bumps against my face. Tjaden is sitting above us in the luggage rack carefully counting out his money – he plans to go straight from the station to a knocking shop. To get himself into the right mood he is already swapping experiences with a couple of riflemen. Nobody thinks there is anything wrong with that sort of conversation – it has nothing to do with the war, and so we all listen in.

A sapper with two fingers missing tells us proudly that his wife gave birth to a baby at seven months, and yet it still weighed nearly eight pounds. Ledderhose laughs and reckons that that would be a miracle. The sapper doesn't understand what he is getting at. He counts on his fingers the months between his last leave and the birth. 'Seven,' he says, 'it must be right.'

Ledderhose hiccups with laughter, a mocking look on his wrinkled lemon of a face. 'Somebody's been doing a bit of work for you.'

The sapper stares at him. 'What ... what are you trying to say?' he stutters.

'Well, it's obvious, isn't it?' says Arthur in his nasal voice, and stretches.

The sapper breaks out in a sweat. He reckons it up over and over again. His lips are trembling. A fat bearded ex-driver from the Service Corps is bent double with laughter by the window. 'Christ, you idiot, you poor bloody idiot!'

Bethke sits up. 'Shut your trap, fat-arse!'

'Why should I?' asks the man with the beard.

'Because you just should,' says Bethke, 'and so should you, Arthur.'

The sapper has gone pale. 'What can anyone do about it?' he asks helplessly, and grips the window frame tightly.

'You should never get married,' says Jupp thoughtfully, 'until the kids are already earning their own keep. Then that sort of thing couldn't happen.'

Outside the evening is gliding past. The woods look like dark herds of cattle on the horizon, the fields are pale and shimmering in the weak light that comes from the train windows. Suddenly we are only two hours away from home. Bethke stands up and gets his pack ready. He lives in a village a few stops outside the town and has to get off before us.

The train stops. Adolf shakes hands with us. He stumbles down onto the narrow platform and looks all round him with a sweeping glance, drinking in the entire landscape in a second, the way a dry field soaks up the rain. Then he turns back towards us. But he can't really hear us any more. Ludwig Breyer is standing by the window, even though he is in pain. 'Come on, Adolf, get moving,' he calls out, 'your wife's waiting for you ...'

Bethke looks up at us and shakes his head. 'There's not that much of a hurry, Ludwig.' You can see how strongly he is being pulled away, but Adolf is Adolf – he stays with us till the very last moment. But when at last the train pulls away, he does a quick about-turn and strides off.

'We'll come and visit you soon,' I shout after him quickly.

We watch him as he walks across the fields. He waves at us for a long time. Smoke from the engine drifts past. There are a few red lights in the distance.

The train goes into a wide bend. Adolf is now only small, a dot, a tiny figure, all alone on the great dark plain over which arches the evening sky, huge, stormy, with streaks of light and shading to a sulphurous yellow on the horizon. I don't know why, and it has nothing to do with Adolf himself, but it moves me to see this solitary human being walking across the broad and level fields, alone in the late evening, set against the vast sky.

Then the trees crowd in and it all gets darker, and soon there is nothing left but the movement of the train, and the sky, and the woods.

It is getting noisy in the compartment. In here there are corners, edges, smells, warmth, spaces and limits; and there are brown, weather-beaten faces, the eyes in lighter patches, and it stinks of earth, sweat, blood and uniforms. Outside, though, the blurred world is rushing past as the train steams onwards, leaving it all further and further behind, that world of trenches, of shell-holes, of darkness, of horror, now nothing more than a jumble outside the windows, something which no longer has any hold on us.

Somebody starts to sing. Others join in. Soon everyone is singing, the whole compartment and the one next to us, the whole carriage, the whole train. We sing louder and louder, with more and more gusto, we are red in the face, the veins standing out on our foreheads as we sing every soldier's song that we know, and we stand up and look at each other, our eyes sparkling as the train wheels pound out the rhythm, and we sing and sing …

I'm jammed in between Ludwig and Kosole and can feel their warmth through my tunic. I move my hands, turn my head, my muscles tense up and a shivering feeling comes up from my knees to my guts, moves into my bones and fizzes like soda water, gets into my lungs, my lips, my eyes, so that the whole compartment is swimming before me, the fizzing inside me is like a telegraph mast in a storm, a thousand wires are buzzing, a thousand pathways are opening – I put my hand on Ludwig's and it feels as if it is about to catch fire, but when he looks up, tired and pale as ever, I can't put into words anything of what is inside me, and all I can get out, hesitantly and with some effort, is: 'Have you got a cigarette, Ludwig?'

He passes me one. The train roars on and we go on singing. Gradually, however, beneath our singing we are aware of a darker undertone than just the rattle of the wheels, and when we stop for a moment we hear a massive crash, which reverberates across the wide plain. The clouds have closed up again and the thunderstorm is over us. Lightning flashes like gunfire. Kosole stands by the window, shaking his head. 'Just what we need right now, lads, another storm,' he murmurs, and leans out of the window. Then suddenly he shouts out sharply: 'Quick, quick, there it is!' We throng around him. In the flashes of lightning we can make out the small, narrow towers of the town right on the horizon, standing out against the night sky. The thundering darkness closes in over them again and again, but with every flash of lightning we see them getting closer.

Our eyes are burning with excitement. A feeling of anticipation suddenly springs up inside us all, looming over us like some great tree.

Kosole gets hold of his things. 'Christ, lads, where are we going to be sitting a year from now?' he says, stretching his arms.

'On our backsides,' says Jupp edgily. But this time nobody laughs. The town has ambushed us, it is pulling us towards itself. There it is, almost like something breathing, coming towards us in the wild light with arms outstretched, and we are rushing towards it, a trainload of soldiers, a trainload of home-comers returning from the void, a trainload of enormous anticipation, closer and closer, we are hurling ourselves at it, the walls are hurtling towards us, surely we shall crash into them, the lightning is flashing, the thunder is roaring – and then there is the station rising up on both sides of the train, full of noise and shouting, the rain is pelting down, the platforms are wet and shining, and we jump down into it all without another moment's thought.

The dog jumps out of the door with me. He sticks closely to me and together we run through the rain, down the steps.

PART TWO

Part Two

1

Outside the station we scatter like water that's been emptied from a bucket and is splashing onto the pavement. Kosole, Bröger and Trosske go storming off down Heinrich Street. Just as quickly, Ludwig and I set off along Station Broadway. Ledderhose has already bolted with his portable grocery store, without even saying goodbye. Tjaden quickly gets Willy to give him directions to the nearest knocking shop, and only Jupp and Valentin take their time. Nobody is waiting for them, and so for now they wander back towards the waiting room to see if they can scrounge some grub. After that they plan to go to the barracks.

The rain is dripping off the trees in the broad avenue that leads from the station and the low clouds are scurrying along. A few soldiers, recent recruits, come towards us. They are wearing red armbands. 'Get those shoulder-flashes off,' shouts one of them, and makes for Ludwig.

'Shut your trap, you bloody rookie,' I say, and push him aside.

Others hurry along and surround us. Ludwig looks calmly at the first of them and walks on. The man gets out of his way. But then two sailors turn up and rush at him.

'You bastards, can't you see he's wounded?' I roar, and chuck down my pack so that I'll have my hands free. But Ludwig is already on the ground, he's as good as helpless with that wounded arm. The sailors tear at his uniform and kick out at him. 'A lieutenant!' shrieks a woman's voice. 'Kick the bloodsucker to death!'

Before I can help him I get a blow in the face that knocks me off balance. 'Son of a bitch!' I gasp, and with all my force I put my boot into my attacker's belly. He wheezes and goes down. At once three more of them are on me. The dog jumps up and goes for the neck of one of them. But the others bring me to the ground. 'Lights out, knives out!' screeches the woman.

Between the trampling legs I see how Ludwig has been able to get one of the sailors down by hitting at the back of his knees, and is throttling him with his left hand.

He won't let go, even though the others are really laying into him. Then someone gets me round the head with a belt buckle and another kicks me in the face. Wolf gets his teeth into the man's leg, but we still can't get up and they go on knocking us down so they can beat us to a pulp. In fury I try to get at my revolver. But at that very moment one of my attackers falls backwards with a crash onto the pavement beside me. Another crash, another one unconscious, and then a third – Willy must have joined the fray.

He had come storming along at full pelt, dropping his pack as he did so, and is now raging away above us. He grabs pairs of them by the collars and hammers their heads together. They pass out straight away, because when Willy is angry, he turns into a human sledgehammer. We break free and I jump up, but the others are already running away. I just manage to get one in the back with my pack, and then go to look after Ludwig.

Willy is already in hot pursuit. He'd seen that it was the two sailors who had started in on Ludwig. Now one of them is lying groaning in the gutter, black and blue, with the dog standing over him and growling, while Willy chases after the other, his hair flying, like a red-headed hurricane.

Ludwig's dressing has been trampled on, blood is oozing through it. His face is smeared, his forehead damaged from a kick in the head. He wipes himself down and gets up slowly. 'Are you hurt much?' I ask. Deathly pale, he shakes his head.

Meanwhile Willy has caught the sailor and hauls him back like a sack. 'You stinking pigs,' he growls. 'You've spent the whole war sitting in the sunshine on your ships and never heard a shot fired – but now you think you can open your traps and have a go at soldiers who've been at the front. Right, get on your knees, you skiver! I'll help you if you like. Beg for forgiveness!' He shoves the man down in front of Ludwig and he looks so grim as he does so that it is actually frightening to see. 'I'll slaughter you,' he snarls, 'I'll tear you to bits, get down on your knees!'

The man whimpers. 'Leave it, Willy,' says Ludwig, and picks up his things.

'What,' he asks, dumbfounded, 'are you crazy? After they trampled all over your arm?'

Ludwig is already walking away. 'Just let him go ...'

Willy stares uncomprehendingly at Ludwig for a moment, then lets the sailor go, shaking his head.

'OK then, move!' But in the exact moment he starts to run, Willy can't resist giving him a kick that sends him head over heels twice.

We walk on. Willy is cursing, because when he's furious he has to talk. Ludwig is silent, though.

Suddenly, at the corner of the next street, we see the whole troop of those that ran away coming back for us. They have fetched reinforcements. Willy gets hold of his rifle. 'Load and prepare to fire,' he says, his eyes narrowing. Ludwig takes out his revolver and I get my own rifle ready to fire. So far it's only been a bit of a roughhouse, but now it's serious. We're not going to be ambushed a second time.

We spread out across the street three paces apart so that we don't present a single target, and we move forward. The dog spots at once what is going on. He crouches in the gutter next to us, growling; he learned at the front how to creep forward under cover.

'We'll open fire at twenty-five yards,' threatens Willy.

The mob in front of us starts to get uneasy. We continue our advance. Rifles are raised against us. With a crack Willy lets off the safety catch, and then takes a hand grenade from his belt – he's kept one as a kind of iron ration. 'I'm going to count to three ...'

At that point an older man wearing an NCO's uniform without the stripes steps out of the crowd. He comes towards us and shouts out: 'Are we comrades or not?'

Willy is so taken aback that he gasps. 'Goddamn it, that's what we're asking you, you bunch of cowards,' he replies indignantly. 'Who was it started this by jumping on wounded men?'

Now the other man is taken aback. 'Did you do that?' he asks the men behind him.

'He wouldn't take his epaulettes off,' says someone from the mob.

The man makes an angry gesture. Then he turns back to us. 'They shouldn't have done that, comrades. But it looks as if you don't know what's going on here. Where have you come from, anyway?'

'From the front, where else?' snarls Willy.

'And where are you heading?'

'We're going where you've been for the whole war – we're going home.'

The man holds up an empty sleeve. 'I didn't lose this at home, mate.'

'That makes it worse,' says Willy, unmoved. 'In that case you should be ashamed of yourself for hanging around with that mob of make-believe soldiers.'

The NCO comes closer. 'There's a revolution going on,' he says calmly, 'and anyone who isn't with us is against us!'

Willy laughs. 'A fine kind of revolution, you and your Union of Epaulette-Strippers! So if that's all you want ...' He spits scornfully.

'No,' says the one-armed man and comes right up to him, 'we do want more! An end to war, an end to oppression! An end to murder! We want to be human beings again and not parts of a war machine!'

Willy lowers his hand grenade. 'Well, that was a really good start,' he says, pointing to the ripped-up dressing on Ludwig's arm. Then he takes a couple of great strides towards the mob. 'Get off home, you half-arsed little brats!' he roars as they give way. 'You want to be human beings? You're not even soldiers! Anyone looking at the way you hold your rifles would be scared you might break a finger.'

The mob disperses. Willy does an about-face, and sets himself in front of the NCO. 'Right, I'm going to tell you something! We're

56

just as sick of all this crap as you are, and obviously there's got to be an end to it! But not like that! If we are going to do something, we'll do it, but never in a million years is someone going to tell us what to do. And now watch this!'

With both hands he rips off his own shoulder-flashes. 'I'm doing this because I want to, and not because you want me to. It's my business. But as for him –' he points at Ludwig – 'he's our lieutenant, and he's keeping them, and woe betide anybody that says anything different.'

The one-armed man nods. You can see him thinking it through. 'I was out there as well, for Christ's sake,' he stutters, 'I know what it was like too! Here –' he gestures agitatedly at the stump of his arm – '20th Infantry Division, Verdun!'

'We were there too,' says Willy laconically. 'Well, cheerio, then ...'

He hoists his pack onto his back and slings his rifle over his shoulder. We march on. But as Ludwig goes past him, the NCO with his red armband suddenly brings his hand up to his cap, and we understand what he is doing. He is not saluting the uniform, or the war – he is saluting his old comrades at the front.

Willy's house is the nearest. He's quite moved as he waves at it from across the road. 'What ho, old hovel! I'll soon be taking possession again!' We want to stop, but Willy says no. 'Let's get Ludwig home first,' he explains, still prepared for trouble. 'I'll get my potato salad and a good nagging from the family soon enough.'

On the way we pause for a moment and tidy ourselves up, so that our parents can't see that we've just been in a fight. I wipe Ludwig's face and we loosen the dressing on his arm to cover up the bloodied places, because otherwise his mother could easily get a shock. Later on he'll have to go to the military hospital anyway so he can get the dressing changed.

We get there without any further trouble. Ludwig still looks pretty battered. 'Don't let it worry you,' I say, and shake hands with him. Willy puts his great paw round his shoulders. 'Could have happened to any of us, old man. If you hadn't been wounded you'd have made mincemeat of them!'

Ludwig nods to us and goes indoors. We watch him to make sure he gets up the stairwell safely. He is halfway up when something else suddenly occurs to Willy. 'Next time, kick 'em, Ludwig,' he calls out as a bit of parting advice, 'just kick 'em! Don't let them get near you!' Then, satisfied, he closes the outer door of the apartment block.

'I'd like to know what's been bothering him for the past few weeks,' I say.

Willy scratches his head. 'Must be the dysentery,' he reckons, 'because you know what Ludwig is like otherwise! Remember how he sorted out that tank at Bixschoote? On his own. That wasn't exactly a piece of cake, was it, mate?'

He hoists up his pack. 'OK then, Ernst, all the best – I'm off to see what the Homeyer family has been up to for the past six months. They'll be pleased to see me for about an hour, then the lectures will start. My mother – what a drill sergeant she'd have been! The old girl's got a heart of gold, only it's wrapped in solid granite!'

I go on alone, and suddenly the world is changed. There is a rushing noise in my ears as if there were a river running beneath the street, and I see and hear nothing more until I am standing in front of our house. Over the door there is a sign that says 'Welcome Home!' and there is a bunch of flowers next to it. They have seen me coming and they are all standing there waiting; my sisters are there, you can see the living room behind them, there is food on the table and it is all very festive. 'What's all this nonsense,' I say, 'flowers and all – what for? – it's not that important – Mother, why are you crying? – I'm back – the war's over – there's no need to cry.' And only then do I notice the salty tears that are running down my own mug.

2

There were potato cakes with eggs and sausage – a fantastic meal. It's been almost two years since I last saw an egg, let alone potato cakes.

Now we are sitting around the big table in the living room, well fed and comfortable, drinking acorn coffee with ersatz sugar. The lamp is on, the canary is singing, even the stove is warm, and Wolf is lying under the table asleep. Things could not be better.

'Well, let's hear about your experiences, Ernst,' says my father.

'Experiences ...' I reply, and think hard. 'I haven't really had any experiences. It was just war all the time, there wasn't any time for experience.'

I rack my brains, but I am completely at a loss over what to say. You can't talk to civilians about things at the front, and I don't know about anything else. 'You've probably experienced a lot more back here,' I say apologetically.

And they have. My sisters tell me how they had to scrimp and save to get tonight's meal together. Twice the regional police took everything off them at the railway station. The third time they had sewn the eggs into the lining of their coats, hidden the sausage in their blouses and stuffed the potatoes into pockets beneath their skirts. That time they got through.

I listen to this slightly absently. My sisters have grown up since I last saw them. Maybe I never took much notice of them before, and that's why it's such a surprise. Ilsa must already be over seventeen. How time flies!

'Did you know that Councillor Pleister died?' asks my father.

I shake my head. 'When was that?'

'In July, around the 20th or so ...'

The kettle on the stove is singing. I play with the fringes on the tablecloth. Yes, I think, in July — in the last five days of that month we lost thirty-six men. But I can hardly remember the names of more than three or four, there were so many more after that. 'What was it,' I ask, already a little sleepy on account of the unusual warmth in the room, 'shrapnel or sniper fire?'

'Ernst,' counters my father in surprise, 'he wasn't a soldier! He caught pneumonia.'

'Oh, right,' I say, and sit up in my chair, 'that sort of thing still goes on.'

They carry on telling me about everything that has happened since my last leave. The butcher on the corner was beaten half to death by hungry housewives. Once, at the end of August, every family got a whole pound of fish. Dr Knott's dog was stolen and probably turned into soap. Miss Mentrup had an illegitimate baby. Potatoes have got dearer again. Next week you might be able to buy stock bones at the abattoir. Aunt Greta's second daughter got married last month, and what's more, her husband's a captain.

Outside the rain is beating on the windowpanes. I hunch my shoulders. It's strange to be in a room again. It's strange to be at home —

My sister breaks off what she is saying. 'Ernst, you're not listening, are you?' she says, surprised.

'Yes, yes of course I am,' I assure her, and get my thoughts together quickly, 'a captain, you say, she's married a captain.'

'Yes, what a piece of luck!' continues my sister eagerly, 'considering her face is covered in freckles! What do you think of that, then?'

What am I supposed to say? If a captain gets a bullet in the head he'll be just as dead as anybody else.

They go on talking, but I can't concentrate properly. My thoughts just drift off elsewhere.

I get up and go and look out of the window. There is a pair of underpants hanging on the line. They are flapping grey and limp in

the twilight. The wavering half-light of the drying yard flickers –
and suddenly another picture rises up behind it, distant and shadowy
– flapping underwear, a solitary mouth organ playing in the evening,
a march forward in the twilight – and a whole lot of dead soldiers,
black men, in faded blue tunics with swollen lips and bloodshot
eyes – gassed. The picture is very clear for a moment, and then it
blurs and vanishes, the underwear is flapping again, the drying yard
is back and behind me I can feel again the room with my parents,
warmth and security. It's over, I think to myself with relief, and
quickly turn round.

'Why are you so fidgety, Ernst?' asks my father. 'You haven't sat
still for more than ten minutes at a time.'

'Perhaps he's overtired,' says my mother.

'No, it's not that,' I reply, slightly confused and trying to think.
'I reckon it's just that I can't sit on a chair for very long now. We
didn't have chairs at the front, we used to lie around wherever we
could. I'm simply not used to it any more.'

'That's a funny thing,' says my father.

I shrug. My mother smiles. 'Have you been to your room yet?'
she asks.

'Not yet,' I reply, and go across to it. My heart is pounding as I
open the door and breathe in the smell of my books in the dark.
Quickly I put the light on. Then I look around. 'It's all just the same
as it was,' says my sister behind me.

'Yes, yes,' I say dismissively, because I would much rather be on
my own at this moment. But the others have come as well. They
stand there in the doorway and look at me encouragingly. I sit
down in my chair and put my hands on the tabletop. It feels smooth
and cool. Yes, everything has stayed the same. Even the brown
marble paperweight that Karl Vogt gave me is still there. It's in its
usual place next to the compass and the inkwell. But Karl Vogt fell
at Kemmel Hill.

'Don't you like your room any more?' asks my sister.

'Of course,' I say hesitantly, 'but it's so small ...'

My father laughs. 'It's the same size as before.'

'Of course it is,' I admit, 'it's just that in my mind it was much bigger ...'

'It's been such a long time since you were last here, Ernst,' says my mother. I nod. 'We'll make the bed up for you,' she goes on. 'You don't need to worry about that now.'

I feel in my pocket. Adolf Bethke gave me a packet of cigars as a parting gift. I need to smoke one now. Everything around me feels disjointed, as if I were dizzy. I draw deeply on the cigar and it makes me feel better.

'You smoke cigars?' asks my father, surprised and almost reproachful.

Taken aback, I look at him. 'Of course,' I reply. 'They were standard issue out at the front. Every day we got three or four. Would you like one?'

He takes one, shaking his head. 'You didn't use to smoke at all back then.'

'Yes, back then ...' I say, and have to smile at the way he is making such a meal out of it. I wouldn't have done that before, either. But any deference we might have had towards our elders just disappeared in the trenches. We were all equals there.

I steal a glance at the clock. I've only been here for a couple of hours, but it seems like weeks since I last saw Willy and Ludwig. What I would really like to do is rush off and find them. I haven't yet got used to the idea that I'm back with my family forever, and I'm still thinking that tomorrow, or the day after, or sometime we'll have to march out again, shoulder to shoulder, cursing, submissive, but close together ...

Eventually I get up and go and fetch my greatcoat from the hallway.

'Don't you want to stay here with us tonight?' asks my mother.

'I've still got to go and report in,' I tell her, because she wouldn't understand my other feelings.

She comes to the stairs with me. 'Wait a moment,' she says, 'it's dark, I'll get a light.'

I stand there in amazement. A light? For a couple of steps? God, how many slippery and slimy shell-holes, how many churned-up and mud-covered approach roads have I had to negotiate without any light and under heavy fire over the past few years – and now a light for some stairs? Mother, Mother! But I wait patiently until she comes back with the lamp to light the way for me, and it's as if she were caressing me in the darkness.

'Be careful, Ernst, make sure nothing happens to you out there,' she calls after me.

'What could happen to me back home in peacetime, Mother?' I reply with a smile, and look up at her.

She leans over the banister. Her small, worried face is golden in the shaded lamplight. Light and shadows make unreal patterns behind her on the landing. And suddenly something moves within me, I'm overcome by a strange and almost painful emotion, as if nothing else in the world existed except for that face, as if I were a child again needing a light to go down the stairs, or if I were a little boy who might come to some harm in the street, and as if everything since then had just been a bad dream ...

But the light of the lamp reflects sharply off my belt buckle. The moment has gone, I am not a child, I'm wearing a uniform. I rush down the stairs three at a time and push open the door of the apartment block, eager to get to my old comrades.

★ ★ ★

I visit Albert Trosske first. His mother has been crying, but that's understandable today and it isn't serious. But Albert is no longer his old self, he's sitting at the table with a hangdog expression. Next to him is his older brother. I haven't seen him for a long time, and only know that he was in a military hospital. He's got fat and has rosy cheeks.

'Hello, Hans,' I say cheerfully, 'up and about again, then? It's always good to be back on your feet.'

63

He mumbles something inaudible. Mrs Trosske sobs and leaves the room. Albert tries to signal something to me with a look. I glance around, wondering what is going on. Then I notice that Hans has a pair of crutches propped by his chair. 'Still not yet right, then?' I say.

'Oh yes,' he says. 'I was discharged from the hospital last week.' He gets hold of his crutches, straightens himself up and swings across to the stove in a couple of movements. He's lost both feet. On the right he just has an iron prosthesis, and on the left he already has a frame with a shoe on.

I feel ashamed of my stupid choice of words. 'I didn't know, Hans,' I say.

He nods. He got frostbite in both feet in the Carpathian campaign, it turned to gangrene and in the end they both had to be amputated.

'Thank God it was only the feet!' Mrs Trosske has fetched a cushion and pushes it under the artificial limbs. 'Don't worry, Hans, we'll manage, you'll learn to walk again.' She sits down by him and strokes his hands.

'Yes,' I put in, just to say something, 'at least you've still got your legs.'

'What happened was quite bad enough for me,' he replies.

I give him a cigarette. What can you do in situations like this? Everything sounds unfeeling, no matter how well meant. We go on talking for a bit anyway, painfully, and with long pauses, but whenever one of us gets up – Albert or me – and walks around we can see that Hans is looking at our feet with a dark and tortured expression, and his mother's eyes do exactly the same, always looking at our feet, you're walking around, you've got feet, I haven't …

Of course it is impossible for him to think anything else at the moment, and their mother is only concerned about him. She doesn't notice that it is also making Albert suffer. He's become completely cowed in the last couple of hours. 'Albert, we've still got to report in,' I say, to give him an excuse to get away.

'Yes,' he agrees quickly.

Outside we both exhale. The evening is reflected softly on the wet paving stones. Lamps are flickering in the wind. Albert stares straight ahead. 'I can't change any of it, Ernst,' he begins hesitantly, 'but when I'm sitting there with them and I see him and Mother with him, then I start to feel guilty and ashamed that I've still got two feet. You feel like a bastard because you're still in one piece. Even if I'd just been wounded in the arm, like Ludwig, then it wouldn't look so much like an insult ...'

I try to reassure him. But he looks away. He is not convinced by anything I have to say, but at least it relieves my own feelings a bit. It's always like that when you try and comfort anyone.

We go to find Willy. Things are a bit chaotic in his room. His bed has been taken to pieces and is propped up against the wall. It has to be made bigger, because Willy grew so much while he was in the army that he no longer fits into it. There are planks of wood, hammers and saws lying around. On a chair there is a massive bowl of potato salad. Willy himself isn't there. His mother tells us that he has been in the wash house for the past hour scrubbing himself clean. We wait.

Mrs Homeyer kneels down by Willy's pack and rummages around in it. Shaking her head, she pulls out a few filthy scraps that once upon a time were a pair of socks. 'Nothing but holes,' she says to herself, and looks reproachfully at Albert and me.

'Wartime quality,' I say with a shrug.

'Wartime quality you think, do you?' she replies crossly. 'Well, that's how much you lot know! That was the best wool! I had to run around for a week before I could get hold of it. And now they're completely done for. But you can't get new stuff anywhere.' She looks indignantly at what is left of the socks. 'Surely when you were at the front you must have had time for a quick change of socks once a week. He took four pairs with him last time. He's only brought two pairs back. And that includes these!' She pokes her hand through the holes.

I'm about to try and defend Willy, but at this point he comes in with a great roar of triumph. 'Now that really is a bit of luck! A candidate for the cooking pot! We'll have chicken stew later on!'

He is carrying a fat cockerel as if it were a flag. Its green-and-gold tail feathers are shining, its comb is purple and there are a few drops of blood on its beak. Even though I have already eaten well, my mouth starts to water.

Willy swings the bird happily to and fro. Mrs Homeyer stands up and lets out a scream. 'Willy, what have you got there?'

Willy reports proudly that he just spotted it behind the shed, caught it and killed it, all in two minutes. He slaps his mother on the back. 'It's a trick we learned out there. Your lad Willy wasn't once temporary acting cook-corporal for nothing!'

She looks at him as if he had an unexploded bomb in his hand. Then she shouts out to her husband: 'Oskar, look what he's done – he's killed Binding's prize rooster!'

'Who's Binding?' asks Willy.

'That bird belongs to Binding next door! The milkman! Oh God, how could you do something like that?' Mrs Homeyer collapses into a chair.

'I'm hardly going to let a roast like that get away,' says Willy in amazement, 'it's a natural reaction.'

Mrs Homeyer can't be calmed down. 'There'll be trouble! That man Binding has a real temper!'

'What do you take me for?' says Willy, now seriously insulted. 'Do you think anyone got the slightest glimpse of me? I'm not an amateur! This is precisely the tenth bird I've managed to get hold of. It's a jubilee cockerel! We can eat it without worries, and your Mr Binding won't know a thing about it.' He gives the bird a cheerful shake. 'You're going to be delicious! Shall we boil it or roast it?'

'Do you think I could even eat a mouthful?' cries out Mrs Homeyer, who is now beside herself. 'Take it back right away!'

'I'd have to be crazy to do that,' replies Willy.

'But you stole it!' she wails despairingly.

'Stole it?' Willy bursts out laughing. 'That's a good one. I requisitioned it! Acquired it! Found it! Stole it? No, if you take money off someone, then you can talk about stealing, but not when it's just getting hold of some grub. We'd all have done a fair bit of stealing then, wouldn't we, Ernst?'

'Of course we would,' I say, 'and that rooster just ran straight into your hands, Willy. Just like the one that belonged to the commander of Number 2 Battery over in Staden. Do you remember how you made chicken stew for the entire company with it? Your equal-parts recipe – one chicken to one horse.'

Willy is flattered and grins, then tests the hotplate on the oven with a finger. 'Cold,' he says disappointedly, and turns to his mother. 'Haven't you got any coal?'

Mrs Homeyer is still speechless with shock. She shakes her head. Willy makes a reassuring gesture. 'I'll sort that out tomorrow too. For now we can just use this old chair, it's not much use now anyway.'

Mrs Homeyer stares at her son, completely flabbergasted once again. Then once she has torn the chair out of his hands she grabs the bird and takes herself off to find Binding, the milkman.

Willy is full of righteous indignation. 'Crestfallen now he leaves, and sings no more,' he declaims gloomily. 'Can you fathom it, Ernst?'

I can just about understand that we might not be allowed to use the chair, even though once at the front we burnt a whole piano in the attempt to get the meat from a dappled horse tender enough to eat. And I suppose I can more or less understand that here at home we can't just give way to temptation when our fingers twitch involuntarily, even though out there anything to do with grub was a matter of luck, not of morals. But even the rawest recruit would surely know that taking the cockerel back once it was already dead could only lead to quite unnecessary shenanigans, and therefore doing that seems completely daft.

'If that sort of thing catches on we're going to starve to death back here, mark my words,' declares Willy, who is still worked up. 'If

67

it had been left to us lot, in half an hour we'd have had the best chicken fricassee going. I'd have made a white sauce for us, too.'

He glances from the oven to the door. 'I think we'd better make ourselves scarce,' I suggest, 'things are getting a bit sticky here.'

But Mrs Homeyer is back already. 'He wasn't in,' she says breathless and agitated, and is about to go on when she notices that Willy has his greatcoat on. This puts everything else out of her mind. 'You're not going away again so soon?'

'Just for a bit of reconnoitring, Ma,' he laughs.

She starts to cry. Willy pats her on the shoulder in an embarrassed fashion. 'Don't worry, I'll be back. We'll always be coming back again now. We'll come back far too often, just you wait …'

* * *

Side by side, striding along with our hands in our pockets, we set off down Castle Street. 'Shouldn't we go and fetch Ludwig?' I ask.

Willy shakes his head. 'No, better let him sleep. It's what he needs.'

The town is far from peaceful. Trucks full of sailors speed through the streets. There are red flags flying.

In front of the town hall great piles of leaflets are being unloaded and distributed. People tear them out of the hands of the sailors and read through them eagerly. Their eyes are shining. A gust of wind hits a stack of them and sends the broadsheets flying up into the air like a flock of pigeons. The pages get caught in the bare branches of the trees, and stay hanging there, rustling noisily.

'Comrades,' says an older man in a grey army greatcoat near us, 'comrades, things are going to get better.' His lips are twitching.

'Hell, something's going on here,' I say.

We move along faster. The closer we get to Cathedral Square, the denser the crowds become. The square is full of people. A soldier is standing on the steps of the theatre making a speech. The chalky light of a carbide lamp flickers on his face. We can't really understand what he is saying because the wind is whistling in long, irregular bursts across the square and carries with it waves of organ music from the cathedral itself, so that the thin, clipped voice is all but drowned out.

Hovering over the square there is a feeling of uncertain, agitated tension. The crowd is like a wall. It's mostly soldiers, many with their wives. Their taciturn, withdrawn faces have the same expression they had under their steel helmets at the front when they were on the lookout for the enemy. But on their faces there is now, suddenly, something else: expectations for the future, the elusive hope for a different kind of life. Shouts come across from the theatre and a dull roar answers them.

'OK, lads, now we're off!' says Willy enthusiastically. Arms are raised. A shudder runs through the crowd. The lines of people start to move. A procession forms. Shouts ring out, 'Forward, comrades!' And the sound of marching feet on the paving stones is like a single massive drawing of breath. We join in without a second thought.

On our right there's a gunner, in front of us a sapper. Groups join up with other groups. Only a few actually know one another. In spite of that, we are immediately at home. Soldiers don't need to know much about each other. They are comrades in arms and that's enough. 'Come on, Otto, come with us!' calls out the sapper just in front of us to one of the others, who has stopped.

He hesitates. He has his wife with him. She tucks her arm beneath his and looks at him. He gives an embarrassed smile. 'Later on, Franz.'

Willy pulls a face. 'As soon as petticoats are involved, proper comradeship is out the window, take it from me!'

'Rubbish,' replies the sapper, and gives him a cigarette. 'Women are one half of your life. But there's a proper time for everything.'

We fall into step automatically. But this is a different kind of marching, not what we are used to. The pavements rumble beneath our feet, and there is a wild, breathless hope which flashes over the marching column like a burst of lightning. It's as if we were marching directly and right now into a life of freedom and justice.

★

But only a few hundred yards later the procession comes to a standstill. It stops by the mayor's house. A couple of workers rattle at the door handle. Everything stays quiet, but behind the closed windows there is a brief glimpse of a woman's pale face. They rattle the door handle a bit harder, and a stone is thrown against the window. Then another. The shattered glass clinks as it falls into the front garden.

At this, the mayor appears on the balcony of the upper floor. He is greeted with shouts. He tries to protest, but nobody listens to him. 'Come on, come with us!' somebody yells.

The mayor shrugs and nods his head. A few moments later he is marching at the head of the procession.

The next one to be dragged out is the director of the Food Registry Office. Then they are joined by a worried-looking bald man, who is supposed to have been profiteering with butter supplies. We don't manage to catch a corn merchant – he heard us coming and scarpered while he could.

The procession marches to Palace Square, and stops at the entrance to the regional headquarters building. A soldier runs up the stairs and goes inside. We wait. The windows are all lit.

Eventually the door opens again. We crane our necks. A man emerges carrying a briefcase. He fishes out a few sheets of paper and begins to read a speech in a monotonous voice. We strain to hear him. Willy puts both hands behind his huge ears. Since he is a head taller than everyone else, he can hear better what is being said, and he repeats it for us. But the words just run off us like water. They ring out and they die away, but they don't touch us, they don't carry us along with them, they don't move us to action, they just run off us.

We start to get impatient. We can't understand it at all. We are used to action. Come on, this is a revolution! Surely something has to happen! But the man up there in front of us just talks and talks. He advises calm and prudence. But nobody has acted imprudently. Eventually he steps down. 'Who was that?' I ask, still disappointed.

The gunner standing near us knows the answer. 'He's the chairman of the workers' and soldiers' council. As far as I know he used to be a dentist.'

'Was he indeed!' rumbles Willy, and shakes his carroty head in irritation. 'What a piece of nonsense! I thought we'd all be marching to the station, and then straight to Berlin.'

There are loud shouts from the crowd and these spark off more shouting. They want the mayor to speak. He is shoved up the steps. He explains in a calm voice that everything will be investigated thoroughly. Beside him, trembling, are the two food profiteers, and they are sweating with fear. In spite of that, nothing at all happens to them. They do get shouted at, but nobody quite wants to raise a fist against them.

'Well,' says Willy, 'at least the mayor has some guts.'

'No, he's just used to it,' says the gunner, 'he gets dragged out every couple of days …'

We stare at him in amazement. 'Does this kind of thing happen regularly, then?' asks Albert.

The other man nods. 'There's always a new lot of troops just back from the front who reckon they have to stir things up. Well, that's as far as it goes.'

'Christ, I really don't get it,' says Albert.

'Neither do I,' declares the gunner with a great yawn, 'I thought it would be different, too. Oh well, cheerio, I'm off to get my head down. Best thing to do.'

Others follow him. The square is getting appreciably emptier. A second delegate is speaking now. Like the others, he calls for calm. The leaders will sort everything out, he says, and they are already working on it. He points up at the lighted windows. The best thing for everyone, he goes on, would be to go home.

'Bloody hell, is that it?' I ask angrily.

We feel almost stupid for having gone along. What did we actually want?

'Shit,' says Willy, disgruntled. We shrug, and drift away.

* * *

We stroll about for a while, then we split up. I walk with Albert back to his house and then go back on my own. But it's curious – now, when I don't have my fellow soldiers around me, everything about me is starting to waver a little and become unreal. So far everything has been obvious and solid, but now things are suddenly beginning to come apart and everything is so disturbingly new and unfamiliar that I am no longer quite sure whether or not I am just dreaming. Am I here? Am I really back here, back at home?

There are the streets, paved and secure, and there are smooth, shiny rooftops without a sign anywhere of gaping holes or shell damage, the walls stand there whole and unbroken in the blue of the night, with the silhouettes of balconies and gable-ends darker against it, and none of it ripped apart by the teeth and claws of the war; all the windowpanes are whole, and behind the bright clouds of their net curtains there is a hushed world, quite different from the howling world of death in which I have been living for such a long time.

I stop in front of a house where the lights are on in the ground-floor windows. Coming from them is the soft sound of music. The drapes are only half closed. You can see in. A woman is sitting playing the piano. She is alone. Only the light from a standard lamp falls on the white sheets of music. The rest of the room is indistinct in the coloured half-light. A sofa and some padded armchairs make up a comfortable picture. A dog is asleep on one of the armchairs. I stare at this picture as if enchanted. Not until the woman gets up from the piano and walks softly and quietly to the table do I step back quickly. My heart is pounding. In the harsh dazzle of the Verey lights and among the shell-shattered villages in the front line I had almost forgotten that things like this still existed – a whole street of solid rooms, rooms full of peace, carpets, warmth, women. I should like to open the door and walk into that room, I'd like to flop down into one of the armchairs, warm my hands by the fire and let it all flow over me, I'd like to talk and let the hardness and violence, all the past melt away under the woman's quiet eyes, so that I could leave it behind me, I should like to cast it off like dirty clothing.

The light in the room goes out. I walk on. But the night is suddenly full of hoarse cries and indistinct voices, full of image and full of the past, full of questions and answers.

I walk a good way out of the town. On the steep pathway up the hill to the Klosterberg I pause. The town is silvery below me, the moon is reflected in the river. The towers seem to be hovering and it is unbelievably still. I stand there for a while, and then turn back, back to the streets and the buildings.

At home I feel my way quietly up the stairs. My parents are already asleep. I can hear them breathing, my mother gently, my father more heavily, and I am ashamed of having come home so late.

I put the light on in my room. In the corner is my bed, freshly made up with white sheets, the covers turned back. I sit down on the bed and stay there for a while, too. Then tiredness overtakes me. Automatically I stretch out and go to pull the covers over me. But suddenly I sit up again, because I have completely forgotten to undress. At the front we always slept with our things on. Slowly I take off my uniform and put my boots in the corner. Then I notice that there is a nightshirt hanging over the end of the bed. I hardly know what it is any more. I put it on. And all at once, as I pull it on over my naked and shivering body, I am overcome with pure sensation, I touch the bedclothes and burrow down into the pillows, I hold them against me and press myself into them, into the pillows, into sleep, and back into life, and what I am feeling now is one thing and one thing only: I am here, yes, I am here!

3

Albert and I are sitting in Cafe Meyer, by the window. In front of us on the round marble table are two cups of what is now cold coffee. We've been here for three hours, and we still can't bring ourselves to drink the bitter stuff. We've been used to all kinds of things at the front, but this can't be anything but boiled-up coal dust.

Only three tables are taken. At one of them a group of black-market dealers are haggling over a truckload of foodstuff; at another sits a married couple reading newspapers; and the third one is where we have plonked our backsides on the plush chairs and where we are still lolling about.

The curtains are dirty, the waitress is yawning, the air is stale and really there isn't much to say for the place; but in spite of all that, for us there is quite a lot to commend it. We are lounging about companionably, we have all the time in the world, a little band is playing and we can gaze out of the window. We haven't experienced all that for a long time.

And so we stay there until the three musicians have packed up their gear and the waitress is walking pointedly around our table with increasing regularity. So we pay and stroll off into the evening. It is a great feeling to be able to wander slowly from one shop window to another, not to worry about anything, and to be free men.

We stop at the end of Stuben Street. 'We could drop in on Becker,' I say.

'Yes, we could,' agrees Albert. 'It'll give him a bit of a surprise.'

When we were at school we spent a good bit of time in Becker's shop. You could buy all sorts of things there, anything you wanted: exercise books, drawing materials, butterfly nets, fish tanks, packets of foreign stamps, second-hand books and little crib sheets with the key to algebra problems. We spent hours at Becker's, smoked illicit cigarettes and had our first covert meetings with girls from the local secondary school. Becker was our greatest confidant. We go in. A couple of schoolboys standing in a corner of the room quickly hide their cigarettes behind cupped hands. We smile and swagger a bit. A girl comes out and asks if she can help us.

'We'd like to talk to Mr Becker,' I say.

The girl hesitates. 'Can't I get something for you?'

'No, miss, you can't,' I reply, 'go and get Mr Becker.'

Off she goes. We glance at each other, put our hands nonchalantly in our pockets and wait expectantly. This is going to shake him!

The familiar bell on the door to the back of the shop tinkles. Becker emerges, small, grey and wrinkled, just the same as he always was. He blinks a couple of times. Then he recognises us. 'Well, well,' he says, 'Birkholz and Trosske. You're back too, then?'

'We are,' we say quickly, and think that now it will all start.

'Very good! And what can I get you?' he asks. 'Cigarettes?'

We're completely taken aback. We didn't actually want to buy anything – that hadn't even crossed our minds. 'Yes, ten please,' I say eventually.

He hands them over. 'See you again!' And with that he starts to shuffle back. We stand there for a moment longer. 'Forgotten something?' he calls out to us from the little step at the back.

'No, no,' we reply and leave the shop.

'Well, Albert,' I say once we are outside, 'he seems to think we'd just been off for a bit of a walk.'

He makes an irritated gesture. 'Bloody civilians ...'

We stroll on. Late in the evening Willy joins us and we all go to the barracks.

On our way there, Willy suddenly jumps to one side. I get a fright too. The unmistakable howling of a shell screams towards us, but then we look at one another in surprise and burst out laughing. It was only the screech of an electric tram.

Jupp and Valentin are lounging around rather forlornly in a large and empty room that used to be for the NCOs. Tjaden hasn't reappeared at all, he's still in the knocking shop. The other two greet us enthusiastically, because now they can set up a proper card game. In the short time since we last saw them Jupp has managed to get himself made a member of the soldiers' council. He simply put himself up, and has hung onto the job because there is such chaos in the barracks that nobody knows what is going on. By doing that he has sorted out his own situation for now, because the civilian job he had before has gone down the pan. The solicitor he worked for in Cologne has written to him to say that the women brought in to replace him have got to grips with the job really well, and are cheaper, and that Jupp himself had probably rather lost touch with office practices while he was at the front. The letter expressed great regret, but times are hard, and it wished Jupp all the best for the future.

'It's a bugger,' says Jupp sadly. 'All those years when the only thing you wanted to do was get away from the army, and now you're happy that you can stay on. They've got you coming and going. I'll go eighteen.'

Willy has a tremendous hand. 'Twenty,' I answer for him. 'What about you, Valentin?'

He shrugs. 'Twenty-four.'

Just as Jupp declares forty, Karl Bröger appears. 'I only wanted to see what you lot were up to,' he says.

'And you came to look for us here, eh?' grins Willy and sits back expansively. 'Oh well, the barracks is a soldier's real home. Forty-one.'

'Forty-six,' challenges Valentin with a snort.

'Forty-eight,' thunders Willy in reply.

Bloody hell, this is high bidding. We all come closer. Willy leans happily against the lockers and shows the two of us with him that he's got a full house. But Valentin has a dangerous grin on his face; he's holding an even better straight flush in his mitts.

It's amazingly cosy in this room here in the barracks. The stump of a candle is flickering on the table. The beds can be seen, pale in the shadows. We scoff great chunks of cheese that Jupp has procured from somewhere. He offers everyone their portion on the end of a bayonet.

'Fifty!' roars Valentin.

Then the door is flung open and Tjaden comes hurtling in. 'Se-Se-' he stutters, and in his excitement is overcome by a massive attack of hiccups. We walk him round the room with his arms up in the air. 'Did the whores nick your money?' asks Willy solicitously.

He shakes his head. 'Se-Se-'

''ten-SHUN!' commands Willy.

Tjaden pulls himself together. The hiccups disappear.

'Seelig,' he says jubilantly, 'I've found Seelig.'

'Christ,' shouts Willy, 'if you're lying I'll chuck you straight out of the window!'

Seelig was our CSM, and an utter bastard. Unfortunately he was transferred two months before the revolution came, and we hadn't been able to get hold of him after that. Tjaden tells us that he's now the landlord of the King of Prussia, and he's got some good beer, too.

'Let's go,' I shout, and we hurry out.

'But not without Ferdinand,' says Willy. 'He's still got a score to settle with Seelig about Schröder.'

We whistle and shout at Kosole's house until he appears crossly at the window in his night things. 'What's the matter with you?' he grumbles. 'It's late. Don't you know I'm a married man?'

'There's a time for everything,' calls Willy, 'but get down here as quick as you can, we've found Seelig!'

Ferdinand comes to life. 'Straight up?' he asks.

'Straight up!' crows Tjaden.

'Right, I'm on my way!' he answers. 'But God help you if you're taking the piss …'

Five minutes later he is downstairs, and gets the details.

We rush off.

As we turn into Haken Street, in his excitement Willy runs into someone and knocks him over. 'Clumsy great oaf,' the man shouts after him from the ground. Willy turns round quickly and stands threateningly over him. 'I beg your pardon, did you say something?' he says, and touches his cap.

The other man gets himself into a sitting position and looks up at him. 'Not that I recall,' he answers in a surly voice.

'Lucky for you,' says Willy. 'You haven't really got the build to be insulting, have you?'

We cross a little garden and stand there in front of the King of Prussia. The old name has already been painted out, and it is now called the Edelweiss. Willy grabs the door handle.

'Wait a minute!' Kosole pulls his great paw away from it. 'Willy,' he says imploringly, 'if it comes to a punch-up, I do the punching! Promise me that!'

'Right you are!' confirms Willy, and tears the door open.

We're met by a sudden mass of noise, smoke and light. Glasses clink. A nickelodeon is belting out the march from *The Merry Widow*. The taps along the counter are gleaming. A burst of laughter echoes round the basin by the bar where two girls are rinsing the dirty beer glasses. They are surrounded by a mob of blokes. Jokes are flying about, the water slops over and distorts their faces as they are reflected in it. A gunner orders a round of schnapps and pats one of the girls on the bottom. 'This is good pre-war stuff, Lina,' he bellows enthusiastically.

We push our way through. 'You're right, there he is,' says Willy. In an open-necked shirt with the sleeves rolled up, sweating and red around the neck, the landlord is behind the bar, pulling pints of beer. Beneath his great fat mitts it flows down into the glasses, brown and gold. Then he looks up. A broad smile spreads across his face. 'Well, well, well! You're back too? What can I get you? Light or dark?'

'Light, sarn't major,' answers Tjaden boldly. The landlord looks to see how many of us there are.

'Seven,' says Willy.

'Seven,' repeats the landlord with a glance at Ferdinand, 'six of you and Kosole as well, as I live.'

Ferdinand pushes forward to the bar and puts his fists on the edge of it.

'Tell me, Seelig, have you got any rum?'

The landlord busies himself behind the shiny nickel. 'Yes, of course I've got rum.'

Kosole looks up at him. 'You like to swig it down yourself, don't you?'

The landlord fills a row of shot glasses. 'Yes, of course I like a drop myself.'

'Do you remember the last time you swigged down a load of it?'

'No ...'

'But I do!' roars Kosole, standing at the bar like a bull in a field. 'Do you remember the name Schröder?'

'Schröder's a pretty common name,' says the landlord casually.

That is too much for Kosole. He goes to jump over the bar, but Willy grabs him and pushes him down onto a seat. 'We'll have a drink first! Seven beers!' he says firmly in the direction of the bar.

Kosole is silent. We sit down around a table. The landlord puts the pints down in front of us himself. 'Cheers!' he says.

'Cheers!' replies Tjaden, and we drink, then he leans back. 'I told you it was true, didn't I?'

Ferdinand looks at the landlord as he turns back to the bar.

'Christ,' he growls, 'when I think of how that bastard stank of rum when we were burying Schröder –'

He breaks off.

'Mind you don't weaken,' says Tjaden.

But it's as if Kosole's words have torn back a veil that had been fluttering and wavering there the whole time, and the bar now seems to fill up with a grey and ghostly desolation. The windows become blurred, shadows rise up out of the floorboards and memories billow out into the smoky room.

Kosole and Seelig could never stand each other. But they didn't become deadly enemies until August 1918. At that time we were in a shot-up section of trench a bit behind the front line, and we had to spend the whole night digging a mass grave. We couldn't make it all that deep because the groundwater soon started to seep in. By the end we were working in thick mud.

Bethke, Wessling and Kosole were shoring up the sides. The rest of us were bringing in the corpses from the surrounding terrain and laying them down side by side in a long row while the grave was being finished. Albert Trosske, the corporal in our section, was collecting up the identity discs and pay books, whenever they still had them.

The faces of some of the dead were already blackened and putrefied, because decay always set in quickly in the wet months. On the other hand, they didn't smell nearly as bad as in the summer. Many of them were soaked, sodden like sponges. We found one lying flat on the ground with his arms outstretched. When we lifted him up we saw that what was actually lying there was mostly bits of uniform, he'd been so completely blown to pieces. There wasn't even any identification. Eventually we worked out from a repair in the trousers that it was Lance Corporal Glaser. He was very light to carry, since most of him was missing.

Any arms, legs or heads that we found separately we put all together on a single tarpaulin. When we brought Glaser along, Bethke said: 'That's enough. We can't get any more in.'

We fetched a couple of sandbags full of quicklime. Jupp scattered it with a flat shovel over the grave. Max Weil, who had been to get a load of crosses from behind the lines, appeared just after that. Then, to our amazement, Seelig also turned up out of the darkness. We gathered that he had been detailed to say the prayers for the dead, because there was no padre available nearby, and both of our officers were ill. He was in a foul mood, because he couldn't stand the sight of blood. He was also pretty fat. On top of that he had night-blindness, and couldn't see much. All this made him so nervous that he misjudged the edge of the grave and fell in. Tjaden burst out laughing and called out in a low voice: 'Quick, start shovelling, start shovelling …'

At that moment Kosole, of all people, was still working in the grave just there and Seelig fell directly on top of him, getting on for two hundredweight of living flesh. Ferdinand swore viciously. Then he saw that it was the sergeant major, but he was an old hand and this didn't make him hold back – this was 1918, after all. The CSM got to his feet, saw that it was his old adversary Kosole, exploded and started to bawl him out. Ferdinand shouted back, and Bethke, who was also still down in the grave, tried to pull them apart. But the sergeant major was spitting with fury and Kosole, still feeling strongly that he was the injured party, gave as good as he got. Now Willy jumped down to join in on Kosole's side. An almighty din came up out of the grave.

Suddenly somebody said: 'That's enough.' Although the words were spoken quietly, the racket stopped at once. Seelig climbed, spluttering, out of the grave. His uniform was white from the lime and he looked like some chubby-faced cherub that had been covered in icing sugar. Kosole and Bethke climbed up after him.

Standing at the top, supported by a walking stick, was Ludwig Breyer. He had been lying by the dugout covered with two greatcoats, because that was the time when he had his first really severe attack of dysentery.

'What's going on?' he asked. Three voices started to explain, all at the same time. Ludwig stopped them wearily. 'It doesn't matter …'

The CSM insisted that Kosole had pushed him in the chest. Kosole started to object furiously once again.

'That's enough,' said Ludwig again. There was a silence. 'Did you get all the identity discs, Albert?' he asked.

'Yes,' answered Trosske, and added under his breath, so that Kosole couldn't hear him, 'One of them was Schröder.'

They looked at each other for a moment. Then Ludwig said: 'So he wasn't taken prisoner, then. Where is he?' Albert led the way along the row of bodies. Bröger and I followed him, because Schröder had been one of our classmates. Trosske stopped by one of the corpses, whose head was covered up with a sandbag. Ludwig bent down. Albert pulled him back. 'Don't look, Ludwig,' he begged. Breyer turned round. 'I have to, Albert,' he said calmly. 'I have to.'

The upper part of Schröder's body was utterly unrecognisable. It was as flat as a pancake. His face had been completely flattened, and a deep, black hole with a ring of teeth round it was the sole indication of where his mouth had been. Breyer covered him up again silently. 'Does he know?' he asked, looking over to where Kosole was working. Albert shook his head. 'We've got to get rid of the CSM,' he said, 'or there'll be trouble.'

Schröder had been Kosole's close friend. In fact we had never understood quite why, because Schröder had been delicate and sickly, still a boy, and Ferdinand was the complete opposite, yet he had looked after him like a mother.

We heard someone puffing and panting behind us. Seelig had caught up with us and was standing there wide-eyed. 'I've never seen anything like it,' he stuttered. 'How did that happen?'

Nobody answered him. In fact Schröder had been due to go off on leave a week ago, but Seelig had scuppered it for him because he couldn't stand him or Kosole. And now Schröder was dead.

We walked away. We couldn't even bear to look at the CSM at that moment. Ludwig went and huddled down under his greatcoats again. Only Albert stayed there. Seelig stared at the body. The moon came out from behind a cloud and cast its light on it. The sergeant major just stood there, his bulky form bent slightly forward, looking down at the pallid faces on which the incomprehensible expression of horror was frozen to a stillness that almost screamed aloud.

Albert said coldly: 'It's best if you say a prayer now, sir, and then get back.'

The sergeant major wiped his forehead. 'I can't do it,' he muttered. The horror had taken hold of him. We knew all about that. For weeks on end you felt nothing and then suddenly something unpredictable would happen and it would knock you flat. He staggered off, green in the face.

'He thought that coming out here would be like a kids' party,' commented Tjaden drily.

The rain came down even harder, and we were getting impatient. The CSM didn't come back. Eventually we fetched Ludwig out from under his coats, and in a quiet voice he said the Lord's Prayer.

We passed the dead down. Weil helped us to do so, and I noticed how much he was shaking. Almost inaudibly he whispered: 'You shall be avenged' over and over again. I stared at him in surprise.

'What's up with you?' I asked. 'These aren't the first you've seen. You'll have a lot of avenging to do.' After that he said no more.

Once we had got the first few rows laid down, Valentin and Jupp came along dragging a tarpaulin.

'This one's still alive,' said Jupp, and pulled back the top of the tarpaulin.

Kosole glanced down at him. 'Not for much longer,' he said. 'We can wait for him.'

The man on the tarpaulin groaned and gasped, and with each breath blood ran down over his chin.

'Should we move him?' asked Jupp.

'If we do that he'll die straight away,' said Albert, and pointed at the blood. We settled him onto his side. Max Weil looked after him and we went on with the work. Valentin was helping me now. We passed Glaser down into the grave. 'Christ, his poor wife ...' murmured Valentin.

'Careful, here's Schröder,' Jupp called out to us, and slid the tarpaulin down.

'Shut up!' hissed Bröger.

Kosole was still holding the body. 'Who?' he asked, bewildered.

'Schröder,' repeated Jupp, who thought that Kosole already knew.

'Don't talk rubbish, you bloody fool,' shouted Kosole furiously, 'he was taken prisoner.'

'No, it's true, Ferdinand,' said Albert Trosske, who was standing nearby. We all held our breath. Without a word Kosole lifted the body out again and climbed up after. Then he shone his pocket torch on it. He bent closely over what was left of the face and looked at it carefully.

'Thank God the sergeant major's out of the way,' whispered Karl.

We waited motionless for the next few seconds. Kosole stood up. 'Give us a spade,' he said sharply. I handed him one. We were expecting murder and mayhem, but Kosole simply began to dig. He dug a separate grave for Schröder, and would not let anyone else help. And then he carried him to the grave himself. He was so preoccupied that he didn't give a thought to Seelig.

By dawn we had finished both graves. Meanwhile, the wounded man had died and we were able to put him in with the rest. Once the earth had been stamped flat we set up the crosses. Kosole wrote Schröder's name on a blank cross with an indelible pencil, and hung his helmet on it.

Ludwig came over again. We took our helmets off and he said another 'Our Father'. Albert was pale as he stood beside him. Schröder had sat next to him at school. But Kosole looked the worst of us all, completely grey and sunken, and he did not say a single word.

We stood there for a while. It was still raining. Then the coffee detail turned up, and we sat down to eat.

In the morning the sergeant major suddenly climbed out of a nearby dugout. We had thought that he had long since cleared off. You could smell the rum on him a mile away and now what he wanted was to get back well behind the lines. Kosole roared out when he spotted him. Luckily Willy was not far off, and he rushed at Ferdinand and held on to him. But it took four of us and all our strength to stop him breaking loose and throttling the CSM. It was a full hour before he calmed down enough to see that he would only make trouble for himself if he went after him. But he swore on Schröder's grave that he would get even with Seelig one day.

And now Seelig is standing by the bar, Kosole is sitting a few yards away, and neither of them is in the army any longer.

The nickelodeon is belting out the march from *The Merry Widow* for the third time in a row.

'Landlord, another round of schnapps,' shouts out Tjaden, with his piggy eyes gleaming. 'Coming up,' answers Seelig, and brings over the glasses. 'Cheers, mates!'

Kosole looks at him with a scowl. 'You're not our mate,' he grunts. Seelig tucks the bottle under his arm. 'OK, suit yourself,' he replies, and goes over to the bar.

Valentin tosses back the schnapps. 'Get it down you, Ferdinand, it's the only thing that matters.'

Willy orders the next round. Tjaden is already pretty tight. 'Well now, Seelig, you old company sergeant maggot,' he growls, 'you can't put us in the jug now, can you? Have a drink with us!' He slaps his one-time superior officer on the back so hard that the man starts to choke. A year earlier he'd have been court-martialled for that, or sent to a lunatic asylum.

Kosole looks away from the bar and into his glass, then from his glass back at the bar and at the tubby, busy fellow operating the beer taps. He shakes his head. 'It's not the same man at all, Ernst,' he says to me.

I feel exactly the same way. He was so much a fixture with his uniform and his notebook that I could hardly have imagined him in his shirtsleeves, let alone as the landlord in a bar. And now he fetches a glass, and doesn't mind when Tjaden – whom he once regarded as the lowest of the low – makes some familiar comments and claps him on the shoulder. My God, things have really moved on!

Willy gives Kosole an encouraging prod in the ribs. 'Well?'

'I don't know, Willy,' says Ferdinand, who is confused. 'Should I give him a smack in the gob or not? I never thought it would be like this. Look at the way he is scurrying around with the glasses, the slimy little shit. It doesn't seem right any more.'

Tjaden keeps on ordering drinks. He is having a whale of a time making his superior officer dance attendance on him.

Seelig has also had a good few by this time. His bulldog face is glowing, partly because of the alcohol, partly because he is doing such good business.

'Why don't we just forget our differences,' he suggests, 'and I'll stand a round of pre-war rum?'

'What?' says Kosole, and sits up straight.

'Rum. I've still got a jar or two under the counter,' says Seelig in a friendly way, and goes to fetch it. Kosole, looking as if he had been slapped in the face, watches him go.

'He doesn't remember it at all, Ferdinand,' says Willy, 'otherwise he wouldn't have dared to do that.'

Seelig comes back and pours the drinks. Kosole snarls at him: 'Don't you remember the way you used to get blotto on rum when you were in a funk? Maybe they could give you a job in a mortuary!'

Seelig waves his hands in a calming-down gesture. 'That was all a long time ago,' he says. 'Things are not the same now.'

Ferdinand goes silent again. If Seelig were to make a single sharp retort, then all hell would break loose. But this unfamiliar conciliatory manner baffles Kosole and leaves him undecided.

Tjaden has a sniff, and we all do the same. It's good-quality rum. Kosole knocks his glass over. 'I'm not taking anything from him.'

'Christ,' shouts Tjaden, 'you could at least have given it to me!' He tries to save some by dipping his fingers in it. He doesn't get much.

The bar is gradually emptying. 'Closing time,' calls Seelig, and pulls the grille down in front of the bar. We get up.

'Well, Ferdinand?' I ask. He shakes his head. He just can't cope. He's not really Seelig any longer, not that potman.

The landlord holds the door open for us. 'Goodnight, gentlemen, and pleasant dreams.'

'Gentlemen,' sniggers Tjaden. 'Gentlemen – he used to call us bastards ...'

Kosole is almost out of the door when he happens to glance down and notices Seelig's legs – he is still wearing the old, familiar puttees. What's more, his trousers are still military issue with piping. His top half is a landlord, but from the waist down he's still a sergeant major. That settles it.

Kosole spins round, and as Seelig retreats, Kosole goes after him. 'Listen to me,' he growls, 'Schröder! Schröder! Schröder! Do you remember him, damn you, you little shit! This one is for Schröder! With best regards from the mass grave!' He lays into him with his fist. The landlord stumbles, runs behind the bar and grabs hold of a wooden mallet. He gets Kosole on the shoulder and in the face with it. But Ferdinand is suddenly so angry that there's no question of backing off. He grabs hold of Seelig, bangs his head down onto the bar so that the glasses all rattle, and turns on all the beer taps.

'Go on, get that lot down you, you rum-soaked bastard!' he snarls. 'Drown in your own bloody booze, I hope you suffocate!'

The beer is pouring down the back of Seelig's neck and shoots straight through his shirt into his trousers, which balloon up. He's roaring with rage, because it'll be hard to replace such decent beer these days. Then he manages to heave himself up and he grabs a glass. He pushes it up under Kosole's chin.

'Wrong move,' comments Willy, who is standing by the door watching with interest. 'What he should have done is headbutt him, and then kick his knee away.' None of us interferes. This is Kosole's business. Even if he was taking a serious beating we still wouldn't be allowed to help. Our role is to hold back anybody who might be inclined to help Seelig. But nobody wants to, because Tjaden has given a quick run-down of the situation.

Ferdinand's face is bleeding copiously. Now he is really furious, and soon finishes Seelig off. He brings him down with a blow across the throat, jumps on top of him and bangs his head on the floor a few times until he has had enough.

Then we leave. Lina is standing ashen-faced beside her boss as he lies there making gurgling noises. 'Best get him to hospital,' Willy calls back to her, 'he'll only be in for two or three weeks. Nothing very serious!'

Outside Kosole smiles like a child who is suddenly free of some sorrow, because Schröder has at last been avenged. 'That was good,' he says, and wipes the blood away from his face. Then he takes his leave of us. 'Right, I'd better get back to the wife as soon as possible, or else she might think I've got myself involved in some kind of a brawl.'

We split up by the market square. Jupp and Valentin go back to the barracks. Their boots clatter on the moonlit paving stones.

'I'd really like to be going with them,' says Albert suddenly.

'I know what you mean,' agrees Willy, probably still thinking about that rooster. 'The folk here are a bit small-minded, aren't they?'

I nod. 'I suppose we'll all have to go back to school before long ...'

We stop and grin at each other. Tjaden is overcome with amusement just thinking about it. Then he runs after Valentin and Jupp, laughing.

Willy scratches his head. 'Do you think they'll be pleased to see us? We're not quite as easy to handle as we used to be ...'

'They liked it better when we were heroes and as far away as possible,' says Karl.

'I'm looking forward to the whole rigmarole,' declares Willy, 'especially with us the way we are now, tempered in the storm of steel ...'

He lifts a leg slightly and lets off an almighty fart. 'An eleven-point-two, high explosive and smoke as well,' he announces with considerable satisfaction.

4

When our company was disbanded we had to take our weapons with us. We were given instructions not to hand them in until we got home. Now we go to the barracks and hand in our rifles. At the same time we collect our demob pay – we all get fifty marks discharge money plus fifteen more for the travelling. In addition, we are entitled to an overcoat, a pair of shoes, underwear and a suit to replace the uniform. We climb up to the top floor to collect our bits and pieces. The quarter-bloke makes a dismissive gesture. 'Sort yourselves out some stuff.'

Willy has a quick sniff around the things that are hanging there. 'Look here,' he says in a fatherly tone, 'this is the sort of thing you can do to recruits. This clobber came off the ark. Show us some new things.'

'Haven't got any,' replies the quartermaster sullenly.

'Well now,' says Willy, and looks at him for a few moments. Then he gets out a metal cigar case. 'Do you smoke?'

The other man shakes his bald head.

'So you like chewing tobacco, then?' Willy puts his hand into his pocket.

'No.'

'OK, then surely you like a drink?' Willy has thought of everything, and his hand moves towards a bulge in the front of his tunic.

'Don't drink either,' says the quarter-bloke offhandedly.

'Then I'm afraid that I have no alternative but to smack you in the face a few times,' Willy explains in a friendly voice, 'because we're not leaving here without some first-class new gear.'

Luckily, Jupp turns up at that very moment, and as a representative on the soldiers' council he's now a force to be reckoned with. He winks at the QM. 'These are mates, Heinrich, old foot-sloggers. Just show them into the salong des monsewers, will you?'

The quarter-bloke livens up a bit. 'Why didn't you tell me who you were in the first place?'

We follow him to a room at the back. This is where the new stuff is hanging. We quickly get out of our old clobber and get dressed in new stuff. Willy explains that he needs two overcoats because he developed anaemia during his spell in the army. The QM hesitates. Jupp takes him off to one side and has a word with him about his own subsistence allowances. When they come back, he is no longer as bothered. He gives no more than a perfunctory glance at Tjaden and Willy, who have become appreciably fatter. 'Oh well,' he growls, 'it's no skin off my nose. Lots of them don't even come and collect their stuff. Got enough dosh. Just so long as my books balance.'

We sign for the fact that we've got all the things we were supposed to get.

'Did you say something about cigars a while back?' the quarter-master asks Willy.

Taken aback, Willy gets his cigar case out with a grin.

'And about chewing tobacco too?' the other man adds.

Willy puts his hand in his pocket. 'But you don't drink, do you?' he says.

'I do actually,' says the QM calmly. 'In fact the doctor tells me I ought to. I'm a bit anaemic too. Just leave the bottle here.'

'Just a sec!' Willy takes a great swig, so that he can at least rescue something. Then he passes the bottle to the stores-wallah; it was full a minute or so ago, and now it is half empty.

Jupp walks down to the barrack gates with us. 'Do you know who else is here?' he says. 'Max Weil, in the soldiers' council.'

'That's where he should be,' reckons Kosole. 'Bit of a cushy job, isn't it?'

'Can be, can be,' says Jupp. 'Valentin and I are keeping things going here for the time being. If any of you need anything, travel papers and things like that, I'm the man in charge.'

'Let me have a rail pass,' I say, 'and then I can go and see Adolf Bethke.'

He pulls out a block of pass-forms and tears one off. 'Fill the details in yourself. And you won't want to travel third, of course, so go second class.'

'Done.'

Outside Willy buttons up his overcoat. He has another one on underneath it. 'Better I've got it than it just goes missing later,' he says cheerfully. 'The army owes them to me anyway for the half-dozen shell splinters I stopped.'

We set off down the high street. Kosole tells us that this afternoon he plans to repair his pigeon loft. Before the war he used to breed carrier pigeons and black-and-white tumblers. He wants to start up again. That was what he used to long for all the time out at the front.

'What else will you do, Ferdinand?' I ask.

'Look for a job,' he says bluntly. 'I'm a married man, after all. Got to buckle down now.'

Suddenly there comes from the area around St Mary's Church the sound of a couple of shots. We listen carefully. 'Service revolvers and a standard issue rifle,' says Willy knowledgeably. 'Two revolvers, I should think.'

'So what?' laughs Tjaden, and swings his new shoes by the laces. 'It's still a damned sight more peaceful here than it was in Flanders.'

Willy stops by the window of a gentlemen's outfitter. On display is a utility suit made of paper and stinging-nettle fibres. But that isn't what interests him. He stares transfixed at a series of faded fashion pictures that have been placed behind the suit. He points excitedly at the picture of an elegantly dressed gentleman with a pointed beard, who is in eternal conversation with someone in hunting gear. 'What do you think that is?'

'It's a shotgun,' says Kosole, who thinks he means the huntsman.

'Rubbish,' interrupts Willy impatiently, 'it's what they call a cuttervay! A swallow-tail morning coat, that's what it is. The very latest thing! And you know what I'm going to do? I'm going to get one made from one of these overcoats. Take it apart, dye it black, remodel it, get rid of some of these bits – and it'll be tray-bloody-bong, I tell you!'

He is more and more taken up with his idea. But Karl puts a damper on it. 'What about the striped trousers to go with it?' he asks after some thought. This stops Willy in his tracks for a moment. 'I'll nick a pair of the old man's out of his wardrobe,' he decides. 'And at the same time I'll have the white waistcoat that he wears for weddings, and how do you think old Willy'll look then, eh?' Beaming with delight he looks at the rest of us. 'Bloody hell, lads, life starts here, right?'

When I get home I give half of the demob money to my mother. 'Ludwig Breyer is here,' she says. 'He's waiting in your room.'

'And he's a lieutenant,' adds my father.

'Yes,' I reply, 'didn't you know?'

Ludwig looks a bit better. The dysentery isn't as bad. He smiles at me. 'I wanted to borrow a couple of books from you, Ernst.'

'Take anything you want, Ludwig,' I tell him.

'Don't you need them yourself?' he asks.

I shake my head. 'Not at the moment. I had a go at reading something yesterday. But it's odd, I can't concentrate properly. A couple of pages and my mind's on something completely different. It was as if I just couldn't think straight. Do you want some novels?'

'No thanks,' he says, and picks out a couple of books. I look at the titles. 'That's heavy stuff, Ludwig, what you want with that?' I ask.

He smiles, embarrassed. Then he says hesitantly: 'When we were at the front so many thoughts went through my head, Ernst, and I could never get things straight in my mind. But now that it's all over there are lots of things I'd like to know. Like why human beings let that kind of thing happen, you know, how it all comes about. There are all sorts of questions, some of them about ourselves. Before the war we had quite a different view of life. There really is a lot I'd like to find out, Ernst ...'

I point to the books. 'Do you think you'll get the answers there?'

'I'm going to try, at least. Nowadays I read from morning to night.'

He soon leaves. I sit there thinking after he has gone. What have I done since we got back? Feeling ashamed, I pick up a book, but I soon put it down again and stare out of the window. I can do that for hours, just gazing at nothing. Before the war it was different, I always knew what I had to do.

My mother comes into the room. 'Ernst, you are going to Uncle Karl's tonight, aren't you?'

'I suppose so,' I reply without enthusiasm.

'He often used to send us food,' she says gently.

I nod. Outside the window it is beginning to get dark. Blue shadows are hanging in the branches of the chestnut trees. I turn to her. 'Did you go for that walk by the poplars much last summer, Mother?' I ask quickly. 'It must have been really nice there ...'

'No, Ernst, we didn't go at all this year.'

'Why not, Mother?' I ask in surprise. 'You used to go there every Sunday.'

'We haven't been going for many walks lately,' she replies quietly. 'It makes you so hungry. And we didn't have anything to eat.'

'Oh, I see ...' I say slowly. 'But Uncle Karl always had enough, didn't he?'

'He quite often sent us things, Ernst.'

Suddenly I become rather sad. 'What was it all for, Mother?' I say.

She strokes my hand. 'There must have been a reason for it all, Ernst. The good Lord will know.'

★ ★ ★

Uncle Karl is our family's one famous relative. He has a villa, and during the war he was senior paymaster in the War Office.

When I go there I take Wolf with me, but he has to stay outside because my aunt doesn't like dogs. I ring the doorbell.

A man in evening dress opens the door. Taken aback I wish him a polite 'good evening'. Then it dawns on me that he must be the butler. In the army I'd forgotten all about that sort of thing.

The man looks me up and down as if he were a lieutenant colonel in mufti. I smile but he doesn't smile back. When I take my coat off he puts out his hand to help me. 'It's OK,' I say, to try and win him round, 'I'm an old soldier, I can manage that by myself.' Then I hang up my clobber on a hook.

But without saying a word he takes it off that peg and with a haughty expression puts it on the one next to it. Arsehole, I think to myself, and go in.

Uncle Karl comes up to me, in mess uniform, with spurs jingling. He greets me somewhat superciliously, because I was only one of the rank and file. I stare at his gleaming full-dress kit in astonishment. 'Are we having horse-steaks tonight, then?' I say, trying to make a joke.

'What do you mean?' he asks, bewildered.

'Well, you're wearing spurs to dinner,' I reply with a laugh.

He looks at me sourly. Quite unintentionally I seem to have touched on a raw nerve. These home-based War Office wallahs do tend to go in for spurs and swords.

Before I can explain that I hadn't meant to be rude, my aunt comes bustling up. She has always been as flat-chested as an ironing board, and her tiny black eyes are glinting just as they have always done, as if someone had polished them up specially. She showers me with a torrent of words, all the time continuing to look sharply all around her.

I'm feeling a bit bemused. Too many people, I think to myself, too many women, and above all too much light. At the front we never had much more than an oil lamp. But these chandeliers are completely unforgiving. You can't hide anything from them.

I scratch my back uneasily.

94

'What on earth are you doing?' asks my aunt, and suddenly stops talking.

'Oh, it's probably just a louse that managed to get away,' I say. 'We had so many lice, and it takes a good week or so before you can get rid of them all …'

She steps back in horror. 'Don't worry,' I tell her soothingly, 'they don't jump, lice are not the same as fleas.'

'Dear God!' She puts her finger to her lips and pulls a face, as if I had just uttered who knows what kind of obscenity. But that's the way these people are. They want us to be heroes, but they don't want to know anything about the lice.

I have to shake hands with a whole lot of people, and I start to sweat. These people here are completely different from us at the front. Compared to them, I feel as clumsy and lumbering as a tank. They all behave as if they were on display, and they talk as if they were on the stage. I try cautiously to hide my hands, because the filth of the trenches is still ingrained in them like a poison. I wipe them surreptitiously on my trouser leg; in spite of that they are invariably damp when I have to shake hands with one of the ladies.

I circulate for a bit, and end up in a group in which a chartered accountant is holding forth pompously. 'Would you believe it,' he says in a tone of indignation, 'a saddle-maker, we've got a saddle-maker as state president! Just picture it for a moment: a gala reception at court, and a saddle-maker is granting audiences! Ludicrous!' He is so worked up that he has a coughing fit. 'What do you think about that, my young warrior!' he calls out to me, and claps me on the shoulder.

I haven't thought about it all, and shrug in embarrassment. 'Maybe he knows a thing or two …'

The accountant looks at me for a moment. Then he gives a delighted chuckle. 'Very good,' he crows, 'maybe he knows a thing or two! No, no, my dear chap, you have to be born to that kind of thing! A saddle-maker! You might as well have a tailor or a shoemaker!'

He turns back to the rest of the group. What he has been saying annoys me, because it rubs me up the wrong way to hear him talking about shoemakers in such a dismissive way. They made just as good soldiers as their social superiors. Adolf Bethke had been a shoemaker, and he knew more about the war than many a staff officer. As far as we were concerned it all depended on the man, not on his job. I look the accountant up and down suspiciously. He is now dropping quotations in all directions, and maybe he has education coming out of his ears; but if I were under heavy fire and had to be brought out, I would much sooner rely on Adolf Bethke.

I am relieved when at last we go in to dinner. Next to me I have a young lady with a feather boa round her neck. She's very attractive, but I have no idea how to talk to her. As soldiers we didn't say much anyway, and certainly not to women. All the others are engaged in lively conversations. I try to listen, so that I can get some ideas.

At the top of the table sits the chartered accountant, who is just explaining to everyone how the war would have been won if we had just held out for two more months. That sort of rubbish almost makes me sick, because every soldier knows that we simply didn't have enough men and munitions. Across the table from him is a lady who is talking about her husband, who was killed in the war, and she is making herself sound so important that you'd think she was the one who had fallen in battle and not the husband. Further down the table the talk is all about shares and about the peace settlement, and of course they all know better than the people who are actually in charge of these things. A man with a hooked nose is telling a tale about a friend's wife with such hypocritical sympathy that you feel like throwing your glass in his face on account of his barely concealed *Schadenfreude*.

I find all this talk completely stultifying, and before long I can't follow what's being said any more. The girl with the feather boa asks me superciliously if I was struck dumb out at the front.

'No,' I answer, and I think to myself that Kosole and Tjaden ought to be sitting here – they'd have a good laugh at all this palaver that everyone is coming out with and that they are so proud of. But it does annoy me a bit that I can't show them with a well-chosen comment what I think of it all.

Mercifully there appears on the table at that moment a plate of crisply done chops. I take a sniff. Real pork chops, cooked in proper fat. The mere sight of them takes away all my discomfort. I secure a decent-sized piece and start to chew at it with full enjoyment. It tastes fantastic. It's been a phenomenally long time since I had a fresh pork chop. The last time was in Flanders – we'd caught a couple of suckling-pigs and we scoffed them down to the bare bones on a wonderfully mild summer's evening. Katczinsky was still alive then, dear old Kat, and Haie Westhus, they were something quite different from this lot back here; I lean on my elbows and become oblivious of everything going on around me because I can see them again so clearly. Those pigs were really tender, we'd made potato pancakes to go with them, and Leer was there and so was Paul Bäumer, yes, Paul Bäumer … I'm deaf and blind to the world, completely lost in my memories …

I'm startled out of it by a giggle. It has gone quiet round the table. Aunt Lina's expression is pure vitriol. The girl sitting next to me stifles a laugh. Everybody is looking at me.

I suddenly break out in a sweat. I'm sitting there just like that time in Flanders, elbows propped on the table, the bone in my paws, fingers covered in fat, absent-mindedly gnawing off the last of the meat – but the others are all eating properly with a knife and fork.

Flushing scarlet, I stare straight ahead and put the bone down. How could I have forgotten myself so much? But I'm just not used to anything else. At the front we always ate like that – we had a spoon or fork at best, but never a plate.

Suddenly my confusion is mixed with fury. Fury at Uncle Karl, damn him, who has just started to talk ostentatiously about war loans; fury at all the rest of them, who behave as if they were so important, with their words of wisdom; and fury at this whole world, these people who go on living their petty little lives so self-assuredly, as if the years of horror had never happened at all, years when there was a single choice: life and death, nothing else.

Silent and resentful I stuff in as much food as I can manage, at least I'm going to have a good meal. As soon as I can I slip out.

In the hall stands the butler in his dress suit. I grab my things and snarl: 'We should have had you at the front, you overdressed baboon! You and all the rest of this mob!' Then I slam the door.

Wolf has been waiting for me outside the house. He jumps up when he sees me. 'Come on, Wolf,' I say, and suddenly I realise that it isn't the faux pas with the chop that has made me feel so bitter, but the old stagnant, self-satisfied attitude that is still there, and still makes so much of itself. 'Come on, Wolf,' I say again, 'these are not our people. We'd get on better with any Tommy or with any old sweat from the French lines! Come on, let's go and find our real mates! It's better with them, even if they do eat the stuff with their fingers and then belch! Come on!'

Off we go, the dog and I, running as hard as we can, faster and faster, gasping, barking, we run like mad things, our eyes blazing – the whole lot can go to hell, but we're alive, aren't we, Wolf, we're alive!

5

Ludwig Breyer, Albert Trosske and I are on our way to school. Classes are supposed to be starting again. We were all training to be teachers before the war, and we weren't covered by the special examination regulations. Those who went from the grammar school into the army were luckier. Many of them were able to take an exam under emergency regulations, either before they joined up or when they were on leave. The ones who didn't do that, of course, also have to go back to the classroom now. Karl Bröger is one of them.

We walk past the cathedral. The green copper plates on the towers have been removed and replaced by grey roofing felt. It looks mouldy and decrepit, and as a result the whole church looks more like a factory. The copper was melted down to make shells.

'I bet the good Lord never dreamt that that would happen,' says Albert.

The two-storey teacher-training unit is in a winding lane by the west side of the cathedral. The grammar school is diagonally opposite. Behind that is the river, and the embankment with the lime trees. Before we went into the army these buildings were our entire world. Then it was the trenches. Now we are here again. But this is not our world any more. The trenches were stronger.

In front of the grammar school we meet our former schoolmate Georg Rahe. He was a lieutenant and a company commander, but when he came home on leave he got drunk and lounged around and never gave a thought to his school-certificate exams. Because of that he has to go back into the fifth form, and he'd already been kept down in that class for two years running.

'Is it true, Georg?' I ask. 'I heard that while you were at the front you got your Latin up to grade-A standard.'

He laughs, and stalks off, long-legged, over to the grammar school.

'You just mind you don't get a C-minus for behaviour!' he calls back to me.

For the last six months of the war he was an airman. He shot down four English planes, but I'm not sure he can still do the proof of Pythagoras' theorem.

We walk on to the college. The lane is full of men in uniform. Faces appear that you have almost forgotten, names that you haven't heard for years. Hans Walldorf hobbles up – we carried him back with a shattered knee in November 1917. He was amputated at the thigh, and now has a heavy artificial leg strapped on, and makes a lot of noise as he stamps along. Kurt Leipold appears, and introduces himself with a laugh as Götz von Berlichingen, Goethe's 'hero with the iron fist'. He's got an artificial right arm.

Then someone comes out of the gate and says in a gurgling voice: 'You don't recognise me, do you?'

I look at his face, insofar as he still has one. Across the forehead there is a broad, livid scar which goes right down into the left eye. The flesh has grown over it so that eye is small and deep-set. But it is still there. The right one is staring, glass. The nose is missing, and there is just a black patch covering the place. The scar that emerges from it splits the mouth in two places. The mouth is thickened and has grown together awkwardly, which accounts for the indistinct speech. The teeth are false, with a metal bridge visible. I look at him, unsure. The gurgling voice says: 'Paul Rademacher.'

Now I recognise him. Yes, that's his grey suit with the stripes. 'Hello, Paul, how's it going?'

'You can see how –' he tries to grimace with his distorted lips – 'two blows with a trenching tool. These went with it.' He raises his hand, which has three fingers missing. His single eye looks at me sadly. The other one stares unfeelingly straight ahead. 'I'd like to know if it would still be possible for me to be a teacher because my speech is so bad. Can you understand me?'

'Of course,' I tell him. 'And it's bound to improve. Anyway, I'm sure they'll be able to operate again later.'

He shrugs and says nothing. He doesn't seem very hopeful. If anything were possible, they would have done it already. Willy now joins us and wants to tell us all the latest. We hear that Borkmann did die from his chest wound after all, the one that got him in the lung. He got raging consumption as a result. Henze shot himself when he found out that his spinal injury meant that he would always be in a wheelchair. It's understandable. He was our best footballer. Meyer was killed in September, Lichtenfeld in July. Lichtenfeld had only been out there for two days.

Suddenly we're all taken aback. A little figure is standing there in front of us.

'No! Westerholt?' says Willy with disbelief.

'Yes, still here, old carrot-top,' comes the answer.

Willy is staggered. 'I thought you were dead.'

'Not yet,' replies Westerholt cheerfully.

'But I read it in the paper – it said you were.'

'Well, they got that one wrong,' says our short-arsed friend, with a grin.

'You really can't trust anyone nowadays,' says Willy, shaking his head. 'I thought the worms had gobbled you up long since.'

'That'll happen well after you, Willy,' replies Westerholt smugly. 'You'll go first, people with red hair never live all that long.'

We go in. The yard, where we used to eat a snack at ten, the classrooms with their blackboards and benches, the corridors with their rows of coat hooks for our caps – everything is just as it was, but it seems to us as if it belongs to another world. Only the smell of these dark rooms is recognisable; it's not as sharp, but it's still a bit like the smell of the barracks.

At the end of the assembly hall is the shiny 100-pipe organ. To the right are the masters. Two pot plants with leathery leaves have been placed on the principal's desk, and in front of it hangs a laurel wreath with a ribbon across it. The principal is wearing his frock coat. That means that there's going to be a ceremonial welcome. We all bunch together. Nobody wants to stand in the front row. Only Willy unconcernedly goes over and places himself there. In the half-dark of the hall his head is as bright as the red lamp outside a knocking shop.

I look at the masters. Once upon a time they were more important to us than any other human beings, not just because they were in a position of authority over us, but because basically we believed what they told us, even when we were making fun of them. Now they are just a random group of older people, whom we can cheerfully dismiss.

So there they stand, and think they are going to lecture to us again. You can see just by looking at them that they're prepared to sacrifice a bit of their former dignified position. But what can they teach us now? We know more about life than they do, we've acquired an entirely different sort of education, hard, bloody, cruel and inescapable. We could teach them things now, but what good would that do? If there were to be a sudden surprise attack on the assembly hall they would scurry around clueless, like frightened rabbits, whereas not a single one of us would lose his head. Calmly and decisively we would take the most necessary precaution, namely to coop them up somewhere where they couldn't get in our way, and then start to defend our position.

The principal clears his throat and starts to speak. The words that spill from his mouth are smooth and rounded, and he is, one has to admit, a first-class speaker. He talks about the heroic struggles of our soldiers, of battle, victory and bravery. But in spite of all the fine words it still feels wrong to me, or maybe it is precisely *because* of those fine words. Things weren't smooth and rounded at all. I look at Ludwig and he looks at me. Albert, Walldorf, Westerholt, Reinersmann – none of them likes this stuff.

But the principal is really getting into his stride. He wants to praise, he says, not just the heroism at the front, but the quieter heroism of those at home.

'Those of us here at home also did our duty to the full, we stinted ourselves and went hungry for our soldiers, we were racked with anxiety and we shook with fear, and getting through it will have been almost more difficult for us than it was for our valiant lads in uniform at the front ...'

'Whoops!' says Westerholt. A low murmuring starts up. The Old Man gives us a look, and then goes on: 'But we can't really make a comparison. You have stared death fearlessly in its steely face and done the great things you had to do, and even if an ultimate victory in arms was not granted to us, we must now desire all the more to stand together in the deepest love for our sorely tried fatherland, and to rebuild our land in spite of all our enemies. We must do so in the spirit of our greatest poet, Goethe, whose pithy message across the centuries to our disturbed age is: "Though enemies 'gainst us raise their hand, yet shall we still undaunted stand."'

The Old Man's voice drops by a major third. By now it's wearing full mourning and dripping with unction. A tremor runs through the black-clad group of masters. Their faces display composure and solemnity. 'And let us above all else think of those former pupils of this institution who fell in battle, who went forth cheerfully to defend their homeland and did not return from the field of honour. Twenty-one comrades are no longer with us, twenty-one warriors have met a glorious death in arms, twenty-one heroes rest now in foreign soil, far from the tumult of battle, and they sleep the eternal sleep beneath the verdant grasses ...'

At this moment there is a brief burst of derisive laughter. The principal stops awkwardly. The snort of derision is from Willy, standing there four-square and solid as a wardrobe. His face is scarlet with fury.

'Verdant grasses – verdant grasses,' he stutters. 'Eternal sleep? They're lying in the filth at the bottom of a shell-hole, shot to pieces, ripped apart, sunk down in a bog – verdant grasses! What do you think this is, hymn practice?' And he waves his arms around like a windmill in a storm. 'A hero's death! What do you think that means? Do you want to know how little Hoyer died? He was caught on the wire the whole day and lay there screaming, and his guts were spilling out like macaroni. Then a shell took off a couple of his fingers, and two hours later a bit of his leg, and he was still alive and trying to stuff his guts back into his belly with his good hand, and it wasn't until nightfall that he was finally done for. When we were able to get to him he was as full of holes as a sieve. Why don't you go and tell his mother how he died, if you think you're brave enough!'

The principal has gone pale. He doesn't know whether to try and maintain discipline or to be conciliatory. In the end he can't bring himself to do either.

'Sir,' says Albert Trosske to the principal, 'we didn't come here for you to tell us that we did our job well, even if unfortunately we didn't quite manage to win the war. We don't give a shit about all that ...'

The principal shudders, and with him all the staff; the great hall shakes, the organ trembles. 'I really must protest at the language ...' he says, quite outraged.

'Shit, shit and shit again!' says Albert. 'And it's about time you realised once and for all that that's been every other word for us over the past few years! When it was all so vile out there and we had long since forgotten all the nonsense you used to talk, we had to grit our teeth and say "shit!" and carry on. You don't seem to have any idea of what's going on here! It's not well-behaved schoolkids you've got in front of you, not your own dear pupils, what you've got are soldiers!'

'But, gentlemen,' the Old Man calls out almost imploringly, 'it's a misunderstanding, an unfortunate misunderstanding –'

He can't go any further. He is interrupted by Helmuth Reinersmann, who carried his wounded brother out of battle under heavy shelling on the Yser, only he was dead when he got him to the clearing station.

'Fell in battle,' he says angrily. 'They didn't fall in battle so that speeches could be made about them. They were our comrades in arms and that's that, and we don't want any nonsense talked about them!'

Everything now descends into complete confusion. The principal stands there horrified and completely helpless. The masters look like a flock of frightened chickens. Only two stay calm. Both of them were in the army.

The Old Man tries to smooth things over at any cost but there are too many of us, and Willy is just too much for him, standing right in front of him and shouting away. Who knows what these wild-men might do next, at any minute they might even start pulling hand grenades out of their pockets. He raises his arms like the wings of an archangel. Only nobody is listening to him.

But all at once the clamour dies away. Ludwig Breyer has stepped forward. Things calm down. 'Principal,' says Ludwig in his clear voice, 'you have your own view of the war, sir. With flag-waving, enthusiasm and military marches. But you only watched it as far as the railway station that we left from. We don't blame you for that. We all thought exactly the same way as you did, after all. But since then we've got to know the other side of things. All the fine feelings of 1914 soon crumbled into dust in the face of what we saw. But in spite of everything we *did* stick it out, because something deeper kept us together, something that only came into being out there at the front, a sense of responsibility of which you can have no concept, and which is impossible to put into words.'

Ludwig stares ahead for a moment. Then he brushes a hand across his forehead and goes on: 'We are not holding you to account – that would be stupid, because nobody knew what was coming. But what we do demand of you is that you no longer try to dictate how we think about these things. We went out there enthusiastically and with the word fatherland on our lips – and we have come back silent, with the sense of fatherland in our hearts. Therefore we are asking you for silence now. Don't make fine speeches. They are not right for us. And they are not right for our dead comrades in arms. We watched them die. That memory is still so close to us that we cannot bear it when you talk about them that way. They died for more than that.'

It has gone completely quiet. The principal presses his hands together. 'But, Breyer,' he says softly, 'it wasn't meant like that ...'

Ludwig says nothing.

After a while the principal continues: 'Could you please tell me yourselves what it is that you want?'

We look at one another. What do we want? Yes, if only that could be answered simply in a single sentence. Seething away within us is a strong, undefined feeling – but putting it into words right now? We don't know the right words to use yet. Perhaps they will come to us later on!

After a moment's silence, however, Westerholt pushes himself forward and stands face-to-face with the principal. 'Let's talk about the practicalities,' he says, 'because that's what we really need. What did you have in mind for us? In this room are seventy soldiers who are expected to go back into the classroom. I'll tell you something right now: we've forgotten pretty well everything of the stuff you taught us, but we haven't the slightest desire to spend much time here.'

The principal pulls himself together. He explains that so far there have been no instructions from the authorities regarding this situation. For the moment, therefore, it looks as if we'll be going back into the classes we were in before we left. He says that we could sort out a course of action later on.

He is answered by murmurings and laughter.

'Surely you don't even believe yourself,' says Willy angrily, 'that we are likely to go and sit in a classroom with kids who haven't been in the army, and put our hands up like good boys when we know the answers? We're sticking together.'

It is only now that we see clearly how ridiculous this whole situation is. For years we've been allowed to shoot, stab and kill – and now it is supposed to be important whether we went out there from the fourth form or the fifth. One lot could already solve equations that had two unknowns, the others could only do equations with one. That's the sort of distinction that counts here.

The principal promises to put in an application for special courses for ex-soldiers.

'We can't wait that long,' says Albert Trosske. 'We'd better take care of it ourselves.'

The principal doesn't comment. He leaves the room without a word. The masters follow him. Then we tramp out as well. Before we do, however, Willy, who thinks the whole business has gone off too quietly, picks up the two pot plants from the podium and smashes them on the floor. 'I never could stand bloody vegetables,' he says grimly. He shoves the laurel wreath onto Westerholt's head. 'You can go and make yourself some soup out of that.'

The smoke from cigars and pipes billows up. We are sitting with the other grammar-school ex-soldiers discussing the matter. More than a hundred soldiers, eighteen lieutenants, thirty sergeants and corporals.

Westerholt has brought with him an old copy of the school regulations, and is reading bits out. It's a slow process, because after every paragraph there is a great roar of laughter. We can't understand that once upon a time it all applied to us.

Westerholt is especially tickled by the fact that before the war we were not allowed to stay out after seven in the evening without the permission of our class teacher. But Willy squashes him. 'You want to be quiet about that, Alwin,' he shouts across to him, 'you've caused your class teacher more trouble than all the rest. You're reported as killed in action, get a moving memorial speech from the principal, you're praised as a hero and a model pupil, and after all that you've got the damned cheek to come back alive! The old boy's really been put on the spot. Now he'll have to take back all the nice things he said about you when you were a corpse, because I bet your algebra and essay-writing are just as bad as before.'

We choose members for a students' council. Our teachers might be good enough to drum a few things into our heads for exam purposes, but we are not going to have them in control of us any longer. From our group we choose Ludwig Breyer, Helmuth Reinersmann and Albert Trosske, and from the grammar school, Georg Rahe and Karl Bröger.

After that we appoint three representatives to set off tomorrow to the provincial authorities and to the ministry to put through our demands for schooling and for the exams. Willy, Westerholt and Albert are chosen. Ludwig can't travel with them because he isn't yet well enough.

All three get military passes and free travel documents, because we have whole blocks of these things. There are also plenty of lieutenants and members of the soldiers' council available to sign them.

Helmuth Reinersmann makes sure that everything looks right. He tells Willy that he has to leave the new tunic that he requisitioned from the stores at home, and instead wear an old one for the journey, one that has been ripped by shrapnel and repaired.

'What for?' asks Willy in surprise.

'Because it will have more effect on the pen-pushers than a hundred well-reasoned arguments,' explains Helmuth.

Willy refuses, because he is proud of his new tunic and wants to show off with it in the capital. 'If I give a good thump on the table at the education commission, that'll be just as effective,' he says.

But Helmuth won't take any argument. 'We can't just bang their heads together, Willy,' he says, 'we need these people on our side. Now, if you thump on the table wearing your old tattered tunic you'll get more out of them for us than if you're wearing your new one. I know what those people are like, trust me.'

Willy gives in. Helmuth turns to Alwin Westerholt and looks him up and down. He seems to be too unadorned. So he gets Ludwig Breyer's decoration pinned to his tunic. 'You'll sound more convincing to a senior ministry official with that on,' adds Helmuth.

This isn't necessary with Albert, because he's got enough tin on his chest already. So the three of them are now properly kitted out. Helmuth looks at his handiwork. 'Excellent,' he says, 'and now off you go! The real front line will soon show those pen-pushing porkers what's what!'

'You can count on that,' declares Willy, who is in good spirits again.

The smoke from the cigars and pipes billows up. Wishes, ideas and desires are bubbling up and mingling. God knows what will come of them. A hundred young soldiers, eighteen lieutenants, thirty sergeants and corporals are sitting here, and they want to start living. Every one of them could bring a company through the most treacherous terrain with the minimum of losses while under fire, not one of them would hesitate for a moment before reacting in the right way to the shout 'they're advancing' if it echoed round their section of trench, every one of them has been forged and tempered by countless merciless days, every one of them is a complete soldier, no more and no less.

But for peace? Are we any good for that? Are we fit for anything other than soldiering?

Part Three

I've come to visit Adolf Bethke. I leave the station, and I know his house as soon as I see it. When we were at the front he described it to me often enough.

A garden with fruit trees. Not all of the apples were picked. There are lots lying on the grass under the trees. There is an open area in front of the door with a huge chestnut tree. The ground around it is thickly covered with red-brown leaves, and so are the stone table and garden seat underneath the tree. Among the leaves there is a pinkish-white shimmer from the insides of the spiky casings of the fruit where they have broken open, and the shiny brown of the chestnuts themselves. I pick up a couple and look at the glossy, veined, mahogany skins with the lighter patch on the underside where it would germinate. So such things still exist, I think to myself, and look around – it's amazing that all these things are still there, these colourful trees, these misty-blue woods, woods rather than just shell-shattered tree stumps; and the wind blowing across the fields, no longer the smell of cordite and the stink of gas, just the oily shimmer of the ploughed and pungent earth, horses pulling ploughs and not munition wagons, and behind them, unarmed and home again, ploughmen, ploughmen in soldiers' uniforms.

The sun is hidden behind the clouds high above a copse, but shafts of silvery light shoot down from behind the cover, children are flying brightly coloured kites which are high up in the sky, your lungs fill up and breathe the cool air in and out, there are no guns any more, no mines, no pack to constrict the chest, no belt hanging heavy around the waist. Gone is the constant feeling of being on your guard, that prickling of the hairs at the back of your head, the need to walk in a half-crouch which at any second could become a fall, a collapse, horror or death – now I can walk freely and upright, with no cares on my shoulders, and I relish the strength of the moment: just to be there, and to be visiting my old comrade Adolf.

The front door is half open. The kitchen is to the right. I knock, but there is no answer. I call out hello, but nothing happens. I go in and open another door. Someone is sitting alone at a table; he looks up, dishevelled, wearing an old uniform, a single glance: it's Bethke.

'Adolf!' I say happily. 'Didn't you hear? Just having a sleep, were you?'

He stays where he is as we shake hands.

'I wanted to come and see you, Adolf.'

'That's nice of you, Ernst,' he says gloomily.

'Is something the matter, Adolf?' I ask, bewildered.

'Oh, forget it, Ernst …'

I sit down next to him. 'Come on, Adolf, what's up?'

He is defensive. 'It's OK, Ernst, never mind. You know, it's good that one of you has come by.' He stands up. 'You can go crazy on your own …'

I look around. His wife is nowhere to be seen.

He says nothing for a while, then he tells me once again 'it's good of you to come'. He digs out some schnapps and cigarettes. We have a drink out of thick glasses with a pink base. Outside the window you can see the garden and the pathway with the fruit trees. The wind is blowing. The garden gate rattles. In the corner a grandfather clock with weights, its wood stained dark, strikes the hour.

'Cheers, Adolf.'

'Cheers, Ernst.'

A cat slips across the room. It jumps up onto the sewing machine and starts to purr. After a time Adolf starts to speak. 'They come here and they talk, parents, in-laws, and they don't understand me and I don't understand them. It's as if we weren't the same people any more.' He puts his head in his hands. 'You understand me, Ernst, and I understand you, but with them it's as if there were a wall between us.'

Eventually I hear the whole story.

Bethke comes home, pack on his back, carrying a sackful of provisions, coffee, chocolate, even a dress-length of silk.

He wants to come in quietly to surprise his wife, but the dog barks like mad and practically pulls his kennel over, so then Adolf can't contain himself any longer and runs along the path between the apple trees – his path, his trees, his house, his wife – and his heart is hammering away in his chest as he comes through the door, a deep breath and he's inside – 'Marie ...'

He sees her, he is overwhelmed by the very sight of her, twilight, home, the clock ticking, the table, the winged armchair, his wife. He wants to take hold of her. But she backs away and stares at him as if he were a ghost.

He still doesn't understand. 'Did you get a fright?' he says with a laugh.

'Yes,' she says nervously.

'It'll pass, Marie,' he answers, trembling with excitement. Now that he is in the room he is shaking all over. It has all been too long.

'I didn't know you'd be coming yet, Adolf,' says his wife. She has backed away to the cupboard and is looking at him with her eyes open wide.

For a moment a sudden chill comes over him and takes his breath away. 'Aren't you pleased to see me?' he asks awkwardly.

'Yes of course, Adolf ...'

'Has something happened?' he asks next, still holding on to all his belongings.

Then the crying starts, she sits down with her head on the table, he might as well know straight away, the others will tell him anyway, she had a fling with somebody, he came on to her, she didn't really want to and always only thought about him, and now he might as well kill her and have done with it.

115

Adolf stands there, just stands there, and in the end realises that he has still got his pack on his back. He unbuckles it, unpacks, he's shaking, and all the time he's thinking: it can't be true, it can't be true – and he goes on unpacking, it's important just to keep calm, the silk crackles in his hand, he holds it out to her – 'I wanted you to have this' – and all the time he's thinking: it can't be true, it can't … Helplessly he holds out the red silk, and still none of all this has really sunk in.

But she is crying and doesn't listen to him. He sits down, and thinks, and suddenly he is terribly hungry. There are some apples there from the trees outside, beautiful russets, he takes one and eats it, because he has to do something. But then his hands go limp and he understands. A raging fury wells up in him, he wants to smash something, and he rushes out to look for the man.

He doesn't find him. He goes into the pub. People greet him, but everyone is walking on eggshells, they avoid his glance and speak very carefully. So they already know about it. He pretends nothing is the matter, but who would be able to keep that up for long? He drinks up quickly and is leaving when somebody asks: 'Have you been home yet?' and there is a silence as he goes out of the bar. He runs around until it gets late. And then he finds himself outside his own house. What is he to do but go in? The lamp is lit, there is coffee on the table, potatoes are frying in the pan on the stove. The pain of all this is overwhelming; how wonderful it would all be if everything were normal – there is even a white tablecloth. But this just makes it worse.

His wife is there and she has stopped crying. When he sits down, she pours him some coffee and puts a plate of sausage and fried potatoes in front of him. But she hasn't laid a place for herself.

He looks at her. She is pale and slim. Then it all wells up again in a surge of incoherent misery. He doesn't want to know any more, he wants to shut himself away and lie on his bed and turn to stone. The coffee is steaming but he pushes it away, and the food too. His wife is frightened. She knows what is coming.

Adolf doesn't get up because he can't. He shakes his head and says: 'Just go, Marie.'

She doesn't question it. She puts her shawl around her shoulders, pushes the plate towards him again and says in a shaky voice: 'At least eat something, Adolf ...' and leaves. She goes, she goes with her light tread, silently, the door closes, the dog is barking outside, the wind is roaring round the windows. Bethke is alone.

And then comes the night.

After a few days, being so alone in a house will start to gnaw away at someone who's just back from the front.

Adolf tries to catch the man and beat the hell out of him. But the man realised in time, and made himself scarce. Adolf looks everywhere, but he can't lay hands on him, and that is the last straw.

Then his in-laws turn up to talk to him and ask him to think it over; they say his wife has long since learned her lesson, and anyway, being alone for four years wasn't easy either, it was all the man's fault, and lots of other things happened during the war ...

'What can you do, Ernst?' – Adolf looks up.

'Goddamn it all,' I say, 'what a shit situation.'

'And that's what you come back home for, Ernst!'

I pour us out some more drinks. There aren't any of the cigars that Adolf smokes in the house, and he doesn't want to go to the pub, so I go and get him some. Adolf is a heavy smoker, and it will help him if he has some cigars. I get him a whole box of 'Woodland Solitude', thick, brown stumpy cigars which are well named, because they are made entirely of beech leaves, but they are still better than nothing.

When I get back somebody is there, and I see at once that it is his wife. She holds herself straight, but her shoulders are soft. There's something moving about a woman's neck, always something childlike, so that you can never be completely angry with them. Apart from the fat ones, of course, with necks like a pig's.

I say hello and take off my cap. The woman doesn't reply. I give Adolf the cigars, but he doesn't take one. The clock ticks. Outside the window the chestnut leaves are rustling down, sometimes one brushes against the glass and the wind holds it there. Five earthy-brown leaves left on one twig look threatening, like an outstretched, grasping hand trying to reach into the room, the dead brown hand of autumn.

Eventually Adolf stirs himself and says in a voice I don't recognise as his: 'You should go now, Marie.'

She gets up, obedient as a schoolchild, and goes, looking straight ahead. The soft neck, the narrow shoulders, how is all this possible?

'Every day she comes in like that, and sits there waiting, and says nothing, and looks at me,' says Adolf bitterly. I'm sorry for him, but now I'm sorry for his wife as well. 'Come back to town with me, Adolf,' I suggest, 'there's no point in sitting around here.'

He doesn't want to. Outside the dog starts barking. The woman is just going out of the garden, back to her parents.

'Does she want to come back?' I ask. He nods. I don't ask any more questions. He has to work things out for himself. 'Why not come with me?' I try again.

'Later, Ernst.'

'At least have a cigar.' I pass him the box and wait until he takes one. Then I shake hands with him and say: 'I'll come and see you again, Adolf.'

He comes down to the gate with me. After a little while I turn round to wave. He is still standing at the gate, and behind him is the darkness of the evening, just as it was when he got off the train and left us. He should have stayed with us. Now he is alone and unhappy and we can't help him, however much we should like to. Yes, it was all so much easier at the front; just as long as you managed to stay alive, everything was all right.

2

I'm lying on the sofa with my legs stretched out, my head against the arm and my eyes shut. While I'm half asleep, my thoughts are wildly confused. My consciousness hovers between waking and dreaming, and the tiredness passes across my brain like a shadow. Somewhere behind it all there is the indistinct noise of artillery fire, shells whistle softly over, and the tinny sound of the gongs warning of a gas attack comes closer; but before I can reach down for my gas mask, the darkness disperses silently, and the earth, into which I have pressed myself, gives way to a warmer, brighter sensation as it becomes the upholstery of the sofa once again, pressing against my cheek, and I realise dimly but deeply that I am at home; and then the gas alarm in the trenches gives way to the gentle clattering of the dishes as my mother quietly sets the table.

Then the darkness rushes in again, and with it comes the grumble of gunfire. But from a distance, as if they had travelled across woods and fields, I can hear words in among it all, words which only gradually start to make sense as they get through to me. 'The sausage was a present from Uncle Karl,' says my mother, her voice penetrating the indistinct thunder of the guns.

The words reach me just as I am slipping down into a shell-hole from its edge. And with them the image of a well-fed, self-satisfied face crosses my mind. 'Oh, him,' I say crossly, and my voice sounds as if I had a mouthful of cotton wool as the weariness still hangs heavily on me, 'that ... miserable ... arsehole.' Then I am falling, falling, falling, and the shadows come back, flooding over me, wave upon wave, darker and darker ...

But I don't fall asleep. There is something missing now that was there before – the regular, light metallic clatter. Slowly I manage to get my thoughts together and open my eyes. My mother is standing there, pale, with a horrified look on her face, staring at me.

'What's the matter?' I shout in alarm and jump up. 'Are you ill?'

'No, no,' she says, shaking her head, 'but how could you say such a thing?'

I think for a moment. What on earth did I say? Oh yes, that business with Uncle Karl. 'Come on, Mother, don't be so sensitive,' I laugh with relief. 'Uncle Karl really is a black marketeer, surely you know that?'

'That's not what I meant,' she replies softly, 'but using expressions like that ...'

What I said when I was half asleep suddenly comes back to me. I'm ashamed that it had to happen in front of my mother, of all people. 'It just slipped out,' I explain by way of apology, 'it really takes a time to get used to not being at the front any more. Things were a lot rougher out there, Mother, rough but honest.'

I run my hand over my hair and button up my battledress tunic. Then I look for my cigarettes. As I do so, I see that my mother is still looking at me and that her hands are shaking.

Astonished, I stop what I'm doing. 'But, Mother,' I say in surprise, and put my arm round her shoulder, 'it really isn't that bad. Soldiers are like that.'

'Yes, yes, I know,' she replies, 'but you ... you too ...'

I laugh. I want to shout 'Of course me too', but suddenly I fall silent and let her go, something has struck me. I sit down on the sofa to try and get my thoughts together.

There before me is an elderly woman with an anxious and worried face. She has folded her hands, tired, overworked hands with soft and wrinkled skin, the blue veins prominent; hands that got that way for my sake. I never noticed before, there are lots of things that I never noticed before, because I was too young. But now I can see why I really am different from all the other soldiers in the world to this careworn little woman: I am her child.

I have always been that to her, even when I was a soldier. She saw the war simply as being like a horde of dangerous animals, threatening the life of her endangered child. It never entered her head that her endangered child might be an equally threatening animal as far as other mothers' children were concerned.

I look away from her hands and down at my own. In May 1917 I stabbed a Frenchman with them. The blood flowed over my fingers, hot and disgusting, as I stabbed him over and over again in mindless, terrified fury. Afterwards I had to throw up, and I cried all through the night. It was already morning before Adolf Bethke could calm me down; I was just eighteen, and it was the first time I'd been in an attack.

Slowly I turn my hands over. During the big push at the start of July I shot three men with those hands. They stayed there for the whole day hanging on the wire. Their limp arms waved around in the blast as the shells impacted, and it sometimes looked as if they were threatening us, but just as often it looked as if they were begging us for help. Once, later on, I threw a hand grenade from twenty yards, and it took both legs off an English captain. His screams were terrible, he had thrown back his head with his mouth wide open and propped himself on his arms, the top part of his body balanced like a seal's. But he quickly bled to death.

And now I sit here in front of my mother, and she is nearly in tears because she can't understand how I have become so coarse as to use a vulgar expression.

'Ernst,' she says softly, 'I've wanted to say this for a long time: you've changed a lot. You've become so restless.'

Yes, I think bitterly, I've changed. How well do you actually know me now, Mother? All you have is a memory, nothing more than the memory of the quiet and dreamy youngster I used to be. You must never, ever find out about the last few years, you must never even suspect what it was really like and what it turned me into. The tiniest fraction of it would break your heart, since you are trembling with shame at a single vulgarity which has already shaken your image of me. 'Things will get better,' I say, feeling rather helpless, and trying to convince myself as well.

She sits down by me and strokes my hands. I take them away. She looks at me anxiously. 'Sometimes you seem like a stranger, Ernst, you get an expression on your face and then I don't even recognise it as you.'

'I've got to get used to things first,' I say, 'I still feel as if I were just here for a visit …'

Dusk falls in the room. My dog comes in from the corridor and lies down on the floor in front of me. His eyes are shining when he looks up at me. He's restless too, he hasn't got used to things either.

My mother leans back. 'But at least you are home, Ernst …'

'Yes, that's the main thing,' I say, and stand up.

She stays where she is, sitting in the corner, a tiny figure in the twilight, and I feel with a sudden softness how our roles have suddenly switched. Now she is the child.

I love her, yes, how could I possibly ever love her more than at this moment, when I know that I can never come to her and be with her and tell her everything and maybe find peace? Have I lost her? All at once I feel how much of a stranger I've become, how alone I really am.

She has closed her eyes. 'I'm getting dressed and going out for a bit,' I whisper, so as not to trouble her. She nods. 'Yes, my boy,' she says – and then after a while, softly, 'my good boy.'

It's as if I'd been stabbed. Carefully I close the door behind me.

3

The fields are wet and the water makes a gurgling noise as it runs off the pathways. I've got a small jam jar in my coat pocket as I walk along the line of poplars. When I was a boy I used to catch fish and butterflies here, and I used to lie under the trees and daydream.

In spring the stream was full of frogspawn and algae. Bright green strands of waterweed waved about in the small, clear eddies, long-legged skater beetles zigzagged between the stems of the reeds, and in the sunshine shoals of sticklebacks cast their rapid little shadows on the gold-glinting sand beneath them.

But now it is cold and damp. The poplars stand there in a long row beside the stream. Their branches are bare, but there is a gentle blue haze around them. One day they will be green and rustling again, and once more the sun will shine down, warm and blessed, on this patch of earth which holds so many of my childhood memories.

I stamp on the bank of the stream. A couple of fish shoot out from under it, and after that I can't stop myself. At a point where the stream gets narrow enough for me to straddle it, I wait until I have caught two sticklebacks in my hand. I put them into my jam jar and look at them.

Backwards and forwards they dart, delicate and perfect, with their three spines on the back, slim brown bodies and flickering front fins. The water is as clear as crystal and the light reflects back onto it from the glass. And suddenly it takes my breath away, so strong is the sensation of how beautiful it is, the water in the jar and the light and the reflections.

Holding it carefully I wander on. I carry it steadily and keep looking at it, my heart beating hard as if I had captured my youth and put it in that jar, and was now taking it home with me. I squat down at the edge of the pool, where there are thick clumps of duckweed, and watch the blue-speckled newts swimming upwards like little contact mines as they come up for air. Caddis-fly grubs crawl slowly through the mud, a water beetle is moving idly across the bottom, and from under a mouldering root a brown frog, quite motionless, gazes at me in amazement. I look at all this, and there is far more in it than you can actually see – memories, longings and past happiness are all there as well.

Still grasping my jam jar firmly, I walk on, seeking, hoping. The wind blows and the hills are blue on the horizon.

But suddenly I'm overcome with panic – down, down, take cover, you're standing in full sight! I shudder in wild fear, and stretch out my hands in front of me so I can rush forward and throw myself behind a tree, I'm trembling and gasping – and then I breathe again. It's passed. I look around in embarrassment – nobody saw me. It takes a while before I calm down. Then I bend over to pick up the jam jar, which had fallen out of my hand. The water has been tipped away, but the fish are still flapping about in it. I go down to the stream again and get some more water.

I walk on slowly, lost in my thoughts. I get closer to the woods. A cat wanders across the path. The railway embankment cuts through the fields as far as the woods. You could make decent dugouts there, I think to myself, proper deep ones with concrete covering ... then the line of the trench would go along to the left, with saps and listening posts, and a few machine guns on top – no, just two, the others would have to be by the wood, and then if you did that the whole terrain would be covered by crossfire. The poplars would have to come down, so that the enemy artillery couldn't use them as landmarks ... and behind, on the hill, there'd be a number of trench mortars ... then just let 'em come!

A train whistles. I look up. What am I doing? I came here to recapture the landscape of my childhood, and now I'm digging trenches through it. It's habit, I think to myself, we can't look at the countryside any longer, we just see terrain, terrain that has to be attacked or defended … the old mill up on the hill over there isn't a mill, it's an objective, the wood isn't a wood, it's artillery cover … the whole business still haunts us …

I shake it off and try to think about what it was like before. But I can't seem to manage it. I'm no longer as happy as I was earlier, and I don't feel like going on. I turn round.

In the distance I see a solitary figure coming towards me. It's Georg Rahe.

'What are you doing here?' he asks in surprise.

'What about you? What are you doing?'

'Nothing.'

'Neither am I,' I reply.

'So what about the jam jar, then?' he asks with a rather amused look. I blush.

'No need to feel ashamed,' he says. 'You wanted to catch a few fish again, didn't you?'

I nod.

'Well?'

I shake my head.

'You're right,' he says thoughtfully. 'That sort of thing doesn't go well with a uniform, does it?'

We sit down on a pile of wood and have a cigarette. Rahe takes his cap off. 'Do you remember how we used to come here and swap stamps?'

'Yes, I remember. The wood depots in the forest used to smell really strongly of tar and resin in the sunshine, and the wind was cool from the water. I can still remember it all, how we used to try and catch frogs, how we used to read books, and talk about the future, and about the life that was waiting for us beyond the blue horizon, calling us like quiet music.'

'And then it changed a bit, didn't it, Ernst?' says Rahe, smiling with the same smile that we all have, weary and slightly bitter. 'We used to catch fish a bit differently when we were at the front, too.

125

One hand grenade into the water and they would be dead and floating on the surface with their white bellies upwards. That was a more practical way of fishing.'

'How did it come to this, Georg,' I ask, 'that we can be sitting around here without any real idea of what we're going to do next?'

'There's something missing, isn't there, Ernst?'

I nod. He taps me on the chest. 'I'll tell you what it is – I've given it a lot of thought. All this –' and he points at the meadows in front of us – 'was life, things were blooming and growing, and we were growing with them. And what we have behind us –' he indicates the far distance with a movement of his head – 'that was death, and the dying destroyed a part of us as well.' He smiles again. 'We need a few repairs, old lad.'

'Maybe it would be better if it were summertime,' I suggest. 'Things are always easier in the summer.'

'That's nothing to do with it,' he says, and blows out some smoke. 'I think it's something quite different.'

'What then?' I ask him.

He shrugs and stands up. 'Let's go home, Ernst. Do you want me to tell you what I've decided?' He bends down to me. 'I'm probably going to join the army again.'

'You're crazy,' I say, aghast.

'Not at all,' he replies, and for a moment he becomes very serious. 'Maybe I'm just being logical.'

I stop in my tracks. 'But, Georg, come on ...'

He walks on. 'Don't forget that I've been back a couple of weeks longer than you have,' he says, and then he starts to talk about something entirely different.

When the first houses come into sight, I take the jam jar with the sticklebacks and tip them back into the stream. The fish swim off rapidly with a flick of their tails. I leave the jar on the bank.

I say goodbye to Georg. He goes off slowly down the street. I stand outside our house and watch him as he walks away. His words have left me strangely unsettled. I have the feeling that there is something indefinite there, something which retreats whenever I try to grasp hold of it, and disappears when I go for it directly, but then creeps up on me again and lies in wait.

The sky is leaden over the low bushes in Queen Luise Square, the trees are bare, an unlatched window is rattling in the wind and there is a damp and miserable twilight lurking in the scrawny elder bushes in the front gardens.

I look at all this, and suddenly it seems as if I am seeing it today for the first time. All at once it is so foreign to me as to be barely recognisable. Did this wet and grubby piece of grass really encompass my childhood years, years that are so golden and glowing in my memory? Is this empty and ordinary square with the factory on one side really the quiet little world that we called home, and which in the flood of horrors out at the front was the only thing that meant hope, and saved us from going under? Wasn't it something quite different from this grey row of ugly houses whose image rose up like a wild and melancholy dream over the shell-holes in the brief intervals between death and more death? In my mind wasn't it brighter, more beautiful, broader and fuller? Is none of it true any more, was my blood full of lies, did my memory cheat me?

I shiver. It is different, but nothing has changed. The clock on the tower of Neubauer's factory is still working and it still strikes the hour, exactly as it did before, when we used to stare at the clock-face to watch the hands moving. The blackamoor figure with the clay pipe is still sitting there in the tobacconist's nearby, where Georg Rahe went and got our first cigarettes. And in the grocer's opposite the adverts for soap powder are still there, the ones where Karl Vogt and I burnt the eyes out with a magnifying glass one really sunny day. I look into the shop window. Yes, you can still see those burn marks. But since then there has been the war, and Karl Vogt fell a long time ago, at Kemmel Hill.

I don't know how I can stand here and not feel the same way as I felt out there in the trenches and in the barracks. What happened to the richness, the liveliness, the brightness, the glow, the things that couldn't be explained? Were my memories really more alive than the reality? Did my memory become the reality, while all this diminished and shrank until there was nothing left but some empty scaffolding which was once covered with colourful bunting? Has my memory detached itself from the reality, so that now it just hovers like a cloud of melancholy? Have the years at the front burnt all the bridges to the past?

Questions, questions, but no answers.

4

The ordinances for school attendance by ex-servicemen have arrived. Our representatives got what we wanted: a shortened period of study, special courses and a relaxing of the exam regulations.

It wasn't easy to push all this through, even though there is a revolution going on, because the whole political upheaval is no more than a few ripples on the surface. It is not very far-reaching. What difference does it make if a few of the people at the very top have changed? Every soldier knows that a company commander can have the best intentions in the world, but if the NCOs don't agree, then he's powerless anyway. In the same way the most progressive minister of education will get nowhere if he is up against a block of reactionary civil servants. And the civil servants in Germany have kept hold of *their* posts. Those paper-pushing little dictators are impossible to get rid of.

★ ★ ★

The first lesson. We're back at our desks. Most of us in uniform. Three with beards. One married.

I find my own name carved on my desk, neatly done with a penknife and inked in. I remember completing this task during a history lesson; but it feels like a hundred years ago, and it is the strangest feeling to be sitting here again. The war has become the past, things have gone full circle. But we are no longer in that circle.

Hollermann, our teacher, comes in, and the first thing he does is to carry out the most important of all tasks – giving us back our old work, stuff of ours that has been kept. Not being able to give the work back before now must have weighed heavily upon his orderly schoolmaster's soul. He unlocks the classroom cupboard and takes the things out, sketch pads, drawing boards, and above all else the thick blue exercise books – with essays, dictations, class tests. A great pile of these soon builds up on the left-hand side of the teacher's desk. The names are called out, we answer and get our books. Willy throws them out to us, so that any loose blotting-paper goes flying.

'Breyer.'

'Here.'

'Bücker.'

'Here.'

'Detlefs.'

No answer. 'Dead,' shouts Willy.

Detlefs, small, blond-haired, bandy-legged, kept down a year. Private First Class, killed in 1917 at Kemmel Hill. His exercise book is passed over to the right-hand side of the teacher's desk.

'Dirker.'

'Here.'

'Dierksmann.'

'Dead.'

Dierksmann, farmer's son, good at cards, bad at singing, fell at Ypres. His book goes onto the right-hand pile.

'Eggers.'

'Not back yet,' calls out Willy. Ludwig explains: 'Shot in the lung, he's in the Reserve Military Hospital in Dortmund, after that he'll be three months convalescing at Lippspringe.'

'Friedrichs.'

'Here.'

'Giesecke.'

'Missing.'

'No he isn't,' declares Westerholt.

'I'm sure he was listed as missing,' says Reinersmann.

'That's true,' replies Westerholt, 'but for the past three weeks he's been back here in the asylum. I've seen him myself.'

'Gehring One.'

'Dead.'

The first of the Gehring twins. Top of the class, wrote poetry, gave private tuition and bought books with the money he earned. Fell at Soissons, together with his brother.

'Gehring Two,' murmurs the teacher, and without saying anything more puts the book with the others on the right. 'Those were really good essays,' he says pensively, flicking through the first Gehring's exercise book again.

A few more books go off to the right-hand side, and when all the names have been called there is a substantial pile. Dr Hollermann looks at it, unsure of what to do. Presumably his innate sense of order is causing him problems because he doesn't know what to do with these books. Eventually he has an idea. The exercise books should be sent to the dead men's parents.

However, Willy doesn't agree. 'Do you really think the parents will be very happy to get an exercise book full of "unsatisfactory" and "must try harder"?' he says. 'Best not to send them.'

Hollermann looks at him round-eyed. 'But what am I to do with them then?'

'Leave them where they are,' says Albert.

Hollermann is almost indignant. 'But that's quite impossible, Trosske, these exercise books don't belong to the school, they can't just be left where they are.'

'God, what a palaver,' groans Willy, running his hand through his hair. 'Just give us the books and we'll sort it out.'

Hollermann passes them over with reluctance. 'But ...' he begins nervously, because after all they don't belong to Willy either.

'Yes, yes,' says Willy, 'you needn't worry about it, it'll all be done in an orderly fashion, duly stamped and signed for, never fear! We must have things done properly, even when it hurts!' He looks back at us and taps his forehead with his forefinger.

After the lesson, we look through our earlier efforts. The last topic we had for an essay was: 'Why is Germany bound to win the war?' That was at the beginning of 1916. Introduction, six separate arguments, and a conclusion. I didn't do very well on the fourth point, the religious justification. In red ink at the side of the page it says: 'thin and unconvincing'. Mind you, the seven-page essay got a B-minus overall, which is not a bad grade in the light of recent events.

Willy is reading out one of his botany essays: 'The Wood Anemone and its Root System'. He looks around with a grin. 'I think we've finished with this stuff, haven't we?'

'Well and truly done with!' says Westerholt.

Yes, it really is over and done with! We've forgotten it all, and that is a judgement in itself. What Bethke and Kosole taught us, that's the stuff we won't forget.

★ ★ ★

That afternoon, Albert and Ludwig come and fetch me. We plan to go and see how our old friend Giesecke is getting on. On the way we meet Georg Rahe, and he joins us, because he knew Giesecke as well.

It's a bright day. From the top of the hill where the institution is you can see for miles across the fields. The inmates, in their blue-and-white-striped jackets, are working under the supervision of uniformed warders. We can hear singing coming from a window in the right-hand wing of the building – 'See the river, broad and shining ...' It must be one of the patients. It sounds odd, coming through the barred window. ''Neath the clouds, high in the sky ...'

Giesecke is in a large ward with some other patients. When we go in, one of them shouts out in a shrill voice: 'Take cover, take cover!' and crawls under the table. The others take no notice of him. Giesecke come towards us at once. He has a narrow, sallow face, and with his pointed chin and sticking-out ears he looks much younger than he is. Only his eyes are restless and old.

Before we can speak to him, someone else pulls us to one side. 'Is there any news?' he asks.

'No, it's all quiet,' I tell him.

'And the front? Have we taken Verdun at last?'

We look at one another. 'The war's been over for a good while,' says Albert reassuringly.

The man gives an unpleasant and bleating laugh. 'Don't let 'em give you that shit! They just want to trick us, then they'll wait till we come out! And then it's "gotcha" and you're on your way back to the front!' Then he adds in a confidential whisper: 'They're not going to get me again!'

Giesecke greets us. We don't know how to react. We had imagined that he might be gibbering like a monkey, or raving and pulling faces, or at least shaking all the time, like the shell-shocked beggars you get on street corners, but he just gives us a poor, crooked smile and says: 'Not what you expected, eh?'

'But you're perfectly well,' I reply. 'What's the problem?'

He runs his hand across his forehead. 'Migraines. It's like an iron ring round my skull. And Fleury ...'

During the fighting at Fleury he was buried alive, and was trapped for hours with another man, a beam of wood jamming his face against the man's side, which had been ripped open as far as his stomach. The other man had his head free and was screaming. Every time he did so, a gush of blood went over Giesecke's face. Eventually the guts were pressed out of the body and threatened to suffocate him. He had to try and squeeze them back so that he could breathe, and whenever he tried he could hear the muffled screams of the other man.

He tells us all this clearly and factually. 'And every night it comes back to me, I'm suffocating and the room is full of slimy white snakes and blood.'

'But if you know the cause, aren't there any steps you can take?' asks Albert.

Giesecke shakes his head. 'Nothing helps, even when I'm awake. They are there as soon as it gets dark.' He shudders. 'When I got home I jumped out of the window and broke my leg. Then they sent me here.'

'What are you lot doing?' he asks after a while. 'Have you done your teaching exams yet?'

'Soon,' says Ludwig.

'I shouldn't think I'll ever be able to,' says Giesecke gloomily. 'They won't let someone like me anywhere near children.'

The man who had shouted 'take cover' creeps up behind Albert and prods him in the back. Albert jumps up angrily, then remembers where he is. 'Passed fit for active service!' cackles the man. 'Passed fit for active service!' He roars with laughter, then suddenly becomes serious again and goes quietly off to his corner.

'Couldn't you write to the major for me?' asks Giesecke.

'What major?' I say in surprise. Ludwig nudges me. 'What do you want us to write?' I go on quickly.

'I want him to let me go to Fleury again,' answers Giesecke agitatedly. 'That would help me, I'm sure of it. It must be nice and quiet there now and I only knew it when it was being blown to blazes. I'd go through Death Valley, past Cold Corner and into Fleury, there wouldn't be any guns and it would be all over. Surely I could get some peace too if I did that, don't you think?'

'It'll pass anyway,' says Ludwig, and puts his hand on Giesecke's arm. 'You just have to tell yourself so.'

Giesecke looks sadly into the distance. 'Please write to the major. Gerhard Giesecke is my name, spelt with a c and a k.' His eyes are set and unseeing. 'Could you bring me some apple purée? I'd so much like to eat apple purée again.'

We promise to do it all, but he isn't listening to us any more – he has suddenly become detached from everything. When we leave he stands up and makes a formal bow to Ludwig. Then he slumps down at the table again with that absent look.

I look back at him from the door. As if he had suddenly woken up he jumps up and runs after us. 'Take me with you,' he says in a strange, high voice, 'they're coming over again.' He comes up close to us, terrified. We have no idea what to do. Then the doctor comes along

134

and takes Giesecke gently by the shoulder. 'Let's go out into the garden,' he says to him quietly, and Giesecke allows himself to be led away.

Outside, the evening sun is shining on the fields. From the barred window comes the singing once more – 'But the castle ... walls are broken ... and the clouds ... go drifting by ...'

We walk along together in silence. The furrows are shimmering in the ploughed fields. A thin, pale sickle moon is hanging in the branches of the trees.

'I think,' says Ludwig after a time, 'that we're all a bit like that ...'

I look at him. His face is lit up by the setting sun. He is serious and thoughtful. I'm about to make a reply, but suddenly a light shudder runs over my skin. I don't know why, or where it has come from.

'We shouldn't talk about it any more,' says Albert.

We walk on. The last sunlight goes and the dusk sets in. The sickle moon becomes brighter. A night wind rises from the fields, and the first lights begin to go on in the windows of the houses. We reach the town.

Georg Rahe has said nothing the whole way back. Only when we stop and are about to take our leave does he seem to wake from his reverie. 'Did you hear what he wanted?' he asks. 'To go to Fleury ... back to Fleury ...'

I don't feel like going home yet. Neither does Albert. We wander slowly along the embankments. Down below us is the sound of the river flowing. We stop by the mill and lean against the railings of the bridge.

'It's strange how you never like being alone, isn't it, Ernst?' says Albert.

'Yes,' I reply, 'it's just not having any real idea where you fit in.'

He nods. 'That's it. But surely we have to fit in somewhere?'

'Maybe when we find a job,' I say.

He shakes his head. 'No, that's not the answer either. You need human contact, somebody else, do you know what I mean ...?'

'Oh, other people,' I reply. 'Now that is one of the chanciest things there is. We've seen often enough how easily other people can cop their lot. You'd need ten or a dozen somebody-elses, just so you've got a few left when the others drop off their perches.'

Albert gazes steadily at the silhouette of the cathedral. 'No, I didn't mean that,' he says, 'I mean somebody who really belongs to you. I think about it a lot, a woman ...'

'God Almighty!' I exclaim, because Adolf Bethke comes into my mind.

'Come on now,' says Albert to me sharply, 'you have to have something to hold on to, can't you see that? I want someone to love me so that we can support each other. Otherwise you might as well go and top yourself!' He is trembling, and turns his back on me.

'But, Albert,' I say softly, 'you've got *us*, haven't you?'

'Yes, yes, but this is something quite different ...' And after a while he adds in a whisper: 'You need to have children ... children who don't know anything about it all ...'

I'm not completely sure what he means. But I don't feel like asking him any more questions, either.

PART FOUR

1

It is all completely different from the way we imagined it would be. We thought that there would be a resounding opening chord and then a vigorous and intensive existence would begin, full of the joys of a life regained. That's how we wanted it to start. But the days and weeks just drift through our fingers, we fill our time with pointless superficialities, and when we stop and look around, nothing has been done. We had been used to thinking and acting quickly – a minute's delay could cost you your life. That's why life is going too slowly for us now, we jump at it, but before it can start to respond and resonate we've already moved on to something else. We had Death as a companion for too long. He played a fast game, and he always played for the highest stakes. That taught us to jump at things, to act swiftly, on an instant's thought, and it has left us empty now, because it isn't appropriate any more. This emptiness has unsettled us, because we have the feeling that nobody understands us, and that even love isn't going to help. An unbridgeable gulf has opened up between soldiers and those who were not soldiers. We shall have to sort it out on our own.

But in our restless days we often hear something else murmuring and grumbling, like the distant thunder of the guns, like a dull threat just beyond the horizon, which we can't identify and which we turn away from, but always with the curious fear that we are missing something – as if something were running away from us. Too much has run away from us already, and for a good few of us it was nothing less than life itself …

* * *

Karl Bröger's room looks positively colourful. All the bookshelves have been emptied. There are great piles of volumes all around, on the tables and on the floor.

Karl used to be crazy about books. He collected books like we collected butterflies or stamps. He was especially fond of the Romantic poet Eichendorff, and he had three separate editions of his works. He knew many of his poems off by heart as well. But now he wants to sell his library to raise the capital to set himself up in business selling wines and spirits. He reckons that there is a lot of money to be made that way. Up to now he has acted as an agent for Ledderhose, but now he wants to branch out on his own.

I glance through the first volume of one of his Eichendorff editions, in a blue full-calf binding. Sunset, woodland and dreams ... summer nights, unexpressed longings, the desire for home ... what an age that was ...

Willy is holding the second volume. He looks at it thoughtfully. 'You ought to offer that to a shoemaker,' he suggests.

'What do you mean?' asks Ludwig with a smile.

'The leather,' replies Willy. 'Shoemakers can't get hold of enough leather these days. Now here –' and he picks up a volume of Goethe's works – 'you've got twenty volumes, you could get at least half a dozen pairs of first-class shoes out of them. I bet the shoemakers will give you more for them than the book dealers will. They're desperate for real leather!'

'Do you want any of them?' asks Karl. 'You can have them at bargain rates.' But none of us want any.

'Give it a bit more thought,' says Ludwig. 'It will be hard to replace them later.'

'Doesn't matter,' laughs Karl. 'Living comes first, that's better than reading. And I don't give a damn about my exams, either. It's all rubbish! I'm starting with the schnapps-sampling tomorrow. Ten marks' profit on a bottle of smuggled brandy, it's an attractive prospect, lads! Money is the only thing you need, then you can get anything else you want.'

He bundles the books together. I remember that in the old days he would rather go hungry than sell one of his books.

'What are you all looking at me like that for?' he says. 'You've got to be practical! Chuck the old ballast overboard and start a new life!'

'Quite right,' agrees Willy. 'I'd flog my books too – well, if I had any.'

Karl claps him on the shoulder. 'An ounce of business is better than a ton of education, Willy. I spent long enough in the mud out at the front, now I want to get something out of life!'

'Actually he's right,' I say. 'What are we all doing anyway? A bit of time at school, that's nothing much …'

'You should chuck it in as well, lads,' Karl urges us, 'you don't really want to go back to the old prison house again, do you?'

'Oh God,' replies Willy, 'you're quite right, it is all nonsense. But at least we're all together. And anyway there are only a few months left before the exams, and it would be a pity not to take them now. Afterwards we can see how things look …'

Karl cuts off a sheet of brown paper from a roll. 'Just watch out, you'll be forever saying that it's only a few months and it would be a pity not to do whatever it was – until in the end you find that you've turned into an old man.'

Willy grins. 'Let's just wait and see.'

Ludwig gets up. 'What does your father say about it, then?'

Karl laughs. 'What all the nervous old people say. You can't take them seriously. Your parents always forget that you've been in the army.'

'What would you have done if you hadn't been a soldier?' I ask.

'I'd probably have been a bookseller, bloody fool that I am,' replies Karl.

★ ★ ★

Karl's decision has made a big impression on Willy. He suggests that we should just drop everything, seize the moment and enjoy ourselves where we can.

But the easiest way of enjoying ourselves is by stuffing our faces, so we decide on a food-foraging expedition. The ration books allow a single person ten ounces of meat, one ounce of butter and two of margarine, four ounces of barley and some bread per week, and that isn't going to fill you up.

Every evening, every night foragers assemble at the railway station ready to go out to the villages early the next morning. We have to be on the first train too, so that nobody gets there before us. There's a sullen air of grey misery in the compartment as we set off. We pick a fairly remote place and split up into pairs so that we can scrounge systematically. After all, we know about reconnaissance patrols.

I'm with Albert. We get to a large farm. The dungheap is steaming, cows are standing in a row in front of the barn and we are met by the warm smell of milk and cowsheds. Chickens are cackling. We look at them hungrily, but control ourselves because there are people round the grain store. We say hello. Nobody takes any notice of us. We stay where we are. Eventually a woman comes and shouts: 'Get off this farm, you bloody beggars!'

The next farmstead. The farmer is standing outside as we get there. He's wearing a long military greatcoat, swishes a whip and says: 'Do you know how many people have been here already today? A dozen.' We're amazed, because we came on the first train. They must have arrived in the evening and slept in barns or in the open. 'Any idea how many we can get in a day?' says the farmer. 'Up to a hundred. What are we supposed to do?'

We see his point. Then he notices Albert's uniform. 'Flanders?' he asks. 'Flanders,' replies Albert. 'Me too,' he says, goes in and gets two eggs for each of us. We go to get some money out but he waves it aside. 'Keep it in your pocket. It's fine.'

'Many thanks, mate.'

'Don't mention it. But don't tell anybody, or half Germany will be here tomorrow.'

The next place. A grubby sign on the fence: 'No foragers. Beware of the Dog.' That's practical.

We move on. A home field with oak trees round it and a big farmhouse. We make it to the kitchen. In the middle of the room there is an ultra-modern cooking stove that would do for a hotel. On both the left- and the right-hand side of it there are pianos. Opposite the stove is a wonderful bookcase with fluted columns and leather-bound gilt-topped volumes. The original farmhouse table and its wooden stools are standing in front of it. It all looks really odd. And two pianos, of all things.

The farmer's wife appears. 'Have you got any yarn? It has to be good stuff, though.'

We look at each other. 'Yarn? No.'

'What about silk? Silk stockings?'

I look at the woman's massive thighs. It dawns on us gradually that she wants to barter, not sell.

'No, we haven't any silk,' I say, 'but we can pay well.'

She shakes her head. 'Money, no, that's just dirty bits of paper. Every day it's worth less.' She shuffles away. There are two buttons missing on her bright red silk blouse.

'Could we at least have a drink of water?' Albert calls after her. She comes back and with bad grace gives us a mug of water.

'Come on, hurry up, I can't stand around all day,' she grumbles. 'You ought to get a job instead of taking up other people's time.'

Albert hurls the mug to the floor. He is too angry to speak. I step in for him. 'I hope you get cancer, you old cow,' I roar. But she turns round and sounds off at us like a navvy at full blast. We run for it. Not even the strongest man could stand up to something like that.

On we march. On the way we encounter swarms of other foragers, buzzing around the farmsteads like starving wasps round a slice of plum tart. We can now see why the farmers are driven mad by this and can get rough with you. But we carry on anyway, get thrown out, get some food, get cursed by other foragers and curse them back.

In the afternoon we all meet up in the local pub. The haul isn't a big one. A few pounds of potatoes, some flour, a few eggs, apples, some cabbage and a bit of meat. Willy is the only one sweating. He turns up last, and is carrying half a pig's head under his arm. He's also got a few other packets sticking out of his pockets. On the other hand, he's no longer wearing his coat. He's bartered it, because he's got another one, supplied by Karl, back at home, and he reckons that spring is bound to come sometime in any case.

We've still got two hours before the train goes. This turns out to be a bit of luck for me. In the bar room there is a piano, and I give them 'The Maiden's Prayer' at full strength. The landlady come in while I'm playing, then beckons me over to come outside. I push my way into the corridor and she tells me that she likes music, but unfortunately nobody plays much now, and she wonders if I might like to come again. She gives me half a pound of butter and indicates that that could be a regular thing. Of course I agree, and arrange to play for two hours for that payment. I go on and play rousing versions of 'The Lonely Grave' and 'By the Beautiful Rhine'.

Then we leave for the station. On the way we meet lots of other foragers who want to catch the same train. They are all frightened of the police. Eventually a whole troop assembles and we wait a little way away from the station, in a dark and windy corner, so that we can't be seen before the train arrives. That's less dangerous.

But we are unlucky. Suddenly there are two policemen with bikes – they cycled up behind us and we didn't hear them.

'Halt! Stay where you are!'

Great agitation, begging and pleading. 'Let us go, we have to get the train.'

'It won't be there for another fifteen minutes,' declares the fatter of the two, unmoved. 'Line up here!' He points to a street lamp, so that they can see better. One of them makes sure that nobody gets away and the other checks what people have. Almost all of the foragers are women, children and old people; most of them line up silently and obediently – they are used to being treated that way, and they have never really dared to believe that they might actually have the luck to make it home with half a pound of off-the-ration butter. I have a good look at the policemen; they are standing there just like the military police used to, pugnacious and domineering, with their green uniforms, red faces, official swords and pistol holsters. It's power, I think, it's always power, and even if they've only got an ounce of it, that's enough.

One woman has a few eggs confiscated, but just as she is moving sadly away the fat one calls her back: 'Stop! What have you got there?' He points at her skirt. 'Out with it!' She brings out a piece of bacon from under her skirt. He puts it to one side. 'You'd have liked to keep that, wouldn't you!' She can't quite believe what is going on and tries to grab hold of it. 'But I paid for that, it cost me all the money I had!'

He pushes her hand away and pulls a chunk of salami from another woman's blouse. 'Off-ration foraging is illegal, you know that.'

The first woman is prepared to lose the eggs, but begs to have the bacon back. 'At least let me have the bacon. What am I going to say when I get home? I need it for the children.'

'Apply to the rations office for a supplementary allowance,' growls the policeman, 'that's not our business. Next!' The woman stumbles away, throws up, and then shouts: 'You mean my husband was killed in the war so that my kids can starve!'

A young woman who is next in line greedily stuffs the butter she had down her throat, her mouth is greasy, her eyes are bulging and she gulps and swallows, so that she's at least had something, rather than let them take it off her. It's not much of a victory – later on she'll be sick too and will have diarrhoea.

'Next!' Nobody moves. The policeman, who had been bending down, shouts out again: 'Next!' He straightens up crossly, and finds himself looking directly at Willy. He calms down noticeably and says: 'Are you next?'

'Not that I know of,' answers Willy coldly.

'What have you got in that package?'

'Half a pig's head,' says Willy, quite openly.

'You'll have to hand it over.'

Willy doesn't move. The policeman hesitates, and glances over at his colleague, who comes across and joins him. This is a serious mistake. Neither of them seems to have much experience in these matters, and they are not used to resistance. The second one ought to have spotted long before that we are all together, even though we weren't talking to one another. Because of that he should have kept to one side so he could cover us with his pistol. Mind you, it wouldn't have bothered us much – it's only a revolver. But instead he stands right next to his colleague in case Willy causes any trouble.

The consequences are immediately apparent, as Willy surrenders his pig's head. The astonished policeman takes it, and is thus rendered as good as defenceless, because he has both of his hands full. At the same time, Willy very calmly punches him in the face and he goes down. Before the second one can react, Kosole brings his hard head against the man's chin from the side, while Valentin gets behind him and squeezes his windpipe so hard that he opens his mouth wide, at which Kosole stuffs some newspaper into it. Both policemen are gurgling, choking and spitting, but they can't do anything, they both have paper crammed into their mouths, their arms are twisted behind them and tied fast with their own belts. It's all over in minutes – but what's to be done with them now?

Albert has the answer. Fifty paces away he has spotted a solitary wooden hut with a heart carved on the door – it's the privy. They are taken there as fast as possible and shoved inside. The door is made of oak and the bolts are large and solid, and it will take a good hour for them to get out. Kosole is not unmerciful, though. He leaves their bicycles propped up outside.

The other foragers have been watching all this apprehensively. 'Pick up your stuff,' grins Ferdinand. The train is whistling in the distance. The others look at us nervously, but need no second bidding. Just one elderly woman is panicky.

'Oh God,' she whimpers, 'you beat up the police, there'll be trouble, trouble ...'

She seems to think that this is a capital crime. The rest of them also seem to be pretty disturbed by it all. The fear of uniforms and of the police is in their very bones.

Willy grins. 'Don't cry, granny – even if the entire government turned up we wouldn't let them take anything off us. Old soldiers giving up grub – that's not likely!'

It's lucky that so many of these rural railway stations are a long way away from the actual villages. Nobody saw anything. It's only now that the stationmaster comes out of his office, yawning and scratching his head. We march up to the barrier. Willy has his pig's head under his arm and is stroking it. 'Part with you? Not a chance!' he murmurs lovingly.

The train pulls out. We wave from the window. The stationmaster thinks we are waving at him and waves back. But we're actually waving at the privy. Willy leans well out of the window and watches the stationmaster's red-banded cap.

'He's gone back into his lair,' he announces triumphantly. 'That means those policemen are going to have a long wait.'

The tension disappears from the faces of the foragers. They are now able to start talking again. The woman with the bacon is laughing with tears of gratitude in her eyes. Only the girl who had to guzzle the butter is crying her eyes out. She was too fast off the mark, and besides, she's already starting to feel ill. But Kosole comes to the rescue. He gives her half of his salami, and she tucks it away in her stocking.

To be on the safe side we get out at the station before the town, and walk across the fields till we get to the main road. We are planning to walk the last part, but a lorry loaded with metal cans comes along. The driver is wearing an army greatcoat and he gives us a lift. And so we roar on through the dark, the stars are twinkling, we are all squatting there together, and from our parcels comes the pleasant smell of pork.

A wet, silvery evening fog covers the high street. The street lamps have great yellow pools of light round them. People seem to be walking on cotton wool. The shop windows to the right and to the left blaze out mysteriously. Wolf the dog swims out of the mist and then into it again. The trees are shining, black and damp against the street lights.

Valentin Laher is with me. He's not exactly complaining, but he can't forget his acrobatics act, the one he performed on stages from Paris to Budapest. 'That's all over now, Ernst,' he says, 'my bones are creaking and I've got a bit of rheumatism too. I trained and trained till I couldn't stand up any longer. There's no point in trying to start up again.'

'What will you do instead, Valentin?' I ask. 'Really you ought to get a state pension, like retired officers.'

'Oh, the state, the state,' says Valentin dismissively, 'the state only gives pensions to those who know how to ask properly. What I'm doing now is working up a couple of things with a dance partner, you know, a demonstration number. It looks pretty good from the audience point of view, but there really isn't much to it, and a proper performer ought to be ashamed of doing that kind of stuff. Still, what can you do? You've got to make a living.'

Valentin has to go to a rehearsal, and I decide to go along with him. On the corner of Haken Street a black bowler hat swims past us through the fog, and beneath it is a bright yellow raincoat and a briefcase. 'Arthur!' I shout.

Ledderhose comes to a halt. 'Bloody hell,' says Valentin, 'you're well turned out.' He fingers Arthur's tie like a connoisseur, a superb item, artificial silk with a pale lilac pattern.

'Not too bad, not too bad,' says Ledderhose, flattered, but still in a hurry.

'And the best Sunday headgear too,' says Valentin admiringly, looking at the bowler.

Ledderhose wants to get away. He taps his briefcase. 'Things to do, things to do ...'

'Haven't you got that cigar shop any more?' I ask.

'Oh yes,' he replies, 'but now I only do wholesale. You don't know of any office accommodation, do you? I can pay top rates.'

'We've got no idea about office accommodation,' says Valentin, 'we haven't got quite that far yet. But what's your wife up to these days?'

'What do you mean?' asks Ledderhose with some reserve.

'Well, out there in the trenches you were always complaining about her. You said she'd got too skinny, and you liked them with a bit more meat on them.'

Arthur shakes his head. 'I really don't remember.' He disappears.

Valentin laughs. 'People can really change, can't they, Ernst? In the trenches he was a miserable little bugger, and now he's a smooth businessman. All the balls he used to talk when we were at the front! And now he doesn't want to know any more.'

'He seems to be doing damned well, though,' I say pensively.

We wander on. The fog drifts about and Wolf plays with it. Faces come and go. In the white light I suddenly see a shiny red patent-leather hat and beneath it a face gently accentuated by the moisture so that the eyes shine even brighter.

I stop. My heart is beating wildly. It is Adele. Memories come flooding in of past evenings when as sixteen-year-old lads we used to hang around by the doors of the gym as it was getting dark and wait until the girls in their white sweaters came out, and then run after them down the street, catch them up and stand there in front of them under a street lamp, panting and out of breath, looking at them and not saying a word until they broke away and the chase started again; memories, too, of afternoons when we had encountered them somewhere or other, and then pursued them shyly but relentlessly, always a few paces behind, too embarrassed to say anything to them, just summoning up all our courage, when they were about to go indoors, to shout out 'Be seeing you!' and then running away.

Valentin looks round. 'I've just got to go back,' I say quickly, 'I have to have a word with someone. I shan't be a minute.' And I run back in pursuit of the red hat, a beacon in the fog, a reminder of the time when we were young, before the uniforms and the trenches.

'Adele …'

She looks round. 'Ernst – you're back then?'

We walk along side by side. The fog drifts between us, Wolf jumps about and barks, bells are jangling on the trams and the world is warm and soft. The old feeling has come back in full, trembling, wavering, the years in between have been swept away and a rainbow has arched into the past, a bright bridge cutting through the fog.

I don't know what we talk about, and it doesn't matter anyway. The main thing is that we are walking side by side, and that the tender, unheard music of the past is there again, rippling cascades of anticipation and longing, and behind them the shimmering silken grass of the meadows, with the silvery rustle of the poplars melodious in the background against the flickering, soft horizon of youth.

Did we walk for long? I have no idea. I walk back on my own. Adele has taken her leave and gone, but a sense of joy is fluttering inside me like a great colourful banner, a sense of hope and abundance, the room I had when I was a boy, the green towers and the wide world.

On my way I bump into Willy, and we go to find Valentin together. We catch up with him just as he is greeting someone effusively with a hearty clap on the shoulder. 'Hey, Kuckhoff, you old devil, where did you spring from?' He puts out his hand. 'Bit of a coincidence, isn't it, meeting up again?'

The other man looks at him rather dismissively for a moment.

'Ah, it's Laher, isn't it?'

'Well, of course it is, we were together on the Somme. Do you remember how we sat there in the middle of all the crap that was going on around us and scoffed those pancakes Lilly had sent me? Georg had brought them up to the front with the mail. Bit bloody risky for him too, wasn't it?'

'Indeed it was,' says the other man.

Valentin is quite carried away by the memories. 'And later he really did stop one, good and proper,' he continues, 'but you'd moved on by then. Lost his right arm well and truly, not the best thing for a coachman like him. I suppose he'll have to be doing something else now. What have you been up to since, you old bugger?'

The other man makes a vague response. Then he says: 'Nice to have met again. And how are things with you, my dear Laher?'

'What?' replies Valentin, taken aback by his formality.

'How are things with you, my dear sir? What is your present occupation?'

'*My dear sir?*' Valentin is still baffled. For a moment he stares at the other man in the elegant overcoat standing there in front of him. Then he looks down at himself, blushes scarlet and moves away quickly. 'Stuck-up pig!'

I feel really sorry for Valentin. It's probably the first time that the idea of social difference has struck him. Up to now we were all just soldiers. And now one toffee-nosed individual has shattered his straightforward and uncomplicated attitude with a single bit of exaggerated formality.

'Forget it, Valentin,' I say. 'People like that boast about how much their father earns. It happens.'

Willy reinforces this with a few rather more vigorous expressions.

'Fine friends we had,' says Valentin bitterly after a time. But he can't get rid of the nasty taste. It keeps coming back to his throat.

★

Luckily we run across Tjaden. He looks as grubby as a dishrag. 'Listen, you,' says Willy, 'the war's over, you really could go and have a decent wash for once.'

'Not today,' says Tjaden with great seriousness, 'but I will on Saturday. In fact I'll even have a bath.'

We are taken aback. Tjaden having a bath? Maybe he is still suffering from shell shock, from the time last August when they all got buried in their trench? Willy cups his hand round his ear and says as if baffled: 'I don't think I quite caught what you said just then. Exactly *what* is it that you're going to do on Saturday?'

'Have a bath,' declares Tjaden proudly. 'Because I'm getting engaged on Saturday night.'

Willy looks at him as if he were some kind of rare and exotic bird. Then he places one of his great paws gently on his shoulder and asks in a fatherly manner: 'Tell me, Tjaden, do you sometimes get stabbing pains in the back of the head? Or peculiar rushing noises in the ears?'

'Only when I'm really hungry,' admits Tjaden, 'and then I get what feels like cannon fire in the gut as well. Not nice. But to come back to my fiancée: she's no beauty, has two left feet and she squints a bit. But she's a game girl, and her father is a butcher.'

A butcher. Now the penny drops. Tjaden is happy to tell us more.

'She's crazy about me. And these days you have to grab what you can. When times are hard, you have to make sacrifices. A butcher is the last person who's going to go hungry. Besides, being engaged is a long way from being married.'

Willy listens to this with growing interest. 'Tjaden,' he begins, 'you know we have always been good friends –'

'OK, Willy,' interrupts Tjaden, 'you can have a few sausages and I reckon I can get you a couple of chops as well. Come round on Monday. We're having a white sale.'

'What?' I ask in amazement. 'Are you selling linen as well?'

'Not exactly. We're slaughtering a white horse.'

We assure him that we'll be there, and continue our jaunt.

★

Valentin goes into the Old Town Inn, which is where performers gather. When we go in, a troupe of midgets are just having their evening meal. On the table are plates of turnip soup, and each one has a chunk of bread.

'I hope at least that lot can fill themselves up with rationed grub,' growls Willy, 'their stomachs are a lot smaller.'

On the walls there are posters and photographs, brightly coloured scraps, half torn off, with pictures of strongmen, lady lion-tamers and clowns. The pictures are old and yellowing; for the past few years the trenches provided the only circus ring for weightlifters, trick-cyclists and acrobats, and they didn't need a playbill.

Valentin points at one of the posters. 'That was me, once.' In the picture a man with a well-proportioned chest is performing a somersault off the bars way up into the big top. But with the best will in the world you wouldn't know it was Valentin.

The dance partner he is going to be working with is already waiting. We go into the small hall attached to the restaurant. There are a few bits of theatrical scenery propped up in the corner. These are left over from the revue *Bye-Bye Little Bi-Plane*, a comic piece with singalong numbers about the lives of our lads in uniform. It was a big hit for two years.

Valentin puts a gramophone onto a stool and sorts out some records. A sultry melody comes crackling out of the sound box, the record is worn, but there is still a hint of wildness, like the hoarse voice of a woman who has been through the mill, but who was once a beauty. 'A tango,' whispers Willy to me like a real connoisseur, not revealing that he has just read the description on the record label.

Valentin is wearing blue trousers and a shirt, the girl a leotard. They practise an Apache dance and then a show number which ends with the girl hanging with her legs around Valentin's neck while he spins as fast as he can.

The pair of them practise without talking and with serious looks on their faces. Only from time to time is there a murmured word. The pale light of the lamp flickers. The gas hisses gently. The

153

shadows of the dancers loom large over the leftover scenery from the revue. Willy shuffles backwards and forwards like a great bear, keeping the gramophone wound up.

Valentin comes to a halt. Willy applauds, but Valentin signals him irritatedly to stop. The girl gets changed without paying us any attention at all. Under the gaslight she slowly takes off her dancing shoes. Her back is supple in her faded leotard as she bends forwards. Then she straightens up and lifts her arms to draw something over her head. Light and shadows alternate on her shoulders. Her legs are long and beautiful.

Willy is poking around in the hall. He comes across a programme for the bi-plane revue. At the back of it are a series of adverts. One sweet-maker is offering shells and grenades made of chocolate, ready-packed as gifts for sending out to the trenches. A firm from Saxony is selling letter-openers made from shell splinters, lavatory paper printed with statements by the great and good about the war, and two series of picture postcards, 'The Soldier's Farewell' and 'On Guard in the Darkest Midnight Hour'.

The dancer is fully dressed. With a coat and hat on she looks completely different. Before, she was a lithe animal, but now she is just like everyone else. You can hardly believe that she only needed to put on a few bits of material to change so much. Funny how much clothes can change you. Especially uniforms.

3

Every evening Willy goes to Waldmann's Lodge. This is a popular place just outside town where they have dances in the afternoons and the evenings. I'm going as well, because Karl Bröger tells me that Adele is often there. And I'd like to see Adele again.

All the windows in the garden room at Waldmann's are lit up. The shadows of the dancers glide across the lowered blinds. I'm standing at the bar looking for Willy. All the tables are full, and there isn't a chair free anywhere. In these post-war months there has been a frantic drive to have fun.

Suddenly I see a gleaming white front and the majestic swoop of a tailcoat. Willy in his cutaway. I stare at him, completely dazzled. The cutaway is black, his waistcoat is white, his hair is red – he's the embodiment of the imperial flag!

Willy acknowledges my amazed look with a dismissive gesture. 'Yes, a bit taken aback, eh?' he says, and turns round like a peacock. 'It's my Kaiser Wilhelm memorial cutaway! You can do some amazing things with an army coat, can't you?'

He claps me on the shoulder. 'Anyway, I'm glad you're here, there's a dance contest tonight, we're all going in for it and there are some first-rate prizes! Starts in half an hour.'

So we've got a little while to practise. Willy's partner looks like an all-in wrestler, massive and solid, strong as a shire horse. He's practising a one-step with her, a dance which depends on being fast. In contrast Karl is dancing with a girl who is covered with necklaces, bracelets and rings like a pony from a sleigh ride, and who works in the Food Registry Office. By dancing with her he combines business and pleasure very nicely indeed. Albert, however, is not at our table. He waves to us rather sheepishly from a corner, where he is sitting with a blonde girl.

'I think we've lost him,' says Willy prophetically.

I look around to see if I can find a decent dance partner. This is no simple task, since quite often somebody who looks as delicate as a fawn while sitting at the table turns into a pregnant elephant on the dance floor. Besides, light-footed dancers are much in demand. But I manage eventually to team up with a little seamstress.

The band plays a flourish. Someone with a chrysanthemum in his buttonhole comes out and explains that a pair of professional dancers from Berlin are going to demonstrate the latest thing for us, a foxtrot. We can't do that yet – we've only heard of it.

We gather round, curious to see this. The band starts up a syncopated tune and the two dancers skip around each other like frisky lambs. From time to time they separate, then get back into hold and spin around jerkily. Willy flexes himself and stares in fascination. This is a dance after his own heart.

The table with the prizes is carried in. We rush over to look. There are three prizes each for the three dances, the one-step, the Boston two-step, and the foxtrot. The foxtrot prizes are out as far as we're concerned, because we can't do it, but for the other two we're going to fight like the generals at Waterloo.

The first prize consists of either ten gulls' eggs or a bottle of schnapps. Willy goes and asks, somewhat dubiously, whether gulls' eggs are actually edible. Reassured on that point, he comes back. The second prize is six gulls' eggs or a woolly hat, the third four eggs or two packs of cigarettes, a brand called Germany's Heroes. 'We're not having them at any price,' says Karl, who knows about that sort of thing.

The contest begins. We've put Karl and Albert in for the Boston, Willy and me for the one-step. Mind you, we don't hold out much hope for Willy. He'll only win if the judges really have a sense of humour.

In the Boston competition, Karl and Albert and three others finish up in the final round. Karl is well in the lead; the high collar of his parade uniform, his patent-leather shoes and the chains and rings of his sleigh-ride-pony partner present an image of dazzling elegance which cannot be resisted. In style and posture he is brilliant, but Albert's sense of rhythm is just as good. The judges pay such close attention that you'd think this competition at Waldmann's was a sudden-death play-off at the Last Judgement. Karl wins and takes the ten gulls' eggs, because he knows too much about the brand of schnapps, and he sold it to them in the first place. Albert gets the second prize. With an embarrassed look at us he passes the six gulls' eggs to the blonde girl. Willy gives a wolf whistle.

In the one-step context I set off well with the little seamstress and we get into the last round. To my astonishment, Willy didn't even get up and didn't enter the competition at all. I show off with a special variation on the heel-turn and reverse chassé, something I've not demonstrated before. The little girl dances as lightly as a feather and we get the second prize, which we split between us.

Proudly I come back to our table with the silver medallion of the National Ballroom Dancing Federation pinned to my coat.

'Willy, you great lump,' I say, 'why didn't you at least give it a go? You might have got the bronze!'

'Yes, really,' says Karl, 'why didn't you join in?'

Willy stands up, stretches, adjusts his cutaway, looks at us magisterially, and says simply: 'You may well ask!'

At that point the man with the chrysanthemum announces the foxtrot competition. Only a few couples enter. Willy doesn't just take to the floor, he positively strides out to it.

'But he hasn't got a clue what he's doing,' snorts Karl.

We are on the edge of our seats with excitement to see what will happen. Willy's all-in wrestler comes and joins him. He offers her his arm with a grand gesture. The music starts.

At that moment Willy is transformed into a wild leaping animal. He jumps into the air, jerks, hops, spins, kicks and flicks, and throws the lady in all directions, then they thunder down the room like the Gadarene swine, his circus strongwoman not in front of him, but at his side, so that she is doing pull-ups on his outstretched right arm, while he is completely free on the other side and is never in any danger of trampling on her feet. Then he does an imitation of a carousel, spinning on the spot so that his coat-tails stick out horizontally, and in the next moment he sets off into a series of delicate little hops across the dance floor like a billy goat that's had a handful of pepper shoved up underneath its tail, he thunders and turns and rampages, and finishes up with a quite unbelievable pirouette, in the course of which he swings the lady high in the air.

Not a soul in the hall is in any doubt that they have just witnessed a hitherto unknown master of the super-foxtrot. Willy spotted his chance and seized it with both hands. His victory is so complete that after him there is a long pause before they even get around to the second prize. Triumphantly he holds his bottle of schnapps out to us. Mind you, he has sweated so much that the dye in the cutaway has run. His shirt and waistcoat are now black, and the cutaway itself looks appreciably lighter in colour.

The contest is over, but the dancing continues. We sit at our table and drink Willy's winnings. Only Albert is missing – he can't be separated from the blonde girl.

Willy nudges me: 'Hey, there's Adele.'

'Where?' I ask quickly.

He points with his thumb into the melee on the dance floor. It's true, she is there, waltzing with a tall dark chap.

'Has she been here long?' I ask, because I want to know whether she saw our triumphs on the floor.

'Turned up five minutes ago,' answers Willy.

'With that beanpole?'

'With that beanpole.'

When she is dancing, Adele holds her head bent back a little. She has one hand on the shoulder of the dark chap. Seeing her face from the side makes me catch my breath because in the dim lights of the dance hall it brings back so strongly my memories of evenings before the war. But seen from the front she looks fuller, and when she laughs she is a stranger.

I take a great swig from Willy's bottle. Just then the little seamstress dances past. She is slimmer and more delicate than Adele. The other day when I saw her in the fog on the high street I didn't notice, but Adele has become a real woman, with full breasts and strong legs. I can't remember if she was like that before; I probably didn't pay enough attention.

'Fine strapping piece she's turned into,' says Willy, as if he had read my thoughts.

'Shut it, you,' I snap back at him.

The waltz is over. Adele is leaning against the door. I go over. She says hello, while continuing to chat and laugh with the dark chap. I stand there and gaze at her. My heart is beating as if I were about to make some great decision.

'Why are you looking at me like that?' she asks.

'No reason,' I say. 'Shall we dance?'

'Not this one, the next one,' she replies, and goes off to the dance floor with her partner.

I wait for her, and then we dance a two-step together. I really make an effort, and she smiles in acknowledgement.

'So you learned to dance at the front?'

'Not exactly,' I say. 'But a little while ago we did win a prize.'

She looks up sharply. 'Pity we couldn't do that together. What did you get?'

'Six gulls' eggs and a medallion,' I tell her, and feel myself blush to the roots of my hair. The violins are playing so softly that you can hear the sliding of the dancers' feet on the floor.

'Well, we're dancing together now,' I say. 'Do you remember how we used to run after each other on the evenings when we went to the gym club?'

She nods. 'Yes, we were still pretty childish in those days. Look, do you see that girl with the red dress? Those flounced blouses are the very latest thing – really chic, isn't it?'

The melody passes from the violins to a cello. They quiver over the deep golden tones of the main tune like barely held-back weeping.

'The first time I ever spoke to you, we both ran away,' I say. 'It was in June by the town wall, I remember as if it were only yesterday ...'

Adele waves at someone. Only then does she turn back to me. 'Yes, wasn't it silly! Can you do the tango? That dark boy over there dances the tango fabulously.'

I don't reply. The music stops. 'Do you want to come over to our table for a bit?' I ask.

She looks across. 'Who's the slim one with the patent-leather shoes?'

'Karl Bröger,' I tell her. She comes and sits with us. Willy offers her a drink and makes a joke. She laughs and looks over at Karl. From time to time she casts a glance at Karl's sleigh-ride pony, who was the girl she'd seen with the latest fashion in blouses. I look at Adele, completely taken aback that she has changed so much. Has my memory tricked me here as well? Did it develop and flourish until it outgrew reality? Here at the table is a rather loud girl, a stranger who talks far too much. Can there be someone else buried inside her, someone I knew better? Can things shift and change so much just because you get older? Perhaps it is the passing of the years, I think, and it really is more than three years ago now, she was sixteen then and still a child, and now she's nineteen and grown up. And suddenly I'm overcome with the nameless melancholy of time, it runs on and on, and if you go back you can't find anything again. Yes, parting is hard, but coming back sometimes seems to be a lot harder.

'What are you pulling that face for, Ernst?' asks Willy. 'Are you hungry or something?'

'He's being boring,' says Adele with a laugh. 'He was always like that in the old days. Why don't you lighten up a bit! That's what girls prefer, not having you sit there as if you were at a funeral!'

It's over, I think, something else that's over. Not because she is flirting with the dark chap or with Karl, and not because she thinks I'm boring, not even because she's different now – no, I realise that the whole thing is pointless. I've been running around everywhere, knocking on all the doors of my youth and wanting to get back in, thinking that they would be bound to let me in, because I'm still young, after all, and wanted so much to forget. But everything has drifted away like a mirage, broken up without a sound, crumbled like dry tinder when I touched it but couldn't get hold of it. Surely here there should be something left, I kept on trying, and made myself ridiculous and that made me sad – but now I see that an unseen and silent war had raged over the landscape of memory, too, and that it would be stupid of me to go on searching. The time between then and now is like a huge abyss, I can't go back and there is nothing else for it, I have to go forward, marching somewhere, I don't know where.

My fingers are tight round my glass as I look up. Adele is sitting there and is still quizzing Karl on where you can get silk stockings on the black market. The dancing goes on as it did before and the music is still playing, the same waltz from the same musical comedy, and I'm still sitting in the same way on the same chair and I'm breathing and I'm still alive. Was there no flash of lightning that tore me away, didn't everything around me suddenly disappear, leaving me behind, all alone, and now with absolutely everything really and truly lost?

Adele gets up and says goodbye to Karl. 'At Meyer and Nickel's, then,' she says in a satisfied voice. 'Yes, I know they do a lot of stuff under the counter. I'll pop along there tomorrow. Bye, Ernst!'

'I'll walk back with you,' I say.

Outside she shakes my hand. 'You can't come with me any further. I'm meeting someone.'

I feel stupid and sentimental, but I can't help myself. I take off my cap and make a deep bow, as if I were very formally taking my leave, not of her, but of the entire past. She looks at me curiously for a moment. 'Sometimes you can be really funny.' And she goes on her way, singing to herself.

The clouds have dispersed and the night is clear over the town. I stare across at it for a long time. Then I go back.

4

The first regimental reunion since we came back from the front is being held in the grand hall at Konersmann's Restaurant. All the old soldiers have been invited. It promises to be a great celebration.

Karl, Albert, Jupp and I get there an hour before it starts. We can hardly wait to see all the old faces again.

In the meantime we sit around in the lounge next to the grand hall waiting for Willy and the others. We are just throwing dice to see who's going to pay for a round of drinks when the door opens and Ferdinand Kosole comes in. We drop the dice in amazement, completely taken aback by his appearance. He's in civvies.

Up to now, like the rest of us, he's been wearing his old uniform; today, however, in honour of the occasion, he's turned up in civvies for the first time. There he stands, in a blue overcoat with a velvet collar, a green hat perched on his head, and a tie and wing collar round his neck. It's turned him into a completely different person.

We haven't quite got over our surprise when Tjaden appears. He's wearing civvies for the first time as well – a striped blazer, two-tone yellow shoes, and he's carrying a walking stick with a silver knob. He makes his entrance into the room with his nose in the air. As soon as he comes across Kosole he stops short. Kosole reacts the same way. Neither of them has ever seen the other out of uniform. They look each other up and down for a moment. Then they both roar with laughter. Each of them finds the other one ludicrously funny out of uniform.

'Bloody hell, Ferdinand, I always used to think you were one of those fine gentlemen,' grins Tjaden.

'What do you mean?' he replies, and stops laughing.

'Well, this.' Tjaden points at Kosole's overcoat. 'Anyone can see that you bought that off the rag-and-bone man.'

'Idiot,' growls Ferdinand angrily and turns away – but I notice that he's actually reddening. I can't believe my eyes – he's really embarrassed, and when he thinks nobody is watching he has a quick glance down at the derided overcoat. And now he's really and truly trying to wipe off a couple of dirty marks with his shabby sleeve; then he stares for a long time at Karl Bröger, who's wearing a top-quality new suit. He doesn't realise that I've been watching him. After a while he asks me: 'What does Karl's father do?'

'He's a magistrate,' I reply.

'Hmm, a magistrate,' he echoes thoughtfully. 'And what about Ludwig's?'

'Tax inspector.'

For a time he is silent. Then he says: 'You lot soon won't want anything more to do with us lot, will you?'

'You're crazy, Ferdinand,' I tell him. He shrugs doubtfully. I'm even more surprised. He doesn't only look different in those damned civvies, he really has changed too. In the old days you couldn't have cared less about that sort of thing, but now he takes off his overcoat and hangs it up in the darkest corner of the place.

'It's too hot here,' he says crossly, when he notices that I'm watching him. I nod. After a time he asks in an irritated voice: 'And your father?'

'He's a bookbinder.'

'Really?' He perks up. 'Albert's, then?'

'He's dead, but he was a locksmith.'

'A locksmith,' he repeats with delight, as if that were on about the same level as being Pope. 'Locksmith, that's great. I'm a metal-turner. We'd have been practically colleagues.'

'That's true,' I say.

I can see that the blood of Kosole the soldier is flowing back into Kosole the civilian. His colour is returning and so is his vigour.

'It would be sad if it weren't,' he assures me with some force. And when Tjaden goes past, pulling a face again, he manages without a word to give him a well-aimed kick, and does so without even getting up. He's his old self again.

The door to the grand hall starts to swing open and shut. The first of the old soldiers are turning up. We go in. The empty room with its paper decorations and the still unoccupied tables doesn't look particularly inviting yet. A few groups are standing around in the corners. I spot Julius Weddekamp in his shabby military tunic and push a couple of chairs out of the way to go and see him.

'How's it going, Julius?' I ask. 'Do you remember that you still owe me a mahogany cross? You were going to make it for me out of a piano lid back then! Best keep it aside for me, old boy!'

'I could have done with it myself, Ernst,' he says sadly. 'My wife died.'

'Damn it all, Julius,' I say, 'what happened?'

He shrugs. 'I think she just wore herself out with all the queuing to get hold of things during the winter. Then the baby came, and she just couldn't take it any longer.'

'What about the child?' I ask him.

'Died too.' He raises his sloping shoulders as if he were suddenly cold. 'Yes, Ernst, Scheffler's dead as well, did you know that?'

I shake my head. 'How come?' Weddekamp lights his pipe. 'He got that head wound in '17, didn't he? Everything healed up well at the time. Then six weeks ago he suddenly got such colossal headaches that he only wanted to smash his head against the wall. It took four of us to get him to the hospital. Some kind of inflammation. By the next day it was all over.' He lights another match. 'And what's more they're even refusing to give his wife a pension.'

'And Gerhard Pohl?' I ask him.

'He can't come. Nor can Fassbender or Fritsch. Out of work. Not enough money for grub. They'd have liked to come, those lads.'

★

By now the room is half full. We meet a good few more who were in our company, but it's strange – the atmosphere doesn't seem to be quite right. We've been looking forward to this gathering for weeks, hoping that it would help get rid of some of the pressures, uncertainties and misunderstandings. Maybe it's the mixture of civvies and old uniforms, or maybe it's because jobs, families or social positions have been forced in between us like wooden wedges. The old spirit of real comradeship just isn't there any more.

Everything has been turned upside down. There's Bosse, the butt of the company jokes, who was always having tricks played on him because he was such a twerp. At the front he was dirty and grimy, and more than once we had to give him a bath under the pump. Now he's sitting there in the middle of us all in a suit of the finest worsted, with a pearl tiepin and spats, a prosperous man, holding forth with authority. And next to him is Adolf Bethke, who towered so far above him when we were at the front that Bosse was happy if he even spoke to him, and suddenly he's just a poor shoemaker with an insignificant smallholding. Ludwig Breyer is wearing the suit he had at school, shabby and too small for him, with a schoolboy's knitted tie askew round his neck, and not his lieutenant's uniform. But his former batman slaps him on the back in a familiar way. He is now running a large plumbing concern, putting in bathrooms, and he has swish premises on the street where all the best businesses are. Valentin is wearing an old blue-and-white sweater under his ragged, unbuttoned tunic and looks like a tramp, but what a soldier he was! And that devious little sod Ledderhose is lording it, sitting there with his shiny top hat and bright yellow coat, smoking English cigarettes. Everything is topsy-turvy.

But even that would be bearable. However, the whole atmosphere is different as well, and that also has something to do with the way people are dressed. Men who wouldn't have said boo to a goose in the old days are now holding court with great speeches. The ones who are dressed well are being a bit patronising, and those who aren't are mostly keeping quiet. A schoolmaster who had been a corporal, and a poor one at that, enquires pompously about Karl's and Ludwig's examinations. Ideally, Ludwig ought to chuck a glass of beer in his face for that, but Karl, thank God, gives him by way of an answer a complete dismissal of education, exams and all that stuff, and then goes on to praise business and trade instead.

All the nonsense that is being talked makes me really sick. We should never have had this kind of reunion, then at least we would have kept our memories. I try in vain to picture all these people wearing dirty uniforms again, and to see Konersmann's Restaurant as a canteen somewhere behind the lines. I can't do it. What is here is more powerful, the unfamiliarity is stronger. What we once had in common is no longer binding. It has disintegrated into the interests of the individual. Sometimes, to be sure, something still shines through from the past, from the time when we all wore the same gear, but already it has become blurred and faded. These are our comrades in arms, and yet they are not our comrades any more, and that is precisely what is so sad. Everything else was wrecked by the war, but we did believe in comradeship. Only now we realise that what death couldn't do, life has achieved: it has split us up.

But we don't want to believe it. We are all grouped round the table, Ludwig, Albert, Karl, Adolf, Willy, Valentin. Our mood is sombre.

'At least we'll all stick together,' says Albert, glancing round the huge room. We agree, and each puts a hand in the middle of the table, while on the other side of the room the good-suits-and-ties are already beginning to close ranks. We don't want to be a part of this new order. We want to start with what they have already rejected. 'Give us your hand too, Adolf,' I say to Bethke. He smiles again for the first time in ages, and puts his great paw on top of ours.

We sit together for a while. Adolf Bethke left pretty early. He didn't look well. I decide that I'll go and visit him in a day or so.

A waiter comes over and whispers to Tjaden, who waves him away, saying, 'Ladies have no business here.' We look at him in surprise. Tjaden smiles, feeling flattered. Then the waiter comes back, and hurrying along two paces behind him is a large and busty girl. Tjaden is taken aback. We grin. But Tjaden is up to the situation. He makes a grand gesture and says: 'My fiancée.'

With that, he assumes that he has done enough, so Willy takes over and introduces us all. He begins with Ludwig and ends with himself. Then he invites the girl to take a seat. She does so, and Willy sits next to her and rests his arm along the back of her chair. By way of an opening he says: 'Your father owns the famous butchery in Neugraben Street, I believe?'

The girl nods. Willy moves his chair closer. Tjaden does not seem to be concerned in the slightest, and happily carries on drinking his beer. Willy's lively and persistent conversation soon gets the girl to relax.

'You know, I've really wanted to get to know you gentlemen,' she tells us. 'Sweetie-pie has talked about you all so much, but whenever I said he should invite you round, he never seemed to want to.'

'What?' Willy glares ferociously at Tjaden. 'Invite us round? But we would all love to come, yes, really very much indeed. The great lump has never said a word to us about it.'

Tjaden has become a little uneasy. Now Kosole leans forward. 'So he's talked about us a lot, has old Sweetie-pie? What sort of things has he been saying?'

'We'd better go, Marie my love,' says Tjaden rapidly, and gets up. Kosole pushes him back down onto his chair. 'Stay where you are, Sweetie-pie. What has he told you, miss?'

Marie-my-love is completely unabashed. She looks coquettishly at Willy. 'Are you Mr Homeyer?' Willy gives a bow, in honour of the butchery. 'Then you're the one whose life he saved,' she chatters on, while Tjaden wriggles around on his chair as if he were sitting on an anthill. 'Don't you remember?'

Willy touches his head. 'I got buried in an explosion later, and that plays hell with the memory. Sadly I seem to have forgotten quite a lot of things.'

'Saved his life?' asks Kosole breathlessly.

'Marie my love, I'm off now, are you coming with me or not?' declares Tjaden. Kosole keeps a firm hand on him.

'Yes, he's so modest,' giggles Marie-my-love, beaming. 'And he killed those three black men who wanted to cut Mr Homeyer down with their machetes. One with his bare hands ...'

'With his bare hands,' echoes Kosole flatly.

'And the others with their own machetes. And then he carried you back behind the line.' Marie-my-love looks at Willy, all six-foot-four of him, and nods encouragingly at her fiancé. 'It's OK now to talk about what you did, Sweetie-pie.'

'Indeed it is,' agrees Kosole, 'it's OK to talk about it now.'

Willy gazes for a moment dreamily into Marie-my-love's eyes. 'Yes, he's a great fellow,' he says. Then he nods across at Tjaden. 'Just come outside with me for a minute.'

Tjaden gets up with some reluctance. But Willy means him no harm. After a few minutes the pair come back arm in arm. Willy bends down to speak to Marie-my-love again. 'Fine, it's all settled. I'm coming to visit you tomorrow evening. After all, I have to show my gratitude for being saved from those black men. But as a matter of fact I once saved your fiancé's life as well.'

'Really?' says Marie-my-love in surprise.

'Maybe he'll tell you the story later,' grins Willy. A relieved Tjaden slips off with his fiancée.

'You see,' Willy says to us, 'they're slaughtering tomorrow night.' But nobody hears him. We've all had to hold it in for too long and now we're all braying like a stable-full of hungry horses. Kosole is laughing so hard that he is nearly sick. It takes a while before Willy can tell us about the favourable arrangement he has made with Tjaden regarding supplies of horsemeat and sausage. 'I've got the lad just where I want him,' he chortles.

5

I spent the whole afternoon sitting at home trying to think of something to do. But it was no use, and for the past hour I've been wandering aimlessly through the streets. In the process I happen to pass the Holland Bar and Dance Hall, the third establishment of that sort to have opened in the past three weeks. These places, with their garish signs, are springing up like mushrooms among the rows of houses. The Holland Bar is the largest and poshest.

In front of the illuminated glass entrance there stands a doorman who looks like a cross between a guards officer and a bishop, a massive chap, with a great gilded staff in his hand. I look at him a little more closely, and then suddenly all his dignity disappears as he prods me in the belly with his stick and chortles: 'What ho, Ernst, you old scruff! Commong savva, as our French friends put it.'

It's Corporal Anton Demuth, who used to be one of our cooks. I give him a full-scale formal salute, because it was drilled into us in the army that you were saluting the uniform, not the wearer. And this fancy-dress uniform is in a class of its own, and worth at least standing to attention in front of it.

'Hey, Anton,' I laugh, 'let's be serious for a minute – have you got any grub available?'

'And how,' he assures me. 'Franz Elstermann is working in this gin joint as well. As a chef!'

'When can I drop in?' I ask, since that last bit of information tells me all I want to know. Elstermann and Demuth were the champion food-scroungers in the whole of France.

'After one o'clock tonight,' Anton tells me. 'We managed to get hold of a dozen geese from one of the inspectors at the food office, under the counter. You can bet your life that old Elstermann will do a couple of advance amputations. Who can say for certain that geese don't also have wars where they might lose a leg?'

'Nobody,' I say, and then I ask, 'Is it busy here?'

'Packed solid every night. Want to have a look?'

He pulls the door curtain aside a little and I peer through the gap into the room. There's a soft, warm light on the tables, blue cigarette smoke is swirling upwards, the carpets are lustrous, the bone china sparkles and the silverware gleams. Women are sitting at the tables, surrounded by waiters, and with them are men who are neither sweating nor embarrassed. They are giving their orders in an amazingly natural manner.

'Well, mate, wouldn't mind a ride on the roller coaster with one of those ladies, eh?' says Anton, and nudges me in the ribs.

I don't reply, because this colourful, smoky segment of life stirs me in a strange way. There's something unreal about it, almost as if I were dreaming it, standing here in the dark street in the damp and slushy snow and peering at it through a chink in the curtain. I'm captivated by it, though I don't forget that this is presumably a bunch of black marketeers spending their money. But we were too long in filthy shell-holes not to be overcome every so often by a fierce and crazy desire for luxury and elegance – because luxury means to be well looked after and well cared for, and that is something we simply aren't familiar with.

'Well, old boy, what about that, then?' asks Anton. 'Nice cuddly little bunnies to share your bed with, eh?'

I feel stupid, but for a moment I can't find an appropriate response. Suddenly this whole line of talk, which for years I've been using as well without even thinking about it, seems unpleasant and coarse. Luckily, Anton is forced back to his original dignified posture when a car pulls up. A slim creature gets out and goes through the door, bending forward a little, clasping a fur stole to her bosom with one hand, her hair shining beneath a bright yellow close-fitting hat, knees close together, with little feet and a narrow face. Smoothly and lightly she walks by me in a cloud of faintly bitter perfume, and suddenly I am overcome with a raging desire to be able to go with this girl, this woman, through the revolving doors to one of the tables in this comfortable and pampered world of colour and light, to stroll without a second thought through a carefree existence bounded by waiters, servants and the protective insulation that money provides, with none of the misery and filth that has been our daily bread for years.

I suppose I must have looked like a schoolboy, because Anton Demuth's bearded face breaks into a great guffaw, he punches me in the side and says with a sly look: 'They might be wearing silk and satin, but in bed they're all the same!'

'Course they are,' I say, and tell him a dirty joke, so that he doesn't notice what's really up.

'See you at one, then, Anton.'

'Right you are,' he says solemnly. 'Or bong-swar, as those French friends of ours put it.'

I walk on, my hands deep in my pockets. The snow is slushy underfoot. I kick it aside irritatedly. After all, what could I do if I really were sitting at one of those tables with a woman like that? I would only be able to stare at her, nothing else. I wouldn't even be able to eat without embarrassing myself. How difficult it must be, I think to myself, to spend an entire day with such a delightful creature. Always on your guard, always on your guard. And at night – then I'd be really lost. Of course I've been with women a bit – but all I know I learned from Jupp and Franz Wagner, and the ladies in question there were certainly not the right sort …

I first went with a woman in June 1917. At the time our company was in barracks behind the lines, it was midday, and we were fooling about in a field with a couple of dogs who had run up to us. The dogs were rushing about through the tall summer grass with their ears flying and their coats shining, the sky was blue, and the war was a long way away.

Then Jupp turned up from the orderly room. The dogs ran over to him and jumped up, but he shook them off and said: 'Orders have come, we're moving out tonight!'

We knew what that meant. For days the steady firing of a big offensive had been rumbling away on the western horizon, and for days we had been watching exhausted regiments come back, and whenever we asked anyone, the only answer was a gesture, as they went on looking blankly ahead; for days transport had been rolling past carrying the wounded, and for days we'd spent every morning digging long pits for mass graves ...

We got up. Bethke and Wessling went over to their packs to find some paper for writing letters, Willy and Tjaden wandered off to the cookhouse, and Franz Wagner and Jupp persuaded me to go with them to a knocking shop.

'Come on, Ernst,' said Wagner, 'you've really got to get some idea of what a woman is for! Who knows, we might all have copped it by the morning, I hear there's a lot of new artillery over there. It would be completely crazy if you copped your lot when you were still a chaste little virgin!'

The military brothel was in a little town about an hour away. We got passes and had to wait for a pretty long time, because other regiments had been ordered up the line as well, and lots of the men wanted a quick bit of it to take with them if they could. We had to give up our passes in a little ante-room. A medical orderly examined us to see if we were clean, then we got a quick shot of Protargol and a sergeant told us that it would cost us three marks and that we wouldn't be allowed more than ten minutes because of the demand. Then we joined the queue on the stairs.

The line went forward slowly. Upstairs a door would slam. Each time someone came out, and then we heard: 'Next!'

'How many cows are there?' Franz Wagner asked a sapper.

'Three,' he replied, 'but you don't get a choice. It's a lottery. If you're unlucky you'll get an old granny.'

I felt almost sick in that stuffy stairwell, which was seething with the heat and sweat of the sex-starved soldiers. I would have liked to clear off, because all my curiosity had left me by now. But I was afraid to do so in case the others laughed at me, so I stayed there and waited.

Eventually it was my turn. The man before me stumbled past and I went into the room. It was low and dark and stank so strongly of carbolic and sweat that it seemed strange to me to see a lime tree outside the window with the wind and the sun playing in its fresh leaves. Everything in the room looked so used up. There was a bowl of pinkish water on a chair, and in the corner a kind of camp bed with a tattered coverlet on it. The woman was fat and she wore a short transparent shift. She didn't even look at me, but just lay down. Only when I failed to join her did she glance up impatiently; then a look of understanding crossed her podgy face. She saw that I was still very young.

I simply couldn't do anything, I shuddered with horror and choking nausea. The woman made a few gestures to get me going, gross and repulsive gestures, and she even gave a coy, saccharine smile as she did so; she really deserved sympathy, because after all she was only a wretched army mattress who had to service twenty or thirty men or more a day, but I just put the money down for her and quickly went out of the room and down the stairs.

Jupp winked at me. 'How was it?'

'OK,' I said, like an old hand, and we wanted to set off, but first we had to report to the medical orderly again and get another shot of Protargol.

'So that's love,' I thought to myself in blank despair, as we got our stuff together, 'that's love, the thing all my books at home were full of, and from which I had expected so much in my youthful and indistinct dreams!' I rolled up my coat and packed my tarpaulin, drew ammunition, and then we marched out; I was silent and melancholy, thinking that there was nothing left of all those high-flying dreams of life and love except a rifle and a fat whore and a dull rumbling on the horizon towards which we were steadily marching. It got dark, and then came the trenches and death – Franz Wagner fell that night, and we lost another twenty-three men as well.

★

Rain is spraying down off the trees and I turn up my collar. I often long for tenderness, for gentle words, for broad and soaring emotions; I want to get out of the dreadful monotony of the past few years. But what would it be like if it were to come back again, the warmth and breadth I once knew, what if someone were to be nice to me in reality, a slim and delicate woman like the one with the bright yellow hat and the light movements, what would it be like if in reality we felt the excitement of a blue and silver evening all around us in an endless self-forgetting? Wouldn't the image of the fat whore interpose itself at the last minute, wouldn't the braying voices of my barrack-room corporals suddenly break in with their obscenities, wouldn't memories, scraps of conversation, army talk, cut into and tear to pieces any decent feelings? We are still more or less chaste, but our imagination has been debauched without our noticing it, and before we had formed any real idea of what love was, we were being lined up and inspected for venereal disease. The breathless, wild emotion, the wind, the darkness, the wondering – they were all there when we were sixteen and we were running after Adele and the other girls in the flickering of the street lights, and they never returned, even at those times when the woman I was with wasn't a whore, and I thought it was different, and the woman held me tightly and I was shaking with desire. I was always sad afterwards.

I find myself marching along more quickly and breathing heavily. I want to get it all back, I must get it back. It all has to come back, or else it won't be worth going on living ...

★ ★ ★

I make my way to where Ludwig Breyer lives. There's still a light on in his room. I throw a handful of stones up at his window. He comes down and lets me in.

Up in his room Georg Rahe is standing in front of the cases where Ludwig has his collection of geological specimens. He's holding a large quartz crystal and turning it so that it sparkles.

'I'm glad I've seen you, Ernst,' he says with a smile. 'I went round to your house earlier. I'm leaving tomorrow.'

He's in uniform. 'Georg,' I say hesitantly, 'you're not really going to ...'

'Yes I am!' He nods. 'Back to the army. It's true. All signed and sealed. I'm off tomorrow.'

'Can you understand that?' I ask Ludwig.

'Yes,' he replies, 'I can understand it. But it won't help him.' He turns to Rahe. 'You're disappointed with things, Georg, but you have to realise that this is perfectly natural. When we were at the front our nerves were always strained to the limit, because it was always a matter of life or death. Now they are as limp as the sails on a becalmed ship; back here it's a matter of making progress by small steps –'

'You're right,' interrupts Rahe, 'I'm sick to death of this petty scrabbling for grub or status, with a couple of second-hand ideals tacked on, and that's why I want to get out.'

'If you really and truly want to do something,' I say, 'you could always join the revolution. Maybe they'll make you minister for war.'

'Oh, the revolution,' answers Georg dismissively. 'It's a revolution led by people standing to attention, party secretaries who are already scared of their own boldness. Just look at the way they are already all at each other's throats, social democrats, independents, Spartacists, communists. And in the meantime those on the other side have calmly killed off the few real thinkers among them, and they haven't even realised what they've done.'

'No, Georg,' says Ludwig, 'that's not the way it is. What's true is that our revolution didn't have enough hate in it, and from the start we wanted to act justly, and that's why everything flopped. A revolution has to rage like wildfire, and then afterwards you can start to sow seeds again. But we wanted a new start without wanting to destroy anything. We didn't even have enough strength left to be able to hate, we were so tired and burnt out by the war. You can be so exhausted that you can fall asleep even under heavy fire, you know that. But maybe it isn't too late to achieve by work what we couldn't take by storm.'

'Work,' says Georg dismissively, letting the light play on the glittering quartz, 'we know how to fight, but we don't know how to work.'

'We'll just have to learn again,' says Ludwig calmly from the corner of the sofa.

'We're no longer capable of that,' counters Georg.

There is silence for a moment. The wind whistles outside the window. Rahe takes great strides around Ludwig's little room, and it seems as if he now really is out of place in this quiet, book-lined study – it's as if his sharp, distinct features over his grey uniform still belong exclusively to the trenches, to battle and to war. He puts his arms on the table and bends down towards Ludwig. The light from the lamp falls on his shoulder-flashes, and behind him the various crystals in Ludwig's collection are sparkling.

'Ludwig,' he says seriously, 'what are we doing here, anyway? Just look around at how limp and hopeless it all is! We're a burden to ourselves and to other people. Our ideals are bankrupt, our dreams shattered, and we're running around in this brave new world of go-getters and profiteers like a lot of Don Quixotes who've been carried off to some foreign country.'

Ludwig gazes at him for a long time. 'I think we're sick, Georg. We've still got the war in our bones.'

Georg nods. 'We'll never be able to get rid of it.'

'We will,' says Ludwig, 'because otherwise it will all have been pointless.'

Georg jumps up and slams his fist on the table. 'It *was* pointless, Ludwig, that's exactly what's driving me mad! Think about what we were like when we marched out in that storm of enthusiasm! It seemed as if a new age had dawned, all the old, rotten, half-baked partisan stuff had been swept away, and we were a new generation like none had ever been before!'

He is gripping the chunk of quartz as if it were a grenade, his hands twitching.

'Ludwig, I've been in lots of dugouts, and we were all young men, hunched round a miserable candle-end waiting, while the barrage was roaring over us like an earthquake – we weren't raw recruits any more and we knew what we were waiting for and we knew what was coming. But, Ludwig, down there under the ground in the half-dark you could see on those faces more than just composure, more than courage, more than simply being prepared for death – in those hard and unmoving faces was the will for a new future, and it was there when we went over the top and it was still there when we died. And where is it now, Ludwig, where is it now? Can you understand how everything has just collapsed into this mishmash of orderliness, duty, women, routine, and all the rest of what they call living nowadays? No, we were alive before, and you can tell me a hundred times that you hate war, but that's when we were really alive, because we were together, and because there was something burning inside us that was better than all this crap!' He is breathing hard. 'It must have had *some* purpose, Ludwig! Once, just for a moment, when I heard the word revolution I thought, yes, now for the breakthrough, the river will flood back and tear stuff down, break its banks and carve out new ones – and by God I'd have been in there! But the river got split up into a thousand little streamlets, and the revolution turned into squabbles about who'd be what and who'd be whose deputy, it just trickled away, muddied, soaked up by jobs, living conditions, families and political parties. I'm going where I'll be able to find proper comradeship again.'

Ludwig stands up. His face is red and his eyes are burning. He looks Rahe directly in the face. 'And why, Georg, why? Because we were deceived, and we know now how we were deceived! Because they abused us completely! They would say "the fatherland", but they meant the annexation plans of greedy industrialists; they talked about honour, and meant the squabbling and the power struggles of a handful of ambitious diplomats and rulers; they said "the nation", and they meant the need for out-of-work generals to be doing something!' He shakes Rahe by the shoulders. 'Can't you understand? They crammed into the word "patriotism" all their overblown rhetoric, their vainglory, their lust for power, their fake romanticism, their stupidity and their commercial greed, and then presented it to us as a shining ideal! And we believed that it was the clarion call to a new, strong and vigorous existence! Don't you understand? We waged war against ourselves without realising it! And every shot that was fired hit one of us! Listen to me, I'll shout it at you as loudly as I can: the youth of the world rose up, and in every country they thought they were fighting for freedom! And in every country they were deceived and abused, in every country they were fighting for vested interests rather than for ideas, in every country they were mown down, and they destroyed each other. Don't you understand? There is only one battle, the one against lies and half-truths, against compromise, the old stuff! But we let ourselves be trapped by their rhetoric and instead of fighting against it we fought for it. We believed that it was all for the future! But it was against the future! Our future is dead, because the young men who carried that future are dead. We are just the remnants, what's left over! But the others are still around, well-fed and contented, living better-fed and more contentedly than ever before! Because the ones who were not contented, who were tempestuous and forceful — they died for them! Think about it! A generation has been wiped out. A generation full of hope, belief, will, strength and ability, all hypnotised into shooting one another down, even though they all had the same goals in all the different countries!'

His voice cracks. His eyes are full of wild tears. We have all jumped up.

'Ludwig,' I say, and put my arm round his shoulders.

Rahe picks up his cap and tosses the quartz back into the cabinet. 'Goodbye, Ludwig, my old comrade in arms.'

Ludwig stands facing him. His lips are pressed tight and his cheekbones stand out. 'You go, Georg,' he manages to say, 'but I'm staying! I'm not giving up yet!'

Rahe gives him a long look. Then he says in a calm voice: 'There's no point,' and straightens his belt buckle.

★

I go downstairs with Georg. When we get to the main door the first leaden glimmers of dawn are already coming through. The stone stairs echo. We go outside as if we were leaving a dugout. The street is grey and completely empty, and stretches off into the distance. Rahe points down it. 'Just another trench, Ernst,' and then he turns to the houses. 'They're all dugouts – the war is still going on, but it's a grubby little war, everyone against everyone ...'

We shake hands. I can't speak. Rahe smiles. 'What's the matter, Ernst? There isn't really a front line over there in the east, not now! Cheer up, we're soldiers, aren't we? And it's not the first time we've had to part.'

'Yes it is, Georg,' I say quickly, 'I think this is the first time we've really had to part.'

He stands there for a moment longer in front of me. Then he nods slowly and walks off down the street without looking back, slim, calm, and for a while I can still hear his footsteps even though I can't see him any more.

PART FIVE

1

A provision has been made for ex-soldiers to be treated with special leniency in the examinations. This is done, and as a result we all pass. The next tranche of candidates, which includes Ludwig and Albert, is not due to be examined for another three months. Both of them will have to wait until then, even though they actually wrote all the essays for four of us.

A few days after the exams we are assigned to temporary teaching posts in the surrounding villages. I'm pleased about that because I was fed up with all the pointless hanging about. It only led to brooding, misery, and pointless, noisy fooling about. Now I want to work.

I pack my bag and set off together with Willy. We've been lucky enough to get neighbouring schools, and our villages are barely an hour apart.

I get lodgings in an old farmhouse. There are oak trees in front of the windows and from the stalls you can hear the gentle bleating of sheep. The farmer's wife sits me down in a high-backed chair and starts right away to set the table. She is convinced that everyone from the town must be half starved, and it isn't far from the truth. I'm quietly moved to see on the table things I had almost forgotten existed: a massive ham, sausages as long as your arm, dazzling white bread from wheat flour, and Tjaden's favourite buckwheat pancakes with great chunks of bacon in them. There's such a spread that it could have fed an entire company.

I dig in, and the farmer's wife stands there, arms akimbo, with a broad smile of pleasure on her face. After an hour I have to give up, groaning, no matter how much Mother Schomaker presses me to have some more.

Just at that moment Willy turns up, looking for me. 'Just watch this,' I say to the farmer's wife, 'now you'll have something worth looking at. Compared to him I'm a lightweight.'

Willy knows what a soldier has to do. He doesn't mess about, he just sets to. On the invitation of Mother Schomaker he starts with the pancakes. By the time he gets to the cheese the farmer's wife is leaning against the cupboard looking wide-eyed at Willy as if he were the eighth wonder of the world. Quite captivated, she fetches out a dish with an enormous pudding and Willy polishes that off as well. 'Right,' he says breathlessly as he puts down his spoon. 'That's given me a bit of an appetite – how about some proper food now?'

With that one sentence he captures the heart of Mother Schomaker forever.

★ ★ ★

Embarrassed and a bit unsure of myself, I sit there at the teacher's desk. There are forty children sitting in front of me. These are the youngest pupils. In rows that might have been drawn with a ruler they are sitting on eight benches, one behind the other, slate pencils and pencil boxes gripped in their small, chubby fists, slates and notebooks in front of them. The youngest are seven, the oldest ten. The school only has three classes, so that different years are combined in all of them.

Their wooden-soled shoes scrape on the floor. In the stove a peat fire is crackling. Many of the children have had a two-hour walk with their woollen scarves and rough leather satchels. Their wet things are beginning to steam in the dry heat of the room.

The smallest, apple-cheeked children are staring at me. A couple of the girls are giggling to themselves. A little blond boy is picking his nose in a concentrated fashion. Another one is scoffing a thick sandwich behind the back of the child in front of him. But the whole class is watching my every move.

I wriggle around on my chair uneasily. Only a week ago I was sitting on a bench myself looking at Hollermann's expansive and old-fashioned gestures as he told us about the poets of the Wars of Liberation. Today I've become Hollermann myself. At least for those sitting in front of me.

'Children, we're going to practise writing a capital L,' I say, and turn to the blackboard. 'Do ten lines of capital Ls, then five of "Lina" and five of "Lark".'

I write the words up carefully with chalk. Behind my back there are rustling and scraping noises. I'm expecting to be laughed at, and I turn round, but it is just the notebooks being opened and the slates put into position. Dutifully the forty heads bend down over their work. I am quite taken aback.

The slate pencils squeak and the pens scratch away. I walk along between the rows.

On the wall there is a crucifix, a stuffed owl and a map of Germany. Outside the window the clouds are scudding rapidly past.

The map of Germany is largely green and brown. I stop in front of it. Borders are in red hatching and they run in a distorted zigzag from top to bottom. Cologne, Aachen – there are the thin black lines marking the railways – Herbesthal, Liège, Brussels, Lille – I stand on tiptoe – Roubaix, Arras, Ostend – where is Kemmel Hill? It isn't there – but there are Langemarck, Ypres, Bixschoote, Staden – how tiny they are on the map, just little dots, quiet little dots – and yet it was there that the heavens roared and the earth shook when the big offensive began on 31 July, and when by nightfall we had lost every single officer ...

I turn round and look over the blond and dark heads, all bent over to concentrate on the words 'Lina' and 'Lark'. It's strange to think that for them these little dots on the map will be nothing more than something they have to study, a few new places and a handful of dates that they will have to learn by heart in a history lesson, just like the Seven Years War or the Roman defeat in the Teutoburg Forest.

A little chap in the second row jumps up and holds out his notebook. He's finished his twenty lines. I go over and show him that he's made the bottom stroke of the capital L just a little bit too long. He beams at me so brightly with his liquid blue eyes that I have to look away for a moment. I go quickly over to the blackboard to write up two words with a different capital letter. 'Karl' and – I hesitate for a moment, but I can't help myself, and it's as if an invisible hand were guiding the chalk – 'Kemmel'.

'So what is "Karl"?' I ask them.

Every hand shoots up. 'A man,' shouts out the same little chap.

'And "Kemmel"?' I ask after a short pause, a little apprehensively.

Silence. Eventually a little girl puts her hand up. 'A place in the Bible?'

I look at her for a while. 'No,' I tell her, 'no, it's not that. You were probably thinking of Carmel, or Lebanon, weren't you?'

The little girl nods shyly. I run my hand over her hair. 'Then why don't we write one of those? Lebanon, that's a very nice word.'

I wander thoughtfully up and down between the benches again. From time to time I spot an inquisitive glance over the top of a notebook. I stop near the stove and look at these young faces. Most of them are decent and ordinary, some are mischievous, others are dull – but in some of them there is a flicker of something brighter. Life won't appear so straightforward to them, and not everything will go smoothly …

Suddenly a great feeling of despondency comes over me. Tomorrow we'll do the prepositions, I think to myself, and next week we'll have dictation, in a year you'll know fifty questions from the catechism by heart and in four years' time you'll have done all your tables, and you'll grow, and life will get its claws into you, maybe gently, maybe savagely, moderately, or in a way that will tear you apart – you'll all have your own destinies, and you'll have to cope with it all one way or another. How can my verb conjugations or giving you a list of German rivers help in any way? There are forty of you, forty separate lives are standing there waiting for you. If I could help you I would be more than glad to do so! But who can really help anyone else in this life? Was I even able to help Adolf Bethke?

The bell goes. The first lesson is over.

* * *

The next day Willy and I put on our formal suits – mine has only just been finished in time – and go to call on the pastor. This is a duty visit.

Our reception is friendly, but reserved, because the fuss we made about our own schooling has left us with a dubious reputation in respectable circles. In the evening we also have to go and see the mayor, another obligation. We come across him, however, in the local pub, which doubles as the post office.

He's a sly old farmer with a lined face, who offers us a couple of large glasses of schnapps. We accept. Two or three other farmers come in, winking at each other, greet us and also buy drinks for us. We clink glasses with them politely. They keep giving us surreptitious looks – the poor saps; we spotted right away, of course, that they want to get us tight so they can make fun of us. They seem to have tried this a few times before, because they grin as they tell us tales about other young teachers who have been here. They think for three reasons that they'll soon have us under the table: first, because they're convinced that people from the town can't hold their liquor as well as they can; second, because schoolteachers are educated people and therefore necessarily less experienced in boozing; and third, because such young lads can't possibly have had any real practice at it. This might well have been the case with earlier probationers from the training college who have been here, but as far as we are concerned there is one thing they haven't reckoned with: that we've spent a few years in the army and are used to drinking schnapps by the billycan-full. So we go into battle. The farmers just want to make us look ridiculous; but we are defending a threefold honour, and that puts extra strength into our powers of attack.

The mayor, the town clerk and a few of the tough old farmers sit there with us. These seem to be the most experienced boozers. They clink glasses with us, their amiable grins full of peasant slyness. Willy behaves as if he is already getting merry. The grins all around us get wider.

We cough up for a round of schnapps with beer chasers, and with that the others hammer down seven more rounds. The farmers reckon that that will finish us off. Already getting a bit baffled, they watch us toss back the drinks without a problem. A small flicker of admiration is visible in the looks we are now getting. With a completely straight face Willy orders another round. 'No beer this time, though, just double schnapps!' he calls out to the landlord.

'Bloody hell, just schnapps?' asks the mayor.

'Of course, otherwise we'll be sitting here till tomorrow morning,' says Willy. 'All the beer does is sober you up every time.'

The astonishment in the mayor's eyes increases. In an unsteady voice he assures one of the farmers that we seem to be damned good at getting it down us. Two others get up and disappear without a word. One or two of our adversaries are trying to empty their glasses under the table without being noticed, but Willy keeps his eyes open to make sure nobody cheats. He makes them put their hands on the table, and the drinks down their throats. Nobody is grinning at us now. We're gaining ground.

After an hour most of them are lying around white-faced in the room, or are stumbling out, defeated. The group at the table has been reduced to just the mayor and the clerk, and a duel between these two and us now starts. We're already seeing double, it's true, but those two have been babbling incomprehensibly for a good while now, and that puts new heart into us.

After half an hour, by which time we are all red in the face, Willy sets things up for the *coup de grâce*.

'Four tumblers of brandy!' he roars across to the bar.

The mayor slumps back in his seat. The glasses arrive. Willy forces two of them into their hands. 'Cheers!'

They stare at us goggle-eyed. 'Get it down!' shouts Willy, his face shining. 'Come on, down in one!' The clerk wants to get out, but Willy won't let him. 'Four gulps!' begs the mayor, already completely subdued. 'Down in one!' insists Willy, and bashes his glass against the clerk's. I jump up as well. 'Here we go! Cheers! Down in one! All the best!' we shout at the dumbfounded pair.

Like lambs to the slaughter they look at us and take a gulp. 'Come on, more! You're not giving in?' cries Willy. 'Everybody on their feet!' They stagger up and drink. They make various attempts to avoid it, but we keep on at them, show them our glasses. 'Cheers!' 'Put it away!' 'Bottoms up!' and they gulp down the rest. Then with a glassy stare they slide slowly but surely to the ground. We've won. If we'd been drinking at a slower rate they might have beaten us, but we're well trained in getting it down us quickly, and we were lucky to be able to force them to go at our pace.

Staggering but proud, we gaze over the battlefield. We are the only ones left standing. The postman, who is also the landlord, has his head down on the bar and is crying about his wife, who died in childbirth while he was at the front. 'Martha, Martha,' he sobs, in a curiously high voice. He does that every night around this time, the barmaid tells us. His weeping hurts our ears. It's time we got out.

Willy picks up the mayor, I take the lighter clerk, and we drag them home. That is our final triumph. We drop the clerk on his doorstep and bang on the door until a light goes on. However, someone has waited up for the mayor. His wife is standing in the doorway.

'Dear God,' she screeches, 'the new teachers! So young and such boozers! That's a fine way to start!'

Willy tries to explain to her that it was all a matter of honour, but he keeps tripping over the words.

In the end I ask: 'Where shall we put him?'

'Put the old soak down over there,' she decides. We dump him onto a sofa. Then with a childlike smile Willy asks her for some coffee. The woman looks at him as if he'd come from another planet.

'But we did bring your husband back,' Willy points out, beaming. In the face of such incredible but unconscious cheek even this hard old biddy has to give way. Shaking her head, she pours us out two huge cups of coffee and gives us a great deal of good advice to go with it. We agree to everything she says, which is the best thing to do on occasions like this.

From that day onward we are seen as real men in the village, and people greet us with respect.

2

The days pass, identical and unvarying. Four hours of school in the mornings, two in the afternoon; apart from that, time stretches out endlessly as I sit around, or wander about, alone with myself and my thoughts.

Sundays are the worst. If you don't want to sit in the pub, they are simply unbearable. The headmaster, the only male teacher apart from me, has been living here for thirty years and in that time has become a first-class pig breeder with a clutch of prizes. But it's almost impossible to talk to him about anything else. Whenever I see him my first inclination is to get out of there for good if I can, because the thought that I might end up like him is so appalling. Besides him there is a lady teacher, a decent, older creature, who shudders if you use a phrase like 'damn it all'. Again, not a very encouraging prospect.

Willy settles in rather better. He is invited as an official figure to every wedding and christening. If the horses get colic or the cows have trouble calving he helps the farmers out with word and deed. And in the evenings he sits with them in the pubs and skins them alive at cards.

I don't want to spend time in the pub, I'd rather stay in my room. But the hours pass so slowly, and often strange thoughts creep out from the corners like blanched and pallid hands which beckon and threaten, or shadows of a ghostly past, strangely transformed, memories which rise up again, grey, anonymous faces, complaints and accusations ...

★

One gloomy Sunday I get up early, dress and go off to the train station so that I can visit Adolf Bethke. It's a good plan. I can spend time again with someone who is really close to me, and when I come back the tedious Sunday will be over.

I get there in the afternoon. The gate squeaks on its hinges. The dog barks in his kennel. I walk quickly along the avenue of fruit trees. Adolf is at home. His wife is there as well. When I go in and shake hands with Adolf, she leaves the room. I sit down. After a while he says: 'You're surprised, aren't you, Ernst?'

'What about, Adolf?'

'Because she's back again.'

'No, that's your business.'

He passes a bowl with fruit in it to me. 'Would you like an apple?' I take one and offer him a cigar. He bites the end off and then says: 'You see, Ernst, I sat here and sat here and it nearly drove me mad. When you're on your own, a house like this is a horrible place. You wander through the rooms – there's one of her blouses still hanging up, there are her sewing things, there's the chair she always used to sit in when she was sewing – and at night there's the other bed, white and abandoned, next to yours, and you keep looking across at it and you toss and turn and you can't sleep – all sorts of things go through your head, Ernst …'

'I can believe it, Adolf.'

'And then you clear out as fast as you can and get sloshed and create mayhem …'

I nod. The clock ticks. The stove crackles. His wife comes in quietly and puts bread and butter on the table. Then she goes out again. Bethke runs his hand over the tablecloth.

'Well, Ernst, it was the same for her, after all. She'd had to sit around too, all those years, and had to lie there alone, and was frightened and uncertain and worried – and then in the end it happened, I'm sure she didn't want it herself at first, but when it did happen she didn't know how to get out of it and so it went on.'

His wife brings some coffee. I want to say hello, but she doesn't look at me.

'Why don't you get a cup for yourself?' asks Adolf.

'I've got things to do in the kitchen,' she says. She has a soft and deep voice.

'So I sat here and said to myself, you've done what honour demands, you've thrown her out. But what good is honour? – it's only a word, you're alone and that won't get any better, honour or not. So I told her that she could stay here – what's the point of it all anyway, you get tired and life is short, and if I hadn't known about it, things wouldn't have changed at all. Who knows how we would behave if we always knew everything that was going on.'

Adolf taps his fingers nervously against the arm of the chair. 'Have some coffee, Ernst, and there's butter, too.'

I pour the coffee and we drink.

'You see, Ernst,' he says quietly, 'you lot have it easier, you've got your books and your education and all that kind of thing. But me, all I've got is my wife, after all ...'

I don't say anything, because I couldn't explain things to him; he's not the same man as he was at the front, and neither am I.

After a bit I ask: 'What does she think about it?'

Adolf drops his hand. 'She doesn't say a lot – you can't get much out of her; she just sits there and looks. At most she cries a bit. She doesn't talk much at all.'

He puts his cup to one side. 'Sometimes she says that it was only so that someone would be there. Then again she sometimes says that she didn't understand, she didn't know that she was hurting me, that it was just as if it had been me there. But that doesn't make sense, surely you have to be able to tell the difference – she's sensible enough otherwise.'

I think about it. 'Perhaps she means that she wasn't really herself then, Adolf, that it was as if she'd been dreaming.'

'Maybe,' he replies. 'But I still can't understand it. I don't think it lasted very long.'

'She's not still interested in the other man?' I ask.

'She says that this is where she belongs.'

I think about this as well. But what else can I say to him? 'Are things better for you now, Adolf?'

He looks at me. 'Not all that much, Ernst, as you can probably guess, not yet. But it'll come, don't you think?'

He doesn't look as if he really believes that himself.

'Of course it'll come, Adolf,' I say, and put a couple of cigars that I had kept for him down on the table. We talk for a bit longer, then I leave. In the corridor I meet his wife, who tries to hurry past me. 'Goodbye, Mrs Bethke,' I say, and hold out my hand. 'Goodbye,' she says, and looks away as she shakes my hand.

Adolf comes to the station with me. The wind is whistling. I give him a sidelong glance, and remember how he always used to smile to himself in the trenches when we talked about peace coming. What's become of it all now?

The train starts to pull out. 'Adolf,' I say from the window, 'I do understand, you know – you wouldn't believe how well I understand it all.'

He goes back alone across the fields to his house.

* * *

The bell goes for long break at ten. I've just had an hour teaching the oldest of the pupils. Now those fourteen-year-olds are hurtling past me to get out into the open. I look at them from the window. In a matter of seconds they have changed completely, shaken off the constraints of school and reclaimed their freshness and spontaneity.

When they are sitting on the benches in front of me they are not really themselves; it's as if they were all idlers or swots or cheats or rebels. Seven years of schooling has taught them to be those things. They came into school from the fields, from their games and their dreams as open, honest and trusting as young animals; the simple rule of life was still valid for them – that the liveliest and the strongest among them would be the leader whom the others would follow. But little by little the weekly ration of education drummed into them a different and more artificial set of values: the one who

194

was most dutiful in taking in the lessons was praised for it and put at the top of the class. The others were supposed to try to be like him. Unsurprisingly, the livelier ones resisted, but they had to conform, because the model pupil is always the ideal in a school. But what sort of an ideal is that, and besides, what is it that always happens to model pupils when they go out into the world? What they enjoyed in the hothouse of the school was brief and illusory – and it is all the more inevitable that later on they'll sink into mediocrity and low-level insignificance. Progress only comes in this world through the efforts of those who were no good at school.

I watch them as they play. They are led by the strong and supple movements of a curly-haired boy called Dammholt, whose energy lets him command the entire playground. His eyes are shining with courage and readiness for action, his muscles and sinews are taut, and the others do what he wants without question. However, in ten minutes' time that very same lad, when he's back behind a desk, will have turned into a sullen and contrary lout who never knows his lessons and who will probably fail after Easter and have to repeat a year. He will be all innocence when I'm looking at him and as soon as my back is turned he'll pull faces, he'll lie through his teeth when I ask him if he's done his homework, and will be just ready with some sort of practical joke, or he'll put a drawing pin on my chair if he gets half a chance. The boy who is top of the class, however, and who cuts a poor figure outside, will grow in stature when he's back in the classroom, he'll confidently put his hand up when Dammholt doesn't know the answer and can only sit there, defeated and angry, waiting for his fail-grade. The star pupil knows everything, and what's more, he knows he knows everything. But I like Dammholt, whom I ought really to punish, a thousand times more than the pallid model pupil.

I shrug. Haven't I seen something like this already? At the regimental reunion in Konersmann's Restaurant? Didn't it suddenly seem as if the man himself counted for nothing and his position as everything, even though things had been different before? I shake my head. What kind of world have we come back to?

Dammholt's voice echoes across the playground. I wonder to myself whether it might be productive to try to establish a more comradely attitude towards the pupils on the teacher's part. It's possible that this would improve the relationship and help avoid some of the problems; but at the end of the day it would just be an illusion. I can still remember from my own schooldays that the young are clear-sighted and can't be deceived. They close ranks and present an impenetrable front to the adult world. They are not sentimental; you can approach them, but they won't let you in. Once you have been evicted from Paradise, there is no going back. All generations have their own rules. With his sharp awareness, Dammholt would cold-bloodedly exploit any comradely attitude on my part to his own best advantage. He might even show a certain amount of affection, but that wouldn't stop him losing sight of the main chance. Any teacher who claims to be in harmony with the pupils has got an overactive imagination. The young don't want to be understood; they want to be left as they are. Adults who try too hard to get close to them make themselves look as ridiculous as if they had suddenly dressed up in children's clothes. We can empathise with the young, but they cannot empathise with us. That is their salvation.

The bell goes. Break time is over. Dammholt reluctantly joins the line at the door.

* * *

I go for a walk through the village, up towards the heath. Wolf is running along ahead of me. Suddenly a bull-mastiff shoots out of a farmyard and goes for him. Wolf hadn't seen the other dog coming, and because of that, its first attack manages to knock Wolf off his feet. The next moment there is just a cloud of swirling dust, bodies going one over the other, and vicious growling.

The farmer comes running out of the house carrying a stick. 'For God's sake, teacher,' he shouts to me, 'call your dog off! Nero will tear him to bits!'

I shake my head.

'Nero! Nero! Here, here, damn you!' he roars in agitation, and gets to them out of breath, ready to beat them apart. But the swirl of dust moves on a hundred yards with furious barking, and the tussle starts again.

'He's done for,' gasps the farmer, and lowers his stick. 'But I'm telling you right now, I'm not paying for your dog. You could easily have called him.'

'Who's done for?' I ask.

'Your dog,' replies the farmer in a resigned voice. 'That bloody mastiff has already finished off a dozen other dogs.'

'Well, let's just wait and see what happens to Wolf,' I say. 'Wolf's no ordinary sheepdog, you know. He's a war-dog, an old soldier.'

The dust settles. The two dogs have finished up in a field. I watch the mastiff trying to hold Wolf down and go for the back of his neck. If he manages to do that, then Wolf has had it, because he could easily snap his spine. But the sheepdog wriggles across the ground like an eel, no more than an inch or so out of reach of the other dog's jaws, throws himself round and goes on the attack again straight away. The mastiff is growling and barking. Wolf, though, fights without making a sound.

'Bloody hell,' says the farmer.

The mastiff shakes himself, makes a leap, snaps at the air, spins round furiously, tries to bite again and misses. It's as if he were there on his own – Wolf is barely visible. He moves close to the ground, like a cat, because he was trained to carry messages that way, so he slips between the mastiff's legs and attacks from below, circles round, feints, then suddenly gets his teeth into the other dog's belly and holds on.

The maddened mastiff howls and throws himself onto the ground to try and get at Wolf that way. But with a single movement, quick as a flash, Wolf has let go and seized the chance to go for the other dog's throat. Only now do I hear Wolf's growl, low and dangerous, now that he has his enemy firmly in his grip, however much the mastiff thrashes about and rolls on the ground.

'For God's sake, teacher,' shouts the farmer, 'call your dog off! He'll tear Nero to bits!'

'I could call him, but he wouldn't take any notice,' I tell him. 'And why should he! He's got to finish bloody Nero off first!'

The mastiff is groaning and whining. The farmer picks up his stick to go and help him. I tear it out of his hand, grab him by his coat and shout: 'Goddamn it, that mangy bastard started it!' It wouldn't take much and I'd let the farmer have it.

Luckily I am standing in such a way that I can see how Wolf suddenly lets go of the mastiff and hurtles across to me because he thinks I'm being attacked. I manage to stop him, otherwise the farmer would at least have needed a new coat.

Meanwhile Nero has cleared off. I pat Wolf on the neck and calm him down. 'That's a devil of a dog,' stutters the farmer, completely deflated.

'Oh yes,' I say proudly, 'he's an old soldier. You really shouldn't mess about with dogs like that.'

We wander on. Beyond the village there are some fields and after that comes the heathland, with junipers and prehistoric burial mounds. Close to a small birch wood there is a flock of sheep grazing. Their fleece is glowing like unpolished gold in the light of the setting sun.

All at once I notice that Wolf has bounded off at full tilt towards the flock. I assume that the business with the mastiff has made him go wild, and sprint after him to prevent a bloodbath among the sheep. 'Hey there! Watch out for the dog!' I shout to the shepherd.

He laughs. 'He's a sheepdog. He's not going to hurt them!'

'He will, he will,' I call back, 'he doesn't know about that kind of thing! He's a war-dog!'

'Nonsense,' says the shepherd. 'War-dog or not, he won't hurt them. There – look – just look at that! Good boy, go, go, fetch them in!'

I can't believe my eyes. Wolf, who has never seen a sheep before now, is rounding up the flock as if he had been doing it all his life.

With long bounds he comes round behind two stray lambs and drives them back, barking. Whenever they try to break away or stop he bars their way or snaps at their legs so that they keep straight ahead.

'Brilliant,' says the shepherd, 'he's only nipping at them, perfect behaviour.'

The dog is transformed. His eyes are shining, his ear – the one ragged from gunfire – is flapping, he circles round the flock carefully, and I can see that he is really excited.

'I'll buy him off you here and now,' says the shepherd, 'my own dog couldn't do better than that. Just look at the way he's driving the flock towards the village! He doesn't need to learn another thing.'

I don't know what's the matter with me. 'Wolf,' I call, 'Wolf,' and I could almost weep, seeing him like that. He grew up under shellfire and now, without anyone having to teach him at all, he knows what his real purpose is.

'I'll give you a hundred marks in cash and slaughter a sheep for you,' says the shepherd.

I shake my head. 'Not for a million, mate,' I tell him.

This time it's the shepherd's turn to shake his head.

★ ★ ★

The tough strands of heather brush against my face. I push them aside and rest my head on my arms. The dog is breathing calmly at my side and from the distance you can just hear the sound of the sheep-bells. Otherwise everything is quiet.

Clouds are drifting slowly across the evening sky. The sun is going down. The dark green of the juniper bushes turns to a deep brown, and I can feel how the night wind is rising gently in the distant woods. Within an hour it will be blowing through the birches. Soldiers are just as familiar with the countryside as farmers and foresters; they haven't lived indoors, they know the way the winds blow, and the cinnamon-coloured feel of hazy evenings, they know the shadows that drift across the ground when the clouds block the light, and they know the patterns of the moon ...

Once in Flanders, after a vicious bombardment, it took a long time before any help turned up for one wounded man. We had all packed our field dressings round him and secured them as far as we could, but he kept on bleeding, and simply bled to death. And the whole time there was one huge cloud in the evening sky behind him, a single cloud, but it looked like a great range of mountains, white, gold, and with a red glow. It rose up, unreal and magnificent, over the shell-shattered brown landscape, quite silent and glowing as the dying man lay there, quite silent and bleeding, as if the two belonged together. And yet I found it incomprehensible that the cloud should be there in the sky, so beautiful and indifferent, while a man was dying ...

The last rays of the sun turn the heath a dusky red. Peewits flutter up making cross noises. Away over at the lake a bittern booms. I gaze out over the broad, deep purple plain. Near Houthulst Forest, north of Langemarck, there was one place where the fields were so thick with poppies that they looked completely red. We called them the fields of blood, because in stormy weather they took on the pale redness of newly spilt and still-fresh blood. That was where Köhler went crazy as we marched past them one clear night, shattered and exhausted. In the uncertain light of the moon he thought they were lakes of blood and wanted to plunge in.

I shiver and look up. What is going on? Why are these memories coming back to me so often now? And in such a strange way, quite different from out there in the trenches. Am I just on my own too much?

Wolf stirs at my side and gives a soft, high bark in his sleep. Is he dreaming about his sheep? I look at him for a long time. Then I wake him up and we go back.

★ ★ ★

It's Saturday. I go over to see Willy and ask him if he feels like going back to town with me on Sunday. But he dismisses the idea out of hand. 'We're having roast goose and all the trimmings,' he says, 'and I'm certainly not going to give that a miss. Why do you want to go, anyway?'

'I can't stand Sundays here,' I tell him.

'I don't get it,' he says, 'not with the food here!'

I take the train on my own. In the evening I go with only the vaguest of expectations to Waldmann's Lodge. Things are pretty lively. I stand around for a while watching the activity. A mob of young lads who just about managed to miss the war are all strutting around on the dance floor. They are sure of themselves and know what they want, their world has a clear beginning and a clear goal: success. They are much more self-possessed than we are, even though they are younger.

Among the dancers I spot the delicate little seamstress who was my partner when we won a prize in the one-step competition. I ask her for a waltz and after that we sit together. I got paid a few days before and so now I order a couple of bottles of sweet, red wine. We drink the wine slowly, and the more I drink, the more I fall into a strange melancholy. What was it Albert had said that time? To have somebody who belongs to you?

Preoccupied with my thoughts, I listen to the girl chattering, twittering away like a little swallow about her fellow workers, about the piecework rates for making underwear, about the latest dances and a thousand other unimportant things. If only the piecework rate would be put up by twenty pfennigs, then she would be able to have lunch in a restaurant and she'd be happy with that. I'm envious of her clear and simple day-to-day existence, and I keep questioning her about it. I'd like to ask every one of these laughing, happy people here how they live. Maybe there would be one who could tell me something that would help me.

Later I take the little swallow home. She lives right at the top of a grey tenement block. We stop by the main door. I can feel the warmth of her hand in mine. Her face shines, uncertain, out of the darkness. A human face, a hand in which there is warmth and life. 'Let me come in with you,' I say quickly. 'Let me come in ...'

We creep carefully up the creaking stairs. I light a match, but she blows it out straight away, takes my hand and leads me along behind her.

A small room. A table, a brown sofa, a bed, a few pictures on the wall, a sewing machine in the corner, a dressmaker's dummy made of cane and a basket full of underwear ready to be made up.

The girl fishes out a Primus stove and makes tea from apple peel and some tea leaves which have been brewed up and dried out again ten times before. Two cups, a laughing, slightly mischievous face, an appealing little blue dress, the friendly poverty of this single room, a little swallow, whose only real possession is her youth – I sit down on the sofa. Is this how love begins? So easily and playfully? I suppose you have to accept that that's the way it is.

The little swallow is very sweet, and it is probably very much part of her little life that someone should come along, take her in his arms and then go away again; the sewing machine hums, someone else comes along, the little swallow laughs, cries and carries on sewing. She throws a small and colourful cover over the machine, turning it from a steel-and-chromium beast of burden into a hill covered with red and blue silk flowers. She doesn't want to be reminded of her everyday life, she snuggles down with my arm round her and chatters and hums and murmurs and sings in her light dress, and she is so slender and pale and almost half starved and so light that she can be carried to bed, to the iron-framed camp bed, and she has such a sweet expression of acquiescence as she holds tight round my neck; she sighs and smiles, a child with her eyes tightly closed, and sighs and shakes and stammers a little, and takes deep breaths and gives little cries, and I look at her, I look at her all the time and I want to be like that too, and I ask over and over in my head: is that the answer, is that the answer? – and then the little swallow calls me all sorts of funny names and is embarrassed and tender and holds me tight, and when I leave, and ask her 'Are you happy, little swallow?' she kisses me over and over again and pulls a face and nods and nods and waves …

But as I go down the stairs I am full of wonder. She is happy – how quickly it can happen. I can't understand it. Isn't she still a different human being with her own life, a life I can never enter? Wouldn't that still be the case even if I were aflame with all the fires of love? Love, love – it's a burning torch which falls into an abyss, and only then can you see how deep it is.

I walk through the streets towards the station. No, that's not the answer, that isn't it either. You're just left feeling more alone than ever …

3

The lamp makes a circle of light on the table. In front of me are piles of blue exercise books. Next to them is a bottle of red ink. I go through the exercise books, underline the mistakes, blot the pages and close the books.

Then I get up. Is this what my life is now? This monotonous regularity of days and lessons? At the end of the day, how unfulfilling it all is! There is far too much time left over for your own thoughts. I had hoped that the uniformity would calm me down. But it just makes me even more agitated. The evenings go on for so long!

I walk across to the cowshed. The cows are snorting and stamping in the dusk. The farm girls are sitting on low stools beside them, busy with the milking. Each one is separate, as if she were sitting in her own little room, the walls formed by the black-and-white sides of the cows. Small lights flicker above them in the warm haze of the cowshed, the milk spurts thinly into the buckets and the breasts of the girls swing gently from side to side under their blue cotton working dresses. They raise their heads and smile and breathe and show their white and healthy teeth. Their eyes sparkle in the darkness. There is a smell of hay and animals.

I stand there at the door for a while, then go back to my room. The blue exercise books are there underneath the lamp – they will always be there – and shall I be sitting there forever as well, until gradually I grow old and then die? I decide to go to bed.

The red moon wanders slowly over the roof of the barn and casts the outline of the window across the floor, a slanting square with a cross in it, and it shifts constantly the higher the moon rises. After an hour it reaches my bed, and the shadowy cross falls across my chest.

I'm lying in the huge farmhouse bed with its blue-and-red-checked covers, and I can't sleep. From time to time my eyes close and I sink with a rush into boundless space, but at the last moment a burst of fear comes over me with a harsh suddenness and drags me back into wakefulness, and once again I hear the church clock striking the hour, and I listen, and wait, and toss from side to side.

Eventually I get up and get dressed again. Then I climb out of the window, lift the dog out after me and walk out onto the heath. The moon is shining, there is a wind, and the plain stretches out into the distance. The railway embankment cuts across it as a dark line.

I sit down by a juniper bush. After a while I see the signal lamps on the railway light up. The night train is coming through. With a soft, metallic sound the rails begin to hum. The headlamps on the front of the locomotive flash on the horizon and drive a swathe of bright light ahead of them. The train roars past, the windows are lit up and for the briefest of moments the compartments with their complement of suitcases and human destinies are really close to me, then they sweep onwards, the rails gleam again in the damp light and from the distance there is nothing but the staring red rear-lamp of the train like a threatening, glowing eye.

I watch the moon turn bright yellow, and walk through the blue twilight of the birch woods, raindrops land on the back of my neck from the twigs, I stumble over roots and stones and a leaden dawn is breaking as I get back. The lamp is still lit – I look in desperation round the room – no, I can't stand it, I would have to be twenty years older to be satisfied with this …

Weary and exhausted I try to undress. I can't manage it. But still, as I fall asleep I clench my fists – I shan't give way, I'm not going to give up …

Then again I sink with a rush into that boundless space …

★

... and I'm crawling carefully along. Slowly, inch by inch. The sun is burning down on the yellow slopes, the gorse is flowering, the air is hot and still, observation balloons and puffs of white signal smoke are hanging there on the horizon. The red petals of a poppy are swaying gently in front of my steel helmet.

There is a very soft, barely perceptible scraping noise ahead of me, coming from behind the bushes. Then it is silent again. I go on waiting. A beetle with greenish-gold wings crawls out from behind a stem of camomile just in front of me. Its feelers run over the jagged leaves. Then again there comes a soft sound in the midday sun. This time the edge of a steel helmet appears behind the bushes. There is a forehead beneath it, bright eyes and a firm mouth – the eyes are scanning the landscape attentively and then looking back down at a white sketch pad. The man is unsuspectingly working on a drawing of the farm across the way.

I pull out a hand grenade. This takes me a long time. Eventually I have it beside me. I pull out the pin with my left hand and count in my head. Then I toss it in a low arc towards the bramble bushes and slide back into my hollow, press my body hard against the ground and open my mouth.

The roar of the explosion tears the air apart, fragments fly about and there is a long-drawn-out scream, full of horror. By now I've got a second grenade in my hand and I peer out from behind the cover. The Englishman is lying on the open ground, the lower parts of his legs blown away and the blood streaming out. The bands of his puttees have unrolled and are trailing behind him like ribbons; he is lying face down, flailing through the grass with his arms, his mouth is wide open and he is shrieking.

He throws himself over and sees me. Then he presses down on his arms and raises himself up like a seal, he screams at me and he's bleeding, bleeding – and then his red face goes pale and falls in on itself, his sight goes, and his eyes and mouth are now just black hollows in a collapsing face which sinks slowly towards the earth, falls forward and sinks into the camomile flowers. It's done.

I push myself up and want to crawl back to our trenches. But I look round once again, and the dead man has suddenly come back to life and is getting up, as if he wants to follow me – I pull the pin on the second grenade and throw it at him. It lands a yard short, rolls along and just lies there – I count and count again – why doesn't it explode? The dead man is standing up now, baring his teeth, so I throw another grenade – that fails to go off as well – and by now the man over there is taking a few steps towards me, walking on the stumps of his legs, grinning and with his arms outstretched towards me. I throw yet another grenade, it hits him in the chest but he brushes it aside ... I try to jump up so that I can run away from him, but my legs won't let me, they have gone as soft as butter, so I pull myself along, desperately slowly, I'm stuck firmly to the ground, I tear at it, hurl myself forward, and I can already hear the rasping noises made by my pursuer as I pull hard on my own useless legs ... but two hands grab me round the neck from behind and pull me backwards onto the ground, the dead man kneels on my chest, snatches up the trailing bands from the puttees on the grass and wraps them round my neck. I twist my head away, I tense all my muscles and throw myself over to the right to escape the noose ... and then there is a jerk, a suffocating pain in my throat and the dead man is dragging me along towards the edge of the chalk pit, he tips me in and I lose my balance, try to hold on, I slip, fall, scream, and I'm falling and falling, screaming, hitting out, screaming ...

Darkness breaks off in lumps beneath my clawing hands, and with a crash something hurtles down beside me, I hit myself against stones, sharp corners, iron, letting out scream after scream, sharp and raucous, I just can't stop. Someone grasps at my arms, I push them away, someone stumbles over me and I grab a rifle from somewhere, try and take cover, raise it to my shoulder and fire, still screaming, and then like a knife cutting through all this I hear 'Birkholz' and then again 'Birkholz', and I jump up, help is on its way and I've got to fight my way through, I tear myself away, start to run, get a blow on the knee and fall into a soft hollow in the light, bright, dazzlingly harsh light. 'Birkholz', 'Birkholz', and then there, in that place, there is nothing left but my own screaming ... and suddenly it breaks off.

The farmer and his wife are standing in front of me. I'm lying half in bed, half on the floor, and at my side the lad who works for them is just getting to his feet. I'm holding a walking stick gripped hard like a rifle, and I must be bleeding, but then I realise that it is just the dog licking my hand.

'Teacher,' says the farmer's wife, trembling, 'what on earth is the matter?'

I don't know what's going on. 'How did I get here?' I ask in a hoarse voice.

'Come on, teacher, wake up. You were dreaming.'

'Dreaming?' I say. 'That's supposed to be a dream?' And suddenly I burst out laughing, laugh so hard that I'm shaking, so hard that it hurts. Then suddenly the laughter dies in me. 'It was the English captain,' I whisper, 'from back then ...'

The serving lad rubs his bruised arm. 'You were having a dream, teacher, and you fell out of bed,' he says, 'you didn't hear us and you beat me half to death ...'

I don't understand, I'm completely drained and miserable. Then I notice the walking stick in my hand. I put it aside and sit down on the bed. The dog pushes his nose in between my knees.

'Just give me a glass of water, Mother Schomaker,' I say, 'and then you can all go back to bed ...'

But I don't lie down again. Instead I stay sitting at my table with a blanket round me. I leave the light on.

I stay that way for a long time, quite still and with an absent look, the way only soldiers can sit when they are on their own. After a while I become uneasy and I start to feel as if there were someone else in the room. I'm aware of how slowly, without my making any movements, sight and sense come back into my eyes. When I open my eyes a little wider I notice that I'm sitting right opposite the mirror which hangs over the small washstand. Out of that slightly distorted glass a face is looking at me, hollow eyes and with black shadows. My own face ...

I get up, take down the mirror and put it in a corner with the glass turned to the wall.

* * *

Morning comes. I walk across to my class. The children are sitting there with their hands folded. The gentle astonishment of childhood is still present in their big eyes. They look at me with such confidence and trust that it suddenly feels like a blow to my heart …

Here I am, standing before you, one of the hundreds of thousands of spiritual bankrupts who had all their beliefs and nearly all of their strength knocked out of them by the war – here I stand before you, and I can feel how much more alive, how much a part of the world you are than I am. Here I stand before you and I'm supposed to be your teacher and your guide. What should I teach you? Should I tell you that in twenty years' time you'll be dried out and hamstrung, your freest feelings inhibited, mercilessly hammered into something off a production line? Should I tell you that all education, all culture and all scholarship are nothing more than a cruel mockery just as long as human beings carry on fighting each other with gas, steel, gunpowder and fire in the name of God and humanity? What can I teach you, you little creatures who still have your innocence in these dreadful times?

So what *can* I teach you? Should I tell you how to pull the pin from a hand grenade so you can throw it at other human beings? Should I show you how to stab someone with a bayonet, kill them with the butt of a rifle or cut them down with a trenching spade? Should I demonstrate for you how to aim the barrel of a gun at the incomprehensible miracle of a breathing body, of pulsing lungs or a living human heart? Should I tell you what tetanus is like, or a spine that's been torn apart, or a head with the top blown away? Should I describe for you what spattered brains, shattered bones or spilt guts look like? Should I demonstrate for you how someone groans when they've been shot in the stomach, or rattles when they've been hit in the lungs, or makes a whistling noise when they've got it in the head? I don't know anything else! I haven't learned anything else!

Should I take you over to that green and grey map on the wall and run my finger over it and tell you that this is where love was murdered? Should I explain to you that the books you are holding in your hands are traps designed to lure your unsuspecting souls into the undergrowth of overblown phrases and the barbed-wire entanglements of fake ideas?

And so I stand before you, sullied and guilty, and I ought to be begging you to stay the way you are, and not let the warm light of childhood be perverted into the sharp flame of hatred! You still have the air of innocence about you – how can I pretend to teach you? The bloody shadows of the past are always at my heels, how can I have the audacity even to be in the same room with you? Surely I have to become human again myself before I can do that.

I feel as if a cramp is spreading through my whole body, as if I am turning to stone and shall crumble and fall to pieces. Slowly I sink down onto my chair and I realise that I can't stay here any longer. I try to fix my mind onto something, but I can't. Only after a time which seems endless to me does the paralysis give way. I stand up. 'Children,' I manage to get out, 'you can go. Today is a holiday.'

The children look at me to see whether I'm joking or not. I nod once again.

'Yes, it's true – today you can go and play, all day, go and play in the woods, or play with your dog or your cat, you don't need to come back till tomorrow.'

With that they bundle their pencil cases noisily into their satchels and rush out, twittering and breathless.

I pack my things together and walk to the next village to say goodbye to Willy. He's standing in his shirtsleeves by the window with his fiddle, practising a folk song about May, springtime and renewal. On the table a substantial meal is laid out. 'Third one today,' he says happily. 'I've discovered that I can put it all away for future use, like a camel.'

I tell him that I'm going to leave that evening. Willy isn't the sort of man who asks many questions. 'I'll tell you one thing, Ernst,' he says thoughtfully, 'yes, it's dull here. However, as long as I've got grub like that' – he points to the table – 'wild horses, or thoroughbred ones for that matter, couldn't drag me away from this place.'

With that he hauls a case of bottled beer out from under the sofa. 'Special Reserve,' he grins, and holds the label up to the light.

I look at him for a long time. 'Hell, Willy, I wish I were like you!' I say.

'I bet you do,' he chuckles, and opens one of the bottles with a snap.

On my way to the station a couple of little girls come running up to me out of the house next door, with dirt on their faces and hair ribbons untied. Apparently they've been in the garden burying a dead mole and saying prayers for it. Then they give little curtseys and hold their hands out to me. 'Goodbye, Mr Teacher sir.'

PART SIX

1

'Ernst, I really have to talk to you,' says my father.

I can already see what's coming. For days now he's been going around with a worried look on his face and he's been dropping hints. But so far I've always managed to keep out of his way, because I'm rarely at home.

We go into my room. He sits down on the sofa and looks anxiously at me. 'We're all concerned about your future, Ernst.'

I fetch a box of cigars from the bookshelf and offer him one. His face lightens up a bit because it's a good cigar – I got them from Karl, and he doesn't smoke ersatz stuff made of beech leaves.

'Have you really given up your teaching post?' he asks.

I nod.

'Why on earth did you do that?'

I shrug. How can I possibly explain it to him? We are completely different, and we've only got on pretty well up to now because we've never understood one another at all.

'And what's going to happen now?'

'Something will,' I reply, 'it doesn't matter much what.'

He gives me a horrified look, and starts to talk about a good, well-respected position, about getting on, about finding one's place in life. Touched and bored at the same time, I listen to him, and all the while I am thinking how strange it is that this man on the sofa is my father, and that he used to be in charge of my whole life. But he wasn't able to protect me in the years at the front, he wasn't even any use in the barracks, where every NCO was more powerful than he was. I had to get through everything on my own, and it was immaterial whether he existed or not.

When he has finished I pour him a brandy. 'Look, Father,' I say, sitting down next to him, 'you may well be right. But what I've learned is how to survive in a shell-hole with a crust of bread and some thin soup. And if nobody was shooting at me at that particular time, then I was happy. Being in an old barracks seemed like a luxury, and a straw paillasse behind the line was paradise. You have to understand that the fact that I'm still alive and no one is shooting any more suits me fine at the moment. I'll manage to get enough together for the bit of food and drink that I need, and there'll be plenty of time for everything else in the rest of my life.'

'Yes, yes,' he counters, 'but that's not a real life, just waiting for something to turn up.'

'It all depends. I don't think it is much of a life if all I can say later is that I've spent thirty years going to the same classroom or to the same office.'

Taken aback, he says: 'I've been going to the same factory for twenty years now, and I've managed to become a master board-maker for the bookbinding trade.'

'But I don't want to manage to become anything, Father, I just want to live.'

'I've lived, and respectably too,' he says, with a touch of pride. 'I wasn't elected a member of the Chamber of Commerce for nothing.'

'You should be pleased that things were that simple for you.'

'But you have to do something,' he complains.

'I can work in the shop that one of my pals from the war has, he's said I can,' I say, to calm him down. 'I'll earn as much as I need that way.'

He shakes his head. 'And for that you're giving up a decent teaching post?'

'I've had to give up a lot of things before now, Father.'

He looks miserably at his cigar. 'And it even carried a pension.'

'Well,' I say, 'how many of us soldiers will make it to sixty? We've got so much in our bones that it's bound to come out later – I'm sure we'll pop off before that.' With the best will in the world I can't imagine living until I'm sixty. I've seen too many men die at twenty.

I go on smoking and look at my father thoughtfully. I'm still aware that he's my father, but at the same time he's a decent, middle-aged man, cautious and pedantic, whose views no longer have any real meaning. I can well imagine what he would have been like at the front; you would always have had to look after him a bit, and he would certainly never have got as far as corporal.

* * *

That afternoon I go and see Ludwig. He's sitting there surrounded by a pile of books and pamphlets. I would really like to talk a lot of things over with him, things that are important to me, because I have the feeling that he might perhaps be able to show me the way through it all. But today he himself is unsettled and agitated. We talk about trivial matters for a bit, and then he says: 'I've got to go and see the doctor …'

'Is it still the dysentery?' I ask.

'No – it's about something else.'

'What else is wrong with you then, Ludwig?' I ask in some surprise.

He is silent for a while. His lips are trembling. Then he says: 'I don't really know.'

'Do you want me to come with you? I'm not doing anything else.'

He looks around for his cap. 'Yes, please come with me.'

On the way he gives me a number of sidelong glances. He seems strangely subdued and taciturn. We turn into Linden Street and come to a house with a small, depressing front garden containing a few small bushes. I read the white enamel plate on the door: Dr Friedrich Schultz, Specialist in Skin, Urinary and Venereal Diseases, and then I stop. 'What is the matter really, Ludwig?'

He looks at me, pale-faced. 'Nothing yet, Ernst. When we were out there I once got a sort of boil. And now something's come back.'

'Well, if that's all it is, Ludwig,' I say with relief. 'I used to get some horrible carbuncles! Massive great things. It's because of all the ersatz rubbish we had to eat.'

We ring the doorbell. A nurse in a white uniform opens the door. We are both colossally embarrassed, and go red-faced into the waiting room. There, thank God, we are alone. There is a pile of copies of the *Weekly News* on the table. We flick through a couple. They are pretty old. They've only just got up to spring 1918 and the Treaty of Brest-Litovsk.

The doctor comes in. His glasses sparkle. The door to his consulting room is half open behind him. In there you can see a tubular-steel and leather chair, depressingly practical and rather unpleasant.

It's funny how so many doctors seem to want to treat their patients like small children. With dentists it's probably part of their training, but this character seems to be just the same.

'Well, Mr Breyer,' says this spectacled cobra with a smirk, 'I think we're going to get to know each other a little better.'

Ludwig stands there like a ghost and manages to say: 'Is it ...?'

The doctor nods encouragingly. 'Yes, the blood test came back. Positive. Now we're really going to have to mount a solid attack on our nasty intruder.'

'Positive,' stammers Ludwig, 'so that means ...'

'Yes,' says the doctor, 'we need a little course of treatment.'

'So it means I've got syphilis?'

'Yes.'

A bluebottle buzzes through the room and bangs against the window. Time stands still. The air between the four walls feels jelly-like and sticky. The world has changed. A dreadful fear has become a dreadful certainty.

'Couldn't it be a mistake?' asks Ludwig. 'Couldn't we do a second blood test?'

The doctor shakes his head. 'It's best if we start the treatment pretty soon. It's in the secondary stage.'

Ludwig gulps. 'Is it curable?'

The doctor becomes animated. He beams reassurance. 'Absolutely. Here, these little tubes – regular injections with these for six months in the first instance. Perhaps after that we shan't even have to do anything else. Syphilis is quite curable these days.'

Syphilis. A horrible word, sounds as if it were a thin, black snake.

'Did you get it when you were at the front?' asks the doctor. Ludwig nods. 'Why didn't you get it treated right away?'

'I didn't know what it was. Nobody ever told us anything about things like that. Anyway, it turned up a lot later and looked harmless. Then it went away of its own accord.'

The doctor shakes his head. 'Yes, that's the other side of the coin,' he says casually.

I feel as if I could bring a chair down onto his skull. How can he have any idea of what it's like when you have a three-day pass for Brussels and you turn up on the evening train straight from all the shell-holes, vomit, filth and blood into a city with streets, lights, illuminations, shops and women, with proper hotel rooms and white bathtubs where you can splash away and scrub off the filth, with light music, terraces and cool, strong wine – how can he have any idea of the enchantment present in the blue haze of the evening, there in that small moment between one lot of horrors and the next? It's like a gap in the clouds, like a wild shout of life in the brief pause between death and death. Who knows whether in a few days' time you won't be hanging on the wire with your bones shattered, roaring out, gasping with thirst, dying. One more mouthful of the heavy wine, one more breath, and a glance into the unreal world of shifting colours, of dreams, of women and of excited whispers, of words, which turn the blood into a dark torrent, sweeping away the years of muck, anger and hopelessness and turning it into a sweet, singing whirlpool of memories and hopes. Tomorrow death will be rushing towards you with guns, grenades, flamethrowers, blood and annihilation, but tonight there is that soft and scented skin, which calls to you like life itself, teasing you and leading you on, mysterious shadows on the shoulders, tender arms, it crackles and flashes and falls and streams down, the skies are on fire ... and who would think for a moment that among these whispers and temptations, the scented skin, that the other thing could be lying in wait, hidden, crouched down, waiting – syphilis. Who would know, who would want to know, who could even think beyond the present moment? Maybe tomorrow it will all be over – the bloody war, it taught us to see and keep hold of the present moment and nothing more.

'What now?' asks Ludwig.

'We should start as soon as possible.'

'Right away, then,' says Ludwig calmly. He goes with the doctor into his consulting room.

I stay in the waiting room and systematically tear up a couple of issues of the *Weekly News*, which are full of nothing but parades, victories and the pompous utterings of clergymen full of enthusiasm for the war.

Ludwig comes back. I whisper to him: 'Why don't you go to another doctor? This one here can't be any good. He hasn't got a clue.' He shakes his head wearily and we go down the steps in silence. When we get to the bottom he turns his face away and says very suddenly: 'Well, cheerio, then ...'

I look up. He's leaning against the railings, his hands plunged hard into his pockets.

'What's the matter?' I ask, taken aback.

'I'm going now,' he replies.

'Well, at least give me your paw,' I say, still bewildered. But his lip trembles as he puts me off: 'You won't want to touch me now, will you ...?'

He is standing by the railings, a shy, slim figure, in exactly the same attitude as when he used to lean against the parados, sad-faced and with his eyes lowered.

'Ludwig, Ludwig, what have they done to us! Not touch you – me? You idiot, you silly goat, look, I'm touching you, I'll touch you a hundred times ...' I'm so affected, damn it, that I could burst into tears myself, fool that I am. And I put my arm round his shoulder and press against him and feel how he is shivering. 'Oh, Ludwig, it's all nonsense, and anyway, maybe I've got it myself, don't worry, that old spectacled cobra of a doctor up there, he'll sort everything out for you …' and he shivers and shivers and I hold him tightly.

2

It has been announced that there will be some kind of demonstration in the town this afternoon. For months prices have been rising, and poverty is worse than it was during the war. Earnings are not enough to provide the absolute basics, and even if you *do* have money, quite often there is nothing to buy with it. But more and more drinking places and dance halls are popping up, and profiteering and fraud is getting more and more common.

Individual groups of striking workers march through the streets. Every so often there is a disturbance. The word is that troops have been mustered in the barracks. However, there haven't been any signs of that yet.

There are shouts in favour of things or against things. Someone is making a speech on a street corner. Then suddenly everything goes quiet.

A procession of men in faded front-line uniforms makes its way slowly along. They are formed into groups, four in a row. Large white placards are carried at the head of the parade: 'Where is the country's gratitude?' 'The war-wounded are starving'.

The placards are being carried by one-armed men. They keep looking round to make sure that the procession is still behind them, because they are the ones that can move fastest.

They are followed by men with guide dogs on short leather leashes. The dogs all have the red cross of the blind on their harnesses. They walk along carefully beside their masters. Whenever the procession stops, they sit down at once. Every so often dogs from the street rush into the procession, yapping and wagging their tails, wanting to play or romp about with them. But they turn their heads aside and take no notice of all the sniffing and barking. Their ears are certainly acute, up and listening, and their eyes are lively; but they walk along as if they never want to run and jump ever again, as if they can really understand what their job is. They are as different from their fellow canines as the Sisters of Mercy would be from a group of cheerful shop girls. And the other dogs don't keep at it for long; after a few minutes they give up and rush off so quickly that it looks as if they are running away from something. Just one great big beast stays there, standing with his forelegs spread wide, barking slowly and deeply and sadly until the procession has gone past.

It's strange – these men have all been blinded in battle and for that reason they move differently from people who were born blind. Their movements are more erratic, but at the same time more cautious, and they haven't yet acquired the sureness that comes from years in the dark. Memories are still alive within them of colours, the sky, the earth, twilight. They are still moving as if they could see; they lift and turn their heads involuntarily, to look at whoever is talking to them. Some of them have black patches or bandages over their eyes, but the majority go without, as if that way they would be just a little bit closer to colours and to the light. The pale red evening sky is shimmering behind their lowered heads. The lights are starting to come on in the shop windows. But these men hardly feel the mild and gentle evening air on their foreheads; they move slowly with their heavy boots through the everlasting darkness that has spread around them like a cloud, and their worried but persistent thoughts revolve constantly around the small sums of money which are supposed to suffice for bread and board and living, but which simply don't. Hunger and poverty move wearily through the darkened chambers of their minds. Helpless and full of dull fear they are aware of them, but they can't see them and are powerless to do anything against them but to march slowly through the streets together and lift their dead faces to the light, silently imploring those who still can see, at least to see them.

Behind the blind come those with one eye, the shattered faces of those with head wounds, mouths crooked and bulging, faces without noses or with their lower jaws shot away, the whole face a mass of scarlet scar tissue with a few holes where the nose and mouth used to be. But above all this destruction there are quiet, sad and questioning human eyes.

These are followed by long lines of those who have lost a leg. Many already have artificial limbs which seem hard to control as they walk, and come down on the pavement with a rattling noise, as if the whole person were artificial, made of hinged metal pieces.

Next come the shell-shocked. Their hands, their heads, their clothes, their whole bodies are shaking as if they were still shivering with horror. They no longer have any control over this shaking, their will has just gone and the muscles and nerves have simply declared war on the brain, their eyes are dulled and impotent.

Those with only one eye or only one arm push along the really seriously wounded in small wicker invalid-carriages with oilcloth covers, the ones who can only survive now in wheelchairs. Among these, some men are pulling along a flat handcart, of the sort joiners use for transporting bedsteads or coffins. On it there is a torso. The legs are completely gone. There is just the top part of a powerfully built man, nothing else. He has a sturdy back and a broad, honest face with a large moustache. He could have been a furniture-removal man. Beside him he has a placard which he probably made himself, which says in crooked writing: 'I'd rather walk too, my friend.' The man sits there with a serious look on his face; only occasionally does he push up on his arms and shift along a little on his cart to change his position.

The procession moves slowly through the streets. There is always a hush when it passes. Once it has to stop for a long time, at the corner of Haken Street. They are building a large, new *palais de danse* there, and the street is blocked with piles of sand, lorryloads of cement, and scaffolding. Between the iron bars of the scaffolding you can already see the name blazing out in bright red lights: The Astoria, Cocktails and Dancing. The handcart with the torso stops directly underneath this and has to wait as a couple of iron scaffolding poles are taken out. The dark glow of the sign shines over the man as he watches silently, turning his face a deep red, as if suffused by some dreadful passion that might burst out at any minute in a terrible scream.

But then the procession gets going again, and once again the face becomes that of a furniture-removal man, hospital-pale in the pale evening, smiling gratefully when one of his pals puts a cigarette between his lips. The groups move on through the streets without any chanting, without indignation, completely composed. This is resignation, not accusation – they know that if you can't shoot any more, then you can't expect much in the way of assistance. They will go to the town hall and stand there for a while, then some minor civil servant will come and say something to them, then they will split up and go back, each to his own room, to their small lodgings, to their pale children and grey poverty, without very much hope – prisoners of a fate imposed on them by other people.

* * *

The later it gets, the more unrest there is in the town. I walk through the streets with Albert. There are groups of people at every corner. Rumours are buzzing around. Soldiers are supposed to have clashed already with a workers' protest march, we hear.

From the area near St Mary's Church there is the sudden sound of gunfire, single shots at first, and then a whole salvo. Albert and I look at each other, then without a word we set off in the direction of the firing.

We meet more and more people coming the other way, towards us. 'Get your weapons, the bastards are shooting,' they scream. We move faster. We wind our way between the groups and push on further and now we are running, a hard, dangerous agitation is driving us forward. We are panting. The rattle increases. 'Ludwig!' I shout.

He's running along with us. His lips are pressed tightly together, his chin jutting out, his eyes cold and tense – his face is the face of the trenches again. So is Albert's. So is mine. We are all running towards the sound of firing as if it were some kind of strange and compelling signal.

The crowds give way to us, screaming. We push our way through. Women hold their aprons over their faces and rush away. There is a roar of rage. A wounded man is carried off.

We get to the market square. The military have taken up a position in front of the town hall. Their steel helmets reflect the pale light. By the steps leading up to the town hall there is a machine gun, ready to fire. The square is empty, but in the streets which lead onto it there are throngs of people. It would be crazy to go any further. The gun has the whole square covered.

But one man walks out there, quite alone. Behind him the masses mill around the ends of the streets, then trickle out around the houses and close up in a solid black group.

But the man is a long way ahead of them. In the middle of the square he steps out of the shadow of the church into the moonlight. A clear, sharp voice calls out: 'Get back!'

The man puts his hands in the air. The moonlight is so strong that you can see his teeth sparkling white in the darkness of his mouth when he begins to speak: 'Comrades ...' Everything goes quiet.

His voice is all alone, there between the church, the massive solidity of the town hall and the shadows, it is alone in the square, a fluttering dove. 'Comrades, put your weapons down! Do you want to shoot at your brothers? Put your weapons down and come over to us!'

The moon has never been so bright. The uniforms on the steps of the town hall are the colour of chalk. The windows reflect the light. The side of the church tower that is lit up by the moon is a mirror of green silk. The stone knights around the portal leap forward out of the bank of shadows with their helmets and visors gleaming.

'Get back or we'll fire!' comes the cold order from the first voice we had heard. I look round at Ludwig and Albert. That was our company commander! That was Heel's voice! A choking apprehension takes hold of me, as if I were being forced to watch an execution. I know that Heel will give the order to shoot.

The dark mass of people shifts about a little in the shadows of the houses, wavering and murmuring. An eternity passes. Then two soldiers with rifles move away from the steps and go straight for the lone man in the middle of the square. It seems an endlessly long time before they get to him, it looks as if they are struggling in grey quicksand, unable to move onward, two shiny rag dolls with their loaded rifles lowered. The man waits for them calmly. When they get to him he repeats: 'Comrades ...'

They grab him under the arms and pull him forward. The man offers no resistance. They drag him along so fast that he stumbles. Then there are harsh cries behind him as the mass of people begins to move and a whole street pushes forward, slowly and jerkily. The high and cold voice gives the order: 'Get him back quickly! I'll give the order to fire!

A warning salvo goes off into the air. Suddenly the man tears himself away, but he doesn't try to save himself, he runs crosswise towards the machine gun. 'Don't shoot, comrades!'

Nothing has happened yet, but when the crowd of people see the unarmed man continuing to run forward, they move forward too. The crowd wriggles along in a narrow line past the side of the church. The next moment an order is barked out over the square and the thunderous rat-tat-tat of machine-gun fire breaks up into a thousand echoes against the buildings, and bullets whistle and splinter as they hit the pavements.

Quick as lightning we have thrown ourselves behind a protruding house-front. A paralysing, cowering terror came over me in the first moments, quite different from anything I ever felt at the front. Then it turns into pure rage. I could still see the lone man spinning round and falling forward. I peer cautiously round the corner. He is trying now to push himself up, but he can't manage it. Slowly his arms give way, his head droops and then, as if he were desperately tired, his whole body slips down onto the pavement – and with that the constriction in my throat disappears and I scream out: 'No! No!' The cry sounds harsh and shrill between the walls of the houses.

Then I feel myself being pushed aside. Ludwig Breyer stands up and walks across the square towards the dark patch of death.

'Ludwig!' I shout.

But he walks further, further. I watch him in horror.

'Get back,' comes the order from the town-hall steps again.

Ludwig pauses for a moment. 'Just give the order to carry on firing, Lieutenant Heel,' he calls across to the town hall. Then he walks forward and bends down over the man lying on the ground.

We see an officer come down from the town-hall steps. Somehow or other we suddenly find ourselves standing beside Ludwig and waiting for the man, whose only weapon is a stick. He does not hesitate for a moment, even though there are three of us and we could easily drag him away, because his troops wouldn't dare to shoot for fear of hitting him.

Ludwig stands up again. 'My congratulations, Lieutenant Heel. The man is dead.'

A stream of blood is running down from under the tunic of the dead man, and trickles into the gaps between the paving stones. A pool of blood, black in the moonlight, gathers around his thin and yellow right hand, which is sticking out of his sleeve.

'Breyer,' says Heel.

'Do you know who the man is?' asks Ludwig.

Heel looks at him and shakes his head.

'Max Weil.'

'I wanted him to get away,' says Heel after a little while, almost pensively.

'He's dead,' says Ludwig.

Heel shrugs.

'He was one of our men,' Ludwig continues.

Heel says nothing.

Ludwig looks at him coldly. 'A fine piece of work.'

Then Heel gets a grip on himself. 'That's not the point,' he says calmly, 'it's only about keeping order.'

'The point ...' repeats Ludwig bitterly. 'Since when did you ever try to justify yourself? The point? You just need to look as if you're doing something, that's all. Call your men off so that there is no more shooting!'

Heel makes an impatient gesture. 'My men are staying where they are. If they pull back now, tomorrow they'd be overrun by a mob ten times the size. In five minutes' time I'm taking control of all the neighbouring streets. You've got till then to take the dead man away.'

'Pick him up,' says Ludwig to us. Then he turns to Heel again. 'If you withdraw now, nobody will attack you. If you stay, there'll be more dead. And it will be your fault. You do know that?'

'Yes, I know that,' replies Heel coldly.

For a second we stand facing each other. Heel looks at us one by one. It is a strange moment. Something snaps.

Then we pick up the limp body of Max Weil and carry him off. The streets are full of people again. A broad pathway opens up for us as we go through. Shouts ring out: 'Reactionary bastards! Hired thugs! Murderers!' Blood drips from Max Weil's back.

We take him to the nearest building. It's the Holland Bar and Dance Hall. A couple of medical orderlies are there already, bandaging up two people who are lying on the dance floor. A woman with blood on her apron is groaning and wanting to go home. They have trouble keeping her there until they can get a stretcher and find a doctor. She's been shot in the stomach. Beside her lies a man who is still wearing his old army tunic. He's been shot in both knees. His wife is crouched down beside him and keeps whimpering: 'He wasn't doing anything! He was just going past! I was just bringing him his dinner!' She points to an enamel billycan. 'Just bringing his dinner ...'

The girls paid to work as dancing partners at the Holland Bar are huddled in one corner. The manager is running about in agitation, asking whether they couldn't take the wounded somewhere else.

His business will be ruined, he says, if this gets around, nobody will want to come there for a dance ever again. Anton Demuth in his magnificent gold-braided porter's uniform has been to find a bottle of brandy and is holding it to the mouth of the wounded man. The manager looks on in horror and tries to wave him away. Anton ignores him. 'Do you think they'll be able to save my legs?' asks the injured man. 'I'm a chauffeur!'

The stretchers arrive. Outside more shots are rattling away. We jump up. Then there are howls, screams and the sound of breaking glass. We run outside. Somebody shouts: 'Rip up the paving stones!' and brings a pickaxe down on them. Mattresses are thrown out, chairs, a pram. There are more shots, flashes from the square. And now shots are being returned from the rooftops.

'Put those lights out!' A man rushes forward and throws a brick. It goes dark at once. 'Kosole!' shouts Albert. He's there. Valentin is with him. The firing has drawn us all in, like a whirlpool. 'Go for them, Ernst, Ludwig, Albert!' roars Kosole. 'The bastards are shooting at women!'

We lie up in doorways, bullets lash the ground, people scream, it takes us over, we are swept along, devastated, raging with hatred, there is blood on the paving stones, we are soldiers again, it has us in its grip once more and the war rages over us, full of noise and fury, and in us, and between us – it's all finished, all the comradeship has been shot to bits by machine-gun fire, soldiers are shooting at soldiers, comrades at comrades, it's over, it's over.

3

Adolf Bethke has sold his house and moved into the town.

After he had let his wife move back in again, things went well for a while. He did his work, she did hers, and it looked as if things would get back to normal.

Only that's when the village malice started. If his wife went into the street after dark things would be called out; lads meeting her would laugh suggestively to her face; the women would twitch their skirts in an unmistakable gesture. She never told Adolf anything of this. But it got her down, and she got paler by the day.

It was the same for Adolf. If he went into the pub, the conversation would stop; if he went to visit anyone, he'd be met with an embarrassed silence. Gradually the unasked questions began to emerge; when people had had a few drinks there would be dubious innuendoes, and sometimes he'd be laughed at behind his back. He didn't really know what to do; why should he have to defend himself against the whole village over something that was his business alone, something not even understood by the pastor, who looked him up and down disapprovingly over his gold-rimmed glasses whenever he met him? It tortured him; but Adolf, too, kept quiet and never spoke to his wife about it.

They lived like this, side by side, until one Sunday evening the mob went further than usual and someone shouted something at his wife in Adolf's presence. Adolf was furious, but she put her hand on his arm. 'Leave it, they do that so often that I don't really notice it any longer.'

'Often?' All at once he understood why she had become so quiet. He leapt up in a rage to grab at least one of the name-callers. But they disappeared behind the others, who closed ranks to help them.

They went home and went to bed in silence. Adolf just stared ahead. Then he heard a soft, suppressed noise. His wife was crying, beneath the bedclothes. Maybe she had lain there like that many a time while he was asleep. 'Don't worry, Marie,' he said quietly, 'it's only talk.' But she went on crying.

He felt helpless and alone. The darkness outside the window was hostile and the trees rustled their leaves like gossipy old women. He laid his hand gently on his wife's shoulder. She looked at him with a tear-stained face. 'Adolf, let me go away, then they'll stop ...'

She got up, the candle was still burning and her shadow loomed up across the room and over the walls; in contrast she herself looked small and feeble in the dim light. She sat down on the edge of the bed and picked up her stockings and her blouse. Like some strange giant her shadow followed her movement, like a silent visitation that had come in through the window from the darkness lurking outside, and that was now imitating her every movement, grotesque, distorted and sniggering with mockery – at any moment it would fall upon its prey and drag her out into the churning darkness.

Adolf jumped up and pulled the thick white curtains across the window, as if that way he could barricade the little room against the night, which was staring through the black squares of the window with greedy, owlish eyes.

His wife had already put on her stockings and was reaching out for her slip. Adolf came and stood in front of her. 'But, Marie ...' She looked up and lowered her hand. The slip fell to the floor. Adolf saw the misery in her eyes, the misery of a dumb creature, the misery of an animal that has been beaten, the utterly hopeless misery of those unable to defend themselves. He put his arm round his wife's shoulder. How soft and warm she was, how could anyone throw stones at her – weren't they both well-meaning people? Why were they tormenting and persecuting them so mercilessly? He

232

pulled her towards him and she did not resist, she put her arms round his neck and laid her head on his chest. And they stood there, both shivering in their nightclothes, and felt the presence of one another and each wanted to find comfort in the warmth of the other. They sat on the bed and spoke little, and when the shadows flickered again on the wall in front of them because the candle's wick had bent and the flame was about to go out, Adolf drew his wife back into bed with a tender gesture that meant: we are staying together, we're going to try again – and he said: 'We're leaving here, Marie.' That was the answer.

'Yes, Adolf, let's get away!' She threw herself onto him and now for the first time she wept out loud. He held her tightly and kept repeating: 'Tomorrow we'll look for a buyer – first thing tomorrow …' And in a confusion of plans, hope, anger and sadness he took her, despair turned into fire, until at last she was quiet, and her weeping gradually subsided like a child's until in the end it died away completely in exhaustion, and she was breathing peacefully.

The candle had gone out, the shadows had disappeared, his wife was asleep, but Adolf lay awake for a long time turning things over in his mind. Late in the night his wife woke up and realised that she was still wearing the stockings she had put on when she was intending to leave. She pulled them off and smoothed them over before putting them on the chair by the bed.

Two days later Adolf sold his house and workshop. A short time after that he found a flat in the town. The furniture was loaded up for removal. The dog had to be left behind. Hardest of all, however, was parting from the garden. It wasn't so easy to leave after all, and Adolf had no idea what would come of it. But his wife was quietly ready.

★ ★ ★

The tenement in the town is damp and dark, the stairwell is dirty and there is a pervasive smell of laundry, the atmosphere thick with feuding between neighbours and badly aired rooms. There isn't

233

much work, so there is that much more time for brooding. Neither of them is happy. It's as if everything had just followed them here.

Adolf sits around in the kitchen and can't understand why things don't change. Whenever they sit facing one another in the evening, after the paper has been read and the meal cleared away from the table, then the emptiness and melancholy of the place returns and Adolf's head spins with listening and thinking about it all. His wife busies herself, cleaning the oven, and when he says, 'Come here, Marie,' she puts down the dishcloth and the scourer and comes to him, and when he draws her down and whispers, pitifully alone, 'We'll get there,' she nods, but she's still quiet, not as cheerful as he would like. He doesn't realise that it is as much to do with him as with her that they drifted apart from each other during those four years of separation, and that now each of them is wearing the other down. He snaps at her: 'Just say something.' She is shocked and says whatever comes into her head; after all, what is she supposed to say, what would ever happen in this house, in this kitchen, that you could talk about? And with two people, when things get to a point where they actually have to try and find something to say to each other, then they will never be able to say enough to make it right. Talking is good when it is based on happiness, when it flows easily and is lively, but how can words – always changeable, always liable to be misunderstood – help when they just have unhappiness at their root? They only make things worse.

Adolf watches his wife's movements, and he sees behind them a different, young, happy woman, the wife of his memory, the one he can't forget. Suspicion flares up in him and he snaps in irritation: 'I suppose you're still thinking of him, then?' And when she looks at him wide-eyed, he realises he's said the wrong thing and it's precisely that which makes him push it even further: 'That must be it, you were a different person before! Why did you come back? After all, you could have stayed with him!'

Every word hurts him too, but what's the point of keeping quiet? He goes on talking until his wife is standing in the corner by the sink where there is no light, and crying again like a lost child. Oh, we're all children, lost, silly children, and all around our house the night is always there.

He can't stand it, he goes out and wanders the streets aimlessly, he stands in front of shop windows without seeing a thing, he goes on to where there is light. The electric trams ring their bells, cars rush past, people bump into him, and there under the yellow light of the lamps are the whores. They wriggle their plump bottoms and laugh and link arms with one another and he asks: 'Are you feeling happy?' and then he goes off with them, just glad to see and hear something different. But afterwards he just stands around, he doesn't want to go home and he would really like to go home, he goes from bar to bar and gets drunk.

That's how I find him, and I listen and I watch him as he sits there dull-eyed, stumbling over words, still drinking: Adolf Bethke, the best and most efficient of soldiers, the truest comrade in arms, who helped so many men and saved so many lives. Protector, comforter, mother and brother – often he was all these things to me at the front, when the Verey lights went up and your nerves were shattered by attacks and death. We slept side by side in wet dugouts, and he covered me up when I was ill, he could do everything, he always knew the answer – but now he's hanging on the wire and his hands and face are torn and the light has already gone from his eyes.

'Christ, Ernst,' he says in a despairing voice, 'if only we'd stayed out there at the front – at least we were all together ...' I don't say anything, I just look down at my sleeve, where there are a couple of fading reddish bloodstains. It's the blood of Max Weil, killed on the orders of Heel. That's how far we've gone. We're at war again, but the old comradeship is dead.

4

Tjaden is celebrating his marriage into the horse-butchery business. It has turned into a real gold mine, and Tjaden's affection for Marie-my-love has grown in direct proportion.

In the morning the happy couple travel to the wedding in a black shiny coach decorated with white silk which is, of course, a four-in-hand, as is only fitting for a business that makes its money from horses. Willy and Kosole have been chosen as groomsmen and witnesses. For the occasion Willy has bought a pair of white gloves in pure cotton. This involved a lot of effort. First of all Karl had to get hold of a dozen clothing coupons for him, and then it took two days to find a pair, since none of the shops stocked any in Willy's size. But it was all worth it, because the dazzling white flour sacks that he eventually got hold of set off amazingly his newly dyed cutaway. Tjaden is wearing tails and Marie-my-love has a wedding dress with a train and a wreath of myrtle.

Just before they set off for the registry office there is another incident. Kosole arrives, sees Tjaden in his tailcoat and can't stop laughing. Hardly has he managed – more or less – to control himself than he looks over at Tjaden again and notices his sticking-out ears pink and glowing over his high collar, and this sets him off all over again. There's nothing for it – he'd be bound to roar with laughter in the middle of the church service later on and put the whole wedding in jeopardy, so at the last minute I have to take over from him as the second groomsman.

The whole horse-butchery establishment has been decorated for the occasion. At the entrance there are tubs of flowers and greenery, and even the slaughterhouse has a great garland of fir branches, onto which Willy, to general acclamation, puts a sign saying 'Welcome!'

It goes without saying that there isn't any horsemeat on the menu; there are dishes of the finest pork, and a huge side of roast beef is carved and ready for us.

After the roast, Tjaden takes off his tailcoat and stiff collar. This allows Kosole to tuck in more effectively, because up to now he hasn't dared to look in that direction for fear of another fit of choking. We all follow Tjaden's example, and things become far more relaxed.

Later on the father-in-law reads out a document which makes Tjaden a partner in the butchery. We congratulate him, and then Willy brings in our wedding present, carrying it carefully with his white gloves on: a brass tray with a set of twelve cut-glass schnapps glasses. With it come three bottles of cognac from Karl's supplies.

In the evening Ludwig drops in for a little while. At the insistence of Tjaden he has come along in uniform, because Tjaden wants to show his people that one of his friends is a real lieutenant. But he soon leaves again. The rest of us stay put, however, till there is nothing left on the table but bones and empty bottles.

★ ★ ★

By the time we are back out in the street it is midnight. Albert suggests we go on to Cafe Gräger.

'That will have closed long ago,' says Willy.

'We can get in round the back,' insists Albert. 'Karl knows the score.'

None of us really fancies it, but Albert keeps on for such a long time that in the end we give in. I'm rather surprised by this, because usually he's the first to want to get off home.

Although it's dark and quiet at the front of the cafe, we find it full and busy when we go through the courtyards and in the back door.

Gräger's is the local for all the black marketeers, and almost every night they keep going until morning.

One part of the room has separate booths with red velvet curtains. That's the wine-drinking section. Most of the curtains are pulled across. Squeals and laughter can be heard from some of them. Willy grins from ear to ear. 'Gräger's own little red-light district.'

We find somewhere to sit nearer to the front of the place. The cafe is packed. On the right are the tables where the whores sit. Wherever business flourishes, so does carnal delight. Because of that, even the twelve tarts here are not enough for the demand. Mind you, they do have some competition. Karl points Mrs Nickel out to us, a dark and voluptuous-looking piece. Her husband is only a small-time opportunist profiteer, and without her he'd have starved. She provides him with valuable assistance by having preliminary meetings with his business partners at their flat on a one-to-one basis, usually for an hour at a time.

At every table there is a lively toing and froing, confidential conversations, whispering, arguments and generally noisy chaos. Men with high-quality English suits and new hats are being drawn aside into corners by others with casual jackets and no collar, packages and samples are mysteriously appearing from pockets, are looked at, rejected, offered again; notebooks come out, pencils are in motion, every so often somebody rushes to the telephone or goes outside, and the air is buzzing with truckloads, kilos, butter, herrings, bacon, medicines, dollars, guilders, shares and figures.

Just beside us a particularly vigorous debate is going on about a truckload of coal. But Karl makes a dismissive gesture. 'That stuff's all just castles in the air. One man has heard something somewhere, another one passes it on, a third gets a fourth interested, they all scurry around and make themselves look big, but there's usually nothing behind it all. These are just hangers-on, trying to pick up a bit of commission. The real kings of the black market will only do business with one middleman, or at the most two, and then only people they know. That fat bloke over there bought two truckloads of eggs in Poland yesterday. They're supposedly being transported to Holland, but on the way the documentation will be altered and then they'll turn up back here as ultra-fresh Dutch new-laid eggs at three times the price. The ones down at the front are cocaine dealers, so of course they're making an absolute mint. Over on the left is Diederichs – he only deals in bacon. That's a pretty good line as well.'

'And because of those bastards we have to go hungry,' growls Willy.

'You'd have to anyway, without their help,' counters Karl. 'Only last week ten barrels of butter from the regular market had to be sold off by the authorities because it had gone rancid by being left standing for so long. Same thing with grain. Bartscher was able to buy up a couple of cartloads of corn for next to nothing because the barn where the officials had had it stored was so decrepit that the rain soaked it and made it go mouldy.'

'What did you say his name was?' asks Albert.

'Bartscher. Julius Bartscher.'

'Does he come here a lot?'

'Yes, I think so,' says Karl. 'Do you want to do business with him?' Albert shakes his head. 'Has he got money?'

'Absolutely rolling in it,' replies Karl, with a certain respect in his voice.

'Hey, look, here comes Arthur Ledderhose,' calls out Willy with a laugh.

The bright yellow raincoat emerges from the background. One or two people get up and hurry towards him. Ledderhose pushes them aside, favours one or two others with a greeting, and walks on through the tables like a general. I am astonished to notice what a hard, unpleasant expression his face now has, and it is still there even when he is smiling.

He greets us rather condescendingly. 'Sit down, Arthur,' grins Willy. Ledderhose hesitates, but he can't resist the temptation, here on his own territory, to show off to us how important he has become.

'Just for a minute, then,' he says, and sits down in Albert's place. Albert is wandering through the cafe as if he were looking for someone. I wonder if I should go after him, but I decide not to because it occurs to me that he might simply need to go out into the yard to find the gents. Ledderhose orders some schnapps, and starts to discuss a deal involving ten thousand army boots and twenty loads of scrap with a man whose hands are flashing with diamonds. Every so often Arthur glances at us to make sure that we are hearing it all.

Albert, however, is walking along past the little curtained-off booths. Someone told him something that he can't believe, but which he hasn't been able to get out of his mind all day. When he peers through a gap into the last booth but one he suddenly feels as if a gigantic axe is falling on him, and he rips the curtain aside.

On the table are champagne glasses, there is a bouquet of roses nearby, the tablecloth has been pushed aside and is half hanging onto the floor. Behind the table there is a blonde girl in a deep armchair. Her dress is half off, her hair rumpled, her breasts still bare. She has her back to Albert and she's humming a popular song as she combs her hair in front of a little mirror.

'Lucie,' says Albert hoarsely.

She spins round and stares at him as if she has seen a ghost. She tries awkwardly to smile, but the attempt dies on her lips as she sees Albert staring at her bare breasts. Lies are not going to help her now. Frightened, she hides herself behind the chair. 'Albert ... it wasn't my fault ...' she stammers, 'him, it was him ...' and then all at once she gabbles out very quickly: 'He got me drunk, Albert, I didn't want to do it, he just kept giving me more to drink, I didn't know what was happening any more, I swear to you.'

Albert doesn't say anything.

'What's going on?' asks someone behind him. Bartscher has come back from the yard and is swaying a bit. He blows a cloud of cigar smoke into Albert's face. 'Trying it on, eh? Go on, piss off!'

Albert stands there in front of him for a moment as if turned to stone. The man's bulging belly, the check pattern of his brown suit, his gold watch chain and his broad, red face burn themselves with awful clarity into Albert's brain.

At that moment Willy happens to glance up from our table, and is on his feet at once and sprinting through the place, knocking people aside. But it is too late. Before he can get there, Albert has his service revolver in his hand and shoots. We all run across.

Bartscher had tried to shield himself with a chair, but he only managed to get it up to the level of his eyes. Albert's shot is half an inch above that, in his forehead. He barely needed to take aim – he was always the best shot in the company, and he's been using small-arms for years.

Bartscher crashes to the floor. His feet twitch. The shot was a fatal one. The girl screams. 'Out of here!' shouts Willy and keeps back the crowd of customers. We grab Albert, who is standing there motionless staring at the girl, and drag him through the courtyard, over the street and round the next corner, where two furniture vans are standing. Willy comes after us. 'You've got to disappear right away, tonight,' he gasps breathlessly.

Albert looks at him as if he has just woken up. Then he pushes us aside. 'It's all right, Willy,' he replies woodenly. 'I know what I've got to do now.'

'Are you crazy?' snorts Kosole.

Albert is a little unsteady on his feet. We hold on to him. He brushes us off again. 'No, Ferdinand,' he says quietly, as if he were just very tired, 'if you start something, then you've got to finish it as well.'

He goes off slowly down the street.

Willy runs after him and tries to talk him round. But he shakes his head and goes round the corner into Mühlen Street. Willy follows him.

'We'll have to drag him back by force,' says Kosole, 'he's quite capable of going straight to the police.'

'I don't think we can do anything, Ferdinand,' says Karl wretchedly, 'I know Albert.'

'But that isn't going to bring the man back to life,' shouts Ferdinand. 'What good will it do? Albert has to get away!'

We sit down, not speaking, waiting for Willy to come back.

'How could he do such a thing?' asks Kosole after a while.

'That girl just meant so much to him,' I tell them.

Willy comes back alone. Kosole leaps up. 'Did he get away?'

Willy doesn't look at us. 'Gone to the police. No one could have stopped him. He was almost ready to shoot *me* when I tried to drag him back.'

'Hell and damnation!' Kosole puts his head down on the edge of a cart. Willy flops down onto the grass verge. Karl and I lean against the sides of furniture vans.

Kosole, Ferdinand Kosole, is sobbing like a child.

5

A shot has been fired, one stone has shaken itself loose, a dark hand has plunged in between us all. We were running away from a shadow, but we were running in a circle and the shadow has caught up with us.

We've complained and we've tried, we've hardened ourselves and we've given way, we've dodged and we've dived straight in, we've lost our way and still carried on – but all the time we felt that shadow close behind us and tried to get away from it. We thought it was chasing after us, and we didn't realise that we had dragged it along with us, that wherever we were, it was there as well, silent, that it wasn't behind us but inside us, in our very selves.

We wanted to build houses, we were longing for gardens and terraces, we wanted to see the sea and feel the wind; but we never gave thought to the fact that houses need foundations. We were like the deserted, shell-cratered battlefields in France; they are just as quiet as the ploughed fields all around them, but deep inside them is all the discarded explosive material, shells and grenades, and for as long as it takes to dig it all out and clear it away, ploughing will be a precarious and perilous activity.

We are still soldiers, even though we didn't realise it. If Albert had had a peaceful and uninterrupted youth he might have had lots of things that were comforting and familiar, which would have grown up with him and sustained him and protected him. But as it is, everything was broken, and when he came back he had nothing – his whole repressed youth, his battered and damaged sense of longing, and his need for a home and for some tenderness, it was all thrown blindly at this one person, with whom he thought he was in love. And when it all fell to pieces he couldn't do anything but shoot – because he had never learned anything else. If he had never been a soldier he might have had lots of other ways of coping. But in the event his hand never even shook – he'd been used to hitting the target for years.

Inside Albert the young dreamer, inside Albert the shy lover, there was still Albert the soldier.

★ ★ ★

The wrinkled old lady can't comprehend it. 'How could he do such a thing? He was always such a quiet boy.' The ribbons on her old-fashioned hat are trembling, her handkerchief is trembling, her black veil is trembling – her whole person is shaking in complete misery. 'Maybe it happened because he hasn't got a father. He was only four when his father died. But he was always such a good, quiet boy ...'

'He still is, Mrs Trosske,' I say. She seizes on this and starts talking about Albert's childhood. She has to talk, she can't cope, the neighbours have been in, people they know, a couple of teachers, none of them can understand it.

'They should all keep their traps shut,' I say, 'they're all partly to blame.'

She looks at me uncomprehendingly. But then she goes on telling me about how Albert learned to walk, how he never screamed like other children, that he was almost too quiet for a boy – and now something like this! How could he do such a thing?

Bewildered, I look at her. She doesn't know anything about Albert. Maybe it would be exactly the same with my own mother. I suppose mothers are only able to love, that's the only understanding they have.

'You have to remember, Mrs Trosske,' I say carefully, 'Albert was in the war ...'

'Yes,' she replies, 'yes, yes …' She doesn't see the connection. 'This Bartscher, he was a bad man, wasn't he?' she asks softly.

'He was a rat,' I assure her at once, because as far as I am concerned that isn't really the point.

She nods, still crying. 'I couldn't even begin to understand it otherwise. He never hurt a fly. Now Hans, he used to pull their wings off, but Albert never did. What are they likely to do to him now?'

'Nothing much can happen to him,' I reassure her, 'he was pretty provoked, and that almost makes it self-defence.'

'Thank God,' she sighs. 'The tailor who lives upstairs, he says he'll get the death penalty.'

'The tailor is an idiot,' I say.

'Yes, and he said that Albert is a murderer.' She breaks down. 'And he isn't one and never could be, never, never!'

'I'll sort out this tailor of yours,' I say angrily.

'I'm frightened to leave the house now,' she sobs, 'he's always standing waiting.'

'I'll see you back home, Mrs Trosske,' I say.

When we get to the block where she lives, the old lady whispers nervously, 'There he is again,' and points to the main door. I brace myself. If he utters a single sound I'll beat him to a pulp, even if I get ten years for it. But he gets out of our way, as do the two women hanging around with him.

In the apartment Albert's mother shows me another picture of him and Hans when they were boys. Then she starts crying again, but soon stops as if she were ashamed of doing so. Old women are like children in that respect; the tears come quickly, but they can equally quickly get over it. In the corridor she asks me: 'He'll get enough to eat, won't he?'

'I'm sure he will,' I tell her. 'Karl Bröger will keep an eye on that – he can get hold of stuff.'

'I've still got some of the griddle cakes he likes so much. Do you think I'd be able to take him some?'

'You could certainly try,' I reply, 'and if they let you, then simply say to him: Albert, I know you're not guilty. Just that.'

She nods. 'Perhaps I didn't give him enough attention. But Hans lost both his feet …'

I comfort her. 'The poor boy,' she says, 'sitting there all alone …'

I give her my hand. 'I'll go and have a word with that tailor now. He won't be bothering you again.'

He's still standing by the main door. A flat, stupid, petty face. He gives me a nasty, goggle-eyed look, ready to open his gob and say all sorts of rubbish behind my back. I get hold of him by the lapels. 'Now listen, you bastard, if you say just one more word to that old lady there, I'll tear you to bits, make sure you remember that, you needle-pushing, gossiping arsehole.' I shake him as if he were a sack of old rags and push him backwards hard against the door handle. 'Otherwise I'll come back and break every bone in your body with your own flat iron, you lousy, bleating little shit!' Then I give him a good hard slap, right and then left.

I'm quite a long way away when I hear him shouting after me. 'I'll report you! That'll cost you a good hundred marks in court!' I turn round and start walking back towards him. He disappears.

★ ★ ★

Grubby and dishevelled from travelling, Georg Rahe is sitting in Ludwig's room. He'd read the news about Albert in the paper and came straight away. 'We have to get him out,' he says.

Ludwig looks up.

'If we can get half a dozen decent lads and a car,' Rahe goes on, 'we could get away with it. The best time would be when he's being taken to the courthouse. We move in, create a disturbance and two of us run off with him back to the car.'

When Ludwig has listened to this for a minute, he shakes his head. 'It's no use, Georg. We'd only cause more trouble for Albert if it went wrong. At the moment he can at least hope that he'll get off relatively lightly. But that's the least of the problems anyway – I'd be with you like a shot, but Albert, we wouldn't get Albert away. He doesn't want to go.'

'Then we'll have to take him by force,' declares Rahe after a while. 'He has to get out of there, even if I die in the attempt ...'

Ludwig doesn't make any comment.

'I don't think it would be any use either, Georg,' I tell him. 'If we did get him out he'd only want to go straight back. He came close to shooting at Willy when he tried to get him away.'

Rahe puts his head in his hands. Ludwig looks grey, his face sunken. 'I reckon we're all lost,' he says miserably.

No one says anything. Silence and sadness hang like death over the room.

Afterwards I sit with Ludwig for a long time. He has his chin in his hands. 'It's all been for nothing, Ernst. We're done for, but the world carries on as if the war never happened. It won't be long before our successors sitting in their classrooms will be listening wide-eyed to tales of the war and wishing that they could escape the boredom of school and be part of it. They're already rushing to join military movements like the Freikorps, and political murders are being committed by boys who are barely seventeen. I am so weary, Ernst ...'

'Ludwig ...' I sit down next to him and put my arm round his thin shoulders.

He smiles sadly. Then he says softly: 'Back then, before the war, there was a girl I was very keen on when I was still at school, Ernst. A week or so ago I met her again. She seemed to have become even more beautiful than she was then. It was as if the past had come back to life again in that one person. We've seen each other a few times since, but now I suddenly feel –' He puts his head down on the table. When he looks up again his eyes are agonised, dead. 'All that business is over for me, Ernst – because I'm ill ...'

He gets up and opens the window. It's a warm night outside and there are plenty of stars. I just sit there, staring dully ahead. Then he turns back to me. 'Do you remember how we used to go off wandering around the woods at night like the Romantic poets, with a volume of Eichendorff?'

'Yes, Ludwig,' I say quickly, pleased that he has a new train of thought. 'It was late in the summer. Once we caught a hedgehog.'

His face relaxes. 'And we used to believe that we could have that sort of adventure with all the trappings, post-coaches, hunting-horns and the bright stars above – remember how we wanted to run away to Italy?'

'Yes, only the post-coach that was supposed to carry us off never turned up, and we couldn't afford to go by train.'

Ludwig's face brightens and it is quite strange how cheerful he looks. 'And then we read *The Sorrows of Young Werther ...*' he says.

'And tried drinking wine,' I remind him.

He smiles. 'And then we read that long novel by Gottfried Keller – remember how we used to whisper about the heroine?'

I nod. 'And later you only ever wanted to read Hölderlin's poetry.'

There is a curious peacefulness about Ludwig now. He speaks softly and gently. 'What plans we had in those days, how noble and good we were going to be. But then we turned into a pretty poor bunch, Ernst.'

'Yes,' I say thoughtfully. 'What happened to it all?'

We lean side by side against the windowsill. The wind is caught in the cherry trees. They are rustling gently. There is a shooting star. The clock strikes twelve.

'We ought to get some sleep.' Ludwig gives me his hand. 'Goodnight, Ernst.'

'Sleep well, Ludwig.'

★ ★ ★

Late in the night I hear someone hammering on my door. Confused, I sit up with a jerk. 'Who's there?'

'It's me, Karl! Open up!'

I jump out of bed.

He rushes in. 'Ludwig ...'

I grab hold of him. 'What's the matter with Ludwig?'

'He's dead ...'

248

The room spins round me. I fall back onto the bed. 'Get a doctor!'
Karl slams a chair down on the ground so hard that it breaks.
'He's dead, Ernst … he slit his wrists.'

I don't know how I managed to get dressed and I don't know how
I got here. Suddenly I'm in a room, harsh light, blood, the unbearable
gleams and flashes from the crystals and pieces of quartz, and in
front of them, in an armchair, the endlessly weary, narrow, shrunken
form, a dreadfully pale face with half-closed eyes from which all the
light has gone …

I don't know what's happening. His mother is there, Karl is there,
someone is saying something to me, I understand I'm to stay here,
I gather that they want to fetch someone, I nod, I huddle down on
the sofa, doors are creaking, I can't move, I can't speak, suddenly I'm
alone with Ludwig and I look at him …

Karl was the last person with him. He found him quiet and almost
happy. After he had gone, Ludwig sorted out a few things and then
wrote for a while. Then he pulled his chair across to the window
and put a basin of warm water on the table beside it. He locked the
door, sat in the chair and opened his veins in the water. The pain
was only slight. He watched the blood flowing, something he had
often pictured to himself: letting this hated, poisoned blood flow
out of his body.

His room became very clear. He saw every book, every nail,
every reflection from his collections of minerals, the lights, the
colours – he experienced his room. It pushed itself forward, entered
into his breath and merged with him as they grew together. Then
it receded again. Indistinct. His youth began in a series of pictures.
Eichendorff, the woods, homesickness. Reconciled, without any
pain. Behind the woods the barbed wire rose up, little clouds of
white smoke from the shrapnel, the impact of heavy artillery fire.
But they no longer frightened him. The noises were muted, almost
like bells. The bells became louder, but the woods were still there.
The bells rang so loudly in his head that he felt he was about to

break into pieces. At the same time it got darker. Then he grew weaker and the evening came in through the window, the clouds drifted along under his feet. He had always wanted just once in his life to see flamingos in flight, and now he knew: here were those flamingos, with broad, pink-and-grey wings, many of them, flying in V-formation – hadn't he once seen wild geese flying in that formation across a red, red moon, red as the Flanders poppies? The landscape grew broader and broader, the woods sank further and further away, silvery rivers glittered, and there were islands, and the pink-and-grey wings flew higher and higher, and the horizon grew brighter and brighter – the sea ... Then suddenly a dark scream rose hotly in his throat, one last thought was sent out by his brain into his fading consciousness: fear, rescue, bind up the cut ... he tried to stagger to his feet, to lift up his hand ... his body twitched, but he was already too weak. Things went round and round, and then everything disappeared and the great bird with the dark pinions came down very softly with slow beats of its wings and folded them silently over him.

Someone's hand pushes me away. People have come back and they are taking hold of Ludwig, I pull the first of them out of the way, nobody else is to touch him. But then I see his face before me and suddenly it is very bright and cold, altered, severe, unknown – I don't recognise him any more and I stagger back and leave.

★ ★ ★

I don't know how I got back to my own room. My head is empty, my arms rest on the sides of the chair and have no strength in them.

Ludwig, I don't want to go on. I don't want to go on either. What am I supposed to do here? None of us belongs here any longer. Rootless, burnt-out, weary – why did you go away on your own?

I get up. My hands are hot. My eyes are burning. I feel feverish. My thoughts are confused. I no longer know what I am doing. 'Come and fetch me,' I whisper, 'please come and take me too!'

My teeth are chattering with the cold. My hands are clammy. I lurch forward. Great black circles appear before my eyes.

Suddenly I go stiff. Wasn't that a door opening? Wasn't that the noise of a window catch? Through the open door of my room I can see in the moonlight that there, hanging next to my violin on the wall, is my old army tunic. I move cautiously towards it, on tiptoe, so that it doesn't notice as I creep up to this grey uniform which wrecked everything – our youth and our lives. I tear it down, I want to throw it away, but then suddenly I run my hand over it and then put it on, and I feel how it takes possession of me through my skin. I shiver, my heart is beating furiously ... then a ringing sound splits the silence, I turn round with a start, take fright and press myself against the wall ...

Because in the pale light from the open door there stands a shadow. It flickers and drifts, then comes closer and waves to me; a figure takes shape, a face with dark, hollow eyes which have a broad cut gaping between them, a mouth, speaking to me soundlessly ... isn't that ...? 'Walter ...' I whisper, Walter Willenbrock, who fell at Passchendaele in August 1917 – have I gone mad? Am I dreaming? Am I ill? But then someone else pushes his way in behind him, pale, bent over, leaning forward ... Friedrich Tomberge, whose back was shattered by bits of a shell at Soissons when he was sitting on the dugout steps ... And now they all come in, with dead eyes, grey and ghostly, a whole host of shadows, they have come back and they fill the room. Franz Kemmerich, legs amputated when he was eighteen, dead three days later. Stanislaus Katczinsky, with his feet dragging and with a thin dark line trickling from his lowered head ... Gerhard Feldkamp, blown to bits by a trench mortar near Ypres, Paul Bäumer, who fell in October 1918, Heinrich Wessling, Anton Heinzmann, Haie Westhus, Otto Mathes, Franz Wagner, shadows, shadows, a long procession, an endless line ... they drift in, they settle down on the books, climb up on the window, they fill the room ...

But suddenly something breaks in on my horror and amazement, because a stronger shadow has slowly risen up, it crawls in through the door, propped up on its arms, it comes to life, grows a skeleton and then a body creeps in, teeth shine chalky-white in the dark face and now there are eyes shining in the eye sockets – raised up like a seal it crawls into the room towards me ... the English captain ... behind him trail his unwound puttees, making a rustling noise. With a slight push he manages to get up and comes towards me with hands like claws ... 'Ludwig! Ludwig!' I scream. 'Ludwig, help me!'

I grab hold of some of the piled-up books and throw them at those hands.

'Grenades, Ludwig!' I groan, then I tear the aquarium from its stand and hurl it against the door, where it smashes noisily ... but he just grins and comes closer, so I chuck the glass case with the butterflies too, then the violin, and then I grab a chair and hit out at that grin, I shout 'Ludwig! Ludwig!' and rush at the figure and burst through the doorway, the chair breaks and I rush on. There are shouts behind me, frightened cries, but the dreadful gasping is stronger and nearer, he's chasing after me, I reach the street, I feel his greedy breath on my neck, I run on, the houses are swaying. 'Help! Help!' Squares, trees, a claw on my shoulder, he's catching up with me, I roar, I howl, I stumble, uniforms, fists, raging, lightning and the dull thunder of the soft axe blades that are cutting me down ...

PART SEVEN

1

Has it been years? Or was it just weeks? The past is hovering on the horizon like a fog, or a distant thunderstorm. I was ill for a long time, and the worried face of my mother was always there after the fever had passed. But then there was a great weariness which took away any hard edges, a wakeful sleep in which all thoughts merged and dissolved, a flat surrender to the gentle song of the blood and to the warmth of the sun.

The meadows are bright in the glow of late summer. Just to lie in the meadow when the grass is higher than your face and makes up the whole world, with nothing else there except the gentle movement of the grass to the rhythms of the wind! In the places where there is only grass the wind has a soft whistling sound, like a scythe being used a long way away; and where there is sorrel is growing too, the sound is darker and deeper. You have to be quiet for a long time and listen carefully before you can hear it.

But then the quietness becomes alive. Tiny flies with red spots on their black wings crowd together on the spikes of sorrel and rock to and fro with the leaves. Bees are humming like miniature aeroplanes in the clover, and a solitary little ladybird is climbing resolutely up to the top of a sprig of shepherd's purse.

An ant crawls onto my wrist and disappears into the tunnel made by my sleeve. The ant is pulling along behind it a piece of dry grass much larger than itself. I feel the light tickling sensation on my skin and I wonder whether it is the ant or the grass on my arm making this gentle little sign of life, which gives way to a light shudder. But then a breeze blows into my sleeve and I feel that even a lover's caress would feel coarse in comparison to this breath on the skin.

Butterflies tumble about, giving themselves up to the wind so completely that it is as if they were swimming in it, white and gold sails on the gentle breeze. They linger on flowers and suddenly I look and see that two of them have settled on my chest, one like a yellow leaf with red spots, the other one with peacock-eye pattern on a deep brown velvet background. Medals awarded by the summer. I breathe out gently and slowly, but my breath still disturbs their wings; however, they stay with me. The sky is bright behind the grasses and a dragonfly is hovering with whirring wings over my shoes.

White threads of gossamer, shimmering in this Indian summer, float in the air. They catch on the stems and leaves, the wind drives them along, they are on my hands, on my clothes, they drift onto my face and over my eyes, they cover me up. My body, while still remaining my body, merges with and becomes part of the meadow. Its outlines become blurred, it no longer exists on its own, the light dissolves its contours and the edges become indistinct.

The breath of the grass rises over the leather of my shoes, the scent of the earth penetrates into the fabric of my clothes, the sky moves through my hair; the wind ... and blood beats against the skin, rising to meet the oncoming forces, my nerve endings become receptive and vibrant, and I can feel the butterflies on my chest and the footfall of the ant echoes through the hollowness of my veins ... then the wave comes over me more strongly still, the last scraps of resistance give way and I am just a nameless mound, meadow, earth ...

The silent currents of the earth circulate in an eternal cycle and my blood circulates with them, it is carried away and becomes part of all things. Through the warm darkness of the earth it flows with the voices of crystal and quartz, it is there in the secret sound of the drops of water as they sink down between the roots and collect together in little rivulets which make their way to the springs. It breaks out, with them, from the earth once again, it is there in the streams and the rivers, in the shiny riverbanks and the wide, wide sea and in the silvery droplets that the sun draws up again into the clouds, it circulates and circulates and takes more and more of me with it and washes it away into the earth and the subterranean streams – my body disappears slowly and painlessly, it has gone, there are only elements, only husks left, all else is the trickling of underground streams, the speech of the grasses, the movement of the wind, the rustle of the leaves, and the silent, sonorous skies. The meadow takes over, flowers grow through, blossoms appear above them, I have sunk away, forgotten, buried under the poppies and the yellow marsh-marigolds with the butterflies and dragonflies hovering above them ...

There is the lightest movement, the most gentle of tremors – is it the last twitch before the end? Is it the poppies and the grass? Is it just the trickle of water between the roots of the trees?

But the movement gets stronger. It becomes regular and breathes and pulses, wave after wave returns and washes everything back, back from the rivers, the trees, the greenery and the earth. The whole cycle begins again, but this time it doesn't take away, and what it brings back remains, it becomes a shudder, a sensation, feelings, hands, bodies, the husks are no longer empty – freely, lightly and with grace, the earth brings back my body ... I open my eyes ...

Where am I? Where have I been? Was I asleep? The mysterious sense of connection is still there; I listen, not daring to move. But that sense remains, and the feelings of happiness, of ease, of floating, of glowing – these all stay with me as I lie there in the meadow; the butterflies have gone, and further off the sorrel sways, and the little ladybird gets to the top of its sprig, the gossamer is still on my clothes, the uplifting feeling is still there, it rises in my breast, in my eyes, I move my hands – what happiness! I flex my legs, I sit up, there is wetness on my face; and then I realise that I am crying, weeping uncontrollably, as if a great many things had passed away and gone ...

★

I rest there for a while. Then I get up and set off in the direction of the cemetery. I haven't been there yet. This is the first time since Ludwig died that I've been allowed to go out on my own.

An old lady comes with me to show me where to find Ludwig's grave. It is behind a box hedge, and is planted with evergreens. The earth is still soft and there is a mound with a few withered wreaths leaning against it. The gold lettering on the ribbons is faded and you can barely make out what it says.

I was a little afraid to come here. But this silence holds no terrors. The wind passes over the graves, the September sky is golden behind the crosses, and a blackbird is singing in the avenue of plane trees.

Ludwig, Ludwig, today for the first time I've had an awareness of homeland and peace, and you are no longer there. I don't quite dare to believe it yet, it still might be just weakness or tiredness – but perhaps one day I'll be able to accept it, perhaps we just have to wait quietly and it will come to us of its own accord, perhaps it is the one thing that never left us; really we just have our bodies and the earth itself – and perhaps we don't need to do anything more than listen to them and follow them.

Ludwig, Ludwig, how we searched and searched, we lost our way and fell, we wanted aims, and we tripped over our own feet, we never found what we were looking for and you broke down in the attempt; and is it possible after all that a breath of wind over grass or the song of a blackbird in the evening can touch us and bring us back home? Can a cloud on the horizon or a tree in summer really have more power than all those things we so fervently wanted?

I don't know, Ludwig. I can't believe it yet, because I had already given up all hope. But then, we don't really know what it is to give ourselves up to something, we don't recognise the power of submissive acceptance. All we know is violence.

But if it were to prove itself to be a way back, Ludwig … what good is it to me if you're not there?

Evening starts to come on behind the trees. It brings back all the restlessness and the sadness. I stare down at the grave.

*

Footsteps crunch on the gravel. I look up. It is Georg Rahe. He gives me a concerned look and says I ought to go home.

'I haven't seen you for ages, Georg,' I say. 'Where have you been?'

He makes a vague gesture. 'I tried a whole lot of jobs ...'

'You're not in the army any more?' I ask.

'No,' he replies sharply.

Two women, dressed in mourning, come along the path between the plane trees. They are carrying small green watering cans, and start watering the flowers on an older grave. The sweet smell of wallflowers and fragrant mignonette wafts across to us.

Rahe looks at me. 'I thought that was where I'd still find some of the old comradeship, Ernst. But there was only a kind of distorted feeling of solidarity, a shadowy caricature of what it was like in the war. There were men who thought that if they had a secret stockpile of a dozen or so rifles they could save the country; there were out-of-work officers who didn't know what to do with themselves except turn up any time there was some kind of disturbance; and there were the eternal squaddies, cut off from everything and actively scared of having to go back to civilian life – altogether the last and the roughest leftovers of the war. In among them there were a few idealists and a whole lot of young and curious lads looking for adventure. Every one of them driven, bitter, despairing, and mistrustful of all the rest. Well, after that ...'

He says nothing for a time, and just stares ahead. I look at his face from the side. He is nervous and worn down, and there are deep shadows round his eyes. Then he shakes himself.

'I might as well tell you, Ernst – it's been going round in my head long enough. One day there we went into action. They said it was against the communists. But when I saw the dead men, they were workers, some of them still wearing their old front-line tunics and army boots, men who'd fought beside us at the front; and then something inside me just snapped. Once I knocked out half an English company in my plane, and that didn't affect me. War was war. But those dead comrades here in Germany, shot down by their own former comrades – that was the last straw for me, Ernst!'

I remember Weil and Heel, and I nod.

A chaffinch breaks into song just above us. The evening sun takes on a deeper shade of gold. Rahe chews on his cigarette. 'Yes, and then ... then a bit later, two of our men suddenly went missing. The word was that they'd been planning to give away the whereabouts of one of our weapon stores. Our so-called comrades in arms had beaten them to death in the woods at night with their rifle butts, without a hearing. They call it lynch-law. One of the two men had been a corporal of mine out at the front. A really decent bloke. So I just chucked it all in.' He looks at me. 'That's what's become of it all, Ernst. And back then, back when we all went off to the front, what a storm of enthusiasm we had then!' He throws away his cigarette. 'Bloody hell, where did it all go!' Then after a while he says quietly: 'That's what I still want to know, Ernst – how could it have turned into all this?'

We get up and walk back between the plane trees towards the gates of the cemetery. The sunlight plays in the leaves and flickers over our faces. It's all so unreal – the things we are saying and the soft, warm, late-summer air, the blackbirds and the cold breath of memory.

'So what are you doing now, Georg?' I ask.

As he walks along he knocks the downy heads off the thistles with his stick. 'I've had a good look at the whole thing, Ernst, work, ideals, politics, only I don't fit in anywhere. What is there, anyway? Everywhere you get profiteering, suspicion, indifference and boundless egotism ...'

The walk has tired me out, and when we get to the Klosterberg we sit down on a bench.

Below us the towers in the town have a green shimmer to them, there is steam coming off the roofs and silver smoke from the chimneys. Georg points down at it. 'They're all lurking there like spiders in their offices, their shops, their workplaces – every one of them ready to suck the lifeblood out of any one of the others. And what else is there, hanging over them? Families, societies, authorities, laws, the state! One spider's web on top of another! Yes, I know you

260

can call it living, and be proud to creep around underneath it all for forty years. But I learned out at the front that life can't really be determined by a length of time. What can I do that will fill up forty years? For years now I've been betting everything on a single card, and the stake was always life itself – I can't change now and play for a few coppers and not very much progress.'

'You weren't in the trenches for the last year of the war, Georg,' I say, 'and it might have been different for airmen. But often we didn't see a single enemy soldier for months on end, we were just cannon fodder. We couldn't place bets on anything, we just had to sit and wait for the bullet with our name on it.'

'But I'm not talking about the war, Ernst – I'm talking about youth and about comradeship.'

'Yes, that's all in the past,' I agree.

'It was like living in a hothouse,' says Georg thoughtfully. 'And now we've already become old men. But it's good to get things clear. I don't regret anything. I just want to draw a line under it all. There isn't any way for me now. The only thing left would be just to vegetate. But I don't want that! I want to stay free.'

'Come on, Georg, you're just saying that we've already had an ending! But now there has to be a beginning for us! I felt it today. Ludwig knew about it, but he was too ill ...'

He puts his arm round my shoulder. 'Yes, yes – you go and become a useful citizen, Ernst ...'

I lean against him. 'When you say that, it sounds slimy and unpleasant. But there must still be some kind of comradeship out there that we can't quite see yet.'

I would really like to tell him something about the feelings I had when I was in the meadow. But I can't find the right words.

We sit side by side in silence. 'What are you really going to do now, Georg?' I ask again, after a while.

He gives a thoughtful smile. 'Me, Ernst? It was only by chance that I wasn't killed – that makes me feel a bit ridiculous.'

I push his hand away and stare at him. He tries to reassure me. 'First of all I'm going away again for a bit.'

He plays with his walking stick and stares for a long time into the distance.

'Do you remember what Giesecke once said? When we visited him in the asylum over there? He wanted to go to Fleury – He wanted to go back, you see. He thought that would help him …'

A light breeze comes up. We look down on the town and at the long row of poplars beneath which once upon a time we used to put up tents and play at being the characters in our favourite Wild West stories. Georg was always the Apache chief and I was his cowboy blood brother, and I loved him without realising it, the way only small boys can.

Our eyes meet. 'Old Shatterhand,' says Georg softly, and smiles.

'Winnetou,' I answer, just as softly.

2

The closer we get to the day of the trial, the more I think about Albert. Then suddenly one day I get a clear and unmistakable picture before me of a mud-wall, a loop-hole, a rifle with telescopic sights, and behind it a cold, tense, ready face: Bruno Mückenhaupt, the best sniper in the battalion, who never missed his target.

I jump up. I have to go and see what he is doing now and how he has come to terms with it all.

It's a large block with a lot of flats. The stairs are dripping wet. It is Saturday, and everywhere there are buckets, scrubbing brushes and women bending over them.

The bell is shrill, far too loud for the door. It is opened hesitantly. I ask for Bruno. His wife lets me in. Mückenhaupt is sitting there in his shirtsleeves on the floor playing with his daughter, a little girl of about five, with a big blue bow in her blonde hair. He's laid out a river made of silver paper on the carpet for her, and put paper boats on it. Some of them have little bits of cotton wool stuck on them, and those are steamships, with small dolls made of celluloid as passengers. Bruno is contentedly puffing at a longish curved pipe. On the porcelain pipe bowl there is a picture of a soldier kneeling to fire and the inscription: 'With Eye and Hand Defend our Land!'

'Ernst, good to see you,' says Bruno, giving the little girl a pat and leaving her to carry on playing on her own. We go into the sitting room. There is a red plush sofa and matching armchairs, all with crocheted antimacassars on the backs, and the floor is so highly polished that I slip around as I walk. Everything is spotless and in its rightful place; there are seashells, trinkets and photographs on the sideboard, and right in the middle, under glass and on red velvet, are Bruno's medals.

We talk a bit about those days. 'Have you still got your tally of hits?' I ask.

'Good God, of course I have,' replies Bruno in a reproachful voice, 'kept in a place of honour!'

He gets his lists out of the sideboard and flicks through them with an air of real enjoyment. 'Summer was always my best time, of course, because you could see for so much longer in the evenings. Here we are – hang on – June the 18th – four shots to the head, 19th, three, 20th one, 21st, two, 22nd, one, none on the twenty-third, nothing doing that day. The bastards realised what was up and started taking more care – although here, look, the 26th, a new lot took over and they hadn't got wind of old Bruno yet, nine direct hits to the head, how about that, then!'

He beams at me. 'In two hours! It was weird, I don't know if it was maybe because I got them from below, just under the chin, but in any case they just went up in the air, one after the other, halfway out of the trench like a load of billy goats. And now, have a look at this – June the 29th, 10.02 p.m., head shot, not a word of lie, Ernst, look, I had it witnessed, there it is: Confirmed, Sergeant Schlie. Ten o'clock at night, almost dark, good shooting, eh? Hey, those were the days!'

'Tell me, Bruno,' I ask, 'it was amazingly good shooting, but now … I mean, don't you sometimes feel a little bit sorry for those poor blokes?'

'What?' he replies, bewildered.

I repeat what I said. 'Back then we were right in the middle of it all, Bruno, but now everything is a bit different.'

He pushes his chair back. 'Christ, are you some kind of Bolshevik or what? It was our duty! We had our orders! Bloody hell …' Offended, he packs his tally book up in its tissue-paper wrapping and puts it back into the sideboard drawer.

I pacify him by giving him a good cigar. He makes a few conciliatory gestures and starts to tell me about the rifle club he goes to, which meets every Saturday. 'We held a ball a little while back. Fantastic, I tell you. And there is a bowling competition with prizes coming up. You ought to come along sometime, Ernst. The pub we meet in has a beer on tap that's better than almost any I've ever drunk. And it's ten pfennigs a pint cheaper than anywhere else. That all adds up over an evening! It's a smart place but it feels comfortable. Here –' and he shows me a gilded chain – 'I'm the club champion! King of the Marksmen, Bruno the First! Pretty good, eh?'

His daughter comes in. One of her paper boats has come apart. Bruno carefully puts it back together and strokes the little girl's hair. The blue ribbon crackles.

Then he takes me over to a chest of drawers, the top of which is covered with all kinds of things. He won them all at the fair, in the shooting galleries. You got three shots for a couple of coppers, and if you hit a certain number of rings you could choose a prize. For the entire day nobody could shift Bruno from those shooting galleries. His marksmanship got him a whole load of teddy bears, crystal vases, bowls, beer mugs, coffee pots, ashtrays, balls and even two wicker chairs.

'In the end they barred me,' he laughs contentedly, 'otherwise I'd have bankrupted the lot of them. Yes, once you learn something, you've learned it for life!'

I walk down the dark street. Light streams from the doorways, and the water from cleaning the stairs spills out. Bruno will be playing with his little girl again. Then his wife will bring in their evening meal. Then he'll go out for a beer. On Sundays he'll have a day out with the family. He's a decent husband, a good father, a respected citizen. There's nothing wrong with that. Nothing wrong with that.

And Albert? And the rest of us?

★ ★ ★

A good hour before Albert's trial starts we're standing waiting in the corridor of the courthouse. At last the witnesses are called. We go in, our hearts pounding. Albert is slumped in the dock, pale and staring straight ahead. We want to signal to him with our eyes: chin up, Albert! We won't let you down! But he doesn't look up at us.

After our names have been read out we have to leave the courtroom again. As we go out we spot Tjaden and Valentin in the front row of the public gallery. They wink at us.

The witnesses are taken one after another. Willy is in there for an especially long time. Then it's my turn. A quick glance at Valentin, who gives an almost imperceptible shake of his head. So Albert has so far refused to testify. I thought that would happen. He's just sitting there, absently, next to his defence counsel. But Willy's face is red.

He's watching the public prosecutor with the eyes of a hungry wolf. The two of them seem to have clashed already.

I take the oath. Then the presiding judge begins his questions. He wants to know whether Albert had ever spoken earlier about sorting out Bartscher. When I say no, he comments that various witnesses observed that Albert had been noticeably calm and collected.

'He always is,' I reply.

'Collected?'

'Calm,' I tell him.

The judge leans forward. 'Even in this kind of situation?'

'Of course,' I say. 'He's managed to stay calm in circumstances quite a lot different from this one.'

'In what circumstances?' asks the prosecutor quickly, pointing a finger at me.

'Under heavy fire.'

He puts his hand down. Willy gives a grunt of satisfaction. The prosecutor gives him a furious look.

'So he was calm?' asks the presiding judge again.

'As calm as he is now,' I reply angrily. 'Can't you see how he's standing there quite calmly while inside he's raging and burning? He was a soldier! That's where he learned that in critical situations you don't jump up and down and wave your arms about in

266

despair. If he'd done that he wouldn't have had them for much longer!'

The prosecutor makes a few notes. The presiding judge looks at me for a moment. 'Why did he have to shoot?' he asks. 'Surely it wasn't such a terrible thing that the girl had gone to the cafe with somebody else?'

'For him it was worse than being shot in the guts,' I say.

'Why?'

'Because the girl was the only person he had.'

'Come on, he had his mother as well,' interjects the prosecutor.

'He can't marry *her*, can he?' I reply.

'Why should he have to marry anyway?' asks the judge. 'Isn't he still too young for that?'

'He wasn't too young to be a soldier,' I say. 'And he wanted to marry because he couldn't come to terms with things after the war, he was afraid of himself and his own memories, and he wanted something to cling on to. And for him that was this girl.'

The judge turns to Albert. 'Prisoner at the bar, will you at last give us an answer? Is what this witness says the truth?'

Albert hesitates for a while. Willy and I stare at him. 'Yes,' he says reluctantly.

'Could you also tell us why you had your service revolver with you?'

Albert says nothing.

'He always has it with him,' I say.

'Always?' asks the judge.

'Of course,' I reply, 'just like his handkerchief and his watch.'

The judge looks at me in astonishment. 'A revolver is hardly the same thing as a handkerchief.'

'That's true,' I say, 'he didn't always need a handkerchief. Quite often he didn't have one of those.'

'And the revolver ...?'

'That saved his life a few times. He's been carrying it for the past three years. It's a habit from being at the front.'

'But he doesn't need it any more now. It's peacetime.'

I shrug. 'It doesn't really feel like that to us.'

The judge turns to Albert again. 'Prisoner, do you not now wish to unburden yourself? Do you have no regrets for your action?'

'No,' says Albert dully.

Everything goes quiet. The jurors listen. The prosecutor leans forward. Willy pulls a face and looks as if he wants to jump on Albert. I stare despairingly at him.

'But you killed a man,' says the judge with some emphasis.

'I've killed lots of men,' replies Albert indifferently.

The prosecutor gives a start at this. The jury member by the door stops chewing his fingernails. 'What have you done?' gasps the judge.

'In the war,' I put in rapidly.

'But that was completely different,' says the prosecutor in a disappointed voice.

Albert raises his head at this point. 'How is that different?'

The prosecutor stands up. 'Are you comparing the battle for your homeland with your action here?'

'No,' replies Albert. 'The men I shot then hadn't done me any harm ...'

'Unbelievable!' exclaims the prosecutor in disgust, and addresses the judge: 'I must protest –'

But the judge is calmer. 'Where would we be if all soldiers were to think like that?' he says.

'It's a point,' I say, 'but that's not our responsibility. If he' – and I point at Albert – 'hadn't been trained to shoot at people, then he wouldn't have done this.'

The prosecutor is red as a beetroot. 'It really is not permissible for a witness to make independent and uncalled-for statements.'

The judge calms him down. 'I think that on this occasion we can deviate a little from the customary procedures.'

For the moment I am told to stand down and the girl is called. Albert twitches and presses his lips together. The girl is wearing a black silk dress and her hair has been newly waved and set. She steps forward confidently. You can see how full of self-importance she is.

The judge asks about her relationships with Albert and with Bartscher. She gives a picture of Albert as someone difficult to get on with, Bartscher on the other hand as amiable. She could, she says, never have thought of marrying Albert, and on the contrary, she was as good as engaged to Bartscher. 'Mr Trosske is still far too young,' she says, and gently moves her hips.

The sweat is pouring down Albert's face, but he doesn't move a muscle. Willy is clenching and unclenching his fists. We can hardly contain ourselves.

The presiding judge asks about her relations with Albert.

'Completely casual,' she says, 'we were just acquaintances.'

'Was the accused agitated at the time?'

'Of course,' she answers eagerly. The idea seems to flatter her.

'Why was that, then?'

'Well, you see ...' she smiles and turns her face a little, 'he was so very much in love with me.'

Willy lets out a dull groan. The prosecutor gives him a piercing look through his pince-nez.

'What a bitch!' comes a shout from the back of the room.

It makes everyone jump. 'Who said that?' demands the presiding judge.

Tjaden stands up proudly.

He is fined fifty marks for contempt.

'Cheap at the price,' he says, and takes out his wallet. 'Do you want me to pay now?'

For that he gets another fifty-mark fine handed down, and he is thrown out of the room.

The girl has become noticeably more modest.

'What had happened between you and Bartscher that evening?' asks the judge.

'Nothing,' she says, rather uncertainly. 'We were just sitting together.'

The judge looks at Albert. 'Do you have anything to say to that?'

I give him a penetrating look. But he replies softly: 'No.'

'The statements are accurate, then?'

Albert smiles bitterly, ashen-faced. The girl stares rigidly at the crucifix hanging on the wall above the judge's seat. 'They may well be accurate,' says Albert. 'It's the first time I've heard them. In that case I must have been mistaken.'

The girl breathes again. But she does so too soon, because now Willy jumps up. 'Lies!' he shouts. 'She's a lying bitch! She'd been well and truly at it with that bloke, she was still half naked when she came out!'

Uproar. The prosecutor makes a protest. The judge issues a reprimand to Willy, but he can't be stopped now, however despairingly Albert looks at him. 'I don't care even if you beg me,' he shouts across to him. 'It has to be said. She'd been at it, and when Albert confronted her she swore that Bartscher had got her drunk, and then he went crazy and shot him! He told me himself when he went to the police to give himself up.'

The defence counsel jumps in on this and the girl screeches in confusion: 'He did do that, he did, he did!' The prosecutor waves his arms about. 'The dignity of the court demands –'

Willy turns on him like an enraged bull. 'Get off your high horse, you pedantic old quibbler, or do you think, sir, that your damn-fool lawyer's gown is going to make us keep our traps shut? Just you try, sir, to have us chucked out! What do you know about us, anyway? That lad there used to be quiet and gentle, just ask his mother! But where in the past he might have thrown stones, now he shoots. Remorse! Remorse! How can he have any remorse when just for once he's done in someone who had ripped his world to shreds? The only mistake he made was that he shot the wrong person! He should have finished off that bloody woman! Do you lot all think you can use that weaselly word "peace" like a wet sponge to wipe four years of killing off the brain? We're all well aware that we can't just shoot down our private enemies when we feel like it, but when we're consumed by real fury and everything goes haywire and it takes us over, then you ought to just think for a moment about where it all came from!'

Pandemonium breaks out. The presiding judge tries in vain to restore order.

We stand close together. Willy looks fearsome, Kosole has clenched his fists, and at this moment there is nothing they can do against us, we are just too dangerous. The one copper on duty in the courtroom is too scared to come near us. I jump across and stand in front of the benches where the jury members are sitting. 'This is about our comrade in arms,' I shout out. 'You mustn't condemn him! He didn't want to become so indifferent to life and death, and nor did we, but out at the front we lost all our values, and nobody helped us! Patriotism, duty, homeland – we kept saying those words to ourselves over and over again to keep us going and to justify it all. But they were only ideas, and there was too much blood flowing out there, and it swept them all away.'

Suddenly Willy is at my side. 'Only a year ago that man –' he points at Albert '– was lying up with two other soldiers in an isolated MG post, the only one left in the whole sector, when there was an attack, but the three of them kept calm, took aim, and waited, so that they didn't fire too early; their sights were set at waist level, and when the oncoming column thought that it was all clear and started the attack, that's when they opened fire and kept on firing, and only much later did they get any reinforcement. The attack was held off. Afterwards we were able to fetch in those who had been cut down in the MG fire, a full twenty-seven of them with clean shots to the stomach, each one as precise as the others, all fatal, and that is quite apart from the rest, wounds to the legs, the balls, the guts, the lungs and the head. That man –' and he points at Albert again '– and his two mates filled a whole military hospital on their own, although of course those hit in the stomach didn't get that far. He got the Iron Cross First Class and a commendation from the colonel. Can you lot understand why this man isn't bound by all the legal niceties of your civilian court? It's not up to you to judge him! He is a soldier, he belongs to us, and we declare him not guilty!'

271

Now, however, the public prosecutor gets a word in. 'This is complete chaos ...' he snorts, and shouts to the policeman to arrest Willy.

Fresh uproar. Willy keeps everyone at bay. I start off again. 'Chaos? Who caused it, then? You lot did! You all deserve to be brought before our court! It's what your war has made out of us. Put the whole lot of us behind bars with him, that's the best thing you could do! What did you do for us when we came back? Nothing! Nothing! You argued about who had won what victories, you dedicated war memorials, you banged on about heroism and ducked any responsibility! You ought to have helped us! But you just abandoned us when things were hardest for us, when we had to find our way back! You should have preached from every pulpit, you should have told us when we were demobbed, and there were countless other times when you should have said to us: "We all made a terrible mistake! Let's try and find the answers together! Be brave! It's especially hard for you because you left nothing behind that you could pick up again! Be patient!" You should have showed us what life was! You should have taught us how to live again! But you just abandoned us! You threw us to the wolves! You should have taught us how to start believing once again in goodness, order, progress and love! But instead of that you set off again with lies and persecution and all your old legal quibbles. One of us has already been destroyed by it! The second one is over there!'

We are beside ourselves. All the fury, all the bitterness, all the disappointment comes boiling up out of us. There is total chaos in the courtroom. It takes a long time before some semblance of order is restored. We are all given one day in jail for disorderly conduct and contempt of court, and are ordered to be taken from the room at once. We could still quite easily push past the single copper, but we don't want to. We want to go to jail with Albert. We walk past him in a solid group, to show that we are all on his side ...

Later on we hear that he's been sentenced to three years, and that he accepted the punishment without a word.

3

Georg Rahe has managed to get a permit for foreign travel and he uses it to cross the border. He has one idea firmly in his head. He wants to confront his past face-to-face once more. He travels through the towns and villages, he waits on the platforms of large and then of small railway stations, and by evening he is at last where he wants to be.

Without any delay he wanders off through the streets of the town and out to the ridge of hills. Workers come towards him, passing him on their way home. Children play in the pools of light thrown by the street lamps. A couple of cars crawl past. Then everything is quiet.

It is still possible to see in the twilight. Besides, Rahe's eyes are used to the dark. He leaves the pathway and sets off across the fields. After a while he trips. A bit of rusty wire has caught in his trouser leg and made a small tear. He bends down to free himself. It's barbed wire from an entanglement that used to run along one of the shell-shattered trenches. Rahe stands up. In front of him are the bare battlefields.

In the uncertain dusk they are like a churned-up and frozen sea, stormy waters turned to stone. Rahe feels the dull, pervasive scent of blood, cordite and earth, the wild smell of death, which is still there, exerting its power over this landscape.

Involuntarily he pulls his head down, his shoulders go up and his arms hang loosely in front of him, his hands and wrists ready for him to drop to the ground – this is no longer the way you walk in town, this is once more the crouched, careful forward movement of an animal, the cautious wariness of the soldier ...

He stops and looks closely at the terrain. Just an hour ago it was still unfamiliar to him, but now he recognises it again, every escarpment, every dip, every valley. He never left it; in the flickering of his memory the months are crumpled together like a screwed-up scrap of paper, they burn up and fly away like smoke – now once again Lieutenant Georg Rahe is creeping forward on a reconnaissance patrol at night, and nothing has changed in the meantime. Around him there is only the silence of the night, and the light wind in the grass; but in his ears the noise of the battle is roaring, he sees the explosions raging, Verey lights hang like gigantic arc lamps above all the destruction, the black sky is boiling, and spurting fountains of earth and sulphurous craters tear up the ground as the thunder rolls from horizon to horizon.

Rahe clenches his teeth. He isn't over-imaginative, but he simply can't help himself. Memories snatch him up like a tornado, there is no peace in this place, not even the fake peace of the rest of the world, in this place there is still war and fighting, in this place all the destruction rages on in ghostly form, only eddying away into the clouds.

The earth takes hold of him, reaching out to grasp him as if it had hands, the thick yellow clay sticks to his shoes and makes it hard to walk, as if the dead were calling this survivor down to themselves with dull and murmuring voices.

He runs across the black, cratered battlefields. The wind gets stronger, the clouds move, and every so often the moon throws a pallid light over the landscape. Every time it does so Rahe stops, his heart beating wildly, throws himself down and clings motionless to the earth. He knows there is nothing there, but all the same the next time he jumps into a shell-hole. Conscious and with his eyes open, he gives way to the laws of this terrain, across which it would be impossible to walk openly and upright.

The moon has turned into an enormous luminescent screen. The stumps of a small copse stand out black against this whiteness. Behind the ruins of a farmhouse there is a narrow gully through which no attack ever came. Rahe crouches down in a trench. There are bits of a belt buckle, a couple of mess tins, a spoon, some hand grenades covered in dirt, cartridge cases, and next to them some wet, greenish-grey cloth, tattered, already half turned to clay, the remains of a soldier.

Georg stretches out on the ground with his face downward, and the silence begins to speak. There is a sullen, monstrous rumbling in the earth, gasps of breath, groans, then rumbling again, rattling and clattering. He digs his fingers into the earth and presses his head against it, he thinks that he can make out voices and cries, he wants to ask questions, to speak, to shout, he listens and waits for an answer, an answer to his life —

But it is just the wind getting stronger, the clouds move more rapidly and are lower than before, and shadow after shadow chase across the fields. Rahe gets up and walks on for a long time without knowing where he is going until he arrives at the black crosses, laid out one after another in long rows just like a company, a battalion, a regiment, an army.

And suddenly he understands it all. In the face of these crosses the whole edifice of fine words and abstract concepts breaks into pieces. Here and only here is where the war still is, not in the minds or in the distorted memories of those who survived it! This is where all the lost years that can never be fulfilled hover like a ghostly mist over the graves, this is where the unlived life that finds no rest screams out in thunderous silence to the heavens, this is where the force and will of youth that died before it could begin to live floods the night like a monstrous lament.

Shudders run over him. Suddenly and harshly he becomes aware of his heroic mistake, of the open gullet in which the faith, the bravery and the life of a whole generation was swallowed up. It chokes and dumbfounds him.

'Comrades in arms!' he shouts into the wind and into the night. 'Comrades! We were betrayed! We must march again! Against it! Against it! Comrades!'

He stands in front of the crosses, the moon breaks through and he sees them shining, they rise up out of the earth with their arms stretched out, and now you can already hear the thunder of their steps, he stands before them and marches on the spot, he lifts up one arm: 'Comrades – march!'

And then he puts a hand in his pocket and raises the arm again ... a tired, lonely shot, the sound of which is caught up by the wind and carried away ... and then he falls to his knees, stretches out his arms and with his last scrap of strength he turns towards the crosses ... he sees them marching, they are beating time as they move, they are marching slowly and they have a long way to go, it will take a long time, but it is the way forward, they will reach their goal and fight their last battle, the battle for life, and they march in silence, a dark army, marching their longest march, the way into all hearts, and it will take many years, but what does time mean to them? They have made a start, they are marching, they are coming.

His head sinks down and there is darkness all around him, he falls forward, and then he is marching in the procession with the others. Like someone who has come home late he lies on the earth, his arms outstretched, his eyes already dulled, one knee drawn in. His body twitches once more, and then there is just sleep; only the wind is left, blowing over the barren, dark spaces, blowing and blowing, past the clouds and the skies, over the fields and the endless plains with their graves and shell-holes and crosses.

LEAVING

1

The ground smells of March days and violets. Primroses are beginning to show under the wet leaves. There is a purple shimmer on the ploughed furrows.

We are walking along a path in the woods. Willy and Kosole are in front, Valentin and I behind them. It's the first time for a long while that we have been together. We don't see much of each other these days.

Karl has lent us his new car for the day. He hasn't come himself, however, because he can't spare the time. For the past few months he's been making a lot of money because the value of the currency is going down, and that's an advantage in his business. His chauffeur drove us out here.

'What are you actually doing these days, Valentin?' I ask.

'I'm going round the fairgrounds,' he replies, 'working the swing boats.'

I look at him in amazement. 'Since when?'

'A good while now. The dancing partner I used to have soon dumped me. She's working in a cafe-bar now, demonstration foxtrots and tangos. There's a lot of demand for that nowadays. Besides, an old army leftover like me wasn't fancy enough.'

'Do you make a living with the swing boats?' I ask.

He makes a dismissive gesture. 'Come on! Not enough to live, too much to die! And all the moving around! I'm back on the road tomorrow. To Krefeld. It really has all gone to the dogs, Ernst! Anyway, where's Jupp?'

I shrug. 'He's moved away. Like Adolf. Neither of them has been in touch since.'

'And Arthur?'

'Soon be a millionaire,' I tell him.

'Yes, he's got the knack,' nods Valentin ruefully.

Kosole stops and stretches his arms out. 'Well, lads, it's a fine thing to be out walking – only it's a pity if you're out of work as well.'

'Don't you think you'll get something before long?' asks Willy.

Ferdinand shakes his head in doubt. 'It's not going to be easy. I'm on the blacklist. Not biddable enough. Still, as long as you're healthy. And at the moment I'm sponging off Tjaden. He's really landed on his feet.'

We take a break in a clearing. Willy gets out a packet of cigarettes that Karl gave him, and Valentin cheers up. We sit and smoke.

There is a gentle creaking in the tops of the trees. A couple of blue tits are twittering. The sun is already strong and warm. Willy gives a hearty yawn and lies back, stretching out on his coat. Kosole makes a kind of headrest from some moss and he lies back as well. Valentin sits there pensively, leaning against the trunk of a beech tree and watching a green beetle.

I look at the familiar faces, and for a moment everything seems to shift focus in a funny way. Here we are again, all down on the ground together as we were so often in the past – it's just that there are fewer of us now. But are we still really together, even us?

Suddenly Kosole pricks up his ears. From the distance come voices. Young voices. It must be some lads from the Wandervogel youth movement, off on their first ramble on this silver-flecked day, with their beribboned guitars. We used to do the same thing before the war – Ludwig Breyer, Georg Rahe and me.

I lean back and think about that time, about the campfire evenings, the folk songs, the guitars and the nights under canvas. That was our youth. In the years up to the war, the romanticism of that youth movement still carried with it a sense of enthusiasm for a new, freer future, and the flame flickered on in the trenches for a little while, until by 1917 it had died away in the horrors of front-line warfare.

The voices come closer. I prop myself on my elbow and raise my head to watch their procession go past. It's strange – a few years ago we were just like that, and now it feels as if there is already a completely new generation in place, a generation after us, who can take up what we had to drop.

There are shouts. A mass of noise, almost like a choir. Then there is a single voice, indistinct, the words not yet understandable. Twigs snap and the ground echoes with the sound of tramping feet. Another shout. Footsteps again. Snapping. Silence. And then, loud and clear, a command: 'Cavalry approaching on the right flank – right about in platoons – quick march!'

Kosole jumps up. I do the same. We stare at each other. Is this some spooky trick to make fools of us? What's all this about?

Then, right in front of us, they break out from the low bushes, running for the edge of the wood, and throw themselves down on the ground. 'Range four hundred,' raps out the voice we heard before. 'Covering fire!'

There is a rattling noise. A long row of boys from fifteen to seventeen are lying in position side by side at the edge of the wood. They are wearing outdoor jackets and have leather belts with military buckles over them. They are all dressed the same way, grey jackets, puttees, caps with a badge – it is obviously intended to look like a uniform. Each of them has a hiker's stick with a spike, and banging these against the tree trunks imitates the noise of machine-gun fire.

Beneath the military caps, though, the faces are young and rosy-cheeked, children's faces. Attentive and excited, they watch out for the cavalry approaching from the right. They don't see the tiny miracle of the violets coming through the leaf mould, nor the promising purple haze on the ploughed field, nor the downy fur of the young hare as it lopes through the furrows. No, they *do* see the hare, but they just aim their sticks at it, and the clattering against the tree trunks gets louder. Behind them is a powerfully built man with a bit of a paunch, also wearing an outdoor jacket and puttees, and he gives them a series of vigorous commands. 'Steady fire! Range two hundred!' He has field glasses and is observing the enemy.

'Christ almighty!' I say, shocked.

Kosole has recovered from his astonishment. 'What's all this bloody nonsense?' he curses, furious.

But he comes off worst. The leader is joined by two other men and he starts to rage and thunder at him. The soft spring air is suddenly full of hard phrases. 'Shut your trap! Malingerers! Betraying your country! Treacherous lot of pansies!'

The boys join in eagerly. One even shakes his small fist at us. 'We'll have to teach you a lesson, then, won't we?' he shouts in a high voice. 'Cowards!' adds another. 'Pacifists!' says a third. 'We have to wipe out the Bolsheviks so the country can be free!' puts in a fourth lad quickly, parroting some slogan.

'Well said!' The leader pats him on the shoulder and moves a step forward. 'See them off, lads!'

At that moment, Willy wakes up. He has been fast asleep. In that respect he's still an old soldier, and if he stretches out on the ground, he's asleep in seconds.

He stands up. The leader stops at once. Willy looks around him, wide-eyed, and then bursts into laughter. 'What's this? A fancy-dress party?' he asks. Then he grasps what is going on. 'Yes, that's about it,' he growls at the leader. 'You lot are just what we've been waiting for! Yes, yes, the fatherland – handed to you as your exclusive property, right? And everybody else is a traitor, right? Funny, that – so three-quarters of the German army must have been traitors, then! Get the hell out of here, you twerps! Can't you let these lads enjoy the few years when they don't need all this stuff?'

The leader has withdrawn his troops, but it has ruined the walk in the woods for us. We go back to the village. Behind us we can hear rhythmic and regular chanting: 'Hurrah for the front! Hurrah for the front! Hurrah for the front!'

'Hurrah for the front' – Willy is tearing his hair. 'What if you'd said that to one of the men out there on the battlefield?'

'Yes,' says Kosole with irritation. 'That's the way it all starts off again.'

★

282

Just outside the village we find a small inn with a garden where there are already a few tables put out. As Valentin has to get back to his swing boats in an hour, we quickly sit down, to make the most of the time left – who knows when we shall all be together again.

The evening sky is a pale red. I can't get that scene in the woods out of my head. 'My God, Willy,' I say, 'we all survived and we've only been out of it for five minutes – how is it possible that there are already people around who can do that sort of thing?'

'There'll always be people like that,' replies Willy, who is unusually serious and reflective. 'But there are still people like us as well. And a whole lot of people think the way we do. Most people, you can count on it. Since that time – you know, with Ludwig and Albert – a lot of things have gone through my mind, and I reckon that everyone can do something about it, even if he's got a turnip for a head. Next week the holidays are over and I'm going back to being the village schoolmaster. I'm really looking forward to it. I want to teach my lads what their fatherland really is. By that I mean their homeland, of course, not something dreamt up by some political party. Homeland means trees, fields, the earth, and not some overblown slogan. I've given a lot of thought to it, and I've come to the conclusion that we are old enough to have a real job to do. That's mine. It's not a great thing, I'll grant you. But it will do for me. I'm no Goethe, anyway.'

I nod, and look at him for a long time. Then we decide to go.

The chauffeur is waiting for us. The car glides quietly through the slowly approaching twilight.

We are already close to the town, and the first lights are visible, then we hear, mixed with the rasp of the car tyres, a long-drawn-out, hoarse and throaty noise – in the evening sky a wedge-shaped formation is flying east, a flock of wild geese –

We look at each other. Kosole is about to say something, but then is silent. We are all thinking the same thing.

And there is the town, with its lights and noise. Valentin gets out. Then Willy. Then Kosole.

I've spent the whole day in the woods. Now I'm tired, I've found a small country inn and taken a room for the night. The bed is turned down and ready for me, but I don't want to go to sleep yet. I sit by the window and listen to the noises of the spring night.

Shadows are flitting between the trees, and there are shouts from the direction of the woods, as if there were wounded men over there. I am calm and composed as I look out into the darkness, because I am no longer afraid of the past. I can look into its eyes without flinching, the fire has gone out of them. I can even face the past, sending my thoughts into the dugouts and shell-holes, and when the images come back to me they no longer bring fear and horror with them, just strength and will.

I had been waiting for a storm that would rescue me and carry me on; but it came softly, without my realising. And yet it is there. While I was despairing and thinking everything was lost, it was quietly growing. I thought that parting was always final. Now I know that growing is a kind of parting. To grow means to leave something behind. And there is no end to it.

One part of my life was spent in the service of the forces of destruction; it belonged to hate, to enemies, to death. But I stayed alive. That alone is almost an aim and a way forward. I want to work on myself and be ready, I want to use my hands and my thoughts, I don't want to take myself too seriously, and I'll carry on even when sometimes I might want just to stop. There is a lot to be built up again, and practically everything to repair, there is work to be done, and things to be dug out again that were buried in the years of shellfire and machine-gun bullets. Not everyone needs to be at the forefront, less powerful hands and smaller strengths will also be needed. That's where I'll look for my place in it all. Then the dead will be silent and the past will stop persecuting me and start to help me.

How simple it all is. But how long it took to find the way! And maybe I might still have lost my way in no man's land and might have fallen prey to the wire traps or the mines if Ludwig's death hadn't shot up like a rocket before our eyes and made the way clear to us. We were in despair when we saw that our combined fellowship, the will of pure life won back from the very edge of death, did not sweep away all the half-truths and selfishness and lead us to new shores, but rather that it just trickled away into the swamp of oblivion, or was diverted off into the marshland of empty words, draining away into the furrows of relationships, worries and work. I know now that everything in life is perhaps only a kind of preparation, working in the individual, in different areas, going off into different channels, each one separate – and just as the different parts and branches of a great tree have to take the sap and move it onwards as it forces itself up, one day for us, too, there will be a rustling of the leaves and sunshine on the crown, and freedom. I want to make a start.

It will not be the fulfilment that we dreamt of when we were young and that we expected when we came back after the years out there. It will be a path like any other, with stony parts and good stretches, with damaged sections and with villages and fields; a pathway of work. I shall be alone. Maybe now and again I might find someone to go along some of the way with me, but probably not for all of it.

And it may well be that I shall often have to hoist up my pack when my shoulders are already weary; and just as often I shall find myself hesitating at a crossroads or at a border, I'll have to leave something behind, I'll stumble and fall; but I'll get up again and not just lie there, I'll go on and not turn round. Perhaps I shall never be able to be really happy again, perhaps the war knocked that out of me and I shall always be a little bit apart, not fully at home anywhere; but I think I shall never be completely unhappy, because there will always be something there to hold me up, even if it is just my own hands, or a tree, or the living earth.

The sap is rising in the trees, buds are opening with a soft noise and the darkness is full of the sounds of growth. The night and the moon are in the room. There is life in the room. The furniture creaks, the table groans and the wardrobe makes a sound. Years ago the wood was felled and cut, planed and put together to make it into serviceable things, chairs and beds; but every spring, in those nights when the sap is rising, there is life in them again, they wake up and stretch, no longer mere things, chairs, just for use, but taking part again in the stream and flow of life outside. The floorboards creak under my feet and move, the wood of the windowsill clicks under my hands, and outside, next to the pathway, even the broken and crumbling trunk of a lime tree is putting out fat brown buds – in a few weeks it will have silky green leaves, just like the broad-sweeping branches of the plane tree that overshadows it.

VINTAGE CLASSICS

Vintage launched in the United Kingdom in 1990, and was originally the paperback home for the Random House Group's literary authors. Now, Vintage is comprised of some of London's oldest and most prestigious literary houses, including Chatto & Windus (1855), Hogarth (1917), Jonathan Cape (1921) and Secker & Warburg (1935), alongside the newer or relaunched hardback and paperback imprints: The Bodley Head, Harvill Secker, Yellow Jersey, Square Peg, Vintage Paperbacks and Vintage Classics.

From Angela Carter, Graham Greene and Aldous Huxley to Toni Morrison, Haruki Murakami and Virginia Woolf, Vintage Classics is renowned for publishing some of the greatest writers and thinkers from around the world and across the ages – all complemented by our beautiful, stylish approach to design. Vintage Classics' authors have won many of the world's most revered literary prizes, including the Nobel, the Man Booker, the Prix Goncourt and the Pulitzer, and through their writing they continue to capture imaginations, inspire new perspectives and incite curiosity.

In 2007 Vintage Classics introduced its distinctive red spine design, and in 2012 Vintage Children's Classics was launched to include the much-loved authors of our childhood. Random House joined forces with the Penguin Group in 2013 to become Penguin Random House, making it the largest trade publisher in the United Kingdom.

@vintagebooks